Paradise Found
By Vivian Arend

Fate is a wind that can change at the drop of a heart...

Paige has enjoyed every no-strings-attached minute with her two Australian lovers, Trent and Mason. Over the past eleven months, they've surfed, hiked...and explored their seemingly limitless sexual chemistry.

Her lovers' invitation to the opening of a new resort comes at the ideal time, because in a few days she's returning to Canada. It'll be a fitting swan song for their easygoing relationship. A chance to fulfill a few fantasies and then escape before her men realize she's broken the rules by falling in love with them both. Better to take flight than be forced to choose.

Unaware of Paige's self-imposed deadline, Trent and Mason scheme to get Paige on their yacht for a once-in-a-lifetime voyage with one goal in mind: break the news that they're ready for something more than casual—and hope she doesn't run like hell.

It's a delicate operation that'll require close attention to which way her emotional winds are blowing. One wrong word, and their paradise-perfect arrangement could be lost in an instant.

Warning: This book starts with the heat turned way up high. Two men entirely focused on one woman's pleasure. One woman stepping outside the box to please her men. An exotic resort suite featuring an erotic piece of furniture that makes ménage a trois even hotter

Tropical Sin
By Lexxie Couper

It takes more than a rock star to rock your world. Sometimes you need a friend.

McKenzie Wood is Australia's star gossip mag journalist, and she's just spied the story of a lifetime: rumor-shrouded rock star, Nick Blackthorne—who thinks he's incognito at Bandicoot Cove resort. The word is Nick's a sex addict about to come out of the closet, and who better to lure Nick out than her BFF, Aiden Rogers—a pulse-poundingly gorgeous firefighter who is always there when she needs him, no matter the challenge.

Aiden admits it's pretty damned pathetic that he can rush into burning buildings, but not have the guts to tell McKenzie he's in love with her. No way can he tell his best friend he'd like to do some seriously sinful things to her, especially since she's never shown one iota of sexual interest.

Nick looks forward to some "unfamous" downtime in his home country. He's surprised to find his creative muse stirred— more like brought to rigid attention—by a couple so sexy that all he can think about is the three of them. Together.

Three bodies move together as one, and the music becomes a smoldering beat that rivals the island's heat. When the truth inevitably comes out, the heat might be enough to save three souls...or end up just another sinner's lament.

Warning: One + one + one = OMG sex, are-you-freaking-kidding-me orgasms and some serious mind-blowing climaxes.

Island Idyll
By Jess Dee

Adolescent fantasies can grow into very adult realities.

Sienna James has come to Bandicoot Cove to mourn the end of her eight-year relationship with Ben Cowley. The last person she expects to meet is the star of every one of her high school fantasies.

Joshua Lye is not only as appealing as he was in high school, he reveals she was the main feature in his adolescent wet dreams. As kids they never got it together. But they're adults now, and there's nothing keeping them apart.

When Ben arrives at the resort determined to win Sienna back, finding another man in her bed kind of throws a spanner in the works. But he isn't deterred. Rather than admit defeat, he comes up with an alternative plan: Let Sienna sleep with both men—at the same time. Then she can make an informed decision as to which man she wants.

Sienna shouldn't want to go through with this shockingly sexy plan, but she does. Desperately. Except after the sexual storm passes, she could have it all...or be left holding an empty heart.

Warning: Contains a suggestion beyond risqué, a solution beyond orgasmic, and two men who know how to play dirty. Really, really dirty.

Tropical Desires

SAMHAIN
PUBLISHING

Samhain Publishing, Ltd.
11821 Mason Montgomery Road, 4B
Cincinnati, OH 45249
www.samhainpublishing.com

Tropical Desires
Print ISBN: 978-1-60928-613-2
Paradise Found Copyright © 2012 by Vivian Arend
Tropical Sin Copyright © 2012 by Lexxie Couper
Island Idyll Copyright © 2012 by Jess Dee

Editing by Jennifer Miller
Cover by Kanaxa

Paradise Found, ISBN 978-1-60928-515-9
First Samhain Publishing, Ltd. electronic publication: August 2011
Tropical Sin, ISBN 978-1-60928-524-1
First Samhain Publishing, Ltd. electronic publication: September 2011
Island Idyll, ISBN 978-1-60928-529-6
First Samhain Publishing, Ltd. electronic publication: September 2011
First Samhain Publishing, Ltd. print publication: July 2012

Contents

Paradise Found

Vivian Arend

Dedication

My world got a whole lot warmer when I started writing, for many reasons. Wonderful friends like Jess Dee and Lexxie Couper keep me hopping, and I'm so pleased to be able to share the world of Bandicoot Cove with them.

Chapter One

You Are Personally and Cordially Invited to Attend The Soft Opening of Australia's Newest FIVE-STAR Luxury Resort BANDICOOT COVE on Bilby Island. Bring a plus one if you desire.

All expenses and needs will be catered for as we test our customer services in preparation for the Grand Opening.

(Hey, brat.

I'm assigning you one of the penthouse suites since you said you needed room for three. What the hell are you up to?

You so owe me.

Love, Kylie)

Trent dropped the engraved invitation back into his shirt pocket and dug out the access code he'd been given for the computerized keypad. The door eased opened as he pressed on it with one shoulder, glancing around at the high-class suite he'd been given to "check for bugs".

He was less interested in finding holes in his sister's service department and more concerned about this being an extended weekend to remember. He needed the setting to be perfect, or Paige would tie his balls in a knot and kick his arse into the drink when she discovered what he and Mason had done.

Vast open space met his gaze, and his first impression of the enormous penthouse suite brought a string of admiring swear words to his lips. He'd never seen a hotel room this size, and he'd barely stepped into the living room. Leather and chrome were everywhere, with thick, cushiony carpeting underfoot. Three luxurious couches were grouped around an enormous coffee table. The entire corner of the room was floor-to-ceiling windows that let in the bright Queensland sunshine and revealed the sparkling waters of the Pacific Ocean.

A perfect place to create some memories, and hopefully do a little convincing.

One final pivot returned him to his starting point. He slung his bag to the floor and strode into the kitchen, passing a huge basket of fruit in a crystal bowl set on the high counter. There were chocolates as well, and a quick peek in the fridge revealed a bottle of champagne nestled beside a wide assortment of cheeses and other goodies. He grabbed the card off the bottle.

Thanks for being there and supporting me along the way, little bro. You're the best.
Kylie

Trent nabbed an apple from the bowl, polished it on his shirt and took a bite of the crisp fruit as he stepped to stare out the windows. A tiny piece of paradise—that's where he was. Thanks to his sister's plum role as manager, he and his best mate, Mason, were in for three full days of rest and relaxation, followed shortly by the trip of a lifetime.

As long as Paige went along with their master plan. She'd always been adaptable before. Of course, this was a little more involved than arranging to get together for a surf-and-sex holiday.

A soft noise disturbed him, and he swung toward the hallway that extended into the back half of the penthouse. An enormous king-plus bed lay behind the first door, plump pillows littering its surface. Luxurious fixtures were everywhere, and through an open door on the far side of the room, a gilded mirror reflected a massive tub. Sunlight streamed in to paint everything with shimmering gold, and once more he was reminded exactly how out of place he was in these surroundings. Of course, he wasn't going to argue with getting to show Paige a good time, but the modest apartment he shared with Mason in Newcastle was more his style. Or the sturdy yacht they'd just bought. This?

Unreal.

The intriguing noises continued, so he stalked deeper into the suite, catching sight of movement behind a slightly ajar door.

Holy fucking moly.

There was a maid still cleaning the room, but he'd always assumed those get-ups were only found in skanky magazines and porn flicks. Black net stockings covered her shapely legs, secured with garter belts that disappeared under the black frill of a skirt circling her flared hips. Strangely familiar hips that twitched back and forth as she strutted around the edge of the room, flickering a feather duster along the picture frames and side table.

The feather duster wasn't nearly as intriguing as the five-inch heels gracing her long legs. And when she walked, her arse wiggled from side to side in time with the lusty song she sang. Dirty words, nicely in tune with the thoughts running through his brain. Oh, she could *take it off* if she wanted to. He'd have no complaints.

Bloody brilliant woman.

He pushed the door open and stepped into the entranceway. Paige twirled and straightened with a gasp, her long black braids flying as one hand snapped up to cover her mouth like some old-fashioned modest heroine. The laughter and smoldering heat in her eyes said there was nothing modest about what she wanted.

Trent drew in a deep breath through his nose, picking up a trace of her perfume. Sweet, yet spicy. He reached over and tugged her ear buds free, the music spilling loose, loud enough to echo off the walls. She licked her lips, then removed the iPod tucked in her waistband and tossed it on the side table.

When she took a deep breath, his cock filled to the point of pain, crowded tight against the front of his boardies. He'd gotten aroused when he spotted the fishnets—any man would. But knowing who was flirting with him, hell, she could arouse him in a freezing rainstorm with only one of her smiles.

And Paige wasn't just smiling. She had wiggled closer, the scoop of her cleavage propped above the edge of her frilly white blouse. Tucked in at the waist, the damn thing emphasized the difference in size between her trim waist and firm tits. God, she had gorgeous tits.

"*Bonjour, monsieur.* I'm sorry, I wasn't quick enough getting things tidied in here. *Un moment.*"

He reached for her, but she'd already spun out of his grasp. Hmm, it seemed she wanted to play. Paige peeked over her shoulder as she approached the bed. Her duster fell unminded to the floor as she leaned way over to adjust the pillows and straighten the cover.

Her skirt rode up to reveal two smooth arse cheeks and a glimpse of a bare mound, and Trent lost it. He tore across the room and covered her with his body. One hand locked her in place, fingers gripping her breast. The other landed on her upper thigh, sneaking under her excuse for a skirt to yank her ass hard against his groin.

"I need you to do a few more things before you leave, if you don't mind."

Paige purred as she undulated against him. "That's exactly what I hoped you'd say."

Waiting for her guys to arrive while wearing nothing but the tiny scraps of fabric in her costume had taken every ounce of courage Paige had, and she'd never considered herself a chicken. Normally the hours before a getaway she was nothing but a quivering mass of anticipation, but this trip was different. The self-imposed deadline on her Australian adventure was rapidly approaching—there were only a few days remaining before she headed home to Canada.

This would be her final chance for fun and frolics with Trent and Mason, and she was going to pull out all the stops, including fulfilling every fantasy she'd ever heard them mention.

Trent's lips touched her neck, unerringly hitting the sensitive spot that caused shivers to race over her skin. He traced tiny circles with his tongue—maddening circles matched by his fingers on the inside of her thigh. She was already wet from imagining being with them. Knowing that the maid outfit was going to get Trent's interest—hell, she'd had to hold back from bringing herself to her first orgasm while she waited for him to arrive.

His voice was a lust-filled rumble. "I didn't know this room came supplied with naughty French maids."

"*Oui, monsieur.* As naughty as you'd like. *Oh—*"

Trent slipped a finger over her clit and rubbed just as a sharp nip struck her neck. Paige arched, torn between grinding

14

her ass on his cock, pulsing her hips harder against his fingers, or turning and giving him access to her breasts.

He stole her decision and slid his fingers into her sheath, heel of his hand pressed hard to her mound. The movement ground her against his groin, and he thrust his hips rhythmically, teasing her with what she had to look forward to. Across the room a wall of mirrors reflected their image, and she smiled in admiration. Trent shone like an ancient sun god. His hair, bleached white from hours spent working outdoors and in the water, contrasted sharply against her black wig. His enormous bicep muscles flexed as his forearm moved over her, bringing unspeakable pleasure bubbling to the surface. The sharp line of his jaw, the flash in his green eyes—God, if only she had a picture of what his eyes looked like as he made love to her.

"As naughty as I want?" he rumbled in her ear. "How about your tits hanging out of that top so I can watch them bounce?"

She shivered with delight. "Of course."

He tugged the elastic at the front of her gypsy blouse and she spilled free, her bra-less breasts escaping the fabric. The warm air of the room caressed her skin for a split second before his free hand covered her again, his groan of approval as he massaged her needy flesh adding to the tension spiking upward. He increased the pace, his fingers spreading her wide, each motion hotter and harder than the last. When he crushed his palm against the apex of her sex, the first wave of pleasure broke, her sheath squeezing hard and sending a lovely dose of endorphins to flood her system.

She went to straighten, expecting him to release her for long enough that she could turn to face him, when she suddenly found herself flat on her back, the mattress bouncing from the weight of him tossing her.

"Whoa, cowboy, let's not get too carried away."

"Open your legs." He growled the order as he yanked off his shirt and discarded it on the floor. She watched in fascination as he unsnapped his button, unzipping and freeing his erection.

God, he was freaking gorgeous. Never mind his clean-cut features, his drool-worthy body, she wasn't ashamed to admit she had it real bad for his cock. Long and hard, and all for her.

She was so going to miss this.

But until she actually had to say good-bye, Paige intended

on enjoying every damn second she could. She grinned and drew her legs wide apart. Knees lifted, insanely high heels balanced on the edge of the mattress. She was completely open and bare, and his gaze devoured her.

"Touch yourself."

Paige instantly covered her breasts.

He rumbled with laughter. "That's not what I meant."

She dropped a hand and touched her sex. The smooth surface of her mound felt so good under her fingers—the time it had taken to do herself up completely clean was worth it. And from the look in Trent's eyes as he stared at her hand, he thought so as well.

With one hand she spread her labia, with the other, she dipped into her wetness. She shuddered as her forefinger skimmed her clit. The tiny nub was hard and hot, wanting more even after the first explosive climax at Trent's hand.

"That's right, love. Show me how you like it."

Paige glanced at him flirtatiously, gasping in a little snatch of air as she became aware of what he was doing. Stroking his cock, firm strokes from root to tip as he stared fixated between her legs.

He'd already slipped on a condom, and she hummed in approval.

"How I like it is for you to bring that thing over here and use it properly."

"Eager for my cock, are you? Aren't you supposed to be getting this room ready?"

She eased her knees farther apart and stroked again, letting a little gasp escape, moaning with pleasure. "Ready. Oh so ready."

Trent dropped to the floor and fastened his hands on her ankles. "Let's make sure of that."

His touch thrilled her, familiar yet exciting, as he smoothed his palms up her stockings. Stroked his way along her thighs, teasing with the promise of more. Making her wait even though he knew exactly how much she wanted him.

They'd been together for over a year. Never longer than a week at a time, but whenever and wherever they could arrange a meeting. From the first almost magical connection, it had been sensual and exciting, and absolutely mind-blowing. She still found it dreamlike—to be involved with not just one, but two guys as hot and vigorous, and willing to give it their all as Trent and Mason. But the affair, as idyllic as it had been, had to end sooner or later.

Damn it, anyway.

"You're drifting, love. Turn those big brown eyes back on me."

Paige eagerly met his gaze as he dipped lower and took a long slow breath. Another rush of desire hit her as his teasing drove her crazy. "Do it already."

Trent raised a brow. "So impatient. You mean this?" He leaned forward and blew across her clit and she wiggled. *Bastard.*

"More."

He tongued her, lapping her slit, rasping against her clit. She let her head collapse back on the mattress to enjoy the ride.

Trent fucked her with his tongue, brought his fingers into play. Again and again he brought her to the edge of a climax before easing off. Her body shook with the need for release, and when he suddenly rose and stabbed his cock at her core, she shouted with approval.

She should have saved the oxygen, because his next thrust split her in two on his hard length, and the final bits of air in her lungs fled. A rapid buzz sounded in her ears until she remember to drag in a breath.

"Fuck me, that feels good."

"I will, and it does." Trent dragged his hips back, the flared head of his cock rubbing her passage so smoothly and wonderfully she couldn't imagine how it could get any better. Until he leaned over her and kissed her, lips soft and tender. Such a contrast to his aggressive plunges into her core. Bringing her higher and higher until she would have sworn the sun shining in the windows wasn't the source of light, but their own bodies glowing, she was so hot.

Paige tangled her fingers in his hair, stroked her tongue alongside his, rocking her hips in an attempt take him farther in. If she arched her back just right, the hair on his chest tugged lightly on her nipples on each pass. Erotic, whisper-soft. Trent picked up the pace slightly, his kisses raining down on her neck, her ear. He sucked the lobe into his mouth and she dug her nails into his back.

"Wrap your legs around me," he ordered.

She managed to obey without stabbing him with one of the deadly spikes on her feet. Her knees hugged his waist, ankles crossed against his lower back. The change in position made his cock drive in deeper.

"Oh yes, do it. Harder. Fuck me."

Trent grunted his approval of her command and drove her back into the mattress. The frilly skirt bobbed around her waist, her breasts bouncing as he braced his hands on either side of her head and pounded in like a madman.

"Yes, yes, *yes...*"

There was nothing left to say. Only sensation to experience as her body flew. Pulses of pleasure radiated out, her passage clenching around him. His breath rang quick and sharp in her ear, the scent of sex rising on the air. It was always like this. Passionate and wild. No regrets, no holds barred. Another series of waves set off in her core as he continued to ravage her. Paige cupped her breasts, squeezing and molding the tips upward. Trent dipped his head and caught a nipple with his teeth, pulsing his lips around the peak and starting a new series of tremors. He froze, body shaking, gasping for air.

"Not...*yet.*" He closed his eyes and grimaced, every muscle in his torso locked tight, bulging in full flexion.

"Trent?"

He took a breath, then another, then sighed. "Fuck, almost too soon."

He pulled out and she felt the loss keenly. His hand smacked against her butt.

"Roll over."

Hmm, they weren't done. Paige leaned on one elbow and eyed his cock, just to make sure. Yup, still at full strength. The condom glistened with her juices. She glanced at his face and caught his grin before he forced a fierce expression. "On your belly, woman."

"Not hands and knees?"

He shoved her, gently enough her fall to the mattress remained controlled but hard enough she had no choice but to go. God, she loved it when he did that. Trent crawled between her legs and nudged her thighs apart with his knees. The air from the conditioning unit kicked on and a waft of cold air brushed her naked sex, wet as it was with moisture, and she shivered.

"Cold, love?"

She shook her head.

"Good." Trent smoothed a hand over her backside before shoving the tiny maid's skirt aside to bare her. His cock nudged between her folds. Barely entering before retreating. He pumped between her legs, rubbing the full crease of her labia. His cock nudged her clit on every pass and the shockwaves registered deep. Paige turned her face into the mattress and grabbed hold of the quilt with clenched fingers.

What was coming next would rock her world.

Two hands, like locking clamps, fastened onto her hips as he lifted her ass into the air. Just far enough his knees fit under her thighs.

"You ready?"

Paige intended on answering, but before the words escaped he'd skewered her on his cock. His balls bounced against her sensitive clit, his shaft spread her wide and she shouted, the sound echoing off the walls.

He wasn't gentle, and she loved it. Trapped under him there was little she could do but cry and moan and squeak when he stroked particularly sensitive spots exactly right. Face hidden against the mattress, her cries were muffled, the only noises his continued grunts and words of approval as he dragged her back onto his shaft again and again.

This time when she came it was with a body-shaking tremor. Trent joined her, his face buried against her as he covered her completely and pulsed into her depths. It was amazing, glorious and heart-wrenching. She smothered the place inside that didn't want to acknowledge this was one of their last times together.

He kissed the side of her neck gently, his body a warm blanket over her. He tousled the edge of the maid's skirt and laughed, a rich satisfied sound. Reaching up, he tugged one of the long black braids. "You wore this for me, didn't you?"

"Uh-hum." Talking was nearly impossible. She was so nicely used, his weight resting on her comfortable and exactly what she'd hoped for. She'd need a little time to recover to be able to greet Mason this afternoon with equal enthusiasm. A little time alone with each of them, a little with all three together, as always.

Before her heart tore apart and she said her final farewells.

"You bloody bastard!" A familiar voice rang out—loud, irate.

Mason?

Paige struggled to rise, but she was pinned under Trent's limbs. The solid *thwack* of a fist meeting flesh rang through the air.

Trent's bulk spun off her, flipping from the bed to land on the floor. "Fuck it, Mason, stop."

Paige scrambled upright to stare with shock into the furious face of her second lover.

Chapter Two

"Paige?" Mason jerked himself to a halt in mid-swing. Trent clutched the edge of the mattress, but it was the woman who drew Mason's attention. He locked eyes on her familiar brown orbs, and shock hit him square in the solar plexus. "What the hell did you do to your hair?"

Fair dinkum, he was in deep shit. His blood still raced from coming across what appeared to be his best mate doing the cleaning staff, not even hours before they were supposed to get together with Paige.

"It's a wig, you idiot." Paige shook her head, two long black braids swinging as she leaned over the mattress toward Trent. With one hand she straightened her blouse and skirt, barely managing to cover her assets, there was so little fabric in the outfit.

"You've never worn a wig before..." he protested.

Trent rose from the ground. All six-foot-four of him looked pissed, although with his dick hanging out of his pants, a little of the overall intimidation factor was lost. Mason snickered in spite of fearing he might be smacked in return.

"Arsehole." Trent dealt with the condom and tucked himself away without a flinch.

"I was protecting Paige's interests," Mason insisted. She knelt on the bed and his mouth watered. Okay, the dress-up thing didn't usually turn him on, but *fuck*.

Paige laughed lightly. "Thank you, but I don't need protecting."

Mason glanced between the two of them and retreated a pace, feeling damn uncomfortable. "Sorry, mates. Misunderstanding. I'll come back in a tic."

"Get over here." Paige pointed to the floor directly in front of her. Bloody hell, now he was in for it. Wouldn't be the first time his good intentions had mucked things up for him. So much for making this weekend the one to be remembered. The one that would change their whole fuck-friends routine into something far better.

As he reluctantly shuffled over, Trent pulled his shirt back on then crossed his arms, a self-satisfied smirk on his face.

Mason glared at his best friend. "What're you grinning about?"

Trent shrugged. "I got pussy, you're gonna get pissy."

Paige reached over and slapped him on the chest even as she laughed. "You! That is so bad."

"True, though."

She grabbed Mason by the shirt front and tugged him closer, leaning in until their noses touched. Then the stern expression she'd pasted on her face melted away and she took a long breath in. Her words came out lusty and low, just for his ears. "That was sweet. Thank you for trying to be my knight in shining armor."

Paige tilted her head to the side and brought their lips together, and he groaned at the taste of her. It had been a couple weeks since he'd gotten to kiss her. Touch her. Laugh with her. He cradled the back of her neck and savored the contact. Stroking his tongue alongside hers. Teasing her lips with tiny nibbles. Pressing his body against hers to share the warmth between them.

It had definitely been too long, and it was time to do something about it. She lived in Sydney, and he and Trent were in Newcastle. Only two hours' drive, but with them all working full-time, they'd barely scratched out time for flings.

No more. It was time to put that lifestyle behind them and shift this relationship to the next level.

Oh God, she could kiss. All his plans to start a more serious discussion evaporated as she kissed her way up his jaw line to his ear and teased with her tongue.

"Damn it, woman, that drives me crazy."

She nipped at his earlobe. "I know. That's why I do it." The words whispered past his ear, and he chuckled.

"Minx."

Then her arms were around him in a tight bear hug. Mason picked her up and returned the squeeze as he attempted to ignore the soft swell of her breasts peeking above the low scoop of her top. Tried to refrain from grinding his half-hard cock against her body and rutting on her like a sex-crazed maniac. It was tough considering the moment her knees left the mattress she'd swung her legs around his hips and now clung to him, an erotic body wrap. The wet heat of her sex sat directly over his dick, and things were not getting any less impressed below his beltline.

"I think I'll leave you two alone for a while. I promised to stop and give Kylie hell for a few." Trent's amusement was clear, but right now Mason was a little occupied.

Paige released him for long enough to turn her face toward Trent. "Say hi to your sis from me. I'll see her later. I need...you know."

"To finish cleaning up?"

Her eyes widened. "Why, what a wonderful idea." She blew a kiss at Trent then tugged on Mason's collar. "Come on. To the bathroom."

Mason glanced at his friend. There was a faint red mark on Trent's jaw, although nothing nearly large enough to match the pain throbbing in his fist. "Sorry, mate. I was a little out of sorts. Not thinking straight."

Trent shook his head. "You meant well. Go, have some fun. I'd better hustle before Kylie starts calling, perfectionist that she is. I've only got a short while to find her." He scooted in close enough to reach over Mason's shoulder and cup Paige's chin. *"Merci."*

Paige grinned and crawled higher to plant a huge kiss on Trent's lips right there over Mason's body.

"Ahh, enough of that. If there's any sandwiches in this relationship, you're the filling, not me." Mason turned away, jostling her upward to get a better grip, and she squealed lightly.

Trent waved one last time and closed the door after him. Mason would have taken more time to look around, but Paige had other ideas.

"What the fuck?"

She'd grabbed his ears and twisted his face in her direction. "Bathroom. Now. I need to ditch this outfit. Unless

23

you want to do a naughty French maid as well?"

"Fuck, no."

She waggled her brows. "Scrub my back for me?"

He wandered into the enormous bathroom, grinning in delight. "Is that all I get to scrub?"

She kissed him again, this time soft and gentle, and he sighed his happiness into her mouth as he lowered her to the floor. Through all the playing and fooling around they'd shared over the past year, he had a spot in his heart that longed for far more. As her soft lips clung to his, he tugged on the elastic collar of her blouse, stripping it from her shoulders to expose a wide expanse of naked skin.

She helped him, opening buttons, undoing snaps. The time it took to get naked passed delightfully quickly, and his mouth watered at the sight of her bare breasts, nipples crinkling tight under his gaze.

"Fuck me, you're a beauty."

She raised a brow and deliberately lowered her gaze over his naked body, ending by staring at his cock. "You're not bad yourself. Wanna fuck me?"

He wanted much more than a fuck, but there would be time to explain that later. Right now his balls were screaming at him to say *yes* and take her right there on the expensive Italian tile. But one thing first.

"Lose the wig."

Paige twirled to face the mirror and laughed out loud. "I'd forgotten about that."

She removed pins, still laughing as he slipped behind her. The touch of her body to his made him groan with the need to speed up. Made him force himself to show some control and go even slower.

So what if it had been a couple weeks since he'd seen her? This was about making the relationship more than a friendly fuck, and it had to start sometime. If he had his way, this was going to be the most important weekend of his life.

He kissed the nape of her neck, fingers stroking softly over her shoulders. "You want the shower or the tub?"

"Definitely the shower. Warm it up for us?"

He was already way overheated, her butt swaying against his hard-on as she laid the final pins on the counter and removed the black monstrosity. Her natural brunette curls bounced into sight and something inside him tightened. God, he wanted her.

"I think we'll be hot enough in a short time. Come on..."

He grabbed her by the hand and tugged her into the enclosure, tucking her against his front before twisting the taps. The water fell from directly overhead, and Paige gave a little shriek as the first drops hit.

Then she twisted under his hands, all that wet skin warm and intimate with his, and contentment rolled over him like a clap of thunder. He wanted this forever, not only for an occasional no-strings bonk. He kissed her nose, eluded her lips and grabbed the soap. He would ignore the ache in his groin long enough to have an adult conversation with her.

Of course that idea got tougher to stick with as soon as he actually touched her skin. He swallowed hard and concentrated. "When did you get in?"

"I took the earliest flight possible. I wanted to surprise Trent, and he'd said he was arriving early. He said he intended to visit with Kylie before too many of the practice customers arrived for the soft opening."

He ran his soapy hands over her curves, loving how she shifted in rhythm with him, seeking his touch. The tips of her nipples beaded against his palms and he shuddered to maintain control. Yeah, Trent had arrived early, but that was because he had wanted to get *Paradise* moored at the marina before the tide turned. Not that he was going to tell Paige that. Yet. "You've got all three days off?"

She hesitated then nodded, her dark wet curls bobbing. "I'm all yours."

He wished. He tugged her against him, the soft curves of her flesh nestled close as he spooned around her. He nibbled on her neck. "I like that idea. Very much."

"Mason?"

"Hmmm?" He was enjoying letting his hands meander over her flesh. Cupping her breasts, gliding over her smooth belly. He played with the jewel in her naval, twirling a finger round the trinket for a moment before continuing the journey southward.

"You want to check out the swimming pool with me?" she asked.

What the hell? "Right now?"

She gasped as his fingers found her core. He probed carefully, uncertain how hard Trent had played her earlier. When Paige eased her legs open farther he smiled. Maybe not that hard.

"Later. After," she gasped.

"After what?" He made a delicate sweep around the tight nub of her clitoris, and she shook in his grasp.

"Bastard."

Mason laughed. "After you come?"

"You too."

"Hmmm, I can wait. How do you want it? Like this?" A single finger slipped into her core, and she breathed out long and slow. Her hips pulsed against his hand, rocking her clit against his palm.

"Yes. Soft and slow. I want..." Paige stiffened slightly. "Wait, I wanted to do something for you."

She would have wiggled free if he hadn't held her in such a tight grip. "Hush. I've been dreaming about making you come all week."

Her tension slowly faded and he laughed to himself. What was she up to?

Slowly she widened her stance, just enough that with the tilt of her hips he cupped her sex softly. Slow motions back and forth followed as the water poured down in a steady stream. He slipped them farther under the deluge, the silky soft caress of the liquid easing his hand's motion against her body. The touch of her teased his senses. Everywhere they came in contact, thrills hit him. His cock nudged her ass, and he canted his hips harder to enjoy a leisurely slide against her skin. Being inside her, against her. Around her—it was all so damn fine.

She leaned her head back on his shoulder and twisted to offer her lips. He dipped down once. Tender and chaste. Lips closed, simply pressed to hers. Pulled back and returned her smile. Approached again, this time sweeping his tongue over the seam of her mouth, only to laugh when she snuck out her tongue and licked his in passing.

Their playfulness continued, grew more heated. She grasped his hips, fingers splayed wide as she rocked back on his dick. The pressure in his balls increased, the base of his spine sending warning signals that he was close to blowing.

All the while his hand continued to caress, circling and massaging her clit. Her breathing grew ragged, the short sharp utterances from her throat making it clear she was close. He thrust his tongue into her mouth and increased the pressure of his fingers, and she came. Body-shaking, fingernails digging into his flesh. Moisture flooded from her core, and he eased his pace, his own release hovering so close he wasn't sure if he should let himself come or prolong the agony for the sake of actually being buried in her body.

Then she stole control from him, dropped to her knees and engulfed his shaft.

The explosive gasp from his lips would have made her smile, but her mouth was too full of cock. Damn if he wasn't the one who always managed to entice her to change her mind about what she wanted in bed. Just when she'd decided it was time for a long, slow assault, Mason would trigger the response that called for nothing less than a hard fuck-me-blind session.

Which, strictly speaking, wasn't a bad talent to have.

She held his cock in her fist and used her mouth on only the head, licking and sucking as she cradled his balls in her other hand. Every motion of her tongue as she teased him dragged a groan from his lips, along with a wide variety of curse words. His Aussie accent and choice swear words made her smile. The way he cradled her head carefully, fingers threaded through her hair—gentle and protective. She pursed her lips tighter and sucked, dragging back, and he shouted, seed leaking from the hot tip of his cock and bathing her tongue with salty essence. Then the gentle, cautious man disappeared and he pressed in farther. Hips pumping toward her, his hands locked her in position as he took complete control, and she savored it all.

The water falling on her shifted away, hitting the backs of her calves and feet instead of pouring in rivulets over her face. She pressed against his hands to try and tilt her head slightly, lifting her gaze.

Mason slowed his pace again, staring at her lips. There was raw hunger on his face and in his brilliant blue eyes, his blond hair plastered to his head. She could picture what he saw—her mouth stretched wide around his cock, her body naked before him. Her nipples were tight in spite of the heat of the water, and she squeezed her legs together, the liquid on her thighs flooding from her core, not the overhead shower.

His voice trembled when he spoke. "Bloody hell, I love how you look on your knees. So giving and—*fuck*."

She'd pressed her tongue harder against his dick as he'd slipped in. His eyes rolled up and his head fell back as he groaned.

Slower still, Mason buried his cock to the back of her throat and she swallowed, grasping his ass cheeks and trapping him. She waited, breathing through her nose, taking in the scent of his skin—clean and masculine. Wanting to store away every possible minute of time, every moment and memory and...

Without another motion he erupted in her mouth, his cock jerking, seed filling her. She swallowed the hot liquid, throat convulsing as she took it all. Mason hissed, his body curled over her, one hand hard against the shower wall as his body shook.

She licked him clean. Caressed his strong leg muscles as she leaned her cheek against the band of muscle above where his thigh and torso met. Her heart pounded, and his touch on her head made her heart leap. It was a caress, a fleeting stroke with his fingers, soft as anything, followed by a delicate brush of his knuckles over her cheek.

How many more times would she have before this weekend was over? How many times to try and tell them without words how much they meant to her? Because falling in love had never been a part of their agreement.

Tears rushed to her eyes and she blinked them away. When he reached down and assisted her to her feet, she twisted to hide under the shower, letting the droplets of water camouflage her sadness.

Mason nestled their bodies together, his semi-hard cock tucked against her.

"That was bloody fine." He kissed her, slow and easy, one hand cupping her face to keep her in position. She wondered if he tasted his seed. The evidence of how much she wanted all of him?

And all of Trent—and that was where she was damned. Because there was no way to possibly choose one of them and say goodbye to the other. Not only because they were "best mates", but because...

She couldn't choose.

"I love doing it. And more." Paige stared into his eyes, enjoying the way they twinkled at her as he leaned in for another round.

Mason kissed her, drawing a moan of satisfaction from her in the way he made love to her mouth. He really was the most fantastic kisser. Plus all the other things he did with that mouth—sinfully good. Both the guys went down on her without any provocation.

She'd never had a boyfriend like that back home in Canada. Hopefully it wasn't a genetic trait only built into Aussie men, because it was another thing she was going to really miss.

Like I need another reason to miss them other than I've fallen in love, two times over...

A soft chuckle interrupted her thoughts. "What's that sigh for?"

Oops—as if she was about to tell him the truth. "You make me happy, Mason."

"And that makes you sigh? Damn. I was going for screaming meant happy."

Paige turned in his arms. "We'll do the screaming bit later. How about we go and take a peek around the resort? Trent can catch up with us once he's done visiting with his sister."

Mason nodded. "She's done alright for herself, hasn't she?"

He reached past Paige and twisted off the water. The towels were fluffy, enormous and heated to perfection on the radiant towel bar.

"This place is incredible. I'm sure Kylie worked hard to make it as manager."

Mason scooped her into his arms and carried her to the main room, ignoring the king-sized bed. She stared longingly after it. Even though she did want to see more of the resort and give Kylie proper congratulations, there was so little time. And while sex wasn't the only thing she enjoyed with the boys, it was definitely one thing she couldn't do over IM or Skype once she was gone.

He lowered her carefully, nuzzling her cheek with his own. "We've all been working hard. Trent, me. You."

"I don't—" The words choked off. She didn't want to tell him about the farewell party her coworkers had given her. Yesterday had been her final day on the job—and while she could bake pastries anywhere, it was another indicator of the countdown clock marking off her final hours.

Mason snagged her chin in his fingers firmly, refusing to let her avoid his gaze. "I swear you spend more time baking than some CEOs of major corps spend in the office."

Because when I'm not with you or Trent, work is all I've got. "That wasn't what I was going to say. We all have to earn a living. I bake—and pastry chefs work strange hours—you should know that by now."

His hands hadn't stopped the entire time since he'd set her on her feet. Every inch he dried not only steamed from the heat of the towel, but the sheer eroticism of his fingers.

His very *thorough* fingers.

"Well, I think you need to consider taking it easy for a little while. Between all the work and the adventuring you've dragged us on, Trent and I, I don't think you've stopped once over the past year."

Her throat closed tight. She'd take it easy when she left Aussie soil. "I just want to be with you guys."

He slid a hand down her torso, admiration in his face. "I'm looking forward to this weekend. I'm going to do everything in my power to ensure you enjoy yourself, more than you ever have before." His lips met hers, a soft, brief caress.

"I always enjoy my time with you."

Mason's grin flashed past sinful as he ogled her body, but his expression as he settled on her face was less lecherous, more caring. "Grab your swimmers, and we'll hit the surf before stuffing our faces with grub. The waves look fun."

Paige retreated to the back bedroom where she'd stashed her suitcase. As she pulled on her swimsuit, her thoughts whirled.

Was she going to enjoy the weekend? Physically, she had no doubts that she'd be sated and completely satisfied long before their time together ended. Emotionally? She needed to brace her few remaining walls, or the coming heartache was going to kill her.

Chapter Three

Trent drummed his fingers on the railing as he leaned over and examined the swimming pool spread below him like a shimmering jewel. "Are you sure she's not there?"

"I'm sorry, Mr. Sullivan, but she's not in the office, and while she's got a mobile phone, it's strictly for emergencies during the soft opening." The woman on the other end of the phone sounded professional, tactful—and controlling as hell. Trent made a mental note to let Kylie know her assistant was certainly on the money for keeping the wolves at bay.

Although as her bro, he wasn't sure he counted as a wolf.

"Fine, leave a message confirming her brother Trent is here, and if she's got a minute, call."

"Very good, sir. Enjoy your stay."

Trent strolled along the smooth walkway, the rich greenery on either side of him lush and full. A deluge of bright red and pink tropical flowers flooded the trails between the resort buildings with their perfume. Combined with the cloudless sky and the distant roar of the ocean, all the elements formed a perfect picture of paradise.

Now if only he had a few reassurances he wasn't going to be kicked out of the Garden of Eden prematurely. Their time with Paige hadn't been nearly long enough. Was suggesting they veer from their original "nothing but fun" commitment going to ruin everything?

A bench tucked into the foliage beside the path attracted him and he paused, sprawling on the curved wood seating. He hadn't left the room that long ago—Mason and Paige were probably still fucking each other's brains out. His dick stirred at the thought of going and watching them, but fair was fair. He'd had some time alone with her. Now he'd be a sport and let Mason have the same.

Funny how the three of them just...fit. They'd never had a major issue, nothing more than a few squabbles, ever since they met. Of course, neither he nor Mason had ever broken the rules with her, certainly not like they'd been discussing privately for the past two months.

Since high school he and Mason had dreamed about taking an extended sailing trip along the Australian coastline. When the perfect yacht had shown up for sale at the harbor, they'd jumped at the chance to buy her. *Paradise* was exactly what they needed for the trip—trim and yet spacious enough for comfort. The timing was right for him to take a sabbatical from his job at customs, and Mason could write anywhere. All their harebrained plans were falling into place but for one major obstacle.

Paige.

They'd never imagined having someone like her in their life back in their original brainstorming days. Leaving her behind as they headed off? Impossible. Not because they wanted her along for sex, but because she would totally get the adventure. The whole trip was something she would appreciate—a way to experience more of the world. Leaving Canada in the first place to come to Australia had proven she had the drive.

But would she be willing to give up her job as a pastry chef to set out into the wild for half a year with them? Part of him said yes—she'd been open and game for so much in the past. Part of him thought he was nuts.

He tilted his head back to stare into the blue sky. A couple of birds warbled at him from an overhead branch and he laughed. It wasn't the idea of inviting her to join them on the ship that freaked him out. It was asking her to change their casual rules to something more intimate. How would she take the news that both he and Mason had fallen in love with her? Most women would run screaming.

Paige wasn't most women—and she'd been happily involved sexually with two men for a year now, but there was a wide gap between casual and permanent. Permanent implied words like family and marriage and all the things not usually associated with fucking-flings.

His mobile phone rang, and when he checked the number

he frowned in confusion. Work? *What the hell do they want?*

"Sullivan here." God, don't let it be work calling him in for another emergency at the docks. There was no way he wanted to leave Bandicoot Cove before they'd told Paige what he and Mason hoped for. They had to muddle their way forward, and soon.

"Hey, Trent. Bad news. Your leave has been approved. I've got the papers here, awaiting your signature."

Relief shot through Trent like an electric zap. "Fuck it—you nearly gave me a heart attack, you bastard. How did you do that so fast? And what do I owe you?"

Charles's deep laugh carried over the line. "It's not rocket science, mate. Admit it, you hate paperwork. Good thing you've got a friend in the government form department. I can get you anything you need, right?"

Trent's head spun. Another step forward to making the trip a reality. "Can you email the form to me? Fax—courier? Whatever the hell you need."

"No worries. You'll have it in the morning. I have one question, though."

"What?"

"When's the wedding?"

Trent choked, snapping upright. "What?"

Silence screamed at him from the other end of the line for a second. "Good one. You had me going for a minute. Mason Wood called and asked me to grab a *Notice of Intended Marriage* form for you as well. If that's not right, I'll leave it out of the package."

His brain had gone numb. With one fell swoop all his grey matter had ceased to function. Why had—? *No, don't ask, just accept it and kill Mason later.* "No, no, that's fine. Sorry, I...misheard you. There's—" Trent glanced around frantically, looking for an excuse. He whipped off his shoe and dragged it against the slats on the back of the bench. The heel made a *thump, thump* noise that echoed nicely. "There's someone working on the fence—it was a little loud for a minute. Distracting. Send everything over, with instructions, and we'll take care of the rest."

"You got it. Catch you for a beer next weekend? Last one before you take off?"

"You bet." Trent gave the shoe another couple of dedicated

drags to ensure the staccato noise registered louder in the phone than his heart, its violent pounding ringing audibly in his ears. "My shout. You're a lifesaver."

Charles hung up and Trent's shoe fell unminded from his fingers as he slammed in the speed dial for Mason's phone. Screw it if he was interrupting anything. The bloke had a lot to answer for.

An Intent of Marriage form? What the hell was Mason doing?

Trent fidgeted, slipping his shoe back on and stomping the path toward the beach area. The phone rang four times before flipping to Mason's voice message and Trent growled, snapping his phone off and shoving it in his pocket.

Marriage. It wasn't as if he'd never thought of the institute. Had no issues with it. His parents were still rock solid, and somewhere down the road he always figured he'd get hitched.

He pictured getting to wake up next to Paige every morning for the rest of his life. Experiencing her enthusiasm, not only for a weekend at a time, but daily. Hourly.

Nightly.

Oh hell yeah.

But the plan he *thought* he and Mason had agreed on was to convince Paige to travel with them, then slowly let her know they wanted more than a casual situation. Allow her to switch gears from this being a fling to something they were serious about. Let her make up her mind about marriage and everything else in her own time.

He reached the end of the path, the greenery giving way to the white sand beach, recliners and sun umbrellas in pristine rows waiting for resort-goers. Trent ditched his shoes and socks, and an attendant appeared out of nowhere to whisk them away to individual cubbies tucked discreetly behind an unobtrusive mesh screen. The man raced back with a chilled water bottle and a towel before offering to assist in finding a chair. Trent waved him off.

The sand warmed the soles of his feet, the midday sun heating the beach and his body nicely. Now if he could find a way to settle the flipping firecrackers going off in his brain.

He grabbed a chair and dragged it partway down the beach. There were only a handful of people around—Kylie had mentioned that Friday morning was going to be slower for the trial run at the resort, with most of the practice guests arriving for the big party in the evening. He'd deliberately brought the yacht in on the morning tide to make the most of every available minute, and while he didn't regret it...*fuck*. How were they going to tell Paige what he and Mason had planned? And what *was* the bloody plan?

The sand flew from under his toes as he aligned his chair with the sun. One leg straddling each side, he sat, the thick cushion under his hips cradling him softly. Here he was in the lap of luxury and he was...

Miserable. Bloody, whacked-out fool.

Two silhouettes darted from the greenery and raced for the ocean, and he watched distractedly, mind racing. If Paige were willing to marry him, he'd have no objections.

Mason—*fuckit*. He'd been the bloke who told Charles to organize a marriage form in the first place. Was there something his best mate and his woman weren't telling him? *Shit*.

The last time they'd made a rendezvous for a weekend get together, he'd had to cancel. He'd been called in to do an emergency job for the customs crew. Normally his position as a customs inspector—scuba diving to examine the hulls of visiting vessels—was a entertaining way to make a living, and rarely did it interfere with his private life, but what if this time something had happened?

He growled at himself, grabbing the bottom of his shirt and yanking it off. Now he was acting like a teenager and imaging all sorts of plots and problems where there was nothing that couldn't be solved with a little conversation.

Trent leaned back and opened the water bottle, chugging thirstily. Images of Paige greeting him in her sexy outfit flitted past and he had to adjust his dick, wiggling in the chair in a losing battle to find a comfortable position.

A rolling line of white broke smoothly along the crest of the wave the swimmers played in. Trent's trained eye measured the speed of the curl—there wasn't enough of a current off Bilby Island to surf, or even body surf. The couple didn't seem to mind. Their bodies glistened in the sunlight, water splashing everywhere as they stood and let the waves knock them over.

Images flashed, a memory of the sun flashing bright against surging water. The day they'd met Paige...

"Done making a fool of yourself, mate?"

Trent raised his middle finger and held it firmly in Mason's direction, smirking as laughter bounced back at him. He gripped the skimboard resolutely, timing his approach. He took a run at the surf, dropped the flat wooden board and stepped on top. The thin layer of water between the board and the sand allowed him to spin lightly in a half circle as he shifted his body weight.

Then he hit something and flipped arse-first to the sand. Again.

This time it wasn't only the sound of Mason's amusement that rang in his ears. There were a couple of long-legged women sunning nearby on the white sands of Bondi Beach. One blonde, one brunette—both smiling admiringly his direction. He pulled himself out of his awkward sprawl and tossed them a wink, rising to dust off the sand.

The women were still watching, and his interest rose. Two of them—that worked, since both he and Mason were without any female companionship at the moment.

"Well done. Still no broken bones." Mason slapped him on the shoulder. "You ready for me to show you how it's really done?"

Trent rolled his eyes and passed over the board. "Drinks on you when you fuck up."

"Deal."

Mason didn't take more than five seconds to eyeball the water before he shouted and raced forward, dancing over the surface as if he had wings on his heels.

Bastard.

After a final flamboyant twirl, Mason snatched up the board and cockily strolled back to Trent's side. "Lessons anytime, mate."

"That offer open to anyone?"

The lightly accented question came from the beachside. The brunette Trent had admired rose to her feet and joined them. Her one-piece suit wasn't the most revealing on the beach, but she had curves in all the right places, and Trent's appreciation was reflected on Mason's face.

Mason made a mock bow. "You brave enough to try?"

Light shrug. "Doesn't look too dangerous. If I fall I'll just get back up." She held out her hand. "Paige Kingston."

"Trent Sullivan." He pointed at his mate. "Mason Wood."

She nodded at Mason, then glanced over her shoulder. "Meg, you want to try?"

The blonde grimaced. "Gad no. You're mad."

Paige turned back to them, muttering "stick in the mud" under her breath.

"Where you from, love?" Mason asked with a grin.

"Canada." She faced him square on. "You going to teach me? I like your technique better than Trent's."

Oh really? Trent eased between them. "All depends what we're doing. I think you'll find I have very good technique."

She lifted her chin and stared him in the eye. The tip of her tongue slipped out to wet her lips, and his dick got hard. "Sounds interesting."

They were still staring at each other when Mason tugged her hand to explain how to ride the skimboard.

The three of them spent the rest of the afternoon playing in the surf, laughing constantly. Someone selling handmade necklaces on the sly wandered past and Trent impulsively bought her one, draping it around her neck with great ceremony. He received a teasing thank-you kiss on the cheek, although her eyes promised more.

Her companion had disappeared when they finally collapsed onto the beach blanket, Trent and Mason on either side of her. His arm lay along side of hers, touching lightly. He'd let his attraction to her remain clear the entire time. Only Mason had been flirting with her just as hard, and she hadn't shown her hand yet as to who she liked better.

"You've been abandoned," Mason noted.

Paige sighed, almost as if in relief. "That's just fine. She's a coworker and kind of tagged along uninvited. She didn't seem to get the part of the conversation when I told her I wanted to have fun."

"Stick in the mud?"

Paige blushed. "You heard that? I wasn't very polite."

Trent lightly nudged her arm. "True through?"

"Damn right. Life isn't for sitting on a beach rotating like a chicken on a spit. It's for grabbing hold of and experiencing everything you can."

That's when Trent noticed Mason was tracing designs on her other arm with his fingertips.

"Any other experiences I can help you with today, Paige Kingston?" Mason asked.

The bloke had balls. Trent copied his example and rolled a little closer, casually letting his thigh make contact with hers.

She glanced back and forth between the two of them, her smile growing broader. "Well, that depends. Is this a package deal?"

"Two for one?" Trent and Mason exchanged a quick look and a nod. Trent was game, even if they'd never done such a thing before. He sat up and let his gaze trickle over her. "If you're interested, I think we can deliver."

"I like the sound of that." She leaned her shoulder against Mason's, checking her watch. "I have one question, though."

The multitude of ideas of what this intriguing Canadian could possibly want to know distracted Trent almost as much as the hand she slipped around his neck. "One question?"

Her smile blinded him. "Either of you want to try skydiving tomorrow? I made a booking, but I need at least one person to go with me."

Trent came back from his daydream to find himself staring at the long, lean lines of the woman as her partner chased her from the water. She looked amazingly familiar, and he cursed.

How the hell did the two of them get down here that fast? He hadn't wandered the grounds for that long.

He lifted a hand off the chair, intending to wave at them. Instead, he let his arm fall back to his side. Mason had caught Paige from behind, and the two shadowy outlines merged into one. Even at a distance Trent knew what they were doing. He'd seen it often enough—seen it that first day on the beach. Paige's arms would rise up to allow her fingers to dig into Mason's hair. Their torsos would be in complete contact, her soft breasts pressed to his chest, his dick to her belly. Trent's own cock filled again as he longed to experience the pressure of contact.

They were kissing. Definitely. Long, slow kisses with lots of tongue, and Trent let his hand fall casually over his lap as he looked around to see if anyone was close by, because if he didn't do something, he was going to explode. His dick swelled, aching for a touch.

There were a couple of people sunbathing twenty-five meters to his left. Too close, still far too close. He abandoned the chair and recovered his shoes, ignoring his demanding cock as it sprang upright inside his boardies. Staying put was out of the question, only which way should he go?

Not even five paces later, Trent had to acknowledge he'd deliberately set an intercept course with his friends. All three of them were headed toward the central core of the resort, Paige tugging Mason along by the hand. So much for letting things progress slowly this weekend. He wanted some answers, and he wanted them now.

The brilliance of Paige's smile when he reached them said nothing but that she was glad to see him. "How's Kylie?"

"Busy as all get-out. Never even caught a glimpse of her."

Mason wrapped an arm around Paige's waist. His mate's move was unpracticed, natural. The flash of frustration that hit Trent had nothing to do with the easy physical intimacy between the two of them and everything to do with his own mental uncertainty about the future. He needed to get Mason alone and ask a few pointed questions.

Paige snatched his wrist in both her hands and actually bounced with excitement. "We're going to the water slide. You want to come?"

Jesus. *No.* Sliding with his cock the size of a cricket bat he was liable to put out an eye.

"That might not be the best idea right now."

Paige gave Mason a kiss on the cheek, then leaned up on tiptoe to whisper in his ear. His brow rose, and he snorted before patting her on the arse and pushing her in Trent's direction. She glanced around before sliding her hands up his abdomen to play with his chest hair.

"I think we need to find somewhere to be alone soon." She rolled her hips against his and any thought of keeping his woody a secret vanished.

He clutched her waist, limiting her motion. If he held her still maybe his cock would relax. "I want to spend time with you outside the bedroom."

It came out gruffer than he'd intended, and a shadow crossed in front of her eyes. *Damn blunderer.* He leaned over and kissed her gently, asking for forgiveness with his lips.

She pressed her full length against him, the moisture

clinging to her two-piece suit transferring to his body. Warm, comfortable and yet tempting. He threaded his fingers through hers before leaning away to stare into her eyes. Yeah, a little more time outside of fucking each other silly would help demonstrate they had something worth using any means possible to maintain. No matter how unorthodox.

"TS?"

A soft, womanly voice intruded on what he had considered a mighty fine personal moment, but he managed to drag his gaze away from Paige's big brown eyes. Then he straightened in surprise, letting go of her completely.

"Sienna?"

Paige wasn't sure what she expected, but for Trent to drop her as if she were a hot potato and reach to envelop the little bit of Aussie beauty right there before her wasn't on the list. At least it was a friendly hug, not a full-body one, or the woman would be getting a dose of Trent's cock pressed against her, and Paige really didn't think she could handle that right now.

She stepped back uncertainly. *Damn*—this was one of those awkward moments she'd managed to avoid until now. All the places they'd met, all the trips the three of them had taken together, had drawn the guys away from their familiar turf.

This getaway was Kylie's gig though, and with Trent invited to the soft opening as her younger brother, Paige should have known there would be others of their group around. She'd met Kylie before, and Mason's twin a couple of times—nice enough woman, although McKenzie seemed totally unaware her brother was sleeping with anyone, let alone sharing a woman with his best friend.

And now little Miss Perfectly-Put-Together with the great set of knockers... Paige glanced at her own chest and wished her sports swimsuit was padded. It wasn't like she was flat or anything, but the tight top compressed her chest until she felt as if she were wearing a training bra.

"Damn, it's good to see you, SJ." Seamlessly, Trent stepped back and Mason stepped forward to embrace the chick, and Paige clenched her teeth together to stop from growling out her ownership.

Holy shit, she was in trouble if she couldn't keep her jealousy under control and hidden. Being green-eyed over her man paying attention to another woman made sense. Being possessive over two men? That would be a hell of a lot harder to explain.

She crossed her arms in front of her chest and tried to look casual. Although with both her men paying full attention to— Sienna?—there wasn't much else she could do.

Then Trent turned back, his expression sharp and focused as he pulled her against his side. From the way he slipped their bodies together it was clear he had no intention of hiding they were a pair, and the knot of jealousy that had sprung up was pacified. A little.

"SJ, I'd like you to meet Paige. She's my special guest here for Kylie's practice run. Paige? This is Sienna, one of the three ladies who made my teenage life hell."

So, this was the one member of the Goddess Pack she hadn't met yet. Kylie, McKenzie and Sienna—inseparable and deadly to the male libido. Mason and Trent had both told her about drooling over this particular woman back in their teens. Paige reached out a hand and politely shook with Sienna, attempting to make her greeting seem pleased and not annoyed.

Even though the other woman wore a happy expression, tiny tired lines marred the corners of Sienna's eyes, and as Trent's hand made a slow circle between Paige's shoulder blades, the rest of her distrust sputtered away. Something wasn't right in the heavens to cause the woman to look so lost.

Paige leaned forward and smiled for real, offering what sympathy she could without a word. "It's nice to finally meet you. Gorgeous resort, isn't it?"

Sienna nodded, adjusting her shorts as she straightened, her chest drawing the attention of not only Paige, but both Mason and Trent. "Absolutely stunning," Sienna agreed with a nod. "And I've only seen my room and the ocean. I'm headed for the pool now." She paused. "Wanna join me?"

Paige opened her mouth to answer when Mason cut in, drawing close to her other side. "We haven't had anything to eat yet. You want to grab some grub with us?"

Sienna shook her head with a grin. "Thanks for the offer, but Ky told me the strawberry daiquiris here are the best in Australia. And they only make them at the pool bar. I'm off to order a double."

Paige's stomach grumbled and Mason laughed.

"If we don't feed Paige soon she's liable to turn on us. Woman is scary when she's hungry."

She shifted without thinking to bump him with her hip. "As good as the daiquiris sound, I think we'd better hit the buffet first."

Paige flushed slightly as she spotted Sienna's one brow raised high, amusement painting her face. Damn, that hadn't looked like a "lover's tap", had it? More a buddy bump? Because Trent had as good as declared them a couple. Explaining why she was acting intimate with Mason as well—not an easy task.

Trent frowned as he stared at Sienna. "Where's Ben?"

Whatever light had glowed in Sienna's eyes flickered and died.

"I'm guessing he's at work," she said. "I wouldn't know though. We broke up."

Both the guys stiffened. Mason muttered something low that sounded like "fucker" "asshole" and "pain".

"Shit, SJ, what the hell?" Trent would have reached for her again, but Paige held him back. This time it wasn't jealousy that made her restrain him from offering a hug. The woman didn't need sympathy right now. She was gorgeous—if Paige wasn't firmly in the loving-the-male camp, she would have been all over Sienna. If a guy was stupid enough to call it off with the Goddess, he was the one who deserved sympathy—along with a swift kick in the balls.

No, the solution was to grab on and seize life with both hands. Like Paige herself intended on doing until the last possible second.

Paige clapped her hands slowly a couple of times, nodding as if in approval before pointing a finger at Sienna. "You know what? Sometimes the best additions to our lives are a few choice subtractions. Assholes, cheats, riffraff..."

Sienna smiled at Trent. "TS, I like the way your woman thinks." She turned to Paige with a shrug. "I wish he had been an arsehole, cheat or riffraff. Unfortunately he wasn't. Isn't. He's just a nice guy who married his job instead of his fiancée." Her voice caught. "It happens."

Mason jammed his hands in his pockets, a dark flush coloring his cheeks. For the second time that day Paige watched her gentle friend show a protective side she'd never witnessed before. "If you need any knees broken, say the word.

Otherwise...drink a few for us, and if you see Mack before me, tell her I need to chat with Aidan as soon as possible. The bloody bastard turned off his mobile."

Sienna nodded, straightening noticeably. That trace of amusement Paige had seen at the start was back, and as she turned, Paige swore that Sienna was making some non-New Year's resolutions. Something that involved kissing her workaholic ex goodbye with more than fruity alcohol. Paige wished her well, even as the sight of the woman's heart-shaped butt swaying from side to side as Sienna disappeared down the path made her sigh.

Why couldn't *she* have an ass like that?

Chapter Four

A resounding groan slipped from his mate's lips, and Mason chuckled under his breath as Trent popped the top button of his trousers and stretched his legs under the table.

"I'm going to explode," Trent complained.

Paige shook her head in mock sympathy. "Really? Why does that not surprise me? Wait, let me guess. Maybe it was the four helpings of crepes you hoovered down? Or the six-egg omelet?"

"I think it was the tarts. I've never seen a selection of pastries like that before." Mason paused, leaning back in his own chair as he winked at Paige. "Except the time you brought us to your shop and let us go wild in your practice batches. I think the whipped cream was the best part. Or maybe the custard. Or—"

Trent groaned for a second time. "Oh God, stop talking about food. And yeah, Paige's baking is better. The tarts were good, but something was missing."

She sparkled at him. "You and your silver tongue. Although..." She frowned briefly, picking up a smidge of crust from her plate and sniffing it lightly. "You're right. I wasn't going to say anything, but if you caught it, I better let someone know they've got a bad batch of butter somewhere."

Paige patted her napkin to her mouth then rose. Mason surged upward instinctively before he caught the confused look she tossed his direction.

"I was just going to the kitchen to chat with the chef. That's what this soft opening business is about, right? To solve problems before the paying customers arrive?"

Mason grabbed her hand and lifted her fingers to his lips,

kissing them softly. "You're exactly right. Go on, then—it's my turn to try and find my sister. Meet you back in our room?"

Her cheeks flushed as she glanced around the room cautiously. She spoke quietly. "You shouldn't be seen kissing me when people think I'm with Trent."

Screw that. "Any polite male can kiss a pretty girl's knuckles." The doubt and worry in her eyes made him crazy. He tilted his head toward the kitchen doors. "Go on. They need you in there."

He watched her retreat across the room, all long, lean lines, and the echo of the words he'd just spoken repeated back in his head. *He* needed her, in his life. They had to make this work.

Time for some last-minute planning.

Mason turned and leaned in close to his friend. "Okay, here's what we've got to—"

"An Intent of Marriage form? What the fuck, Mason?"

Sudden relief rushed him. "Charles got one for us? Fantastic." That was one less thing to worry about, then.

Trent's elbows hit the tabletop and his gaze narrowed. "You bloody arsehole. What the hell were you thinking? We weren't going to ask her to marry anyone, not right off the bat."

Oh shit. Mason frowned in confusion. Hadn't he told Trent about this? Hmm, maybe not, since his buddy seemed intent on brooding about how everything was going to tip into shit at any moment.

"Now wait a minute, I merely intended it as an emergency back-up. I thought we should have it to be able to prove how serious we are. I mean, it's a pretty big deal to switch the rules around at this point in our relationship. Although, I frankly don't think there are going to be any problems." *Yeah, yeah, that was pure positive thinking and shit.* Mason ignored the expression of disbelief on Trent's face. "But it struck me that if she did have any concerns it would be on the long-term part of the situation. Having the ability to get married quickly, when she wants to, could be the deciding factor that makes this work. It's good for eighteen months."

"But now the people at work know I've got the form."

Mason's mind swirled in confusion. "Bastard. Don't you want to marry her?"

Trent's entire attitude shifted as his grin stretched wide. "Oh hell, I'd love to marry her, and you've just handed me the keys to be the one to get first crack at asking. I have no objections."

Strangely enough, neither did Mason, although he still had to share that with Trent. "Keep it quiet for now. I'm going to get Aidan to help with a final clean-up on *Paradise* this afternoon. I thought we could take Paige out tonight after the party and show her around."

"That's when we'll tell her our plans?"

"And ask her to join us."

Trent relaxed back, shaking his head slightly. "Are we fucked in the head or what?"

Oh man. How to explain this? Mason poured a little more coffee into his cup and decided to simply go for broke. If anyone could handle it, his best mate should.

"You remember when your folks planned that trip to America over the Christmas hols that year, and you got chicken pox and couldn't go?"

Trent groaned loudly. "Bloody hell, are you going to break out the pictures again?"

"Just give me a minute. You stayed with us. That was the start of us being best mates—you fit in with the family like a glove. I got along better with you than with my horde of brothers."

"Your family is insanity to the nth degree. The whole damn shooting match of you. Freaking Christmas morning started at three a.m., and your father was the first one awake, shrieking at the top of his lungs as he threw his stocking around."

Mason snorted. "Yeah, the old man is hilarious. He actually calmed down a lot that year out of deference to your sensitive presence."

"Bullshit." Trent smiled wryly. "What mystical thing do you need to remind me of that occurred when I moved into Chaos Central of Woodville?"

Mason picked his words carefully. "Did you ever feel as if you were an outsider? Did any of my brothers, or McKenzie, or Mum and Dad do anything but welcome you in and treat you like family?"

"At thirteen, McKenzie treating me like family was not what I wanted. Back then I had the hots for her."

Mason faked a gag. "Please, my sister? Talking about sex

and Mack in the same sentence—you know those topics are off limits."

His best mate poked back mercilessly. "Yeah, tell me Aidan isn't fucking her mindless."

Arghhh, the images flashing through his mind were enough to make him purse his mouth.

"Stop joking around, I don't want to have to bleach my brain." Mason threw a leftover pastry at Trent. "Can we stick to the conversation at hand? You came, spent Christmas, and never really left. You've been a part of the family ever since. You and me—we've crashed down mountainsides, gotten stuck up creeks without a paddle. Gone without food for days when we got lost."

Trent nodded. "What's your point?"

Mason took a deep breath. "I like doing stuff with you. It's...right. We fit, and I don't see any reason why we can't just keep doing things together. Even the important things like getting married and having a family."

Trent's jaw swung open. "Holy fuck, are you hitting on me?"

Oh shit. "No! Bloody hell, I mean with Paige. I see no reason why we can't both be with her, for good. If she wants a marriage license to make it official, that's fine with me, but I don't care if it's your name on the piece of paper next to hers, or mine. There's enough room for me to care for her, and you—in a totally nonsexual way—and I just..."

Mason trailed off. The look of amusement on Trent's face pissed him off a little. "What?"

Trent sniffed dramatically. "My first marriage proposal. Mason, I'm touched."

Mason resisted the urge to smack his mate's head with his fist. "Arsehole."

Trent raised a brow. "You have to carry the bouquet. And there's no fucking way I'm wearing a garter belt."

"Bastard."

"Also, no veil. Kissing through those things is nasty—"

"Enough."

Trent's big hand slammed down between his shoulders, and Mason breathed a huge sigh of relief. It appeared he had dodged the bullet of having his face rearranged. Best mate or not, Trent and he had rumbled often enough Mason preferred to settle matters without getting fists involved.

"I won't kick your arse for moving on the marriage form without me, but Mason, let's not blow this. Take our time, don't rush. I don't want to lose her." Trent rumbled out the words and Mason nodded in agreement.

They rose, heading for the exit door as one. Once outside, Mason paused at the split in the path. "I won't say a word to Paige without you there. Let me organize things with Aidan, then I'll meet you back at the room. Paige should be there soon."

Trent raised a brow. "Still say that bloke's nailing your sister. If he's not, he's an idiot."

Of all the people to join into the madness of the Wood household, Aidan Rogers was a prime example of why Mason knew his idea of extended relationships would work. The big dude was nothing but heart when it came down to it. "Bloody dickless wonder."

"Aidan?"

"You, if you keep jawing about my sister like that."

"Whatever."

Mason stuck his middle finger in his Trent's face. His mate grinned as he shoved the hand away, then turned without another word and headed back into the resort building towering over them.

Mason stood for a minute and let relief sweep over him. Trent had actually taken that announcement a lot better than anticipated. Mason had fully expected the revelation of his ease with unusual marital arrangements to be met with a little more physical violence.

Things were looking up. Mason turned, whistling lightly as he headed back toward the pool and made a mental to-do list.

Track down his sister, Mack.

Get Aidan, her constant sidekick, to supply a little muscle.

Spend a little free time with Paige in the afternoon.

Hit the evening party then arrange to change their entire future.

It was looking like a busy day, and he could hardly wait.

A steady stream of supplies passed by as Trent held the

suite door open. He gawked, speechless, until the seventh white uniform was followed by Paige's arrival.

He caught her by the arm. "Umm, Paige?"

"Just a second." She patted his fingers distractedly, slipping into the kitchen and pointing as she tossed out orders. "Put the cooler over there. Baking sheets on the stovetop. Thank you, and tell Leo that if the rest of the mascarpone doesn't arrive on the supply barge, he has to let me know immediately, so I can make alternate plans."

The server she spoke to dipped his head and scurried away, the long line of uniforms disappearing out the door like a host of silent ghosts.

Trent stared in consternation at the piles of cooking supplies now littering the counter. "Do I want to know what's happening?"

Paige pushed up her sleeves and headed for the sink. "I got shanghaied. Kylie's pastry chef came down with the mumps. That's why they were serving stale-dated boxed pastries. Somehow the sous chef sweet-talked me into prepping the desserts for the head table at a formal wedding tomorrow."

Ah, fuckit. Not an interruption to their already limited time. Although...Mason wasn't back yet, and his mate had mentioned he needed to finish getting *Paradise* ready for the grand reveal.

Maybe having Paige occupied for a little while this afternoon would be a good thing.

Trent leaned against the fridge and admired Paige as she moved effortlessly, organizing her workstations. "Anything I can help with? Hey, are you allowed to do this here? I thought all food products for public consumption had to be made in sterile, stainless-steel settings."

Paige raised a brow. "I may be a pushover, but I'm not stupid. The only thing we're doing right is figuring out what they can make. Elevation and humidity affect the dryness and consistency of pastry. The recipes I use in Sydney might not turn out properly, so I need to tweak them. Whatever I bake now, we'll eat. Then I'll give the kitchen directions, and they'll take over tomorrow. They have enough staff, just not the ability to deal with this specific circumstance."

Trent slipped to her side and hugged her close, kissing her nape gently. "Thank you."

She leaned back on him easily, twisting to catch hold of his lips for a quick kiss. "What for?"

"For offering to help and making my sister's job a little easier. I bet she was thrilled to have your assistance."

Paige reached for a block of cream cheese and laughed as she dumped it into a large bowl. "Kylie was appreciative, although also a little distracted."

"That makes sense. She's responsible for a lot right now."

Her laughter increased. "Oh yeah, I'm sure that broom closet I saw her getting dragged into by Mr. Tall, Dark and Studly was high on the priority list for the soft opening."

Trent jerked upright, her warm body rocking against him as she worked the cheese into a soft ball in the bowl. "My sister?"

"Uh-huh. And I don't think she was inspecting mops."

Oh fuck. There was a nasty taste in his mouth as he tried not to think about Kylie getting intimate with anyone. A touch of guilt hit for having teased Mason about *his* sister earlier in the day. "Enough. I don't think I need to know any details."

"But I was planning to tell you where his hands were—"

He rapidly slipped his own hands two directions, one over her mouth, one covering her chest. "Minx."

She pressed a kiss to his palm and giggled lightly. He released her mouth but nuzzled in tighter to her body. His cock rose again, and he rocked his hips against her.

"Hey, help first, play later," she protested. "Where's Mason?"

He kissed her once more, then reluctantly stepped away to wash his hands. "Still tracking down his sis and her best friend. He should be here soon."

Paige nodded, a wicked light shining in her eyes, and Trent's body reacted. "You've got something naughty going on in that head of yours. What's up?"

Her gaze darted around the room, falling on the middle couch in the living space. "I had an interesting conversation with Kylie before her little broom closet disappearance, and I want to ask Mason a few questions."

Trent stared at the strangely shaped leather couch. It looked like a slightly flattened fancy "M", the first bump higher than the second, a smooth dip between them. "Is that a courting chair? One of those old fashioned designs done up new? It looks uncomfortable."

Paige pressed the mixing bowl into his arms. "Fold, please, slowly. Turn the ingredients over together until they blend. That's right. But no, it's not a settee. From what Kylie said, it's extremely comfortable, if you use it right."

Trent frowned, mindlessly following her directions as Paige poured additional ingredients into the bowl. He stared again. The cream-colored leather looked soft enough, and he could imagine sitting in the middle of the scooped central section, but the two humps at either end? One high, the other low...how the hell would you comfortably sit on that?

"There's no backrest, and it's not symmetrical."

Paige laughed softy, bumping into his side as she moved. He ignored the mystery and concentrated instead on giving her a hand until she finished her Good Samaritan task and they were free to move to the next stage of the day. And the first thing on the list would involve Paige helping him with his dick, its length rising involuntarily with every moment in her presence.

He tried to focus on the task at hand and not get distracted. This was part of his goal—to spend time together outside of the bedroom. He asked her questions, chatting about everyday things. She smiled and responded smoothly, laughing and letting their bodies touch even as she stayed intent on the task before her.

Hell, even cooking she was sex personified. How was he supposed to concentrate on the things he liked about her that didn't involve his body wanting to take her against the nearest wall when he couldn't get enough of that? The aroma rising from the mixing bowl was delicious, but it was the underlying scent of her skin that made his mouth water.

She rolled a thin sheet of pastry, held it to the light and smiled with satisfaction.

"What are we making?"

Her mouth opened, then shut as she flushed. "You know, I'm not sure what to call them. It's a common dessert dish I would take to a potluck back in Canada, but instead of serving it in slabs, I'll make individual pastry pockets."

Trent nodded. He wasn't letting this opportunity slip past. "Single servings are best for public parties, you've told me that before. But why the blush?"

Paige stared him in the eye. "Sex in a pan."

He laughed. "That's the dessert?"

"The name is a mutation from six in a pan, for the original six layers, but the taste is downright orgasmic, if you make it right." She ran a finger along the edge of the bowl, scooped up a smear of the chocolate sauce onto her fingertip and offered it to him.

He swallowed hard.

"This isn't a good time for you to stop what you're doing, is it?" He forced the words past a throat suddenly tight with need.

She shook her head.

Fuckit. He sucked her finger into his mouth and moaned. The dessert was tasty, but having her finger to suck and tease, to be able to watch her eyes widen and hear her breath catch as he twirled his tongue around the digit? Torture.

He let her pull back, her finger escaping with a *pop.* He shook off the haze of lust threatening the production of the delicacies. *Hold off, caveman.*

Instead, he grinned at her. "If they're individual sex servings, does that make them masturbation pies?"

Paige rolled her eyes. "*God.* You are not helping me name them."

"Jerk tarts?"

"Trent!"

"Cream—"

The shot of, appropriately enough—whipped cream—hit him in the mouth, and he sputtered to a stop, eyeing her evilly.

She lowered the piping bag, fists dropping to her hips. "Behave. Let me pop these crusts in the oven, and then we can talk about your fascination with self-pleasure."

Hmm, now there's an idea. Not his pleasure, but hers. That was something he could get into. He stepped back complacently, licking his lips. Paige poked him as she passed by to re-wash her hands thoroughly. She returned to the counter, working quickly with the pastry dough. Effortlessly, she formed intricate flowerlike cups, one after another resting on the paper lining the cookie sheets.

He studied her face, loving the way her intent concentration made a tiny furrow appear between her eyes. She was smiling, nodding as she placed another edible art form onto the tray, and he realized this was a form of artistic expression. The beauty she created not only pleased the eyes but the palate and all the rest of his senses. She was a fully sensual creature, and he loved being around her. Enthusiasm and sensuality shone through everything she did.

He couldn't be any more certain. This thing between them was far more than a physical attraction. He was head-over-fucking-heels with the slim seductress. He would do everything he could to make sure she stayed in his life—even if it meant a few more unusual solutions, like those offered by Mason's gung-ho, madcap, anything-goes, both-feet-forward attitude.

Hmm, an attitude that was remarkably like Paige's.

"I bet that's why you guys get along so well."

She straightened after placing the second pan in the oven, that little secretive smile teasing the corner of her mouth again. "What are you talking about? Who?"

"You and Mason. You're both totally open and game for anything."

Paige's heartbeat leaped upward again as he caught her fingers. She'd slipped them under the faucet, adding a shot of soap to clean off the butter clinging to them. He lathered her up, threading his fingers through hers, his touch firm and yet sexual as he touched each digit in turn. Her mouth went absolutely dry.

They didn't seem to be able to be in the same room without wanting each other. "You're not such a prude yourself, Trent."

He crowded closer, his arms caging her, hands rocking over hers again and again. Splashes rose to soak the front of her blouse. He planted kisses along her neckline, and she leaned to the side to allow him to maneuver.

Instead he spun her and locked his lips on hers. Oh Lord, she couldn't think when he did that thing with his tongue. Taking total control of her mouth as if he were starving and only she could satisfy his hunger. He licked and nibbled and explored—ownership in every touch. The sound of the running water grew faint below the roaring of the blood in her ears. His wet hands slipped onto her back, the fabric sticking to her skin. He held her by the upper arms and slowly separated their bodies, his lips clinging with heat and moisture until the last possible second.

They stared at each other. She knew she was grinning, and the expression on his face—sheer happiness. As if he was exactly where he wanted to be, and life was good.

She'd put that expression in his eyes, at least partially, and for one wild second she nearly blurted out that she loved him.

"Knock knock."

They both spun toward the door, Trent settling her tightly against his chest. The warmth of his body heated the wet spots on her clothing.

Mason raised a brow as he approached. "Am I interrupting? Fair dinkum, it smells delicious in here."

"Paige is cooking up a storm."

Mason walked the length of the room with any hesitation, not stopping until he was pressed firmly against her.

"She always cooks up the most mouth-watering mischief." He lifted her chin with his fingers and kissed her. A momentary buss on the lips, just enough for her to taste him, tease her senses. "What's next on the menu? That's what I want to know."

He dipped his head again and took his time opening her lips to his caress. A series of small kisses along her jaw, a butterfly soft touch to the corner of her mouth. A tantalizing stroke of his tongue over her lower lip.

A low level of excitement and delight accompanied his teasing touch. She was totally surrounded, boxed in by two solid male torsos. Trent's erection pressed hard into her right butt cheek, and the longer Mason kissed her, the more his interest rose as well. She tangled her fingers in his hair and held him tight. Twisted her hips slightly, rubbing both of them, slow and deliberate. She might be encircled, but she still had a say in this adventure. It looked as if there was no need to prolong the wait for one of her favorite parts.

Being totally cared for by two men. Four hands bringing her delight, stroking and guiding her pleasure in ways she'd never dreamed possible before getting involved with them.

Paige pulled her lips free and Mason leaned his forehead against hers. Trent's fingers caressed her hip slowly. They both waited, patiently. Time paused, their three bodies slowly becoming more attuned to each other as their breathing synchronized. Her anticipation rose—there *was* some specific mischief she had in mind, although it was actually Mason who was the engineer of this afternoon's coming escapade.

She could hardly wait to see him explain the sex chair that graced the center of their suite. Forget the details of how it got there, she wanted to know everything possible about using the chair itself.

Chapter Five

Paige twisted free of their hands. She smoothed her fingers along their forearms and tugged them out of the kitchen area toward the tall windows. The view of the Pacific caught her eye again, and she stared for a moment, distracted by the crystal blue meeting of sky and sea.

"It's so gorgeous." Mason and Trent stood on her left and right, joining her in admiring the view. "Sometimes, I just want to take off. Find where the end of the water is. And you know what? When you get there? In my mind, you don't bump into North and South America. It's a brand-new land, with new things to see and places to explore."

Mason's fingers threaded through hers. "And every time you make land the colors are more vibrant, and the smells are more intense than the last place you left, because everything that happened before was merely a dream, and you're finally awake and experiencing the real world."

Paige's heart skipped. *Oh God, yes.* Exactly. If there were a magical pill she could swallow to make it happen, or a spell to chant, she would in an instant.

She turned her back on the dream floating outside the room, twisting to face the reality she had for another forty-eight hours. Her lovers, here. An experience as vibrant and desirable as any pipe dream she might wish for—in fact, far better since it was real. She could touch them, hold them tight in her fist. Love them—*both*—for today.

It wasn't nearly enough, but it was all that was offered.

She looked into their faces and stopped, momentarily confused by what she witnessed. Mason was motioning crazily toward her, staring intently at Trent. Trent shook his head and frowned. She opened her mouth to ask what the hell they were doing—

Buzzzzzz.

She darted past the guys, opened the oven and exposed trays of beautifully browned crusts. It only took a moment before the two pans were carefully arranged to cool, the heat turned off and the buzzer dealt with. She'd fill them a little bit later, but now?

Now was time to work Mason over until he 'fessed up.

She pivoted on the spot, catching him in her sights. "I talked to Kylie after lunch."

His brilliant blue gaze followed her fingers as she undid the top button of her blouse. Both Trent and Mason groaned as she made quick work of the row and let the sides fall apart to reveal the push-up bra she'd slipped on before their trip to the buffet. It had done wonders for her ego after seeing Sienna, and their response now? The icing on the cake.

"Kylie was in high spirits and gave me a message to pass on to Trent."

Her other lover frowned. "You never told me any—"

She shrugged the soft blouse from her shoulders, letting it flutter to the floor before reaching for the snap on her skirt. He swallowed the rest of his words as lust raced over his face, his gaze glued to her fingers.

Powerful. There was nothing on earth comparable to holding two passionate men in the palm of her hand like this.

If only I also held their hearts.

"It was a little too cryptic—the message—so I asked for clarification. She ended up being very forthcoming regarding the identity of our mystery object here in the living room."

She watched Mason closely as she strutted to the curved leather bench, stepped past the knee-height first bump to caress her fingers in long slow sweeps over the leather-covered surface of the hip-level one. His jaw dropped open, and for one incredible second, she could have sworn he blushed.

Then his eyes lit up and she saw the promise of an incredible experience.

"Mason? You want to explain why you were in a position to act as a sex consultant for Kylie and the resort?"

"Bloody hell! You've been doing *what* with my sister?" The

words tore from Trent, and Mason backed away from him, as if in self-preservation.

He held up a restraining hand. "Consultant only. She'd...read one of my books, and wanted to know if part of the story was fiction or reality. This bench. That's all."

Paige hopped up on the top bump before swinging her legs to straddle the bench. Leaning back, she slid into the central dip until her butt rested firmly on the broad surface. "You really have to stop being so secretive and tell me what you write, Mason. It's driving me crazy wondering what kinds of novels you sell that include chairs like this."

The smooth curve of the bench let her lie back comfortably, fully supported, yet at the same time the gentle arc of the higher "M" bump thrust her breasts into the air. She stroked a hand down her torso, ignoring them both as she carried her fingers down and under the elastic of her panties.

Well, ignoring everything but the sound of them simultaneously groaning.

Mason strode to her side and squatted at the base of the lower leather-covered hump. He stroked her skin with his gaze, seemingly fascinated with her fingers.

"Does it matter what I write?"

She moaned lightly, widening her legs. "Of course it doesn't. Just curious."

He stroked a finger down her torso. "Fine. I write romance novels. Real ones, with happy endings."

Paige smiled at him. "Cool. They must be fascinating."

He didn't answer, his gaze following his hand as he caressed her thigh reverently. She leaned willingly into his touch.

"I like this chair. So soft on my skin. As if there's a world of possibilities just waiting—Mason!"

He lifted her as he stood and stepped to the far right of the bench, returning her to perch on the highest point, only this time facing outward. His hands were gentle on her hips as he slid her into position. Her legs remained touching Mason's as he stood behind the raised section. A soothing sound came from his lips as he encouraged her to relax, leaning her back against the soft leather, draping her belly upward over the top bump.

She was flat on her back, or she would have been if the couch had been level. As it was, her head hung towards the central dip, slightly lower than her hips, but she remained firmly supported on the wide bench. She let herself settle against the comfortable leather. All thoughts about occupations—writing, baking or otherwise—vanished. "I'm going to end up with my head spinning."

"Oh God, I hope so." Dark, low. The words curled from his throat as he stripped away the fabric covering her mound and lowered his mouth to her sex.

Whisper-light caresses taunted her. His tongue darted in and out, small strokes around her core without giving her nearly enough pressure against her clit to allow her to get off in a hurry.

"Bastard. You're going to leave me hanging, aren't you?"

Warm air disappeared as he changed his approach from open-mouthed intimate kisses to blowing a steady stream of air, cool against her wetness.

"Mason, oh hell. Stop it. Don't tease. Please—"

"Trent, give me a hand with the lady. She's a little noisy. You want to deal with that?"

Oh shit. Trent straddled the curved central section and smiled at her evilly as he sat. His head was higher than hers, and his upside-down expression made her laugh, at least until Mason picked up his assault again and tore a gasp from her lips.

Trent cupped her face in both hands. Tenderly leaning closer, he brushed his thumb over her cheekbone. "You okay?" he whispered.

Mason chose that moment to add fingers to his repertoire. Smooth pressure filled her sex, stretching her wide as his tongue finally, oh yes—finally, found her clit.

Somehow she managed to speak. "I'm grand. You want to join in?"

Trent stared at the couch in admiration. "A sex toy. Never thought it was possible. I agree, I think it's time for Mason to spill a few more beans regarding his work."

"You don't even know—?"

"But not this instant," he interrupted, standing and staring down at her as he unzipped his pants. "I'm getting the idea behind this bench. It's all about comfort and convenience. You're comfortable, and right now..."

His cock was in his hand. Hard, skin stretched taut over the beautiful length.

"...very well positioned."

Trent stroked, once, twice. Each time the foreskin of his cock slipped back and revealed the purplish head, the slit glistening with a drop of moisture. Paige licked her lips as he grasped himself at the base then directed the length of his shaft toward her.

He didn't have to do anything but stand over the bench. With her draped over the upper bump, her mouth was exactly in line with his erect cock.

The even pleasure Mason stirred in her contrasted nicely with the zing of dirty delight that struck when Trent's cock contacted her lips. She darted out her tongue to lap eagerly. Even as the salty essence of his seed hit her taste buds, he took total advantage of her soft sigh of happiness and pressed his hips forward. His shaft slipped between her lips, familiar and yet totally brand new.

She'd never given a blowjob upside-down before.

Instead of feeling the thick ridge of vein lining the bottom of his cock, her tongue met the smoother upper surface. When he retreated slowly, the crested head was more distinct, with a larger rise between the width of his cock and the flared head.

"Fucking-A, that's incredible." Trent continued to caress her cheek, working his cock in and out of her mouth. She couldn't move over him, her head comfortably but firmly supported on the soft leather of the chair. All she could do was take him in and allow him control of her mouth. Use her for his own pleasure.

Of course, Mason was still treating her wonderfully. If Trent was taking, right now Mason was all about giving. She couldn't move to enhance the sensations as Mason touched her, but he was doing fine on his own. The insistent and rhythmic press into her core changed slightly as he corkscrewed his fingers, the pressure varying in intensity and location, and she groaned loudly, trying to tell him how much she liked it.

"Mason, goddamn, whatever you just did, do it some more. She nearly took my head off when she hummed like that. Come on, beautiful. Nearly there?"

Paige rocked her head slightly. She was ready to go off, but she was going to take him with her. She grasped his hips, digging her fingernails into his jean-covered buttocks. She opened wider and encouraged him deeper on the next thrust.

His cock slipped all the way to the back of her throat, her nose nestled against his tight sac.

"Paige, *bloody hell*. Oh fuck, fuck, *fuck*..."

She swallowed and Trent continued to curse, the first of his seed splashing into her mouth. He dragged himself back, slipped from her lips and squeezed his cock at the base. His face was scrunched in a grimace as he fought to hold off his release.

Then her own vision grew hazy as Mason dragged her over the edge, his lips locked around her clit, pulsing in a firm, demanding rhythm. Her sex tightened around his fingers and he slowed, just the way she liked. The first seconds after coming she was far too sensitive, but his careful consideration allowed her to relax and enjoy. The waves of pleasure rolled up one side of her then down the other. Happy moans escaped her, and that was when he increased the pressure, removing his fingers and tonguing the hypersensitive outer edge of her core to prolong the tingling.

The leather sighed as Trent sat on the lower swell of the chair, his breathing back to something near normal. Mason helped her to sit upright on the top hump once again instead of being draped over it. His mouth and chin were still wet from her sex. She grabbed him by the ears and kissed him hungrily, the moisture of her pleasure mixing with their kiss and the lingering tease of Trent's seed.

More. It was a start, but not nearly enough.

Their tongues fought for dominance, his torso pressing hard against hers. That wasn't the only hard thing between them, the rocky length of his cock tight to her soft and ready sex. If he'd removed his clothes before starting, he'd be exactly the right height to slip into her body right now.

A hand slipped down her back. Trent, his fingers trailing along her spine as his deep voice buzzed through her, coaxing her anticipation higher.

"I understand this chair more and more. Mason could fuck you right now, pounding into you until you scream with pleasure. I could lay you over the lower section, facedown, and on my knees I'd be the perfect height to slip into your pussy or fuck your ass."

A shiver raced over her skin. Images of him taking her, loving her so thoroughly, filled her mind and she longed for him to act them out. Mason covered her hands with his and tugged them free from his ears, lowering both their arms. He eased off the kiss, nipping and teasing now, stealing her breath.

Her bra was unhooked—*Trent*—and the straps were pressed slowly from her shoulders. Kisses landed everywhere his fingertips brushed. Mason stepped back enough that when Trent's big palms slipped around her torso, her bra fell away and there was nothing to impede him from totally enclosing her in his hands.

Her breasts felt heavy, achy. Needy. So much that when Mason's kisses descended past her neckline she arched upward, hoping he would take the hint. Trent rubbed and massaged, his fingertips teasing her nipples into tight buds, disappearing a split second before Mason lapped the surface.

One side, then the other. Again. Again.

"Oh God, that feels incredible." Two hands—no, four—caressed her. Mason closed his mouth over one aching peak and pulsed, hard. A bolt of lightning flew from his lips to the center of her sex, liquid heat flooding from her body. "Please, someone fuck me. I need you. I need you both."

"Shhh, you'll have us both. Let us have a little fun first. Mason's enjoying himself. You want to take that away from him?"

"Yes." As good as it was having Mason play with her nipples, she wanted more.

Trent laughed. "Too bad. You'll just have to wait."

"Strip. Guys, get naked. Mason…"

Paige locked her legs around his hips and rocked as hard as possible. Ground against his clothed body—she smeared him with her juices, but that was his own damn fault for not giving her what she wanted.

Mason sucked harder and she squeaked, partly in pain, partly in pleasure. He pulled off with a soft *plop* and stared down, looking immensely satisfied.

"Fucking love your tits."

Her legs dropped as her body shook with laughter. They drove her mad with lust, and filled her heart with happiness at the same time. "Please get naked? *Please*?"

Mason cupped her face, those gorgeous blue eyes sparkling

at her. "There's my Canadian girl. Of course. When you ask so politely, how could we possibly refuse?"

He held her hand and turned her, letting her pivot on the higher of the two bumps until she faced Trent who stood to the side of the chair removing his clothing. Mason pushed on her hips, and she slipped into the central dip.

"Lean back and relax, because we're about to show you how this chair can really work."

Oh boy. Naked, waiting. Warm leather against her skin, she watched the erotic strip show with her mouth watering. Shirts peeled off to reveal toned muscles. Trent's firm upper body was marred with minute scars from scuba incidents. The thin silver lines didn't detract in the least from how amazingly attractive he was. Trent's chest, and the thighs he revealed as his jeans fell to the floor were thicker and broader than Mason's. Trent was her muscle man, and she leaned forward to touch his quadriceps, fingers splayed over the solid mass in admiration.

"You want something to grab, reach a little to the right, darling."

She grinned at him. His boxer briefs were wet where the tip of his cock continued to leak his desire. "Why didn't you let me finish that off for you earlier?"

"Didn't think trying to swallow uphill was a good idea."

Mason snorted. "Sorry, hadn't thought of that."

She turned to nod at Mason, and got totally distracted. He'd already stripped to nothing, and while he wasn't as bulky as his best friend, his muscles were well-defined. There was nothing soft about his erection either, reaching skyward until it bumped his belly. His cock had a gentle slope to the left that somehow made sex with him even more incredible when it hit usually neglected spots deep inside.

"I love how you look at me. As if I'm more delicious than anything you've ever cooked up in the kitchen." Mason's voice trembled with lust.

"You two are far more appealing to my taste buds."

Mason and Trent exchanged glances, then moved on her with perfect synchronization, and Paige opened her arms wide to embrace them and the experience.

It was a little bit of paradise in one perfect package. Having Paige there, willing to give everything of herself to him, and to

Trent.

He was the luckiest bastard on the entire fucking planet.

Mason locked gazes with Paige, trapping her brown orbs and refusing to let her look away. "I want in your sweet heat. I want to feel you surround me and then you're going to come around my cock and freak my mind. Deal?"

She nodded rapidly, the edge of her pink tongue slipping out for just an instant. "And what's Trent going to do? Watch us?"

The sudden intake of air from Trent was impossible to ignore. Paige had caught that kink of Trent's had she? Mason winked so his best mate couldn't see. "He does like to watch, doesn't he?"

Trent growled at them. "He also likes to bury his dick in someone's tight arse."

Paige's eyes widened, and she was the one who winked secretively this time. "Is there something you two aren't telling me about?"

Trent sputtered. "Your arse, your arse. *Jesus Christ*, woman, do I need to spell it out?"

"Well, I didn't want to get in the way if you two were doing the nasty. I'm fine with it, as long as I get to be in the audience."

Trent sat on the lower swell of the bench and threaded his fingers into her hair. He brought her face close until she had nowhere to escape. She was still grinning like a maniac.

"I am one hundred and ten percent heterosexual, and so is Mason. The only backside I'm sticking my dick in is yours. Now, get ready to be fucked, woman."

He kissed her madly, dragging her against his chest. Mason had to admit that Trent wasn't the only one of them who liked to watch. Seeing them explore each other's mouths with bruising kisses, observing Paige as she scrambled into his best mate's lap—hell, it might make him a pervert, but it fucking well turned his crank.

Mason dragged himself away for long enough to grab two condoms. He rolled his own on, thrusting into his hands as Paige and Trent gyrated together breathlessly. It was time. If he didn't take control of the situation now he was going to blow before he even got a chance to slip inside her.

He stepped to the foot of the chair and knelt. "Paige, come

here. Lie on your belly and face me."

Trent reluctantly released her. Mason slipped him a condom and the lube, motioning with his head for Trent to back up. His friend frowned, then slid into the dip. Comprehension crossed his face as Paige obeyed Mason's instructions, draping herself over the lower end of the bench.

The position left her hips raised slightly, her legs spread on either side of the couch, backside presented in Trent's direction. He rubbed a hand slowly over her bare cheeks, sheer delight in his expression.

"You have the most fucking fantastic body." Trent squeezed the flesh under his hands and Paige moaned out her pleasure.

This was going to be the shortest double fuck in history. Mason's balls ached, and he figured he was going to last two, maybe three thrusts tops.

Good thing he could still orchestrate it to be fun for Paige.

He leaned in and kissed her. She had rested her elbows on the cushioning of the lower hump, and with him kneeling before her, their mouths lined up perfectly. He sighed into her mouth with happiness. The chair had simply been a research discovery he'd slipped into a story. Getting to actually use one? The rest of his writing buddies didn't need to know that the chair was this successful.

Her lips under his, completely soft and pliable. It was partly diversion—he didn't think Trent needed any advice of what to do while he was distracting her.

When she let out a little gasp he smiled. Nope. No instructions needed.

"So fucking gorgeous. You like my finger in your arse don't you?" Trent continued to talk, his dirty descriptions of adding another finger perfectly coinciding with the minute tensing then relaxing of Paige under Mason's lips.

He pulled back to admire her more closely. She rested her cheek on her hands and hummed softly as Trent spread her on his fingers. Trent rose slightly and placed the head of his cock to her opening. Both Paige and Mason let out long groans as Trent slowly pressed forward.

When the head of his cock disappeared he paused. "Good?"

Paige nodded even as she blew out a long uneven breath. "I swear you get bigger every time."

Way to stroke a guy's ego. Trent grinned at Mason before

turning his full concentration back to slipping into her sweet body. Mason's dick jerked at the sight, and if he hadn't had the damn condom on he would have been dripping everywhere. He was ready to go off at the slightest provocation.

While Trent's cock disappeared into her backside, Paige reached for them. One hand caught hold of Mason, one Trent. She linked her fingers through theirs and held on as if she was afraid she was going to be forcibly removed.

Mason had no intention of letting her go anywhere, and with every minute that passed, they got that much closer to letting her know exactly how permanent they wanted this arrangement to be.

Loud groans from both Trent and Paige announced their complete connection. Hips tight to her arse, Trent squeezed his eyes closed then sighed. "I'm gonna die."

Mason knew the damn feeling. "Lie back."

Trent nodded but dragged his hips away for one more stroke. His thrust back in was accompanied by a long, enthusiastic cry from Paige.

"So, so good. God, why does that feel so good?"

Trent wrapped an arm around her and pulled her upright with him. The change in position left them sitting vertically with her arse resting tight to his groin.

"Fuck." Trent panted, obviously fighting for control. "That's..."

"...deeper. Oh God, *oh God.* Mason? Hurry..."

Trent leaned back on the smooth slope of the higher swell. Paige panted a couple of times before joining him.

Her knees were spread wide, her legs resting on the outside of Trent's. She basically lay on top of him, speared on his cock as they reclined on the couch. His feet were planted firmly on the floor and the position left her sex wide open. Cream coated her labia, painted the inside of her thighs. She was so wet she glistened with it. She rested her head on Trent's shoulder and her perfect breasts thrust at Mason.

He could have stared for hours.

"Hurry the fuck up," Trent ordered.

"Yes, now. Oh, please, now." Paige writhed and Trent swore, the motion obviously squeezing her tight passage around his shaft.

Mason couldn't wait any longer even if he'd wanted to draw it out. He straddled the bench as well, his arse resting on the warm leather. He held the base of his cock and tilted it toward her sex.

Warm. Slick. He rubbed the hard cock head between her labia, scooting high enough to nick her clit on every pass.

Paige's brown orbs opened wide, her chest rising and falling in rapid succession. She reached down and took hold of him and on the next rock, guided the head of his cock into her heat.

That was the end of his control. Mason pressed in slowly, the tightness of her passage compounded by the thickness of Trent's dick in her arse. She was filled to the brim, and when he finally forced his cock all the way in, all three of them moaned in unison.

"You have to do all the work," Trent gritted out. "I can't shift, but I can freaking feel every move you make. Make love to her for both of us."

That he could do. The sun shining in the window fell across the chair like a spotlight on their erotic tableau. Mason withdrew his dick and thrust in once, then again. Both times, air escaped from Paige's lungs on an exhale full of pleasure and heat.

Harder, he plunged in, the force shoving her back against Trent, and both of them voiced their approval. The sticky sweet scent in the air from Paige's baking was covered by the rising smell of sex. Hard, dirty, needy as all get-out. Mason pumped again and again until his balls were tucked so tight to his body they felt like rocks, barely budging as his hips slammed against Paige's.

Mason leaned his torso out of the way to reach to capture her clit between his fingers, even as he kept drilling into her sex.

One touch—that was all it took—and she was gone, calling his name, Trent's.

Game over. She scratched her nails down his back, and he shot like a drunken fool, no finesse, simple need racing through his body and exploding out the end of his dick. Trent must have lost control at the same time, and they both held Paige in place as their cocks emptied.

His brain muddled.

Mason panted, leaning back on the lower bump, his heart

racing, mind fogged. Before him, Paige sprawled, boneless in Trent's arms. Mason's cock still filled her, and he slipped a finger softly along the crease between them. A series of aftershocks took her, her passage tightening around him so hard she pressed him free.

Oh God, that had been incredible. He struggled to find something to say. His tongue didn't seem to be working anymore. Mason wavered slightly, his brain too numb with pleasure to control his balance.

Okay. Here was one problem with the chair he'd never dreamed of. Trent and Paige were totally supported as they reclined, but he was in danger of falling to the floor on his arse.

Then a soft sound, a rumble, made him peel his eyes open and he chuckled.

"What?" Trent sounded as mindless as Mason felt.

He managed to drag himself back to the raised lower end of the couch, staring at Paige's beautiful face for a moment before winking at his best friend.

"We've fucked her senseless."

Trent's eyes widened for a second then crinkled with laughter as another soft purr of sleep escaped from Paige's lips.

Chapter Six

Waking in the middle of the big bed, completely naked and cleaned up, proved the whole experience had been more intense than she expected. If she didn't feel so deliciously used, Paige would have been a lot more embarrassed to realize she'd fallen asleep with the two men still buried in her body. It was too hilarious to be upset about though, and man-oh-man, she had enjoyed every minute of it.

She stretched her arms over her head and arched her back, loosening the minor kinks and aches in her limbs. Her cheeks warmed as she smiled to herself, remembering what caused them.

"You look like a cat when you do that."

Paige rolled to her belly to discover Trent watching her from the easy chair beside the bed, his gaze roaming approvingly over her naked flesh.

She *meowed* lightly and he laughed.

They stared at each other for a moment until Paige forced herself to break eye contact and drag herself from the bed to find some clothes.

"Where's Mason?"

Trent pointed below them. "He's going to meet us at the soft opening first-night party in thirty minutes."

Hmm. She hesitated between the limited articles in her bag to choose from. "It's not formal dress, is it?"

"Hell no. It's at Bar Evoke. Although, Kylie did mention she had some kind of incredible surprise planned. I have to say, she's done a bloody good job, even if she is my sister."

Paige stared at herself in the mirror as she fixed her hair. There didn't seem to be any time when she had them together that they could just talk. Maybe that was a good thing. So far she'd managed to keep her mouth shut and not ruin this weekend.

She double-checked her desserts, and after Trent taste-tested one and expressed his approval, she sent off the modified recipe to the chef via email.

It seemed only a moment later they were in one of the long hallways connecting the various parts of the resort. Ahead, Mason lazed against the wall and her heart fluttered at the sight of him. The fluttering changed to intense pulsing centered between her legs as he peeled himself off the wall, cupped her face in his hands and proceeded to kiss her breathless.

When she'd finally remembered she wasn't supposed to be his date for the weekend, she forced her hands between their bodies and reluctantly pushed him away.

"Hey, we don't want to get our butts kicked by any of Trent's family or friends who think we're cheating on him. Right?"

"I just..." Mason sighed. "Right."

She tugged the neckline of her dress back into place—it was as if he couldn't resist touching her. Trent either, but he could get away with it. Mason had to demonstrate a little restraint or they were going to face all kinds of impossible questions.

Trent linked his fingers through hers, giving Mason a mock dirty look. "Yeah. Hands off my girl."

Mason bumped his shoulder, and the two of them laughed at each other as they escorted her the rest of the way to the party.

Music spilled from the entrance of Bar Evoke. The decor was gorgeous, the long bank of windows facing the Pacific sparkling with the reflected light off the water. Sunset approached, and very shortly the hall's occupants would be treated to the most spectacular light display.

"Miss Kingston?"

A soft touch on her arm distracted her from the incredible setting. "Leo? What's up?"

The head chef dipped his head politely. "If I could have a moment?"

Paige nodded and turned to the guys. "Go ahead—I'll join you in a minute."

Trent hesitated. Mason frowned.

She pushed them away. "Go. Grab us chairs. I'm fine."

Reluctantly, they stepped into the bar and disappeared behind a shimmering silver column.

Leo waited patiently until she turned her attention on him.

"I wanted to let you know our supply barge arrived. It had everything you listed as required in the modified recipe you sent to the kitchen. Thank you so much for your assistance. We'll take care of the desserts tomorrow—don't let us interrupt your holiday any further."

She smiled at him. "I'm glad I could help. You're fortunate to receive fresh ingredients on a regular basis. I wondered if being so remote was going to make your deliveries more erratic."

"Twice daily."

"Twice?" Paige was impressed.

He nodded. "There are two barges. They drop supplies then head back to the mainland about an hour later. The most recent landed about half an hour ago and sent the groceries in first thing."

Paige accepted his hearty handshake before slipping into the bar.

In the distance, voices rose above the noise and chaos of the rest of the partygoers. Paige spotted not only Mason and Trent in the middle of it, but Kylie and Mason's sister, McKenzie. A massive man followed her like a shadow. Aidan, maybe? Paige was pretty sure that was the name Mason had mentioned a few times. People slapped each other on the back, shared hugs, and familiar laughter rang on the air.

Paige was still too far away to hear what they were saying, and she approached slowly, loath to intrude as Kylie squeezed McKenzie in another bear hug. The only one of the Goddess Pack she didn't spot was Sienna.

Since she only knew the receiving parties a little, Paige was far more interested in watching her guys, soaking in every memory possible. Trent's grin was so wide he was almost smirking. Mason shook the enormous man's hand enthusiastically, then in his typical off-the-wall manner, reached up and gave him a noogie.

Death wish much?

Aidan didn't do anything in response but flash a sheepish grin.

Paige waited to the side, hoping she could get through the evening without making a fool of herself, or the guys. Maybe she should just go hide in the kitchen. That would work—Leo would probably welcome her with open arms.

Running away from the guys she loved to go play in the kitchen. *Smart plan, idiot.*

"What's that smile for?" Trent appeared beside her, sliding his hand around her waist.

She picked part of the truth to share. "I'm happy I could help Kylie in the kitchen. Feel as if I've earned my way."

He pressed a kiss to her cheek, the warmth of his body wrapping her in security. "You didn't owe anyone anything, but I'm pleased you stepped in."

He guided her back to the table they'd nabbed and pulled out one of the chairs.

A trace of fear and regret washed over her. Honestly? She didn't want to officially meet all the family and friends before fading off into the sunset. It was going to make things that much harder when she left.

Good memories. Positive experiences. She had to concentrate on them instead, and up to now that's exactly what this day had been about. The most incredible start to a final weekend. Paige leaned back, crossed her legs and let her ankle bounce with the rhythm of the music playing quietly in the background.

The others settled at the table, conversation continuing to flow.

Mason leaned in on her right, resting his chin lightly on her shoulder. He stared at her legs before giving a low growl. "I'm so going to strip those stockings off with my teeth."

"Stop it," she whispered. "You need to behave."

"I am behaving. I'm treating my girl to a preview of what she can expect later."

His girl. Paige sighed, happiness and pain mingling to torment her. She wiggled her shoulder until he was forced to retreat.

Paige shuffled a little farther out of the banter swelling and falling like waves around the group of tight-knit friends. If she were staying and truly going with Trent, she'd be right in there, sharing smiles and good wishes. Learning more about them as people, and not just names mentioned in passing during stories told by her guys. Things like discovering why Kylie seemed to have a different man with her here at the party than the one who had been groping her madly as they disappeared into that broom closet.

She caught herself frowning and forced a smile back on her face. Wasn't this the most awkward thing? Hanging around people, most of whom had no idea of her real identity, and all of them unaware even those tenuous threads were about to be severed.

This whole party was a bad idea.

She managed to stay out of any deep discussions without making it appear as if she was dodging questions and avoiding truly joining into the swing of the party. Her sudden relief at the announcement the buffet line was open was so sharp she fought down giggles.

The group rose from the table, a moving mass of happiness and camaraderie, and Paige ached a little harder. It was made just that much worse when she ended up next to Mason's sister, who overflowed with sheer happiness. Her beaming face made Paige feel even guiltier.

She'd never thought herself the jealous type, but between her reaction earlier to Sienna, and her current response to McKenzie's enthusiasm, it seemed the green-eyed monster was firmly riding her back.

Having her dreams about to swirl down the toilet made it difficult to watch others head into their futures full of shining optimism.

McKenzie handed her a plate. "Isn't the resort the most amazing place?"

Good. The resort and the weather. Those were nice, safe topics. Paige nodded. "Kylie's found a little bit of paradise to live and work in."

McKenzie waved her free hand, her adorable button nose wrinkling slightly. "I can't imagine living here all the time, though, too quiet for me. It's fantastic to visit, but I enjoy the city better. Could never do things like Mason and Trent. Pack it all in and explore the wilds for months on end? Not for me."

Months on end? "Getting out and seeing new things is

something I've always loved."

"Whee, they have shrimp! Oh, I know. Mason told us about you joining him and Trent on getaways. I'm glad you found a couple of like-minded people to explore Australia with." McKenzie passed the serving spoon to Paige. "I'm surprised you're not going with them on their often-discussed, finally-happening, travel-to-the-ends-of-the-earth experience. When they told me they'd bought a freaking ship I thought they'd gone off the deep end."

The serving ladle slipped from her fingers, back into the salad bowl. Paige retrieved it as smoothly as she could. What the hell? The guys had bought a ship? McKenzie obviously considered this common knowledge. Paige didn't have the energy to explain the ins and outs of casual fucks versus family and lovers. She glanced over her shoulder, but both her guys were deep in discussion with Kylie a few meters back down the line, and out of earshot.

She scrambled to find something to say to get more information without revealing she had no idea what McKenzie was talking about. "Well, it's not always easy to get time off."

"Believe me, even if I could make the arrangements, there's no way Mason could convince me to go sailing for six months, destination unknown." McKenzie shook her head. "No bloody way, not even with my best friend."

Paige felt a touch nauseous.

Mason and Trent had bought a boat and were going on a sailing adventure for six months?

The pain that hit froze her to immobility. She'd admitted to herself she'd fallen in love, but she hadn't been honest about one thing—the part inside her that still hoped that the affectionate way the guys had been behaving meant they had felt more for her as well. More than she was a good bud they could screw.

They hadn't bothered to tell her their plans. This couldn't have occurred in the two weeks since she'd seen them last. All the while she'd been storing up memories to last her when she left, they'd been preparing for an adventure of a lifetime that didn't include her.

Fair enough. They didn't have to tell her. The rules of the relationship were clear, and she'd stood by them every second. She'd known coming here it was to say goodbye before she messed things up. Announcing to them both that she was head over heels in love—wouldn't that be the most awkward thing ever? Especially since it was crystal clear she was only a fling to them?

"Paige?"

Her head snapped up as McKenzie's voice broke through. The other woman was already a step farther down the buffet line, frowning in concern. Paige shook herself slightly and stepped forward. "Shit, sorry. Woolgathering."

Somehow Paige found the energy to carry on and not drop her plate. Not run and disappear like she wanted to. She'd been strong this long, she was more than capable of finishing this façade.

Everything around her was a blur, though, as her mind raced. Her feet may have been slowly following the shuffle of the person in front of her, but her brain whirled with images. Memories. All the things she and Trent and Mason had done together over the past year. The hikes and excursions. The practical jokes they'd played on one another as they worked through boring sections on the trail, or the times of sheer adrenaline during tense and dangerous adventures. It wasn't just about sex, not to her, and, she could have sworn, not to them.

She placed her plate on the table and sat gingerly. Voices continued to swell around her. She pasted a smile on her face and silently picked at her food, but no one seemed to notice. They were busy with happy laughter and smiling faces. Old reminiscences, and "Do you remember the time...?"

Through it all, the heat from Trent's body warmed her left side. He'd casually draped his arm over the back of her chair and leaned her direction as he spoke across the table to Aidan. Mason pressed on her other side, his chair close, the seating allowing him to be right freaking there in her personal space.

It was exactly where she wanted to be, and exactly what she couldn't have. Had never had? To be surrounded by them both. Her body.

Her heart.

The overhead speakers clicked on and a sexy, rough-tinged voice broke through the cheerful rumble of conversation. All heads turned toward the stage where a lone male was spotlighted. He perched on a tall stool, a beat-up guitar casually held in his lap.

Nick Blackthorne strummed the strings, just a gentle brush, and the room fell silent. Oh man, this was Kylie's surprise for the evening? A famous rock star providing the music?

A sudden memory of making love with Mason and Trent as one of the singer's songs played in the background burned through her and she squeezed her eyes shut. The rush of blood pounding in her ears drowned out everything else. From the shadow-filled stage, Nick uttered something about love, something about life, but the screw twisting in her belly blurred the words together into incomprehensible babble.

An involuntary gasp of pain escaped.

Trent squeezed in tighter to whisper in her ear. "You okay?"

She hesitated, longing to ask him about the ship. About why they hadn't mentioned it. To beg to be allowed to come along and join them. Paige took a deep breath and frantically considered her options.

Nick caressed the strings again then started singing, and like a torn balloon, she let her hopes shrivel. It was too late, and this was no longer the time or the place.

Paige whispered in Trent's direction. "I need a breath of air. Going to the washroom."

She pushed back her chair quickly, trying not to disturb the others at the table. She needn't have worried. Everyone's gazes but Trent's and Mason's were fixed on the stage. Trent squeezed her hand before returning his attention to the singer. Mason frowned, concern creasing his forehead, a mirror image of McKenzie's a scant time ago. Paige forced herself to smile and nod before turning her back on them and heading for the exit.

The haunting words of the song pierced her ears. Stabbed her heart. Pain rolled over her, flattening her completely, and all she could think about was to get as far away as possible from the hurt.

The adventure had been wonderful while it lasted, but it wasn't for forever. And right now she couldn't handle staying and faking it through two more days knowing when Sunday was over, she had nothing more to look forward to.

She turned in the doorway, cursing her need for one last look back. Her guys' faces were offered in profile as they stared at the stage. Trent nodded his head in time with the music.

Mason had rested his hand on the back of her empty chair, the clean lines of his cheekbones and jaw making her mouth water and her heart ache.

He turned to look at her. Even across the room his brilliant blue eyes were mesmerizing. He blew her a kiss, winked, then faced the performance.

Paige clutched her hand over her chest in an attempt to hold in the broken pieces threatening to burst out. She twirled, and left her soul behind as she fled.

The music was over. His sister and Mason's were wiping their eyes. Low conversations resumed, but Trent had no interest in any of them. He looked back at the door and wondered for the millionth time where the hell Paige was.

"Where did she say she was going?" Mason leaned across the empty chair—Paige's empty chair—and Trent swore.

"She said bathroom. Or fresh air? Damn, what if she's sick? I'm going to look."

"*We're* going to look."

Trent's legs wouldn't work fast enough. She'd been fine this afternoon. More than fine. It had taken everything he'd had to force himself to stick to the agreement he'd committed to with Mason and wait until tonight to tell her about the ship.

It was time. Enough with dragging this out any longer.

Of course, when they made it to the washrooms he realized their mistake.

Ah fuckit. "We can't go in there."

Mason rolled his eyes. "You're such a feckwit at times. Guard the door."

He stuck his head past the doorway and gave a shout. No female voices answered back, so Mason slipped into the room. Trent eyed the hallway, hoping that Paige was okay.

There was a quick tap on his shoulder as Mason rejoined him.

"She's not in there. You think she went outside for a walk? You said fresh air."

"But why wouldn't she ask us to go with her?"

Mason shrugged. "She's not a trained puppy, Sullivan. She's got a mind of her own."

The doors to Bar Evoke popped open and the merriment spilled out. Trent's concern rose. "We need to find her."

"Fine, you want to take the front paths, and I'll take the back?"

"Maybe she's gone to our room. You want to check there? Got your mobile?"

"Yeah."

Trent couldn't explain the heaviness he felt as he ran the path toward the ocean. It had been a simply amazing day. Everything was in place for a wonderful evening. Was this sensation haunting him a foreboding of what Paige's response was going to be to their suggestion of switching their relationship in a new direction? Mason seemed positive she'd be okay with it, but he still had his doubts.

He turned the corner and examined the beach. A few couples strolled together, hand in hand or arms around waists. No lone female figures waited for him to swoop in to carry her off into the sunset.

Although that was exactly what he wanted to do.

Trent looped past the swimming pool. This was frustratingly stupid. For all he knew Paige was wandering in a circle directly in front of him. He was never going to find her this way. He turned back to the resort, ready to interrupt the party and get his family to help him search. If she was sick, he wanted to find her fast.

He raced around a corner and jerked to a stop. "Ah, Kylie?"

Shit.

His sister untangled herself from the guy she'd been lip-locked with. "Trent. Hey, umm, did you meet Brad?"

That wasn't the same bloke she'd had at her side during the party. Trent's brain was on overload. "Oh God, I'm not even going to ask what the hell is going on. I don't have time. Have you seen Paige?"

Kylie frowned. "Not since dinner. My chef is singing her praises, by the way. He's halfway in love with her. He said any woman who could—"

"That's great, but she's missing."

The man at Kylie's side straightened. "What do you mean, missing?"

Trent's pocket rang and he held up a finger as he snapped

the line open. "Wood? She there?"

Mason's voice shot from the phone like a lightning bolt. "I checked the kitchen first before I came up, just on the off-chance. She wasn't there, so I hit the room. Bloody hell, she's not here and her flipping suitcase is gone as well."

Trent's stomach fell. She wasn't wandering somewhere just out of reach. "Why would she take her suitcase?"

"She's disappeared, Sullivan. Vanished. And she left behind that necklace you gave her. You know the shell one, from the first day we got together?"

Trent shook his head in disbelief. "She loves that necklace. Did she drop it accidentally or something?"

"I doubt it. It's on the freaking sex chair laid out in the shape of a heart."

What the bloody hell is going on?

"Trent—what's happened?" The concern in Kylie's voice dragged him back to the path. The romantic setting felt colder than he thought possible.

"It's Mason. He says it looks as if Paige packed up and left."

"How could she leave? Does she have a boat in the harbor?" Brad asked.

Trent shook his head, "She flew in."

"*Why* would she leave?" Kylie poked him in the chest. "Did you do something to upset her?"

"Of course not." Trent pushed down his indignation for a second to double-check his actions. Nope. Couldn't think of a single thing. "She was happy enough this afternoon when Mason, she and I used that—"

He slammed his mouth shut.

Kylie's brows shot skyward. "Oh dear. Don't think we want to have that conversation if you were about to tell me what I think. Didn't you say that *you* were going out with her?"

All his hesitation at telling anyone about their unusual situation fled, driven out with the rising fear that he'd somehow fucked things up royally. "We're both seeing her. Mason and I. We're both in love with her. Happy? Now help me figure out where the hell she's gone."

Kylie leaned back against the tall tower of man beside her. "Okay, don't panic. The only flights are regularly scheduled—there's no way she could leave that way. Unless she knows someone with a speedboat, the only other ships belong to guests, like your *Paradise*, and the regular supply barge."

Oh God. "Paige would know about the supply barge, wouldn't she?"

"Possibly. She did help me with the kitchen problem. I'm not sure what—"

"How can I find out? Is there a radio?" What mattered now was not figuring out how Paige knew, but if she was even on the thing.

"Come on." Kylie indicated the main resort building. "There's a radio in the kitchen. We can check if she's on board. In the meantime, I'll get the staff to do a grounds check. It's a good test of the emergency search system, although I hate the idea we're using it to find someone you love."

Trent's heart hovered somewhere in his throat the entire trip to the kitchen. He filled Mason in on their idea before shoving his phone into his pocket and urging Kylie forward. By the time she'd gotten through to the barge and explained what she needed, Mason had joined them.

"She ran off on us? Why the hell did she leave without saying a word?" Mason dragged a hand through his hair.

"I have no idea."

Mason held up the necklace. "Is this some kind of message? Because I'm totally too stupid to get it."

"I have no idea."

"She's there," Kylie announced, hand covering the mic.

"Oh, thank God." Trent stepped back. "I'm going to get her."

"*We're* going. But with *Paradise*? Paige will be on the mainland before we even get the ship under way," Mason protested.

Brad stepped forward. "If you need a rapid means of transportation, allow me to offer a solution." He held up keys.

Kylie nodded. "Take him up on the offer, guys. If you're serious about catching up with Paige, Brad's boat is bloody fast."

The water didn't just rise on either side of the sleek craft, it parted like the Red Sea, spray flying up and landing far behind in their wake. Trent adjusted the wheel slightly, following the

GPS designations Kylie had obtained from the captain.

"She bloody well left without saying goodbye." Mason shouted to be heard over the roar of the engine.

"That's the tenth fucking time you've said that. Yes, she left. I don't know why. Now shut up and let me steer."

"I'm telling her everything when we see her. No more waiting."

Trent nodded. "Agreed."

They sat in silence, the loud buzz of the engine the only thing cutting through the constant repeat flipping through his brain.

She left you. She left you.

The ache in his heart was going to kill him. Paige leaving was not an option. He'd been afraid she wasn't going to accept their offer, but now that he'd actually thought about living without her in his life, he'd come to an even more radical conclusion. If she did have an issue with the threesome continuing, he'd do anything to make her happy. Anything.

Even—and the thought made his entire body turn to stone—even let her be with Mason alone if that's what she wanted. He'd still get to see her, spend time with her. Be able to enjoy seeing her laugh and live life with enthusiasm. It would kill a part of him to not be able to hold her, touch her. Make love to her.

But if that was what she wanted, then that was what he would agree to.

The slow-moving bulk of the barge appeared on the horizon, its shining starboard lights twinkling in flashes as he propelled the speedboat through the waves in an intercept path.

There were only a few meters to go before they took the next huge step. And right now he was totally unsure whether he was going to shake her to pieces or kiss her to death.

Chapter Seven

Paige hadn't noticed when the engines stopped, too caught up in her world of gloom and pain. Hours remained before she could totally escape Australia. Maybe time would eventually help her forget.

Something stirred in her peripheral vision, and Paige stared in shock as two familiar figures crawled over the edge of the rail to stand on the deck, their heads twisting side to side frantically.

No. It wasn't possible. She wanted to cower farther into the corner. Hide herself away and disappear, because she simply couldn't take any more heartache.

Then something flipped inside, and she got mad.

She stormed from the storage room onto the deck, her feet pounding on the sturdy metal. The limited lighting left her partly in the shadows.

"What the hell are you doing here?" she yelled as loudly as she could. Shouting released a tiny bit of the rage racing through her veins. Here she'd managed to pull herself away. Cut the cord and run before the tortuous pain could take her. And now they were back, and she would have to do it all over again?

No. Fucking. Way.

Mason reached her first. Ignoring her outstretched arm, he yanked her against his body. He kissed her wildly, one hand looping around her lower back and dragging her tight to his torso. His other hand caught her nape, holding her fast so his mouth could ravage hers.

Oh God, she was going to die. His touch undid her. She longed for this, wanted it.

Couldn't accept it unless it was going to be forever.

She thrust him away, only to be trapped by Trent for an equally bruising kiss of possession. There on the flat open deck, with crates and boxes scattered around them, she was kissed mindless, the simmering anger inside her fighting with the longing for passion, the need to tell them exactly what she wanted from them both.

Them both.

Paige ripped herself from Trent's arms. He let her go—there was no way she could have escaped him if he'd continued to cling as tight as he'd been holding.

She stepped back and fought the tears, working to maintain the heat racing through her veins. Anger was going to be the only way to survive this.

Mason stood with his arms crossed in front of his chest. "You left us without saying a word."

Trent glared at his friend. "I'm going to rip your freaking head off if you so much as utter that phrase ever again."

Mason turned and flipped him the bird. "She did, and I want to know why. And I want to know why this was left behind like some pagan offering."

He held out his arm and opened his fist. The long string of her abandoned shell necklace poured out to dangle from his fingers.

Paige held her hand to her chest, again trying to slow the desperate beating, slow her breathing enough she didn't pass out right here and now. "I'm not explaining anything to you."

At her back, someone cleared his throat, and she twirled to find the nice captain who had agreed to give her passage across to the mainland.

"Miss. I've just gotten word from the resort. They would very much like me to keep moving forward, so if you could go with the gentlemen and hold your discussion elsewhere, that would be best. I can't stop the engines for any longer."

Oh God, no. "But I can't..."

"I'm sorry, but I've been told no resort passengers allowed on board. I didn't know that, or I would have turned you down at the start." His face scrunched with concern as he leaned nearer. "Are you afraid to go with them, miss? If so, I'll break the rules. In fact, I'll have me boyos throw the blokes into the drink for you."

There were crewmen now visible in the wings, and Paige wished she could be vindictive enough to simply turn her back and escape. But she couldn't do that, not destroy the good memories of their times together in such a cruel way.

"I'm fine. I'll go with them. Thank you."

She grabbed her bag from the cabin, and stepped over to where Trent and Mason waited for her. "I need a ride to the mainland, please."

Trent hesitated. "I don't know how much petrol the boat has. The island is closer."

Oh God. She would have to find some other way to leave early. "Fine."

"And we'll talk about—"

Paige shoved her bag at Mason. "Shut up and get in the boat. I will talk about exactly what I want, when I choose. Now can we take this show off the deck of the supply barge? I don't want this to become any more public than it already is."

Trent went down the ladder first. Helped her into the speedboat. Found her a comfortable seat before Mason took the wheel and turned them back toward Bilby Island.

Every time one of them tried to talk, she held up a hand. It was bad enough having to explain why she'd chickened out and left. She didn't want to have to do the whole conversation at a shouting level, over the roar of the motor.

Paige stared at the ocean and ignored the part inside that wanted to crawl into Trent's arms and cry. He'd be warm, and he would hug her, and...that wasn't what she needed.

Not with their plans for the future.

Her mind hurt. Did she tell them the truth and end up putting a damper on their trip?

Did she really give a shit?

The damning thing was—she did. There was no way she could destroy something they were so excited about. McKenzie had said they'd planned to do this forever. Who was she to take their dream and force it to become even a tiny bit bitter? All the mental images she had of standing on the deck and shouting at them with righteous anger dissipated like the foam swirling in circles in their wake, breaking up and being carried off on the smooth evening tide.

Should she tell them the truth? Paige sighed. She still

didn't know, and with the lights of the resort growing closer, she didn't have much time left to decide.

Mason turned the wheel at the last minute. There was a far better place to hold a private conversation than back at the docks where by now all their family and friends could potentially be gathered, waiting to discover what happened. Then again, maybe Kylie had managed to keep it hush-hush—a disappearance wasn't the sort of thing that needed to be bandied about during the soft opening.

The harbor lights approached and he maneuvered his way carefully, ignoring the jetty where Brad had moored his speedboat. Instead, he took the next channel between the buoys and headed toward *Paradise.*

They needed to be on board, where she could understand the implications of at least part of what they were asking. And if by some chance she didn't want to join them...

Thoughts of shanghaiing her and lashing her to the mast until she changed her mind were probably not responsible ones to act on, but as far as a plan, they were about as good as he could get right now.

Trent stood to help as they came alongside, the bulky *Paradise* nowhere near as trim and sleek beside the powerboat they currently rode, but she was a living vessel, not a playing one.

Paige's face as she gazed up at the ship held the most curious expression. As if she was finding it tough to swallow, her eyes full of moisture.

Oh damn, she's going to cry. Mason turned off the motor and rushed to her side. She restrained him.

"I'm walking a thin line here, Mason. Just...take me aboard and we can talk about why I left. Don't touch me. I need space to think."

He backed off, hands held up in submission.

Once they'd dealt with the mooring and scrambled aboard, Mason continued to observe Paige closely. She wandered the deck of *Paradise* silently. She ran one hand slowly over the railing before disappearing below deck.

"What's she doing? Why aren't we telling her what we want?" Trent made as if to follow Paige into the living quarters, and Mason held him back.

"Let her look around. I have a feeling this is all tied together with why she left."

He sat on one of the deck seats and stared over the harbor toward the resort. Somehow the whole thing had come down to this moment...

And he still didn't have a bloody clue what the hell was going on.

He and Trent waited for another minute. Another.

"What's taking her so long?" Trent paced the deck. "The galley and stateroom are smaller than the penthouse suite. There's no reason for this."

His own hard-won patience vanished when Mason realized the faint sound coming from below sounded suspiciously like crying. He raced down the stairs, Trent on his heels.

The galley was empty, which only left the head or the stateroom. The ship was big enough to have space for an actual king-sized mattress, and as they pressed open the door it was to discover Paige perched on the edge. The picture of the three of them that had been displayed above the headboard was in her hand, and tears poured down her cheeks.

His heart broke.

"Oh God, Paige. Don't. Don't cry. Don't tell me not to hold you. Let—"

Whatever else he wanted to say disappeared as she leapt into his arms and buried her face in his neck, the photo abandoned on the bed. She wept, her chest heaving as he maneuvered them until he was able to sit on a galley bench with her still clinging tight.

Trent stood helplessly at their side. He rubbed Paige's back and leaned close to whisper soothing things.

What the hell was wrong?

It was the only thing he hadn't thought of until now. "Paige? Did you get bad news about family or something? Do you need to be contacting someone—?"

"No." She gasped between sobs. "It's not...that. Oh fuck, I'm an ass. Just...give me...a minute."

He'd give her all the time in the world if it would get her back to smiling and being with them.

Her crying slowly faded, and Trent passed her a tissue. She

laughed uneasily and cleaned herself up, squeezing his neck tight for a final second.

"Nice ship, guys. She looks comfortable. You must be looking forward to your trip."

"We are—" *Oh hell.*

Paige slipped off his lap and onto the seat next to him, wiping at her teary eyes.

Trent spoke slowly. "You know about the trip?"

She nodded.

"Then why…?" Mason paused. "Paige, this is fucked up. If you knew about *Paradise*, why did you leave without talking to us?"

She had her fingers clenched together so tight her knuckles had turned white. Trent reached out and soothed them, rubbing until she let go and grasped his fingers instead.

"God, you must think I'm such a girl right now."

"I pretty much know you're a girl, one hundred percent of the time. It's one of the things I love about you." Trent played with her fingers, his voice soft and teasing.

Mason was watching her face as Trent spoke, and the instant flash to white made him wonder if she was going to faint. Paige opened and shut her mouth a couple times before clearing her throat.

"Guys, I left because McKenzie told me about your trip. I didn't want to interrupt something you'd been planning forever with all kinds of melodrama." She snorted. "Of course, I screwed that up royally, so I may as well throw myself off the plank all the way. I've got a ticket booked to return to Canada. My five years are up. I always intended to return home then."

Mason's world fell apart. "You're leaving Australia? Not just Bandicoot Cove, but Sydney and Australia?"

She nodded. "That was the plan. But the reason I left…I didn't want to make the mistake of telling you…"

Pause. Hard swallow. Paige squared her shoulders and lifted her chin—the same moves he'd seen her make as she gathered her courage to join them on a risky maneuver in the wilds. Before taking on a fast zipline, or a dangerous section of rapids.

She tugged on Trent's fingers where he held her captive, pulling one hand free and reaching it to Mason. He snatched it up immediately, rubbing warmth back into her cold digits.

"I wanted to be angry. I wanted to be able to hold off and not tell you this, but I'm not strong enough. I'm sorry..."

Mason clung to her fingers. "What? God, you're killing me."

"Not telling us is worse than anything you could say," Trent agreed. "I'm thinking of all sorts of terrible things. Like you're dying, or—"

Paige swung her head his direction. "Oh damn, no, that's not it. It's just that—I love you."

Trent froze in surprise. Mason stilled as well, his hopes hovering like a bird in a windstorm looking for a safe place to rest.

She turned to face Mason, squeezing his fingers. "But I love you too."

He closed his eyes and let the blessed relief sweep over him. There wasn't anything in his brain except this buzzing sound repeating *thank God, thank God*, over and over again.

Paige wiggled her hands free. "And...that's about why I left. I'm sorry, guys, I didn't mean to ruin—"

Trent grunted. "Holy crap, woman, you Canadians take apologizing far too seriously. We're not sitting here in shock thinking, 'What the hell are we going to do next?'"

Mason's brain finally reengaged. He scooped her off the bench and back into his lap. He needed to be touching her while he explained. "I love you. So does that dickhead over there."

"Hey—" Trent protested.

"But we were waiting to be able to show you the ship before we asked if you'd like to travel with us."

It was Paige's turn to flap her jaw wordlessly.

Trent leaned across and snatched up her hand again. "Just as proof I can talk for myself, I love you, Paige. While the past year has been incredible, it's not enough anymore. I want it all. I want to introduce you to my family and have you sleeping in my bed all the time."

"All the time you're not sleeping in *my* bed, or we're not in yours." Mason caught her chin in his hand and turned her face toward his. "But it's about more than the bedroom. We want you to join us as we laugh with our friends, and kick back over the holidays with my brothers and sister."

Paige shook her head. "Both of you? I thought it was impossible, that's why I left. I mean, it *is* impossible."

"Not if we *want* it to work. It's true, you can't marry both of us—"

"Marry?" The word squeaked out, and Trent punched Mason in the shoulder.

"You have fucking lousy timing for someone who claims to be a romantic."

"Never said I was a romantic."

"Then what the hell are you doing writing romance novels?"

Paige laughed. It was still a little shaky, and Mason tucked her tight against his chest and cradled her close.

"Yeah, yeah, I suck dingo balls. But it's part of this discussion. We've all been keeping secrets from each other out of good intentions. Enough of that."

Trent nodded. "If we're going to make things work with three of us in the picture we're going to have to cut the crap."

Paige sniffed. "And I have to stop being such a girl."

Mason chuckled. "The fact you're a girl is part of your charm, love."

She squeezed her eyes tight for a moment, her lashes wet with moisture from her tears. "I've never been so scared in my life. When McKenzie said you two were going away and I wasn't going to be part of it, I couldn't even stick to my plan to fulfill all your final fantasies this weekend. I just thought about escaping."

The pain in her voice dragged daggers down Mason's back. "I'm sorry my big idea of making it a surprise ended up hurting you."

"Me too." Trent squatted on the floor in front of them and looked into her eyes. "So as a part of being a threesome and not a duo—we obviously need more total disclosure. Mason and I both love you, and that means the whole deal. We're not doing this all romantic and shit and actually proposing right now because we don't want you to feel pressured into anything. But down the road? We want it all." He frowned. "You were leaving...I thought you had a full visa? You don't have to leave Australia, do you?"

Paige shook her head. "I got my immigration status years ago. Pastry chefs are in high demand."

"But you quit?"

"Yeah."

Trent grinned, then cleared his throat. "Paige Kingston, since you're unemployed and all, would you do us the honor of accompanying us on a trip up the coast of Australia for the next six months? Unscheduled stops to include sandy beaches, hiking trails, kayaking spots of interests, and wherever catches our eyes."

A small smile appeared on the corner of her mouth. "I don't know. Does that include having to put up with you calling me *Sheila* when you're cranky?"

Mason snorted. "Does it include us having to put up with you asking if we're going to *throw another couple of shrimp on the barbie?*"

She raised a brow. "Don't all you Aussie men do that? And carry big knives and—" Paige let out a huge sigh and cuddled up to him again. "Oh God, I'm so exhausted. My mind is numb, as if I've been walking on the edge of a cliff and one wrong move would send me falling to my death. And now—I can't believe that we're not only okay, but together even better. It's...so incredible."

Mason squeezed her tight, relieved as well, but highly amused. "You really are being a girl today."

Trent smacked him one.

"What?"

"Arsehole."

"Wanker." Mason grinned at his best mate. After nearly fucking the whole thing up, it appeared they still might get a chance for everything they'd dreamed of to come true.

They sat, the three of them curled close together. Paige in his lap, Trent at their feet caressing her hands with a slow, smooth repetition. The ship swayed gently, rocking them as peace filled the cabin.

Then Paige stood and turned to face them. There was a light shining in her eyes that he'd missed seeing lately, the one that reflected her sheer joy and enthusiasm for life. It was good to see it back where it belonged.

She lifted her chin resolutely. "I would love to travel with you. I need to make a few calls and cancel my flight. And we need to talk about other details, like how will your families take the idea of me being the scarlet woman who led you astray into a terrible, wicked lifestyle?"

Trent raised a brow. "Is that what you're planning on doing? Terrible, wicked things? Because I'm totally good with that."

"Me too. Wicked gets my vote." Mason leaned back in his chair and ogled her. "Plus naughty. And if you really feel up to it, evil acts of perversion—I could use a little research for my next novel."

"You're not going to put me into a book, are you?" she asked.

Mason drew an X over his chest. "Not anymore, darling."

Paige narrowed her gaze. "What does that mean?"

He grinned, letting all the worry and fear of the past hours slip away, reveling in the joy rising on her face. "You were the inspiration for my last three heroines. I'm going to have to find a new prototype, or my fans will get sick of reading about strong-willed, gorgeous brunettes tangling the sheets with their Aussie lovers."

Paige stuck out her tongue at him and he retaliated by sticking his fingers in his mouth and tugging on his cheeks as he crossed his eyes.

"I want to know if the offer still stands..." Trent interrupted their oh-so-grownup argument.

Paige giggled. "Mason, you win—you were uglier to start."

"Hey—"

She turned to Trent. "What offer?"

Trent rose and approached her. "The one where you planned on making all our fantasies come true."

"Oh..."

Trent guided her toward the stairs leading to the deck. "Because I have this one fantasy that's just begging to be fulfilled."

Mason followed closely, intrigued. There were still many questions to deal with, but at least they'd be moving forward together. Unified. Not trying to spare one another's feelings and stupidly hurting the others more in the end.

The harbor was silent—deserted. Kylie must have heard from the boat captain they'd retrieved Paige and was giving them time to deal with the situation. Sunset had long ago faded from the sky, and the light from the silver crescent overhead splashed across the deck.

Trent took Paige by the hand and pulled her against him for a long, slow kiss. Mason watched contentedly, the shimmering moonlight turning the display into something of unearthly beauty. Trent opened her buttons as their tongues tangled, and Mason stepped closer, needing to be a part of them. Then it was his turn to kiss her, and Paige slipped her fingers into his hair as always, and his heart thumped with pleasure as he realized how many more times they'd be able to do this.

Daily, for months.

Years.

There in the moonlight they made love. The three of them. Trent, touching and caressing her. Mason, caring and soothing. Paige, accepting and thrilling under their combined touch. The way it should be, the way it was meant to be. It was as if heaven had opened its gates and let them in. They'd been given the access key and they were going to spend the rest of their lives finding a way to remain exactly where they were.

With each other.

Paradise, found.

About the Author

Vivian Arend has hiked, biked, skied and paddled her way around most of North America and parts of Europe. Throughout all the wandering in the wilderness, stories have been planted and they are bursting out in vivid colour. Paranormal, twisted fairytales, red-hot contemporaries—the genres are all over.

Between times of living with no running water, she home schools her teenaged children and tries to keep up with her husband—the instigator of most of the wilderness adventures.

She loves to hear from readers: vivarend@gmail.com. You can also drop by www.vivianarend.com for more information on what is coming next.

Oh, and Paige wants you to know that she's posted the sex in a pan recipe at www.bandicootcove.com, along with other interesting tidbits about the resort. Enjoy!

Look for these titles by
Vivian Arend

Now Available:

Granite Lake Wolves
Wolf Signs
Wolf Flight
Wolf Games
Wolf Tracks
Wolf Line

Forces of Nature
Tidal Wave
Whirlpool

Turner Twins
Turn It On
Turn It Up

Pacific Passion
Stormchild
Stormy Seduction
Silent Storm

Takhini Wolves
Black Gold

Six Pack Ranch
Rocky Mountain Heat
Rocky Mountain Haven
Rocky Mountain Desire

Xtreme Adventures
Falling, Freestyle
Rising, Freestyle

Bandicoot Cove
Exotic Indulgence
Paradise Found

Print Anthologies
Under the Northern Lights
Under the Midnight Sun
Breaking Waves
Storm Swept
Freestyle

Tropical Sin

Lexxie Couper

Dedication

To the man who was once "just" my friend.

Chapter One

You Are Personally and Cordially Invited to Attend The Soft Opening of Australia's Newest FIVE-STAR Luxury Resort BANDICOOT COVE on Bilby Island. Bring a plus one if you desire.

All expenses and needs will be catered for as we test our customer services in preparation for the Grand Opening.

(P.S. Can you believe I got this job, guys? Wow!! Mack, if you don't bring Aidan I will thump you. Just saying. See you soon,
Love, Kylie
XXXX)

"Holy shit!" McKenzie Wood grabbed at her best friend's sleeve, almost yanking Aidan off his seat and into her lap. "Did you see who that was?"

She swiveled in her own seat, trying like hell to catch a glimpse of the tall-dark-and-freaking-gorgeous man through the restaurant's crowd.

Aidan, bless his little cotton socks—well, not that little, since the guy had size thirteen feet—didn't smack her back. Instead, her best friend since she was fourteen disengaged his shirt sleeve from her fist, righted himself on his chair and turned to look in the general direction she was gawking.

"Hugh Jackman?" he guessed, his deep voice rumbling with mirth. "Russell Crowe? Russell Brand? Brandon Routh?" He shot her a sideward glance, a grin pulling at the corners of his mouth. "Care to throw me a bone here, Mack, 'cause I haven't got a bloody clue."

McKenzie twisted back to him and gave him a wide grin. "Nick Blackthorne."

Aidan's mouth fell open. He smacked his palms to the sides of his face, his green eyes wide. "No!" he burst out. "Nick Blackthorne? *The* Nick Blackthorne?"

McKenzie whacked the back of her right hand against his chest, hiding her grunt of pain under a scowl of exasperation. Damn it, the man's chest was harder than concrete. "Yeah, yeah, yeah—" she rolled her eyes, "—funny bastard, aren't you? The last time anyone saw Nick Blackthorne, he was supposedly checking into a sex rehab clinic in Germany for being an addict."

Aidan cocked an eyebrow. "Sex addict? The guy's a bloody rock star. The biggest rock star this country has produced. Isn't he *meant* to have sex with just about everything in a dress that throws herself at him?"

"No, no, no, no." McKenzie shook her head. "God, don't you actually read the rags I write for? He supposedly checked into a sex rehab center because he can't stop having sex with *men.*"

Aidan studied her for a long second. Followed by another one.

She sat and waited for him to say something, her hands on his knees, her gaze holding his.

Finally, he shrugged. "Well, to each his own."

McKenzie leaned closer to him. "You're missing the point, Rogers. If Nick Blackthorne is here, when everyone thinks he's in Germany, I could get the scoop."

"The scoop?"

She grinned, squirming closer to the edge of her seat. "The scoop."

Aidan let out a sharp breath, turning back to their table and reaching for his beer. "McKenzie," he said, his voice level, "we are at the soft opening of your friend's resort. If you go all tabloid-journalist and stalk a guest, Kylie will kill you. Then I will have to explain to Mason why I let his twin sister get killed. And then Mason will probably try to punch me."

"And what would you do in return?"

Aidan gave her a steady sideward glance. "Depends. Do you like your twin today or not?"

McKenzie thought about that question for a moment,

struggling to keep her face composed. Aidan always, *always* seemed to make her want to grin, even when he was telling her she was being horrible. Prick. "Better not punch him back," she answered. "He did, after all, pay for the flights up here."

"Good point." Aidan took a mouthful of beer before picking up his fork and stabbing at the lobster bisque on his plate. "Although I coulda done without the blackmail to help clean that boat of his he just bought with Trent. Seriously, if Trent wanted to sail up the Australian coastline, how come I get stuck with scraping the barnacles off the hull of the damn rust bucket?"

"'Cause you lost that stupid bet at the airport about whose bag was the lightest—his or yours, remember?" McKenzie offered, picking up her own fork. She had to hand it to Kylie; the girl knew how to throw a party, and the soft opening hadn't even started yet. Lobster for brunch? Bring it on. "Oh, and you can hold your breath the longest?"

Aidan snorted again, the sound making her grin wider. "Next time Kylie launches a resort opening, I want it to be in the Outback." He took another mouthful of beer. "Or the Snowies."

McKenzie laughed. "Don't tempt her. You know what she's like. Besides, it was nice to have Mason on the flight with us, even if he did sucker you into cleaning *Paradise*. At least this way I don't have to call Mum. She still hasn't forgiven me for my article on—" A tall man walked past the entrance to the restaurant, oozing brooding sexuality, phenomenal good looks and smoldering arrogance. Nick Blackthorne. In the flesh. She grabbed Aidan's arm just as he was about to take a drink, sploshing beer over his hand and wrist. "Oh God, it *is* him, Rogers. It is him! Look. *Look*!"

Before Aidan could do such a thing, McKenzie jumped to her feet, sending her chair tumbling to the ground. The rather overweight and ridiculously overdressed woman sitting at the table behind her muttered something that sounded very much like "inconsiderate cow", but McKenzie didn't care. Nick Blackthorne *was* here. At Bandicoot Cove Resort. Walking around without any sign of bodyguards, groupies or entourage.

Nick Blackthorne. The world's biggest rock star.

Here. Within twenty meters of her.

She watched him amble through the opulent foyer, his stunning light grey eyes concealed by a pair of pitch-black sunglasses, his tall, lean frame wrapped in a pair of snug, faded Levis and an R2-D2 T-shirt. Sinewy muscles coiled and flexed as he walked, each stride almost rhythmic, as if he moved to music no one else but he could hear.

A little flutter of something entirely sexual stirred in McKenzie's core, a tiny throb of base, instinctual interest. For a brief second an image of him throwing her on the massive bed in her resort room filled her mind. His long-fingered hands tore her clothes from her body before, with fluid ease, he sank what was rumored to be a solid and very impressive ten inches into her sodden and very willing pussy.

Her nipples pinched tight and she huffed into her fringe, tracking his path past the reception desk and out of sight.

"We gotta go." She hooked her fingers under Aidan's arm and tugged him to his feet. Well, tried to. Shifting a six-foot-three firefighter wasn't easy, especially when he was looking up at her like she'd lost her mind. "Quick quick," she begged, resorting to both hands wrapped around his biceps. Bloody hell, when had Rogers bulked up so much? "I need to see where he's going."

Aidan—stubbornly—stayed put. "Stalking now? Didn't you tell me you wanted out of the tabloid business? That it was time to start your serious journalist career?"

McKenzie slapped the back of his head and then snared his arm again, her fingers barely curling halfway around its muscled width. "Shut up. He's getting away."

Aidan made a move to pick up his fork again. "Good for him."

A surge of hot anger stabbed into McKenzie's chest and she bit back a curse. Aidan was correct. She *had* told him and Mason on the flight up that she was going to quit her job at Goss when she got back. She *had* said it was time to actually use her degree in journalism for the greater good. But then Nick Blackthorne had walked past, and really, wasn't it for the world's greater good to know just what he was doing here and where he'd been? And if that "where" had anything to do with the secret activities of ten inches of flesh?

She pulled at Aidan's arm once more, an ineffectual tug she was almost ashamed of. Almost. "Please, Aidan?" she begged, giving him her most wounded-puppy expression. The kind that always, always made him bail on one of his stubborn standoffs. "Please? For me?"

He looked up at her, his jaw square, his expression unreadable. He'd been her best friend since before she had her first boyfriend. He'd been her rock, her anchor. Her voice of reason when her journalist's mind got carried away with her. She didn't want him upset with her. She needed him with her on this.

He studied her with those deep, direct eyes of his. Eyes that missed nothing. Eyes that seemed to see nothing in the world but her.

A soft flutter constricted in McKenzie's sex, unexpected and just as eager as her earlier response to Blackthorne.

She hitched in a silent breath and let his arm go, a lump forming in her throat. "Please," she muttered, looking everywhere but at the man sitting before her. "Please come with me, Aidan."

"Fuck it," she heard him grumble, half a second before his chair scraped over the polished bamboo floor and he stood.

A wave of impish relief surged through her, destroying the wholly unsettling...*thing*...she'd just felt. Aidan was Aidan. Yes, he was pretty okay to look at and just about every woman within a ten-mile radius threw herself at him whenever she hit the clubs with him, but he was Aidan. That was it.

Grinning up at him, she snared his arm again with her fingers, giving his hard biceps a small squeeze. "You are so bloody awesome, Rogers."

"I know," he growled, moving away from the table and taking her with him. "Just promise me no muck-slinging, no trash-flinging and no lies. We follow the guy, you ask him for a comment and we leave. All over, Red Rover, in ten minutes. Deal?"

"Deal."

He pointed a finger at her nose, a stern glower darkening his otherwise friendly face. "And no asking him if he's gay. A bloke doesn't like being asked such a thing whether he is or not, got it?"

McKenzie cocked her head, quickening her step to stay abreast of him. "Are you gay, Rogers?"

His eyebrows shot up. "What?"

"I only ask 'cause you've never gone out with anyone for more than a day or two. Like, ever."

Aidan let out a harsh breath and turned his glare forward, all but pulling her out of the restaurant. "I've had girlfriends."

"Really? When? The longest you ever went out with a woman was that police officer from Newcastle Command and that lasted for a little less than a week."

His fingers curled harder into her arm, his stride lengthening. "Why the hell do I put myself in these situations?"

McKenzie skipped into step with him. "'Cause they're fun?"

"Yeah," he grunted, not looking at her. "Like a root canal."

They walked through the foyer, McKenzie's stomach flipping and flopping in a strange little way she didn't understand. Part of her wanted to slide Aidan a little sideward glance, just to be sure it was still Aidan storming along beside her. She'd known him forever, well, what felt like forever. She'd met him in her second year of high school when his family had moved to Newcastle. The minute he'd walked into the science lab, towering over just about every boy in the class, and the teacher as well, she'd smiled. It had nothing to do with the way he looked—which even at fourteen she knew was pretty damn good. She'd smiled because his eyes said, *there's mischief to be had. Who wants in?*

The rest of the girls in her year, and quite a few above and below, threw themselves at him straightaway, but he never took any of them up on their far-from-unsubtle advances. It wasn't until he'd been at school for a week when she finally spoke to him—right after she'd accidently kicked a soccer ball straight into his groin during a Phys Ed class.

Of course, she'd run over straightaway and dropped to her knees, rubbing his groin and making sorry sounds before she realized what she was doing. She had six brothers, after all, one of them being Mason, her twin. Male anatomy wasn't something mysterious or dangerous to her. She'd seen more penises by the time she was fourteen than she could remember—especially Mason's. Damn, her brother had zero interest in personal privacy. When Aidan had looked up at her, squirming under her palm, his face red with pain, his eyes wide with stunned shock, she'd realized what she was doing and promptly burst out laughing. She'd laughed all the way to the principal's office after being sent there by her mortified Phys Ed teacher for inappropriate touching of a fellow class member. Aidan had found her at lunch, plonked down beside her on the rickety metal bench, said, "You know, I don't think I've ever had a handjob quite like that before," and that had been it. They'd been best friends since.

She'd never *ever* thought of him in any kind of sexual way. Ever. So why had her belly done that weird squirmy thing just now in the restaurant?

Because you're excited. You've just seen Nick Blackthorne. The Nick Blackthorne. Of course, you're going to be all squirmy. Not just 'cause the guy's as freaking hot as sin, but because he's your ticket. One exclusive exposé about Nick Blackthorne's sexual tendencies, and you can write your own meal ticket out of tabloid trash hell and land yourself that serious job you've ached for forever.

The reasoning made little sense. Write trash to stop writing trash? But McKenzie wouldn't let herself analyze it any more. If there *was* more to the way her belly was behaving, she'd deal with it later. Nick Blackthorne was in front of her and Aidan was beside her. Currently, the two most important men in her life.

Huh. You really are one for the dramatic, aren't you?

Shut up. Focus. You've got a story to write. How exactly are you going to do that, Ms. I'm-Such-A-Clever-Serious-Journalist?

Her eyes, of their own accord, slid to Aidan and her belly flip-flopped again. She grabbed at her bottom lip with her teeth, an idea coming to her.

If the rumors about Nick Blackthorne *were* true, she had the most perfect, *perfect* bait to get her story. Now, all she had to do was convince Aidan of that.

Do you really want to do that, McKenzie? Ask him to...

She cut the thought dead. She wouldn't just ask him to do it for a story. She would ask him to do it for fun. Aidan had always been one to leap into life. Hell, he'd taken her kicking and screaming on more than one harebrained adventure. Why should this be any different?

Yeah, but you're going to ask him to...

"I still can't believe I'm doing this."

Aidan's low grumble played over her senses and she started, her stomach tightening again. And not just her stomach this time, but all sorts of other parts of her anatomy: parts of her anatomy that had no right getting tight over Aidan Rogers.

"I remember when you'd do anything for fun, Rogers." She shoved him with her shoulder, giving his arm a squeeze at the same time. Seriously, when had he become so muscular?

"Fun I can do. Fun I like doing. Stalking celebrities—" he gave her a steady and very pointed sideward stare, "—not so much fun."

She flashed a grin at him. "You're looking at this all wrong, Aidan. All you're doing is walking through a hotel in the same direction as another guy. That's not stalking."

"Is this how you live with yourself, McKenzie Wood?" He turned his attention back to the foyer and the broad back of the world's most Googled rock star. "Delude yourself into believing you're *not* being a horrible creep?"

"Yep."

Her one word answer made him snort, but for a brief second McKenzie glimpsed a hint of a dimple in his left cheek.

Bingo! She had him.

"Just go with me on this one, will you?" She turned her own stare to Blackthorne, her stomach knotting. This time the physical reaction was from nervous excitement. "All I'm going to do to start with is say g'day."

Aidan snorted again. "Why do I not believe you?"

McKenzie laughed. "I have no idea."

Nick Blackthorne weaved his way through the smattering of guests milling around the Bandicoot Resort's massive reception area, a small smile curling at the corners of his mouth. It wasn't the fact he was here, at the soft opening of the resort, that made him happy, nor the fact he was walking around without a minder or bodyguard or groupie to be seen. It was simply because the woman laughing behind him had a delightfully throaty, infectious laugh.

He stopped himself from shooting a look over his shoulder, concentrating instead on finding the correct passageway that would lead him to the Oasis Bar. He was a touch jetlagged and needed something more than coffee to wake up.

A touch? You've been on one plane or the other for the last three days. You're more than jetlagged, you're jet-fucking-dragged-through-the-turbines stoned. Besides, the need for something more than caffeine has nothing to do with jetlag. You just want to sit out in the sun and pretend you're a normal person for a short while, don't you?

He smiled wider. The truth was always less sensational. It had been a long time since he'd been able to sit at a bar and relax. When his agent had offered him the chance to attend the resort's soft opening he'd jumped at it. Minimum number of guests, all hand-picked by the hotel's manager, all—his agent assured him—too discreet or important in their own rights to worry about him being in their presence. A nice change from where he'd just been, that was for sure.

The thought made his smile falter. A little. He wasn't going to let his mind turn to where he'd just been. Not when he was walking through Eden.

Ah, so the romantic you used to be is still buried in that craven pit you call a soul, is he?

Behind him the woman laughed again, another low, throaty chuckle and, before he could help himself, Nick turned.

Whoa.

She was only a few feet behind, grinning up at a guy almost half again her height, her long, strawberry blonde hair a flaming halo in the sun's warm rays, her pink lips stretched in a grin that said very clearly, "Yes, I am completely in charge of this situation."

Nick let his gaze flick to her companion, noting with an experienced eye the man's latent strength in his six-foot-plus form, his fluid, steady movements, and his utter adoration for the woman gripping his arm.

Fuck, they were a sexy couple. Damn sexy.

His prick twitched in his jeans and he scowled, turning away from the young lovers. There was a time he'd have walked straight on up to them and suggested something far more depraved than either could probably imagine. Something very dirty and very enjoyable. That time had passed, however.

The woman laughed again, the delicious sound accompanied by a lower, deeper chuckle. The guy's laugh. Relaxed. Easygoing. Coming up from his chest to slip past his lips in a humored rumble. Equally as infectious as hers.

Nick's cock gave an eager spasm, rubbing with a certain amount of pleasant insistency against the denim of his favorite jeans.

He drove his nails into his palms and scanned the lush gardens on the other side of the glass wall. Where the hell was this bar? Somewhere outside beside a pool? He needed a drink.

No, not a drink. You need—

A face of an angel with filth on her mind,

I pray to burn in her fire, I pray to die in her arms.

The words—lyrics of a song he hadn't written yet—whispered through Nick's head and he raised his eyebrows, his heartbeat quickening. Just as it had been too long since he could relax in public, it had been even longer since words of music came to him. Whoever the redhead was, she stirred something in him.

Yet the arms of her lover reach out for more.

Like a sinner I will burn in his fire,

I will die in his fire as she pleads for more.

Nick came to a halt, the unexpected lyrics floating through his head. It seemed they'd *both* stirred something in him he hadn't felt for a long time, not just the woman.

The whisper of a rhythm teased him and he closed his eyes, a familiar sensation stirring in the pit of his gut. Carnal thoughts and lyrics? Coming to Bandicoot Cove really was a good—

"Excuse me, but can I ask you a question?"

The soft, husky voice speaking beside him could only belong to one person. Opening his eyes, Nick turned around, leaving his sunglasses firmly in place as he fixed his gaze on the flame-haired woman smiling up at him. This close she wasn't just sexy, she was stunning. Stunning and gorgeous. As was the man standing next to her, his expression unreadable, that sleeping strength radiating from him in waves of...

Like a sinner I will burn in his fire,

I will die in his fire and beg her for—

"You're Nick Blackthorne, yes?"

The woman's question took Nick by jarring surprise. It shouldn't have, but with the words of a hidden song taunting him and the unexpected lick of sexual interest teasing him, he wasn't prepared. Especially for what she said next.

"I'm McKenzie Wood from Goss Weekly." Her clear blue eyes turned direct. Intent. "I'm wondering if you'd like to comment on your stay at the *Vergnügen* sex clinic in Germany?"

Chapter Two

Biting back a groan—damn it, she said she was going to be subtle!—Aidan watched Blackthorne stiffen. No, not just stiffen. Every muscle in the man's body coiled, as if he were about to attack. And why wouldn't he? He was minding his own business when out of nowhere, bam, a little thing with beguiling blue eyes and an attitude the size of Uluru smacks into his peace with a question about his sex life. If it were Aidan in the rock star's shoes, he'd stiffen too.

But it wasn't Aidan, and the little thing with the beguiling blue eyes and attitude was McKenzie. Which meant Blackthorne was in a world of pain if he so much as raised his hand to her.

"No." The singer's voice was a liquid-smooth purr. "I don't think I do want to comment."

A strange accent—not quite Australian anymore but not quite American either—made the words sound tight. Strained.

"So, nothing about the rumors you checked in to Vergnügen to try and cure your—"

Aidan reached out and pressed his hand over McKenzie's open mouth, grabbing her around the waist and tugging her against his body as he did so. He looked at the tall man standing stock still before him, eyes still concealed by pitch-black sunglasses, body still tense.

"Sorry," he said, ignoring McKenzie's attempts to disengage herself from his hold. It wasn't easy—she was the only daughter of seven offspring. She knew how to get herself out of a death grip if she needed to. He, on the other hand, was a firefighter. And he'd been wrestling with McKenzie—in some way or another—since before his balls dropped.

When the hell are you going to tell her how you—

"Sorry," he said again, giving Blackthorne an embarrassed smile. "She kinda forgets not everyone's open to her type of charm."

The rock star didn't say a word. Nor did the tension leave his body.

Aidan pulled McKenzie—still squirming in his arms—harder to his body. It was a bad idea, of course. The way her toned backside kept rubbing against his dick, the way her full breasts kept pushing against his forearm, he was going to be in a rather stiff situation any second now. Better that, however, than Blackthorne taking a swipe at the tabloid journalist bugging him on his holiday. If that happened, Aidan was likely to do something very foolish. Knocking out the world's most famous musician wasn't on his bucket list.

Telling McKenzie how you feel? That's on your bucket list though, isn't it? Ever since you almost—

"Like your last album, by the way," he burst out, shutting the unnerving thought down. Far too unnerving when the woman in question was writhing against his crotch in an attempt to break free. Jesus, he could feel his semi already. With every wriggle and squirm from McKenzie the damn thing got bigger. "Wasn't that fussed on track number five, though."

Oh, you bloody moron. Has all the blood from your brain gone south?

Blackthorne didn't move. "Savage Lust? Not one of my favorites either."

Aidan laughed, the man's answer surprising him.

They stood looking at each other for a second, McKenzie's muffled protests filling the awkward silence. "Well," Aidan finally said, his cock now so hard there wasn't a hope in hell McKenzie could miss it, "I better boat this marlin and mount her on my wall."

An image of McKenzie—naked and waiting for him on all fours—flashed through Aidan's head and he bit back a groan. Fuck, that's what he got for trying to be funny. Why the hell did he have to use the word "mount"?

Another image of naked McKenzie popped into his head—this one of her bent over a black velvet cube with her wrists cuffed to her—

"I'm sure that will be...entertaining."

Blackthorne's strangely accented drawl jerked Aidan's mind from the wholly arousing and unsettling image. The man looked at him, black sunglasses hiding whatever was going through his mind. His expression never changed, his body never relaxed.

Just get her outta here, Rogers. Take her as far away from him as you can. Now. Before she bites your hand or you come on the small of her back.

It was the last thought that did it. With a nod and an embarrassingly sheepish grin, Aidan hauled McKenzie off her feet and carried her in the opposite direction of Blackthorne. Jesus Christ, what a debacle.

He strode through the foyer, ignoring the curious glances and questioning stares of the resort's guests and staff. Thank God Mason wasn't about. The guy knew what his sister was like. He'd probably offer to lend Aidan a hand and that'd end them all up shit creek.

No, what he needed to do now was take her back to her room, deposit her on her bed and then—

Fuck her senseless?

—go find Kylie and apologize in advance for harassing one of her guests. After that, he'd find a bar and order himself a bloody stiff drink. To go with his bloody stiff dick.

Two seconds later, McKenzie did what he suspected she'd do much earlier. She bit his palm. Hard.

"Oww." He dropped her, shaking his hand before giving the bright red teeth marks indented in his skin an angry inspection. "That hurt."

McKenzie glared at him. "Serves you right. What the hell were you doing?"

"Saving you from a lawsuit," he shot back, shaking his hand again. Damn, she knew how to bite. "*And* saving your friendship with Kylie. Do you think she'd be happy you pissed off one of her guests? Not just one of them, either. Nick bloody Blackthorne. Think for a second here, Mack. Yeah, there may be a story to be had, but Christ, this is your friend's job on the line. A soft opening like this comes with all sorts of expectations and conditions. You stuff up Kylie's event and she'll suffer, long after you've written your story and moved onto the next one."

For the first time since he'd known her, McKenzie seemed lost for words. She stared up at him, her bottom lip caught between her teeth, her eyes wide. She looked confused. Fragile.

So completely kissable.

Do it. Do it now. For fuck's sake, man, how long are you going to wait? Do you need to almost die in another fire before you tell her?

He took a step toward her.

"Where the hell have you two been?" a male voice boomed from behind Aidan, and he turned around, his gut sinking to find Mason approaching them both. "I've been looking everywhere for you."

McKenzie let out a soft breath, the sound ragged, and he flicked her a quick look, frustration stabbing into him. Whatever expression had been on her face when she sighed, it was no longer there, replaced instead with a wide grin as she watched Mason walk toward them.

What do you think it was, Rogers? Do you really think she wanted you to kiss her? The whole reason you never have is 'cause she's never shown an iota of sexual interest in you. What would change that? Manhandling her like you did? Hardly.

"Aidan, you bloody bastard," Mason continued, throwing him a laughing glower, "you turned your mobile phone off."

His balls throbbing and his cock an aching rod, Aidan turned toward McKenzie's twin. "You think I wanna clean that boat of yours so early in the morning?"

Mason gave him a wide grin, his eyes as blue as McKenzie's—and just as full of irrepressible charm. "Hey, what else are you going to do?"

What else indeed?

"I can tell what *you've* been doing," Aidan said, knowing very well the statement would shut Mason up in a heartbeat. McKenzie's twin was in a rather unusual...relationship...with his best friend, Trent and the cute little Canadian pastry chef they'd met a while ago, but he wasn't overly forthcoming about it when he was around McKenzie. In fact, Aidan would say Mason was doing everything he could to keep his sister in the dark.

For a quick second, panic flickered across the other man's face and then he gave them both another patented Mason Wood smirk. "Don't try and wheedle out of it, Rogers. You owe me a boat clean-up."

"What *have* you been doing all morning?" McKenzie asked, giving her brother a curious look. "We didn't see either you or

Trent at breakfast."

A very faint pink tinged Mason's cheeks as he looked everywhere but at his sister. "Err, housekeeping."

"That'd be right." She rolled her eyes. "In your hotel room for less than an hour and it's already a mess. I hope you're not making Paige clean it up. She's far too nice to be doing your dirty work."

Mason didn't say a word, but Aidan noticed his cheeks got a little pinker.

"How long has she been going out with Trent for?" McKenzie asked, and Aidan had to bite the inside of his cheek to stop himself bursting out laughing. It seemed that while he may be the only one not scoring, at least he wasn't the only one feeling awkward at the moment—Mason's cheeks were almost red.

"Did you know Josh Lye is here? Installing the resort's IT system."

Mason's hurried question made Aidan blink. And McKenzie laughed. "Josh Lie-With-Si? Really? Does Sienna know he's here? She's going to freak when she finds out. Especially now she's finally starting to live her life again." A wide grin pulled at her lips and she rubbed her hands together. "Wow, I just remembered I still owe that bugger a thump in the arm."

Mason rolled his eyes. "You're not *still* holding a grudge over the AFL Grand final are you? Bloody hell, sis, that was *twelve* years ago."

McKenzie jutted out her chin, the stubborn action making the pit of Aidan's gut tighten and his balls—still throbbing from their earlier unintended stimulation—ache anew. Jesus Christ, he was pathetic. "Doesn't matter," she said. "Josh's team lost. I get to thump him. That was the bet."

Mason gave her an exasperated look. "How old are you?"

"Same age as you. So shut up."

"No, you're not," he shot back, lips twitching. "I'm five minutes older."

"Freak."

"Lunatic."

"Maniac."

"Girl."

It was Aidan's turn to roll his eyes. "Alright you two, break it up."

Mason poked his tongue out at his sister before giving Aidan a firm stare. "I need you at the yacht in a couple of hours, mate. Don't be late."

Aidan raised his eyebrows.

"Okay, okay." Mason shrugged. "*Please* can you come to the yacht, Aidan? Trent and I are taking Paige out later this evening and we need your help."

McKenzie laughed. "You mean his muscles?"

Mason flicked Aidan a quick look, a small grin pulling at his lips. Aidan resisted the urge to shuffle his feet. The way McKenzie's twin was looking at him made Aidan wonder if the way he felt about her wasn't as secret as he thought.

His gut knotted. If Mason suspected he had a thing—a *big* thing—for his sister, what would the guy do? Hit him? Hug him? Tell him to fuck off?

And if you die before she finds out? What does that achieve?

"No," Mason drawled, a gleam in his eye that made Aidan's stomach knot some more. "We need his firefighting skills." He gave McKenzie a "duh" look. "Of course his bloody muscles, you moron."

It was McKenzie's turn to poke her tongue out at Mason. "I don't like you. Go away, please."

Mason grinned again, the smile so like his sister's it was a little freaky. "Gladly. Places to go, people to do."

McKenzie pretended to make herself gag. "You're disgusting."

With a wave and another uncomfortably ambiguous smile at Aidan, Mason left them alone, swinging open the nearest exit door in the glass-walled passageway and ambling through the gardens outside.

"I've always wondered what sex on a boat would be like?"

The question was out before Aidan realized where his mind had taken him. Or that he'd spoken aloud.

"Who's having sex on a boat?" McKenzie turned her head, tracking her brother with a narrowed-eyed stare through the glass until the tropical gardens swallowed him up.

"Err..."

She turned back to Aidan, giving him a disgusted look. "Mason? Really? Sex with Mason? Who would have sex with

Mason?" She pulled a face. "That's just gross."

Aidan cocked an eyebrow. "Not that it's any of my business, but I'm pretty sure your brother has a dick and you know what we blokes are like—have dick, will use it."

For a very brief moment, McKenzie's gaze slid down Aidan's chest, over his stomach to his groin before, with an almost imperceptible shake of her head, she looked up into his face again. A faint frown pulled at her eyebrows and she caught her bottom lip with her teeth again. "Umm...there's something I need to ask you."

Aidan's throat slammed shut. He stared down into her clear blue eyes, his dick—all too easily remembering what it had been worked up over only a short while ago—growing hard again. His blood roared in his ears and he tried to swallow, his mouth dry. "What?" he asked, more than a little dismayed at how croaky his voice came out.

"Something kinda...odd," she continued, the frown pulling deeper at her eyebrows until a tiny crease formed in the middle of the smooth space between them. "But important."

Aidan drew a slow breath through his nose. This couldn't be happening, could it? What he'd hoped for, for so bloody long? Had McKenzie Wood finally seen him as something other than—

"Will you hit on Nick Blackthorne for me?"

McKenzie waited for Aidan to say something. He didn't.

Not straight away.

"Umm..."

"I know I'm asking a lot." She placed her palms on his broad chest and gave him a crooked smile. "But it's just one little conversation with the guy at a bar."

He looked down at her, an expression she had no hope of deciphering falling over his face. "Ummm..."

Oh, my God, Wood. Are you really doing this?

"Please?"

Yes. It seemed she really was.

You're pathetic, you know that?

No. Pathetic she wasn't. Confused. That's what she was. Confused about the new and totally unexpected way her body was reacting to Aidan. *Aidan.* Her best friend. The guy who'd held her hand after every break-up she'd ever had. The guy who'd helped pick out what she was going to wear on just about every first date she'd ever had. Aidan freaking Rogers. She didn't get horny over Aidan Rogers. She didn't.

Yeah, that's why the second he uttered the word "dick" you wondered what his was like. And don't go pretending you didn't feel it when he was holding you against his body earlier. In fact, don't go pretending you weren't squirming against him more than you needed to. You liked the way his dick got hard rubbing against your arse. You liked it a lot.

"Let me get this clear." His voice was just as unreadable as his expression. "You want me to try and pick up the world's biggest rock star so you can get a story?"

McKenzie's belly flip-flopped. She wanted to take it back. She wanted to say, *No, it was just a joke, what I want you to do is kiss me.*

The unexpected thought hit her. Blindsided her, in fact. Made her pussy clench and her pulse pound.

She nodded, not trusting herself to say or do anything else.

Aidan's jaw bunched. His nostrils flared. "If I do this, will you do something for me?"

McKenzie nodded again. A quick single nod of her head.

"Quit Goss."

The request was like a physical slap. And not because he'd asked her to give up her job, a job she didn't want anymore. Because he hadn't asked her to...

What? Kiss him? Sleep with him? Marry him?

Oh, for Pete's sake. What the hell was going on with her?

For the third time, she nodded.

Aidan's nostrils flared again. "And when he turns me down?"

She looked up at him, her sex constricting, her heart hammering. "He won't."

Because who in their right mind would?

Chapter Three

Nick studied the sweating glass in his hand, his stare following the paths of individual beads of water even as his mind played seven lines of lyrics over and over again.

A face of an angel with filth on her mind,
I pray to burn in her fire, I pray to die in her arms.
Yet the arms of her lover reach out for more.
Like a sinner I will burn in his fire,
I will die in his fire as she pleads for more.

Like a sinner I will burn in his fire,
I will die in his fire and beg her for—

What? What did he beg for?

He didn't know yet. He didn't know and it pissed him off. And intrigued him.

As did McKenzie Wood from Goss Weekly and her unnamed, completely enamored male companion.

Intrigued? Is that the word you're going with?

It was for now. When he finished his drink, however...

"Is it just water?" A familiar male voice spoke beside him and Nick twisted on his barstool, watching as McKenzie Wood's unnamed, completely enamored male companion slid onto the stool beside him. "Or something a little stronger?"

Nick swung his attention back to the glass in his hand, regarded it for a second and then turned back to the man next to him. "Water. Very icy."

His new friend perched himself on the edge of the stool,

and Nick couldn't help but note how tense he was. Every muscle in his body seemed sculpted from rock, lovingly carved by a master artist, each one sublime in that latent strength he'd noticed earlier, but rock all the same. Whatever was going on, the man was on edge.

Nick waved a finger at the barkeeper, keeping his gaze on McKenzie Wood's companion as the woman dressed in little but a string bikini and lip gloss hurried over to them. "Give my friend what I'm having. Straight up."

The man flinched at the word "straight", a barely-there tightening of the corners of his eyes, and Nick chuckled. He took a sip of his drink, let the cool water slide down his throat and then turned back to his new friend. "Can I ask a question?"

If it was even possible, the man's muscles coiled tighter. "Sure."

"What's the first thing to come into your head when I say, 'I will die in his fire and beg her for...'"

"A chance."

The two words passed the man's lips without hesitation and Nick chuckled again. Yep. Here was a love story ready to be told. Or sung about.

He straightened back to the bar, closed his eyes and held up his glass. "*A face of an angel with filth on her mind,*" he sang, his voice low. "*I pray to burn in her fire, I pray to die in her arms.*"

He heard the man shift on the stool, but he didn't open his eyes, the words and the rhythm—far more haunted than anything he'd created before—claiming him for the moment.

"*Yet the arms of her lover reach out for more.*
"*Like a sinner I will burn in his fire,*
"*I will die in his fire as she pleads for more.*

"*Like a sinner I will burn in his fire,*
"*I will die in his fire and beg her for a chance.*"

It worked. On more levels than Nick expected.

A chance? Isn't that what you've been looking for, for the last lifetime? A chance at something else? Something you once had?

He ignored the ambivalent question, opening his eyes instead and holding out his hand to the man beside him. "Nick Blackthorne." He smiled. "But you already know that. Who might you be?"

The man closed firm fingers around Nick's grip, his skin callused. "Aidan Rogers."

"And what do you do for a living, Aidan Rogers? Apart from boating marlin and helping tired rock stars write song lyrics."

Aidan snorted, the sound far more self-deprecating than Nick believed he intended. "I'm a firefighter."

"Dealing with enflamed situations a specialty, 'ey? But today, you're on a different mission? Feeling the heat for a different reason?"

Aidan cocked an eyebrow. "What makes you say that?"

Nick grinned. "You're here to ask me out."

Silence followed his statement. Stretching silence. He shot Aidan a quick look, taking another drink as he did.

The man studied him, his expression steady. For all intents and purposes, Nick could have said Aidan was here to sell him a fire extinguisher. Nothing about his face registered any kind of shock or reaction. "So," the man finally said, his voice steady. Calm. "Can I buy you something stronger than water?"

Unable to help himself, Nick burst out laughing. "Oh, mate." He clapped a hand on Aidan's very broad shoulder—what did the guy do? Shoulder-press Mack trucks in his spare time? "You have no idea how far from my type you are."

A face of an angel with filth on her mind...

The song lyric came to him, lilting and soft, a teasing caress on the part of him he'd thought long dead, and with it came an image of McKenzie Wood, her entirely kissable lips curled in a challenging smile, her direct gaze presenting its own challenge.

His prick moved in his jeans, an eager spasm he felt both in his balls and at the base of his spine. What he wanted right now...right at this very moment...

Aidan cleared his throat, and as if someone had released a valve somewhere on his well-built body, a fluid ease rolled through him. "Didn't think I was."

"So, what are you going to tell her?"

A frown pulled at Aidan's eyebrows. "How do you know it

was Mack who put me up to this?"

Nick shrugged, Aidan's answer confirming more than one suspicion. "Who else would it be? You're here at the resort with a tabloid journalist. A journalist with the balls to ask me straight out about Germany."

"That doesn't really answer my question." Aidan's gaze was direct. "Who's to say I didn't find you attractive back in the corridor?"

Nick laughed again. "I do. I saw the way you looked at her, even when you were trying to shut her up. You don't write over twenty rock ballads about unrequited love without being able to recognize it."

He waited for the man to say something, wondering if he should also point out the way Aidan had looked when the little journo with the brass balls and sexy-as-sin body squirmed against him?

Before he could, though, Aidan shook his head, another one of those self-deprecating snorts escaping him. "Unrequited love. Yeah. That's one way of putting it."

Nick chuckled. "Ever thought of telling her?"

"About a million times a day."

"And instead you're here?"

Aidan let out a huff. "Yeah. I'm here. Of course, she'll accuse me of not trying to pick you up hard enough." He tilted his head a little, casting Nick a gaze part curious, part uncertain. "What *were* you doing in Germany, if I might ask? If not because of the whole..." He made a funny, fumbling gesture with his hand, his cheeks growing pink and Nick had to laugh again. Aidan Rogers was, if nothing else, an open, honest and somehow altogether innocent bugger.

"Gay thing?" Nick finished for him, grinning.

"Yeah, that." Aidan raised his own ice water to his lips and took a drink. "Are you bi?"

Nick let out his own snort. "Nope."

"So the sex clinic thing is just a rumor?"

The pit of his gut tightened and he swallowed a mouthful. "Nope."

Once again, Aidan didn't say anything. Not for a good couple of minutes at least. "Fair enough," he eventually said with a nod. "Just out of interest, if I were to say to you, 'I will die in his fire and beg her for', what's the first thing that comes into *your* head?"

Life.

The word—simple but with so much weight he could barely draw breath—came to Nick straightaway, accompanied by an image of McKenzie Wood naked and slicked in perspiration, her lithe little body wrapped in the strong, muscled arms of an equally naked, sweat-slicked Aidan Rogers.

How could two people he'd never met until today stir something so firmly believed dead?

And what was he going to do about it?

The sound of metal scrapping on granite jerked Nick back from the brooding thought and he turned towards Aidan, surprised—and more than a touch disappointed—to find the man on his feet. "So, you're going to give her the bad news, are you?"

Aidan let out a short chuckle. "You know what?" An ambivalent expression claimed his face. "I think it's time I give her something else."

Nick raised an eyebrow, his pulse thumping quite hard in his neck. "Why today?"

"Because a month ago I almost died in a fire." Aidan's lips pulled into a small, lopsided smile. "I think a chance is exactly what I've been given."

With another one of those strangely communicative nods the man walked away, his massive back straight, his shoulders so broad his T-shirt barely stretched over them.

Nick watched him go, his throat far too dry for a man drinking ice water. "Give her one for me, mate," he muttered, reaching for his drink, knowing full well he was thirsty for something else.

McKenzie chewed on her thumbnail, her stare fixed on the closed door of her luxurious room. It was a disgusting habit she'd promised herself she wouldn't indulge in anymore—nail chewing, not door staring—but at the moment, she was so damn nervous she didn't know what else to do.

Damn it, what if Aidan didn't come back?

What if Nick Blackthorne accepted his drink offer?

What if they were both right at this very minute removing

each other's clothing in Nick's room?

Why are you so worried about this, McKenzie? Why now? What's going on in your head to make you worry about who Aidan Rogers sleeps with?

She didn't know. But something about the way he'd looked at her earlier, like she was the only thing that mattered to him in the world... God, what if she'd made a mistake asking him to—

The sound of a lock releasing shattered the suffocating silence, and McKenzie started on her chair, her pulse flying as the ultra-chic chrome doorknob turned.

The door swung inward, Aidan filling the frame for the split second he took to cross the threshold. The sun streaming through the room's main window bathed him in warm light, picking out the copper-gold in his light brown hair and turning his green eyes brilliant jade. The white T-shirt he wore clung to his body, snug enough to emphasize his perfectly fit physique, loose enough to highlight how little attention he paid to his appearance. Even his almost baggy cargo pants—hanging low on lean hips and faded to a washed-out olive—were a season late, but on Aidan they just looked...

Sexy.

McKenzie's heart slammed into her throat, a hot prickling sensation she didn't want to analyze racing through her at the sight of his towering presence.

Face it, Wood. The guy's sex on legs. Why have you never seen this before?

Tossing the suite's key card on the nearby table, he gave her a steady look, walking deeper into their luxurious suite's living room, drawing closer to her with slow steady steps.

"Soooo?" she asked around her thumbnail.

"He said no."

"No?" She scrambled from her chair, her heart beating harder. Faster. "How could he say no? How could anyone with a pulse say no to you?"

Aidan's face became still, a small muscle twitching in his jaw. "I don't know, Mack. How can you?"

McKenzie's heart didn't just thump harder in her chest. It tried to smash its way out of her chest cavity. She looked up at him, lost for a thing to say.

"Ah, fuck it." The words were almost a guttural growl. In two steps he destroyed the small space left between them, pressed his large hands on either side of her face and took her lips with his.

They were warm. Warm and soft and confident. He didn't hesitate. He didn't just test the waters. He kissed her. The way a lover kisses. There was nothing chaste or friendly about the way his lips took hers. First with just his lips, his hands framing her face, holding her motionless, and then with his tongue, dipping into her mouth with a determined assurance she liked so very, very much.

Aidan Rogers is kissing you. You are kissing Aidan Rogers.

The thought should have terrified her. He was her best friend. What if it went all wrong?

His tongue stroked against hers, a slow, thorough mating that made her pussy constrict and the ridiculous notion of things going wrong went out the window. Along with the temporary paralysis for some reason claiming her.

With a low groan, she snaked her arms up around his neck, closing her eyes as she pressed her body to his. He was hard. Everywhere. Hard and big. Her sex constricted again, a demanding throb that made her whimper.

"Jesus, you have no idea how long..." he murmured against her lips, nipping at them with gentle bites. He didn't finish the statement, instead plunging his tongue back into her mouth, a groan closer to a growl rumbling in his chest as his hands raked down her back and grabbed her arse.

He was six-foot-three and built like a warrior. She was five-foot-six and resembled a waif. He had no difficulty whatsoever hauling her off the floor, even less spinning around and taking the two steps needed to press her back against the door. His hands cupped her butt, his legs splaying just enough to balance them both as his lips and tongue continued to worship hers.

McKenzie's head swam. Hot fingers of raw sensations threaded through her, twisting and turning through the center of her heat as Aidan made love to her mouth. She rolled her hips, wanting to feel the solid thickness of his erection rub over her spread pussy lips. Even with the damn barrier of their clothes, the bulbous shape of his cock head nudging her folds made her pulse quicken and her nipples pucker. She'd touched that cock once—sixteen years ago. She'd rubbed it and laughed and never thought twice about touching it again.

And yet, here she was. Aching to not just touch it, but impale herself on it. Have it stretch her to her limits, fill her completely. No laughing involved.

What if this is a mistake?

The unspoken question hung between them and she pulled away from his kiss, her heart racing. She couldn't believe this was really happening. How could she? One minute Aidan was just her best friend, now...they were about to have sex?

He waited, watching her but not saying a word, his eyes blazing his desire—and, she was somehow glad to see—his confusion as well. Had he always wanted this? Or was it an island thing? God, she didn't know.

Does it matter?

Yes, it did. This was huge. She wanted him to make love to her, but hell, was she just letting her body do the thinking now? Their relationship was on the line here. What happened next could destroy it. Irrevocably.

Or take it to a level you never imagined.

Or realized you wanted.

"Aidan..." she whispered, wishing she could see inside his head. Was this just sex for him? Or something else? Something...

"You truly have no idea how long I've ached for this, Mack."

His proclamation, spoken with an almost dazed disbelief, sent a shiver through her. Not just through her sex, but through *her*. All of her.

"What?" She needed to know. "What have you ached for?"

"You."

The answer was simple. Honest.

"Why didn't you tell me before?"

"Because I almost...because the thought of you rejecting me..." He left the sentences unfinished, but what he didn't say made her belly flip.

Oh God. This wasn't just two friends fooling around now. This was...huge.

"If you want me to stop..." he continued, dragging his hands up her waist only to halt them at the curve of her ribcage just below her breasts. His face was tight with tension, his jaw clenched. "I will. But you need to tell me now."

Stop? Was he kidding?

Her reaction was instant and raw and it told her what her stupid brain couldn't. The second he'd even uttered the word "stop" she knew she didn't want him to.

She buried her fingers in his choppy mess of hair to stare into his eyes. "If you stop, I will be forced to slap you senseless."

A soft chuckle vibrated through him, the dimples in his cheeks flashing into existence. "I thought of doing something else to you until you were senseless only a little while ago."

She cocked an eyebrow at him, rolling her hips again in an attempt to stroke her sex over the confined pole of his cock. Damn, she wanted to feel that inside her. Wanted it so much she actually ached. "And what was that, Rogers?"

His eyes twinkled green fire. "This."

He spun her away from the door and, three strides later, threw her on to the suite's main bed, a massive king-sized number covered in silk and cushions. She squealed in shocked delight, the sound captured by his mouth as he dropped on top of her.

His hands roamed her torso, up to her throat, back down to her hips. He squeezed her arse cheeks before raking one hand down the back of her thigh and tugging her leg up. She willingly obeyed his unspoken direction, wrapping her leg around his hip to grind her pussy up and down his still-constrained cock.

"I want to make love to you, Mack." His breath was ragged, his eyes ablaze. "Right now." He slipped one hand under the hemline of her shirt, his fingers brushing her bare flesh beneath.

She sucked in a swift gasp, the contact somehow more electric, more arousing than any she'd ever had before.

Of course it is, McKenzie. This isn't just anyone. This is Aidan. The guy's had your heart in his pocket since you were kids. Even if you didn't know it.

She whimpered, bringing her hand to his as she arched her back. She wanted him to touch her breasts. Not just touch them, but cup them, squeeze them. She wanted to feel the callused strength of his hands mold her soft flesh, hands skilled in extinguishing heat now on the verge of setting her on fire. She wanted to feel him possess her.

"Then what the hell are you waiting any longer for?" she

asked, directing his hand up to her breast. Over it.

"Oh God, McKenzie." He moaned, his body stiffening as his fingers found her pleasure-swollen flesh.

He dragged his thumb over her rock-hard nipple, teasing it through the thin lace of her bra. It puckered harder to his touch, as if it too said, "Yes, why *have* you taken so long to do this?"

Her breaths grew shallow, more rapid with every stroke of his thumb pad. But it wasn't enough. It was torture.

"Please..."

Like he always knew when she wanted popcorn at the movies, like he always knew when she needed chocolate, like he always *always* knew when she needed to hear his voice and called her from the fire station, now it seemed he knew exactly what she wanted him to do to her.

God, it was wonderful. More than wonderful. It was amazing. Sublime. It was...

Right. So goddamn right.

His erection pressing to the sodden junction of her thighs, Aidan hooked the edge of her bra with his fingers, and with one swift move of his arm, pulled the lace from her breast and raised her shirt up her torso.

He looked at what he'd revealed for a short—and at the same time, agonizingly long—second before his gaze found her face. "Are you sure?" he whispered, the words almost strangled.

Was she? This wasn't just a quick fuck. Not even a one-night stand—well, a one-morning stand. There was no coming back from this. Sex with Aidan. Everything changed after that. Whether it was good or horrendously bad, it changed everything.

Horrendously bad? Are you serious? You've never felt so freaking aroused, so consumed with...with...hell, so consumed with real pleasure and all he's done is kiss you.

Was she sure?

She nodded, swallowing at the thick anticipation rising in her throat. "I've never been surer."

The muscles in his body tensed, his nostrils flared again, and then he lowered his head and took her nipple in his mouth.

Exquisite pleasure shot through her, and she cried out, her pussy not just throbbing but contracting with such eager want she thrust her hips harder to his body. She'd had her breasts sucked before, but what Aidan was doing...

His tongue rolled over her nipple, short stabbing strokes followed by shorter, sharper sucks that sent shards of squirming pressure straight through her. She moaned, fisting her hands in his hair and shoving her sex closer to his cock. "Oh, Aidan..." She closed her eyes, close to sensory overload. "That feels..."

"I'm in hell here, Mack," he growled, his lips and breath hot on her breast. "I want to make this last forever—for as long as I've wanted to do it—but I'm so close to coming..."

The torment she heard in his voice, the raw truth, flayed McKenzie's tenuous control. God, why had she never known he felt this way? Why hadn't she realized she felt the same? Her pussy squeezed a cock that wasn't there. She opened her eyes and gazed up at him, the pain etching his face, the desire, making her sex flood.

She'd always been one for foreplay. Long sessions of foreplay followed by longer sessions of fucking, but Aidan—as always—seemed to know exactly what she needed. She needed him inside her. Now.

"Sixteen years of foreplay and I didn't even know it," she murmured.

Aidan's jaw bunched, his cock nudging her sex with a jerking spasm. "I fucking did."

She laughed, a shallow burst of awestruck breath, and he seized on the moment to rise up between her legs, grab the waistline of her shorts and yank them off her body, taking her sodden undies with them.

"I'm going to fuck you with my tongue later," he rasped, tossing her clothing aside, his voice not altogether steady. "I promise, but right now..."

He tore open his fly, his cock springing free of its imprisonment immediately. McKenzie's breath left her in a whimpering moan. God, he was huge.

Precome glistened on the tip of his shaft, a perfect bead of pleasure. Her mouth filled with moisture at the thought of licking it off with her tongue.

Later. Later. But now...now...

"Condom?" The single word passed Aidan's lips in a low question, his breath ragged, his oh-so-very-impressive stomach muscles hitching.

McKenzie laughed. "I've known you for sixteen years, Rogers." She raised herself off the bed, just enough to trace her fingertip up the length of his cock, its satiny heat making her pussy contract. "I trust you more than I trust any other living soul. I know you will always protect me and you know I would never do anything to hurt you, but if you think there's a reason to use a condom, then use one."

His nostrils flared again and McKenzie could see his throat work up and down as he swallowed.

"Babies?"

His question was barely more than choked moan. She knew exactly how he felt—she was burning up herself.

"Pill."

Green fire danced in his eyes and he lowered himself toward her, his hands planting on either side of her ribcage, his lips brushing hers. "So is this where I should say coming, ready or not?"

She grinned, her heart warm. Aidan—the man she'd never seen before, the man turning her on so much she could barely think, was still *her* Aidan. The bloke that made her laugh. "Oh, I'm *more* than ready."

Aidan stared into her face. "So am I."

And in one single, fluid move, he buried himself to the balls inside her.

"Oh God, yes!" she cried out, arching herself into the searing thrust. He was inside her. Completely and totally. Filling her like no one before, and for a surreal moment all she could think about was how bloody perfectly they fit together and how bloody stupid she'd been not to see that before now.

And then he slammed into her again, again and again, his face buried into the side of her neck, his hands balling the silk duvet beneath her, and rational thought deserted her.

There was nothing tender or gentle or even romantic about the way he took her. It was raw and desperate. His breath left him in strangled moans, in shaking hisses through clenched teeth. His penetrations grew faster, harder, and McKenzie rode each one, a frantic need for a connection so long denied, so long ignored, consuming her. There was a power in his thrust, an urgent force she'd never experienced before. It was amazing. It altered everything, as she knew it would, but on such a monumental scale, her mind was lost to it, overwhelmed by it.

"Yes." She bucked into his strokes, pulled him into each one, driving his thick length deeper, deeper into her center. "Oh God, God, yes, yes."

Her climax claimed her, her orgasm an exquisite eruption. She drove her nails into Aidan's back, her voice hoarse, just as his savage rhythm broke and he came in thick wads of liquid release she felt fill her very soul.

Aidan Rogers. Her best friend.

His strokes grew wilder, erratic, and then, with one last driving thrust, he let out a moan, the sound vibrating through him, turning into a long groan as he slumped on top of her.

They both lay like that, McKenzie's mind reeling, her body still thrumming from the pleasure he'd wrought upon her. God, there was no turning back now, was there? No matter what Aidan said next, he'd just given her the most mind-blowing orgasm of her life.

"Jesus, Mack," he finally whispered, his face still pressed to her neck, his lips brushing her flesh, "I'm sorry. I'm so sorry."

Her heart stilled, her blood roaring in her ears. She lay motionless, unsure she'd just heard him correctly. Sorry?

He's realized he's made a mistake. After all these years of wanting you, now he's realized he was wrong. Just when you've finally realized just how right for you he is.

Her stomach lurched, and she ground her teeth. Tears stung at the back of her eyes, hot and burning.

Oh, McKenzie, what do you do now?

"I'm sorry," Aidan said again, his voice muffled. "I wanted to last longer. I wanted—" he shook his head against her neck, "—to give you so much more."

A short, sharp laugh burst from her, relief not just sweeping through her but turning her chilled blood hot. She wriggled beneath him, shifting him enough so she could cup his jaw in her hands. With a no-nonsense push, she raised his head, giving him a hard stare. "Don't you bloody dare apologize."

He gave her a wry smile. "That wasn't exactly how I planned this to go."

McKenzie chuckled. The gravity of their situation beat at her but she didn't let it take her. Not when she felt this totally, utterly awesome. "Well, considering I pictured you naked and in bed with Nick Blackthorne less than thirty minutes ago, I think the afternoon's gone pretty well, don't—"

A knock on the suite's door stopped her. She and Aidan looked at each other, a small grin playing with the corners of Aidan's mouth. "That'll be Mason."

"Oh, let me open the door." McKenzie scrambled away from him, almost falling off the bed as she did so. She was happy, so damn happy she wanted to shout it to the world, no matter how clichéd the notion. "I wanna see his face when he sees what we've been up to."

"Mack!" Aidan burst out, throwing a pillow at her as she all but sprinted for the door.

She dodged it, throwing him a wide smile over her shoulder as she messed her hair up more and smoothed out her rumpled T-shirt until the hem fell just below her backside. She wrapped her fingers around the doorknob and gave Aidan one last look over her shoulder. "Wanna bet he threatens to tell Mum?"

Before Aidan could answer, she flung open the door.

And found Nick Blackthorne leaning against the doorframe, his pitch-black sunglasses perched atop his ink-black hair, his piercing grey eyes fixed completely on her.

"Hello, McKenzie Wood from Goss Weekly. Any chance I can join in?"

Chapter Four

Aidan didn't just scramble from the bed; he leapt from it. He stared hard at the rock star leaning in the threshold, his heart thumping fast. "What the fuck are—?" he began, a second before Nick's gaze slid to him and he realized he was standing in the middle of a hotel room with his tackle—still semi-hard and probably glistening with McKenzie's juices—on show.

Jaw clamping shut, glare locked on Nick's smiling face, he shoved his dick back into his cargos and yanked up his fly. What the hell was Nick Blackthorne doing here? And what the *hell* did he mean "join in"?

"Nick?" McKenzie's startled voice shattered the suffocating silence, and from the corner of Aidan's eye he saw her step back from the open door, her eyebrows dipping in a stunned frown. "I...we...you..."

She stammered over the personal pronouns, each one passing her lips in a short, breathless hiccup, her normal poise nowhere to be seen.

The rock star raised his eyebrows, a grin Aidan would have sworn was cheeky playing with his lips, if not for the hesitation in his eyes. And the uncertainty.

Nick himself, it seemed, didn't really know why he was here. Or what was going to happen next.

"How can we help you, Nick?" Aidan held the man's stare, a heavy beat thumping in his temple, his throat. If what the singer was going to suggest was what Aidan suspected...

An unbidden image flickered through his head, McKenzie, naked, pressed between them both, her head thrown back as both Nick's mouth and his own explored the perfection of her throat, her breasts.

His pulse quickened and his balls—so recently depleted—grew hard. Jesus Christ, what was he thinking?

"I came to ask…" Nick paused, rubbing at his mouth with a hand before raking it through his hair; hair, Aidan couldn't help but notice, much more messy than it had been at the bar. "I wanted…" He let out a harsh breath, shaking his head and stepping backward. "Fuck," he muttered, turning his face away, "where's the cool fucking rock star when I need him?"

Aidan's pulse beat faster. He narrowed his eyes, knowing he should do something, say something. But what? What exactly did he want to say?

Before he could work that out, however, Nick swung his stare back to them both, looking first at McKenzie and then Aidan, a calm resolution falling over his face. A face hundreds of thousands of women—and likely a few men—fantasized about over and over again. A face, when combined with a voice unlike any the world had heard, that elevated Nick Blackthorne beyond fantasies.

"I want to have a threesome," he said, that ambiguous accent almost all Australian now. "So fucking much I'm aching all over."

McKenzie's mouth fell open, but not before Aidan was at her side, his stare locked on Nick. "I think—" he started, but Nick cut him off, his gaze holding Aidan's with just as much force.

"I haven't heard music, lyrics, for a long time. Too long to remember." He let out a ragged sigh. "I haven't felt alive for a long time either. I've been dead inside for so long I'd forgotten what it was like to feel *anything.* But the second I heard McKenzie laugh—" he closed his eyes for a moment, an expression of sheer rapture crossing his face, "—the second I saw her in your arms…"

He opened his eyes and looked at Aidan, and that haunted, hesitant torment was back on his face. "I want to be a part of your intimacy."

Something heavy and hot surged through Aidan's veins, though his body. "What you're saying," he said, keeping his voice calm, modulated, "is you want to make love to the one woman you know I've wanted forever?"

McKenzie gasped. Nick's nostrils flared. "Yes," he nodded. "While you do as well."

"You want to..." McKenzie's unfinished question, uttered on a shaking breath, should have torn Aidan's stare from Nick's. But it didn't.

"I want to lose myself in the magic of your desire for each other," Nick continued, the words low and smooth, and yet at the same time rough and husky. "Just standing here now, looking at you both, looking at the room behind you...the rumpled sheets, the rumpled hair...the scent of your pleasure streaming into my body with each breath I take..." He closed his eyes again for a split second, shaking his head as if moved by something Aidan couldn't experience.

Or maybe already had?

"Arousing," Nick growled, and it was a growl. Guttural and barely controlled, it was the horniest sound Aidan had ever heard a man make. "So damn arousing."

He looked at them again. "I'm assailed by images of you both together. Ever since you left me at the bar, Aidan, ever since I knew you were coming back here to claim the woman of your dreams, I can't stop seeing you together, moving together... Fuck me, I can't stop wanting to be a part of that."

Aidan's mouth went dry.

"I don't want to intrude on your intimacy." Nick shook his head again, even as he moved his stare to McKenzie, his eyes beseeching. "I know you need time alone, but damn it, just for once, I want to be a part of something so very few people in the world ever get the chance to experience: true bliss."

He returned his stare to Aidan. "McKenzie is so fucking gorgeous." The sides of his lips twitched a little in a small smile. "And God help me, the thought of you making love to her..."

He left the rest of the sentence dangling between them, saying instead, "I hear music again. I feel it in my soul, but the song isn't finished." He paused again, his Adam's apple rolling up and down in his throat. "Just one day, that's all I ask. Just one day, the rest of *this* day. Please."

Aidan stood motionless, the heat of McKenzie's body seeping into his side, his stare locked on Nick Blackthorne's haunted face. His ears rang with a low roar, his heart thumped a wild tattoo. He didn't know what to say.

But surely, that is answer enough? As is Mack's silence?

He pulled a swift breath. McKenzie hadn't said a word either. Not one. Her uncharacteristic failure to respond to the rock star made his throat tight. And not just his throat. His balls grew hard, his cock twitching with interest. He turned to face her, the delicate scent of her release still lingering on the suite's still air.

Nick was correct. She *was* fucking gorgeous. He'd known that forever. Every night when he'd closed his eyes he'd seen her, imagined her moving over him, riding his shaft, her hair rumpled like it was now, gorgeous and sexy and his, all his. But now, right now, right at this very moment in time, it wasn't *just* he and McKenzie he saw in his head.

And by the shaky way she drew breath, by the way her eyes were dilated and the way her nipples were erect and hard beneath the thin cotton of her shirt, he suspected Nick was in her head as well.

Which should have made him jealous as all hell, but instead made him so fucking aroused his cock was a rod of agonized steel.

The world's most lusted-after celebrity, the man described by *Rolling Stone* magazine as "sin and sex and soul", was inspired by what he and McKenzie had. How could he not be turned on?

Aidan gazed at her, unable to find the words to vocalize his thoughts.

She studied him, her eyes wide, her lips parted, the tiny pulse at the base of her neck beating so quickly he could see it fluttering beneath her smooth skin.

Did he ask her? Did he dare?

He didn't have to. A small smile began to pull at her lips, the kind he recognized so very well: the kind that said she was with him. No matter what, she was with him. He'd seen it so many times since he'd first met her that if he were an artist, he could draw it with his eyes closed. But he wasn't an artist, he was a firefighter. And a man. The luckiest fucking man on the planet.

He cocked an eyebrow at her and let his own smile stretch his lips. *I'm with you too.*

Without a word to either him or Nick, McKenzie turned and crossed the suite's carpeted floor, her hips swaying in that naturally sensual way he knew was unpracticed or contrived, her naked butt barely hidden by the hemline of the shirt she wore.

She stopped at the expensive iPod docking station that was part of the suite's luxurious inclusions, bending a little at the waist until her fingertips swirled over the iPod she'd placed there on checking in.

He heard Nick suck in a swift breath at the teasing glimpse of her perfect arse peeking out at them from beneath the rising hem of her shirt. Heard the man's feet shuffle a little, and then the room filled with the low, muted sounds of Nick Blackthorne singing the love ballad that catapulted him onto the world's music stage and gave him his first number one selling, multi-platinum release: "Night Whispers".

The smoldering lyrics wafted from speakers embedded in the walls, Nick's voice husky and raw, the lyrics lamenting the loss of love when courage failed.

Aidan sucked in his own breath. He knew this song so very well. He'd danced with McKenzie at their high school formal to this song. The only slow dance they'd ever shared.

"And I want to beg but I can't find the words," Nick from fifteen years ago sang, the evocative sound of an acoustic guitar his only accompaniment.

"And I want to cry but I can't find the tears.

"And all that's left is the shadow of your heart and the ghost of your smile...

"And the whispers in the night."

Aidan's throat grew tighter. Thicker.

As did his cock.

But no more so than when McKenzie—her back still to him and Nick—crossed her arms in front of her body and slowly, without turning to face them, lifted her shirt up over her head.

Aidan's heart skipped a beat.

Jesus Christ.

Her back was beautiful. He devoured its sublime perfection with greedy eyes, following the subtle curve of her spine from the smooth column of her neck down to the equally smooth curves of her arse cheeks. His mouth filled with water at the sight of the twin dimples denting her flesh just above the swell of each one, his cock jerking with insistent need.

"Bloody hell," he heard Nick murmur behind him.

"And all that's left is the shadow of your heart and the ghost of your smile..." Nick crooned from the iPod, his voice cracking,

the guitar strings echoing his torment. *"And the whispers in the night."*

McKenzie turned to face them.

Two sets of eyes moved over her naked body. Two men staring at her with undeniable, molten want.

McKenzie stood still. Erect. The suite's cool, air-conditioned air slipped over her exposed flesh, between her thighs, over the folds of her sex and her taut nipples. A ripple of wanton delight claimed her, making her pleasure-swollen breasts grow rounder, pinching her nipples tighter. She lifted her chin, catching her bottom lip with her teeth.

Her iPod continued to play, the sounds of Nick singing "Night Whispers" slipping over her nerve endings. Her heart didn't just hammer in her chest, it beat out a rhythm so wild, so frantic she could barely draw breath.

Was she really doing this?

Yes, she was.

She was about to let two men make love to her at once. Her firefighter and the world's most desired rock star.

It was Aidan who moved first.

With a growl, he crossed the floor, nostrils flaring, his hands removing his shirt as he did so.

McKenzie only had a second to gaze in stunned rapture at the sheer strength of his naked torso, its muscled width marked by a stunning tattoo of a heart set alight with deep red flames directly above where his real heart sat, before his mouth was crushing hers and his hands were on her body.

His tongue delved past her lips, finding hers and battling with it. His hands roamed up her back, the line of her neck and into her hair, fisting in the strands at her nape, holding her head motionless as his mouth turned hungrier, more demanding.

Liquid heat pooled in McKenzie's sex at his dominating possession. His teeth nipped at her bottom lip, his tongue swirled inside her mouth. He sucked and plundered and fucked her mouth, and all the while his massive erection ground against her belly, making her head spin and her pussy constrict and her pulse pound.

She pressed her hands to his hard chest, her fingertips

resting on the pebbled points of his nipples. The contact drew a low groan from Aidan, the sound vibrating through her body. It was a wild sound, desperate and aggressive at once. She liked it. A lot. She stroked her fingers over his nipples, her pussy fluttering as Aidan groaned again, his cock jerking against her.

"Jesus, Mack," he ground out against her lips, "tease me like that and I'm going to lose it."

The confession sent shards of squirming tension into the junction of her thighs. She rubbed them together, her clit throbbing in her folds. A simple kiss and she was almost insane with need. A simple kiss. She flicked at his nipples, catching his tongue with her lips and sucking it with ungentle force, giddy with mounting want. And the very moment she thought she would pass out from the sheer pleasure Aidan's lips and tongue wrought on her senses, another set of hands moved over her body.

"You smell just like I knew you would." Nick's deep murmur caressed the side of her throat, his lips journeying up to her ear as his fingers skimmed up the length of her arms. "Like spring flowers and summer breezes." He snared her wrists, pressing his body against her back as he moved her hands up Aidan's chest to link her fingers behind Aidan's neck.

In the background, the next song on her playlist began, Nick's husky-smooth voice wafting from the speakers, the lyrics a carnal declaration of lust for a woman called Heartbreak.

McKenzie's heart slammed faster, her pussy lips growing engorged with fresh blood. At some stage since Aidan had begun his ravishment of her mouth, Nick had removed his clothes. His tall, lean form touched her from shoulder blades to thighs, the soft hair on his chest tickling her back, the soft curls at his groin kissing the cheeks of her arse. McKenzie whimpered. The rigid pole of his cock nudged at the crevice of her backside, parting it with insistent force just as Aidan's cock—still trapped in his cargo pants—pushed harder at her belly.

Oh God, she thought, squirming against them both, *I'm the filling in a manwich.*

Nick's hands smoothed back down her arms and over her shoulders, his lips exploring the sensitive dip below her ear as his fingers brushed the side swell of her breasts. "You feel just like I knew you would, soft and warm and heavenly." He feathered his fingertips over breasts and down her ribcage, sending a ripple of concentrated pleasure over her flesh. "And so, so fucking sinful."

The growled proclamation made McKenzie's pussy contract, her anus squeezing with equal pressure. She tore her lips from Aidan's, rolling her head until it rested on Nick's shoulder. "Can I quote you on that?" she asked on a moan.

He chuckled, curling his fingers over her hips and pressing his thick cock harder to her butt. "The face of an angel with filth on her mind..." he sang, his voice husky.

Aidan's lips curled in a slow, crooked smile as he gazed down into McKenzie's face. "I'm thinking this song's on its way to being my all-time favorite."

Before she could respond, he stepped away from her, his fingers slipping from her hair, his nostrils flaring at her soft cry of protest. "I need to feel your flesh on mine, Mack." His chest heaved and his hands moved to the waistband of his cargos. "*All* my flesh."

"Do you see how much she wants you, Aidan?" Nick's hands took advantage of Aidan's absence against her body. They roamed her belly, skimming over the shallow dent of her navel, the angles of her hips. She hitched in a breath as his fingertips brushed over the trimmed curls of her pubic hair, her stare locked on Aidan's eyes.

"Jesus, Nick," he groaned, jaw bunching, "I didn't think I could be this turned on watching someone else touch Mack like that."

Nick chuckled behind her, his warm breath tickling her ear. "What if I touch her like this?" His fingers dipped lower over her mound, parting her folds to stroke her clit with one slow caress.

Warm tension speared into McKenzie's core and she let out another whimper.

Aidan's eyes burned, his stomach muscles coiling. "Oh, yeah."

Nick's fingers played over McKenzie's clit once more. "She's wet for us already, mate."

"Good."

The simple word left Aidan in a low breath, his fingers playing with the button on his waistband and, her pussy squeezing in greedy impatience, McKenzie watched as he released it with a quick flick and then lowered the zipper.

Oh, yes.

Her heart beat harder, faster, against her breastbone, her stare devouring the sight of his distended shaft jutting free of his parting fly. If possible, it was bigger, thicker than before. Its head topped the venous length like a taut, purple dome, tiny beads of precome glistening on its very tip, slicking his flesh.

The need to taste those pearls of Aidan's pleasure filled McKenzie's mouth with saliva and she writhed in Nick's embrace. "Please..." she whispered.

"Tell me what you want to do to him, McKenzie," Nick murmured in her ear, his lips hot on her skin.

She stared at Aidan where he stood, motionless, but a mere meter away from her. The tattoo over his heart seemed to throb, his broad chest and sculptured stomach highlighting the sheer perfection of his body. He didn't move, waiting for her, his hands fisted at his side, his cock standing ramrod straight from the thatch of dark blond curls peeking from his open fly.

Nick's fingers slipped over her clit, dipping in to her sodden heat. "Tell me."

McKenzie's head swam. Her breath grew shallow. Rapid. She gazed at Aidan, every fiber in her body aching for him. Needing him. Needing this. "I want to suck his cock."

Aidan groaned at her hoarse confession, his eyes closing for a brief moment, his rigid shaft jerking against his stomach. "Jesus, Mack."

"*A face of an angel with filth on her mind,*" Nick sang, his throaty voice tormenting McKenzie's nerve endings. He slid his fingers deeper into her sex, his other hand smoothing up her stomach to capture her right breast.

"Please," McKenzie begged, writhing in his embrace. "Oh, please, Nick, let me...give me..."

Nick wriggled his fingers in her pussy, sending ribbons of exquisite sensations through her very core. "Tell Mack what you want, Aidan."

Aidan's nostrils flared and he swallowed, flicking his smoldering green gaze to the rock star's face. "I want to feel her lips slide over my dick, Nick, while you bury your cock into her."

At the calm declaration, McKenzie climaxed. Or maybe it was Nick's seeking fingers, stroking the sweetest spot on her feminine walls over and over again. Or maybe it was both. Whatever it was, she could not control the strangled cry bursting past her lips, nor the shuddering contractions squeezing her sex.

"Oh God." She bucked into Nick's penetrations, her own hands moving to his, helping him cup her breast and bury into her dripping cleft. "Oh God, yes." She felt herself through Nick's hands, her abrupt orgasm rocking through her, her stare holding Aidan's.

"Now, Aidan," she heard Nick pant, a second before Aidan yanked his cargos from his thickly muscled legs and destroyed the distance between them.

He fisted his hands in her hair, hungry desire burning in his eyes. His cock pressed to her hitching stomach, painting her heated flesh with precome. He stared into her face and crushed her mouth with his lips, his kiss neither gentle nor sweet.

It was a declaration: of what, McKenzie didn't know. Or care. She'd never been kissed with such brutal need. That Nick's hands worked her pussy and her breast at the same time only heightened the rising tension already rebuilding in her center.

Her head swirled. She was going to come again. How could that be? How could she come again so—

Another orgasm claimed her, just as abruptly, just as violently as the first. Nick pinched her clit as it did so, rolled her nipple between his fingers, torturing her pleasure-torn body with new waves of rapture. And still, Aidan plundered her mouth, his tongue lashing inside, his teeth nipping and biting her bottom lip, drawing moan after moan from her chest.

The two men were relentless. Unstoppable. She bucked and whimpered and pleaded with them to stop, begged them for more.

Just when her legs began to tremble, just when the third orgasm threatened to consume her, just when her pussy seemed to flow with rivers of her cream, Nick released his hold on her and stepped backward.

"No!" she cried out, but the word was muffled in Aidan's kiss.

Aidan tore his lips from hers. "Climb on the bed, Nick."

It was Aidan's turn to growl commands. He stood before McKenzie, his jaw clenched, his right hand slowly pumping up and down his turgid erection.

Nick did as Aidan ordered, and it was all McKenzie could do *not* to moan at the sight of him moving atop of the king-sized mattress.

Instead, she kept her attention on her best friend, in awe and more than a little apprehensive of this new side of him she'd never seen before. There was nothing jovial or sardonic about Aidan right at that moment: he was a base male, wanting one thing from his woman and doing exactly what he needed to get it.

His nostrils flared as he pulled a slow breath. "Go and climb onto the bed, Mack. On your knees with your back to him."

A shiver raced up McKenzie's spine at the blunt order. Her nipples puckered hard. Her clit throbbed. She moved to the bed, her gaze connecting with Nick's for a tantalizing second as she climbed onto the mattress's edge. He studied her, his stunning grey eyes half lidded, his world-famous languid smile nowhere to be seen.

McKenzie swallowed, her pulse quickening. Nick's cock jutted up from the dense thatch of black curls covering his groin, long and thick and bowed in a slight arc. Like Aidan's, its tip was anointed with tiny beads of pleasure. Like Aidan's, each drop made her more aroused.

Movement from the corner of her eye made her turn back to her best friend, and her breath caught in her throat as she watched him retrieve his wallet from his discarded trousers and withdraw a small thin foil square from inside it.

She knew what it was. She knew what it meant.

The world's most desired singer was going to fuck her very soon.

Her mouth went dry and she rubbed her thighs together, her clit not just throbbing but prickling with fresh need.

"Put this on." Aidan tossed the condom packet to Nick, his stare never leaving McKenzie's face.

At the faint sound of foil tearing, she sucked in a ragged breath. This was really happening. She was going to have a threesome with Nick Blackthorne and Aidan Rogers. This was really, really happening.

A low chuckle rumbled behind her and she tore her gaze from Aidan to risk a glance over her shoulder. Nick's fingers were slowly sliding down his length, sheathing it in a bright red condom. "Should have known a firefighter would go for red." He smirked, a flash of his famous smile playing with his lips.

McKenzie licked her lips at the sight of his erection straining within the tight red latex. That was going to be inside her. Soon. Oh, so—

"I'm going to fuck your mouth now, Mack."

Aidan's soft words jerked her attention from Nick's cock and she turned back to find Aidan standing before her. He towered over her, as he always did, his imposing height making her pussy constrict. She'd had a thing for tall, bear-like men since she was a teenager and now she knew why—Aidan. It was Aidan. For years she'd been trying to make love to him without even knowing it. She looked up at him, wanting him to see the elemental desire he'd awakened in her.

"I'm going to fill your mouth with my cock while Nick buries his cock in your cunt."

His use of the word made her gasp. She'd never, ever known him to use such raw language. Ever. It was the horniest fucking thing she'd heard.

He studied her, every muscle in his body coiled. "Are you ready?"

She let out a ragged breath, snaring his fingers in hers and pressing his hand to her sodden, throbbing sex. "Do you have to ask?"

A shuddering spasm made his cock twitch and he lifted his stare to Nick. "Take her," he said.

And with one fluid move, Nick slid his hands up McKenzie's back and bent her forward, the tip of his cock parting her drenched folds as her palms came to rest on the end of the bed and her head lowered to Aidan's straining erection.

Nick sank his dick into heaven. Tight, hot, wet heaven. He felt McKenzie's pussy muscles squeeze around his length, gripping him as he slowly pushed deep into her sex. He was big; he knew that. More than one "anonymous source" in more than one tabloid magazine boasted of his "impressive package" and "porn-star length" and while the number of his lovers was much smaller than those trash rags would have the world believe, the size of his dick wasn't. He'd been worried McKenzie wouldn't be able to accommodate his length, but at the sound of her moan, a low gnarr of undeniable pleasure as he buried himself to the balls in her heat, all doubt and fear vanished. Replaced with a sheer rush of carnal joy a second before he watched her lips slide down Aidan's equally impressive erection.

"Fuck, Mack," Aidan groaned, his eyes rolling back in his head. His hands came up to McKenzie's head, his fingers tangling in the wild copper-fire mane as a shudder wracked his body.

Nick felt it course through McKenzie and into his cock, the sensation beyond wild. He'd participated in more than his fair share of threesomes in his day, but none came with the unadulterated passion and desire of this one. What Aidan and McKenzie felt for each other...what they were allowing him to share...

It soothed the hollow grief of his heart. And made him so fucking hard he wondered if there was any blood left in his brain.

Withdrawing slowly from McKenzie, he stopped just as the head of his cock crowned the sodden folds of her tight pussy. She whimpered, pushing her backside to him, her fingers driving into Aidan's hips.

"Christ, that feels amazing," Aidan ground out, his stare locked on McKenzie's mouth. Nick understood his rapt focus. Watching her lips stretched over Aidan's engorged dick, seeing those lips glisten with the moisture of her mouth... Holy crap, there were no words.

He let his own gaze linger on the sight for a long moment before dropping his attention to the equally amazing vision of his cock sliding in and out of her pussy. Her juices coated his red-sheathed length, filling the air with the musky scent of her pleasure.

"Oh, Mack," Aidan groaned, lifting Nick's stare. "I'm going to come soon, babe. I can't hold on much longer."

Nick's heart leapt faster. He knew exactly what the man meant. McKenzie's pussy enveloped him like a glove. With every thrust into her center his balls slapped against her soft mound. With every withdrawal, she gripped him tighter. His blood surged through his veins, his breath ripped from his throat in shallow pants. He wasn't just going to come soon, he was going to fucking erupt.

"I hope to God you have more than one condom in that

wallet of yours, mate," he rasped, flicking Aidan a look, "'cause I'm about to blow myself."

McKenzie's pussy fluttered around his cock. She moaned around Aidan's dick, her grip on his hips growing harder, her knuckles growing white.

"Babe." Aidan's moan sent a shard of hot tension into Nick's groin. "Oh, fuck, babe, you need to stop if you don't want me to..."

McKenzie didn't stop. Nick could see it in the way Aidan threw back his head, in the way his sweat-slicked muscles coiled.

He stared at the man on the verge of sexual implosion, and—a mere heartbeat from destruction himself—felt McKenzie's sex contract. Not just once, but twice, three times, four.

"Oh, Jesus, yes!" Aidan burst out. "Yes."

It was enough. It was too much. As McKenzie's pussy pulsed around his dick, as her nails gouged into Aidan's bucking hip, as Aidan's cry tore through the air, Nick's orgasm smashed through him. Scalding through his soul, searing through his veins and pouring into Aidan's fire-red condom. And as it did, the words poured through him too.

I will die in his fire and beg her for life.

Beg her for soul, beg her for heat.

I will die in his fire and live in their love.

Live in their love until...

And then, even the words were lost to his release.

Chapter Five

McKenzie slowly lifted her head from Aidan's spent cock in time to see his chest heave and his body shudder. His eyes were closed, his nostrils flaring. His semi-stiff length jerked in her hand, a small wad of his seed—the last of his orgasm—spurting from its tip. The raw sight made her own ebbing climax pulse with increased force in response, squeezing Nick's cock still embedded deep within her.

Nick groaned. "Don't do that, McKenzie." He smoothed his hands over her back before dropping a soft kiss between her shoulder blades. "Give me a moment."

"A moment?" Aidan brushed his knuckles over her cheek. His eyes seemed to burn into her soul, a small smile—*his* smile—curling the edges of his mouth. "Think I might need a lifetime to recover from that."

McKenzie chuckled. "Wuss."

Giving Aidan her own smile back, she slowly straightened to an upright position, the sound of Nick's tortured groan as his length slipped from her sex making her pulse flutter.

She climbed off the bed and stepped away from both men— or at least, tried to. Aidan's arms snaked out around her waist, drawing her to his body as Nick came up behind her, his hands smoothing over the front of her thighs. "Wait a minute," Aidan rumbled, tilting her chin up to gaze down into her face, "I said '*might*', not 'will'."

"And if you think *I'm* done," Nick murmured in her ear, his fingers skimming up her legs to traced a gentle caress over her swollen pussy lips, "you don't know the staying power of us rock stars."

McKenzie's pulse kicked up another notch. She couldn't

believe what she'd just experienced with these two men and they were already talking about more?

Oh God, yes please.

The entirely wanton thought didn't just whisper through her head, it pleaded.

Aidan's hands slid up her back, a heady passion glinting in his eyes as he feathered his fingertip around her ribcage to stroke her breasts. "I'm pretty certain Kylie left a packet of condoms in the bathroom, Nick."

McKenzie drew in a ragged breath. The tops of her thighs were still wet from her oh-so recent orgasm, her juices dribbling onto her flushed skin. An orgasm that had rocked her to the very core. Hell, she'd almost come the second Aidan's thick, long cock slid past her lips, let alone when Nick's equally impressive appendage stretched her to the limit. Did she even have the energy to succumb to another climax so soon?

Behind her, Nick chuckled, and she hiccupped in a gasp when he fingered her still-sensitive clit. "Red ones?"

Aidan returned his laugh with his own, the sound vibrating through McKenzie like a thrumming caress. Oh God, it was making her horny again.

"Doubt it." Aidan's grin curled his lips. "But knowing Kylie Sullivan, they won't be the standard issue."

"Any chance she's left any toys?"

Nick's question, spoken in a gravelly growl, filled McKenzie's cheek with tingling heat, and sent squirming pressure into her pussy.

She caught her bottom lip with her teeth, her nipples tight. Yep, she was horny again. So horny her sex throbbed and ached with an insistent, undeniable need.

Aidan looked down into her face, his thumb rolling little circles over her erect nipples. "Who knows with Kylie? The woman has always been one for surprises."

McKenzie gazed back at him, her womb heavy with want. Surprises? Oh Lordy, this whole island had been full of surprises.

With a gentle pinch on her clit, Nick slipped away and she had to bite back her whimper of dismay at his sudden absence. "Let me see what I can find."

McKenzie barely heard him. Not with her blood roaring in

her ears. Not with her heart hammering so powerfully. Not with Aidan's hands stroking and massaging and teasing her breasts.

Surprises. Like having a threesome with the very guy only a few hours ago she was sure was gay. Like discovering her best friend was more than the platonic mate she'd believed him to be. Like realizing she was in...

"Are you okay?"

Aidan's soft question made her blink. She frowned, pulling away from him a little. "Yes." Her voice cracked. "Why?"

He gave her a lopsided smile, the kind that said, *bullshit, Wood.* "You kinda looked like a rabbit trapped in headlights there for a sec."

McKenzie shook her head, her pulse beating fast in her neck. "A little shocked is all. I was planning on writing an award-winning exposé on Nick Blackthorne's sexual secrets...now I seem to be a part of them."

Aidan chuckled, tracing the line of her nose with the tip of one of his fingers. "Maybe he'll give you an exclusive?"

"Good idea, Aidan."

McKenzie started at Nick's murmur so close behind her. She turned to him, the sight of his lean, sinewy naked body making her pussy constrict. Damn, he truly was sex and sin and soul. A treble cleft tattoo sat just below his shallow navel, its curled bottom hooking over the root of his shaft. At least, that's where she assumed it was. She really couldn't see, seeing as his dick was jutting upright—thick and long and obviously ready.

"I do have an exclusive for you, McKenzie." He walked toward her and Aidan. "But later."

"Later?" Her voice cracked again.

He nodded, a slow dip of his head that didn't break eye contact. "After we find a use for these." He held up his right hand, showing them the packet of condoms, Rough Rider ridged condoms to be precise. "And this." He cocked an eyebrow as he held up his left hand.

McKenzie's mouth went dry. *Oh God.*

The glass dildo reflected the muted light of her suite, its long surface covered in subtle dimples, its end a wide, pointed mushroom shape. A small tube of lube rested on Nick's palm, white and clean, but it was the dildo that made her pulse pound.

"Now that's a surprise and a half," Aidan murmured behind her. "It seems Kylie remembered our conversation about toys last New Year's Eve, Mack."

"I think I like this Kylie friend of yours." Nick grinned, closing the distance between her and Aidan. He stopped directly before her, just as Aidan's large body pressed against her back. His grin turned sultry, his eyes holding hers as he lifted the dildo and traced its tip along her bottom lip.

McKenzie's breath caught in her throat. She stared up at him, unable to move, even when Aidan's hands smoothed over her hips, one nestling between her thighs, the other moving up to cup her left breast.

"She's definitely not the shy type." Aidan chuckled, dipping one finger, then another into McKenzie's sopping folds.

Who was he talking about? McKenzie couldn't remember. Her brain didn't seem to be working anymore.

Nick traced the tip of the glass dildo over her chin, down the column of her throat. Its cool surface was so smooth it almost felt slick, and a ripple of base lust claimed her. "Tell me about this New Year's Eve conversation." Nick circled her right nipple with the dildo's end. Her nipple distended into a rock-hard peak, the response eliciting a hum of appreciation from the rock star.

Aidan's fingers in her pussy wriggled a little deeper, his breath fanning the side of her throat.

"I told Kylie I wanted to try a glass dildo once," McKenzie croaked, the simple pleasure of Aidan's intimate touch and the insane caress of smooth, cool glass on her breast almost stealing her ability to speak. "And Kylie suggested Aidan be the one to..." she faltered.

"To what, McKenzie?" Nick prompted.

Behind her, Aidan drew a ragged breath, his erection like a rod of steel pushing at the base of her spine.

"To use it on me," she finished on a whisper, her stare fixed on Nick's piercing grey eyes.

"What did you do?"

His question made her cheeks fill with heat. "I laughed."

He studied her. "Are you laughing now?"

All she could do was shake her head. And swallow.

Without a word, he passed the dildo to Aidan.

The glass was hard against Aidan's palm, cool against his flushed flesh. He closed his fingers around its dimpled length, his dick jerking at the somehow carnal contact.

There was no denying what the object in his hand was designed for—the giving of pleasure.

Mack's pleasure.

His head swam and he ground his teeth, gazing at Nick over the top of McKenzie's head. He remembered the conversation with Kylie and Mack so very, very well. The second Kylie—not anywhere near as tipsy on champagne as McKenzie—had uttered the suggestion he help his best friend out with her unexpected sexual curiosity, his prick had jumped to aching attention and his heart had slammed into his throat.

Much like they did now, although he doubted his cock could get any harder than it already was.

He curled his fingers tighter around the dildo's dimpled girth, his head swimming some more. From the corner of his eye he saw Nick move, rolling a fresh condom down the length of his erection, but the sight barely registered in his rapture-fogged brain. "Babe..." he murmured against McKenzie's temple.

"Oh God, Aidan." She arched into his fingers still sheathed inside her sweet, wet pussy. "If you don't fuck me with that now..."

He didn't need her to finish.

Neither it seemed, did Nick.

With one simple move, the singer scooped McKenzie's right leg up into the crook of his elbow, spreading her folds wide.

The heady scent of her musk filled Aidan's breath, and, impossible as it was, his cock pulsed with fresh blood, growing thicker and longer and harder.

Jesus, how could he be in this much pain and feel this goddamn good?

"She is so ready for you, mate."

Nick's low statement speared into his groin. The man was correct—McKenzie's juices flowed from her spread pussy, coating Aidan's fingers. He withdrew them from her tight heat, stopping at the swollen nub of her clit. She hissed as he rolled the tiny button of flesh under his fingertips, her hips bucking upward once in a violent thrust. "Aidan..."

She hadn't finished calling his name when he slid the glass dildo into her sodden channel. Burying its dimpled length into her.

"Oh God!" she cried out, her arms reaching up behind her, snaring around his neck and shoulders. "Oh God, yes."

He withdrew the dildo a little, McKenzie's hitching whimpers telling him exactly what those tiny beads all over its length were doing to her, and then plunged it back into her, squeezing her breast and fingering her clit as he did so.

"Fuck!" The word left her on a breathless scream, followed by nonsensical moans as Nick stepped closer into her spread legs and closed his free hand over her other breast.

"Tell me how you feel, McKenzie," Nick commanded, his lips roaming her cheek, her jaw. "Tell me what Aidan is doing to you."

She shook her head, her body quivering against Aidan's, her pussy weeping her pleasure. "I can't...I can't..." she panted, clinging tighter to Aidan's shoulders. The position thrust her breasts upward, a fact he reveled in as he watched Nick capture her nipple with his thumb and forefinger. Aidan's mouth watered, the need to suck on that pebbled form so great he growled.

"Yes, you can," Nick ground out, and it was only the raw tone of his voice that told Aidan the man was on a tightrope of control as well. "Tell me how good Aidan is making you feel and he will let you come."

"I..." McKenzie's gasp was barely a word. She pushed her hips upward, riding the dildo as much as Nick's hold on her leg would let her. Her heart hammered—Aidan could feel its frantic rhythm pound through her body into his. It was an intoxicating beat he felt all the way to his soul.

"Tell me, babe," he whispered against her temple. "Please...please, tell me."

"Oh God," she panted, writhing into each thrust and stroke and penetration he made with the glass dick. "Oh God, Aidan, I...you..."

Nick dipped his head, and Aidan let out a growl of arousal at the sight of the man closing his lips over one of McKenzie's erect nipples. He saw Nick's cheeks concave, he heard McKenzie whimper immediately after. His cock jerked some more, so engorged with need it was excruciating.

"Tell me, Mack." He slid the dildo in and out of her gripping sex. "Tell me how I make you feel."

She bucked, one hand burying in Nick's hair. "I..." Her voice grew higher. Her breath grew shallower. "I..., oh, Aidan, oh God...I...I...too good...this is...so..."

He plunged the dildo back inside her, his body on fire. "Oh babe, I need to be inside you now."

His declaration tore from his throat.

"Fuck, so do I," Nick groaned, lifting his head from her breast. "Will you let us take you both at the same time, McKenzie?"

Her grip on the back of Aidan's neck grew fierce. His mouth went dry.

"Yes," she gasped. "Yes, I want that. I want that so badly."

"Aidan's going to fuck your arse, McKenzie." Nick's voice was barely more than a rasping breath. "Aidan's going to bury that massive dick of his into your tight arse and I'm going to fill you with mine. Is that okay?"

"Yes," she moaned, squirming on the dildo impaled in her sex. "Yes."

Aidan's cock throbbed. His ears roared. He withdrew the thick, glass length one last time, pinching her clit as he did so.

"Oh God, I'm coming," McKenzie screamed.

Warm cream gushed from her pussy, coating his hand, his fingers. She clung to him, to Nick, making nonsensical noises as her climax detonated through her. It poured from her, turning the air to sweet musk, filling the room with the wet sounds of her release.

He thrust the dildo in once more, his balls full with need, his heart smashing in his chest, and then, unable to control himself any more, he pulled it free of her folds, threw it aside and swiped his drenched fingers from her pussy up to her anus. Spreading her wet pleasure to the tightest opening of her body.

"Lube?" He flicked Nick a harried look. He was coming undone here. He wouldn't hold on much longer. He couldn't—

Nick held up the tube, and Aidan couldn't help but note the man had already removed the lid. He lifted his own hand and without a word, Nick squeezed some of the cool, thick liquid onto his fingers. Fingers that trembled when he applied the lubrication to his straining cock.

"Gonna try to take it slow, Mack." He pressed his face to the side of her neck. "Gonna try."

She shook her head, fisting her hand in the sweat-matted hair at his nape. "Don't."

The command was all it took to push him to the edge. He wrapped his fingers around his cock, dragged his thumb over its tip, painting his already lubricated flesh with his viscous precome, and then pressed it to McKenzie's cream-slicked anus.

"Now, Aidan," she gasped, trembling. "Now."

He penetrated her tightness. One ring of muscle, the other, the other. Fighting to go slow. Almost losing. Almost.

"Oh. My. Fucking. God!" she cried, her spine arching, her nails digging into his scalp. "That feels so fucking good."

"As will this," Aidan heard Nick promise, a second before he saw the man shift his position slightly, his hips rolling upward.

And then Aidan felt Nick's cock sink into McKenzie's pussy. Felt Nick's cock slide against his through the thin wall of McKenzie's heat. And then all rational, cohesive thought deserted him and he became a creature of elemental pleasure.

McKenzie's name falling from his lips.

McKenzie's mind was consumed with utter and total rapture. She'd never ever experienced anything like it. She wasn't an anal virgin, but nothing, nothing could have prepared her for the insanely amazing feel of Aidan's and Nick's erections sliding in and out of her at the same time.

Without words, they moved in perfect sync, Aidan penetrating her arse, stretching her to an exquisite burning point, while Nick withdrew from her pussy, the textured condom he wore grazing the inside of her most feminine walls. And then they would reverse their wonderfully torturous strokes and it would be Nick sinking into her heat as Aidan slowly withdrew almost free of her anus.

And then they would do it again. And again.

And, God help her, again.

She clung to them both, one fist knotted in the hair at Aidan's nape, the other in Nick's. The rock star's elbow still supported her leg, still held her motionless between them— spreading her folds to accommodate his famous cock, balancing her for Aidan's deep thrusts.

Moans and shallow pants filled the room—hers, Aidan's, Nick's. Behind her, Aidan rained a slew of hot kisses over her jaw, her cheek, her temple, his hands roaming her body as he did so, his strokes growing faster. She whimpered, the wicked sensation of his cock in her arse flooding her pussy with new, wet pleasure.

Before her, Nick dragged his free hand up her ribcage to capture her breast, his thumb rolling over her nipple until she gasped. A low chuckle slipped from him, the sound echoed by Aidan's. If she didn't know any better, she could believe them psychically linked. How else did they move so perfectly together to make her feel so...so...was there even a word to describe how she felt?

"Oh..." she breathed, the mounting pressure inside her very core growing heavier. Tighter. "I can't...this is..."

Aidan captured her breast with one large hand, the friction of his callused fingers on her soft flesh making her whimper again. With Nick cupping one breast and Aidan massaging the other, their erections sliding in and out of her, their lips on her throat, her face...

"Just..." she begged, her pussy and arse constricting. "Oh, just..."

"Jesus, you feel so tight, babe." Aidan groaned in her ear, pinching her nipple as the words flayed her senses. "So tight. So tight and so good."

The last word left him in a drawn-out tremble, his cock pulsing inside her. Its massive girth stretched her anus and she let out a strangled cry. Only to have the sound captured by Nick's seeking mouth.

"So good," he growled against her lips before his tongue invaded her mouth again. His rhythm increased, each stroke of his cock into her pussy faster, deeper. The root of his cock rubbed her clit, sending shards of searing tension into her center.

The world began to spin, her mind incapable of comprehending the concentrated pleasure being wrought upon her body. Her eyes fluttered closed and she lolled her head back onto Aidan's chest, her breath tearing from her thick throat in soft mews.

She was there. There. All it would take was one more...

Aidan's tongue dipped into her ear as his rough fingers found her clit.

"Oh God!" She bucked, her orgasm detonating through her like a fireball. "Oh God, yes, yes!"

"Fuck, yes." Nick's groan raked over her a second before she felt his cock spasm. Rhythm deserted him, his thrusts into her sex becoming wild. Savage. He threw back his head, his spine arching, his cock grinding harder to her clit even as Aidan's fingers rolled over the tiny button of flesh.

And then Aidan, too, was coming, his breaths ragged and barely restrained, his seed filling McKenzie's arse in thick wads of pleasure. His hands dug into her hips, his thrusts frenetic. "Christ, Mack," he choked out, "I didn't...I never..."

But before the words could form, another orgasm slammed through McKenzie, followed by another. She cried out, all control of her body lost, all strength robbed of her muscles except those surrounding Aidan and Nick's stabbing lengths, and soon, even that was too much and she gave herself over to absolute pleasure.

For a long moment, they stood still. Aidan's heart slammed against her back, Nick's thumped against her breast. The two men held her closely before, with a gentle shift of his arm, Nick released her leg from his elbow and allowed her foot to return to the floor. There was a moment of prickling heat as the blood rushed into her toes, the sensation adding to the waves of warmth radiating through her, and then she slumped against Nick's chest. "Oh..." she began, her throat dry. "Wow."

The singer chuckled at her highly eloquent, whispered exclamation. "Well, that's one word I would use."

"Amazing," Aidan murmured, his lips pressed to the back of her neck. "That's the word this poor firefighter is going to use."

"Yeah." Nick laughed again, his hips shifting just enough to let his spent shaft slip from McKenzie's still-throbbing sex. "I'd agree with that one too."

He took a step backward, giving McKenzie a slow smile. "Don't move."

She gave him a weak snort, letting her weight rest against Aidan's solid form. "Are you kidding? I don't think I can."

Aidan smoothed his arms more snuggly around her body, his hands—with almost hesitant uncertainty—skimming over the underside of her breasts. "I've got you, babe."

McKenzie's heart fluttered. Yes, he did. On so many levels. Levels she didn't imagine possible only six hours ago.

Nick studied them both, his sharp grey eyes unreadable in the suite's dimming light—where had the day gone?—before he turned on his heel and disappeared into the bathroom.

McKenzie closed her eyes, content to stand against Aidan's hardness. The fading beat of her orgasm—*don't you mean orgasms, Wood?*—still constricted the inner muscles of her sex, sending soft pulses of delicious pleasure to her brain. The tops of her thighs were slicked wet with the sticky juices of her climax, a wholly carnal aftermath of sex she'd never enjoyed until this very moment.

"Did I hurt you?"

Aidan's low murmur in her ear made her turn her head and she raised her eyebrows at him. "Yes." She smiled, touching her fingertips to his bunched jaw. "And it felt so so good so don't you dare say sorry."

"That's twice you've told me not to apologize to you today." He narrowed his eyes. "If you keep this up I'm going to think I've been too nice to you all these years."

She laughed, the vibration working its way through her body, reminding her he was still buried in her arse. The realization sent a wicked little shiver through her, pinching her nipples tight.

God, I've become an Aidan addict.

Her heart beat quicker at the notion. She had. It felt...right.

"Okay." Nick's deep voice rumbled before her and she turned her attention back to the singer, but not before seeing an ambiguous tension pass over Aidan's face.

Something warm and moist stroked at the junction of her thighs and she blinked, more than a little surprised to discover Nick was wiping her sex clean. "Turn around and give the firefighter a kiss, McKenzie," he ordered.

She grinned. "Yes, sir."

She twisted in Aidan's embrace, the friction of his shaft sliding from her anus making her moan. A moan echoed by Aidan as she raised herself up on to tiptoe and lifted her face to him. "Kiss me, Rog—"

The rest of his name was cut off by his lips claiming hers, his tongue dipping into her mouth as Nick briskly, albeit gently, cleaned her backside with the washcloth.

Chapter Six

"Now, I don't know if either of you have noticed," Nick said behind McKenzie, and it took Aidan a second to realize he had finished tending to her hygienic cleanliness, "but we missed lunch. May I suggest we sojourn to my bungalow for a quick supper before picking this up where we left off?"

With far more reluctance than he expected, Aidan broke off his exploration of McKenzie's lips. He wanted to taste them again. He couldn't seem to get enough of their soft warmth moving under his.

He looked down into her face, wondering what she would say, what Nick would say if he was to announce he was quite satisfied feasting on McKenzie's kisses.

What would they both say if you told them you didn't want to go anywhere at all? Not even to the big party at Bar Evoke tonight? That you quite cheerfully would stay here with McKenzie. Just McKenzie, forever?

McKenzie stared at him. As if waiting for him to say something.

"Sounds great," he blurted out.

Idiot.

Before he could take it back, Nick nodded and scooped his discarded clothes up from the floor. "I'm performing tonight at Evoke." The rock star shoved his long legs into his jeans. "But there's still something we need to do before then."

Aidan's heart thumped a little harder.

A quiet stillness seemed to claim McKenzie as she turned to face the singer. "What's that?"

Nick gave her a wide smile. "Where would the fun be in me telling you that?" He snatched up his boots and slung them over his shoulder, stuffing his T-shirt into the back pocket of his snug jeans, leaving his upper body bare. To Aidan, he'd never appeared more the sexual celebrity.

With another smile and a nod to Aidan, he was gone, humming the song Aidan knew was unfolding in his soul softly as he went.

"Bloody celebrities," McKenzie muttered, disengaging herself from Aidan's arms. She padded on bare feet over to her own clothes lying in a crumpled heap on the floor. "Think the world bows down to their every whim."

Retrieving his own clothes from their scattered locations, Aidan forced a jovial chuckle from his chest. "Kinda getting the feeling we just did, Mack."

She didn't answer him. Instead, she yanked her T-shirt over her head and thrust her legs into her cutoff white denim shorts, shorts, Aidan couldn't deny, that had always driven him to distraction

"Aidan?" McKenzie lifted her attention from her fly, giving him a curious glance over her shoulder.

He grinned, zipping his fly up. "Yes?"

"Why did you finally decide to show me how you felt?"

The question wasn't what he was expecting. He blinked, a heavy knot rolling in his gut. How did he answer this?

His hesitation must have been enough to trigger McKenzie's suspicious journalist's mind. Eyes narrowing, she turned to face him, crossing her arms over her breasts, her expression part expectant, part impatient. "Well?"

Aidan swallowed, a tornado of colors and sound and smells assaulting him—greys and blacks, the pop and hiss of incinerating wood, the stench of burning flesh... If it hadn't been for his sheer strength and a fellow firefighter...

He let out a sigh, knowing exactly how McKenzie was going to react. "I almost died in the fire that destroyed the Newcastle Town Hall."

Her face drained of color. "You what?"

The words burst from her in a choked whisper, her eyes growing wide.

"I didn't tell you because I didn't want you to—"

"If you say worry—" she cut him off, her arms dropping from her chest, her eyes thunderous, "—I will smack the shit out of you."

Aidan chuckled, a wry laugh he knew was going to piss her off even more. "Okay." He reached for his shirt where it hung perilously from the edge of the suite's writing desk. "I didn't want you to freak out, how's that?"

McKenzie slumped onto the foot of the bed, as if his statement had robbed her body of its strength. She shook her head, her stare locked on his face, her eyebrows pulling into a deep frown. Or was it a scowl? "Details. I want details. Now."

Letting out a sigh, Aidan slipped one arm and then the other into his shirt, shucking it over his head and down his torso. "There isn't much to tell you, Mack." He walked over to her, stopping a mere inch before her bent knees and lowering himself into a crouch. "A support beam collapsed while I was underneath it. For a while, I was wearing the second floor as a hat. It crushed the airways on my gear and I was breathing nothing but smoke until I passed out. Beaso found me under the rubble and pulled me out." He shrugged. "As far as onsite accidents go, it was pretty uneventful."

The thunder in her eyes grew angrier. "Uneventful?"

Aidan released another sigh, smoothing his hands up the tops of her thighs. Her muscles tensed under his palms and she pulled her legs away from his touch, glaring at him.

Uh-oh.

"Why didn't you tell me?" she asked, and his chest tightened at the controlled anger in her voice. "Is that why I couldn't get in contact with you for those four days?" Her jaw bunched. "Those four days you told me you were on a training run up the coast?"

He didn't answer.

She stared at him. "You were in hospital?"

Jesus, Rogers. Probably should have told her before now.

The anger in her eyes turned seismic. And icy. She stood, the abrupt move sending him tumbling backward. He landed on his arse, his elbows hitting the floor a second before she stepped over him and stormed across the room.

"You were in hospital, almost dead, and you didn't tell me?" Her voice cracked on the word *me.* "You were in fucking hospital and you didn't tell me?"

He scrambled to his feet, watching her pace back and forth in a short line in front of the suite's large flat-screen television.

Yeah, he probably should have told her before now.

She spun to him, fists clenched, fury etching her face. "You selfish prick," she snarled, striding back to him again. "What did you think I'd do? Cry on your chest and beg God not to take you?" She stopped directly before him, chin tilted upward, glare firmly in place. "Go all weepy and wussy and burst into—"

She burst into tears. Just like that.

"Hey!" Aidan was shocked. No, more than shocked. Stunned. He couldn't remember the last time he'd seen Mack cry. Maybe when Lachlan Wilson called her a "frigid bitch" when she wouldn't pay out at the school dance? How old were they when that happened? Sixteen? "Hey hey hey."

He stepped forward, wrapping his arms around her back and pulling her into his body. She fought him, trying to wriggle out of his embrace, still grumbling about him being a prick, stating quite firmly as she hiccupped around her tears that she hated him and wished she'd known he was in hospital so she could have come into his room and changed his chart to read "castration required".

And in amongst all the bluster and foot stamping and repeated "God, I hate you, Rogers, I really hate you", her struggle to escape his hold turned into her pressing herself closer to his body, her cheek resting on his chest, her arms circling his waist, the words "What if I'd lost you before I knew?" slipping from her in a soft sigh.

"Knew what?" he asked, his lips against the top of her head, her hair like cool silk on his warm face.

"About this?"

He closed his eyes, wanting to ask just what *this* meant. He loved her. He had no doubt of that. Unconditionally and unreservedly. But she had yet to utter the L-word and he didn't want to push her, not after the way she'd just reacted to the revelation that he'd almost lost his life. Risking his life every day came with the whole firefighter job description, but risking McKenzie...?

He pulled a slow breath, taking the subtle scent of her— clean soap, fruity shampoo, musky perfume—into his very soul. Was what they'd just done here, on the island, more dangerous than what he did every workday?

What happened after Nick Blackthorne left their lives and it was just the two of them again? Aidan the fiery and Mack the journo? What happened then?

What happens if Nick doesn't want to leave, Rogers? What happens if he decides he wants McKenzie for himself? What do you do then? How do you compete with the world's biggest rock star with a dick the size of a rhino's?

A tight chill rippled through him. A second before a hard slap struck him on the shoulder.

"Hey!" He pulled away, looking down into McKenzie's upturned face. "What was that for this time?"

"For being a jerk." She scowled. "Next time you decide to try and wear a building for a hat, remember that slap, okay?"

He laughed. He couldn't help himself. "I'll try." He grinned, snuggling her closer to his body, his hands cupping her backside with a gentle squeeze. His cock twitched in his cargo pants, more than happy to go along with the fondling.

She scowled a little harder. "Do."

Before he could stop himself—and why would he?—he dipped his head and brushed his lips over hers. "Anyone tell you you're kinda pushy, Ms. Wood?" he murmured, squeezing her arse again as he rolled his hips forward.

She gazed up at him, her hands resting on his chest, her lips parting. The silence stretched between them, heavy, thick. She touched the tip of her tongue to her bottom lip and her eyes widened, as if she'd just realized something very, very important.

"I—"

The suite's phone rang.

You've got to be bloody kidding me.

An ambiguous frown flittered across McKenzie's face and, with a gentle shove, she disentangled herself from Aidan's arms and crossed the room.

Leaving him standing motionless, his dick growing stiff and his heart thumping harder than ever.

Chewing on her bottom lip, McKenzie snatched up the phone's hand piece from the cradle and pressed it to her ear. "H—"

"What the hell are you doing?" Kylie yelled on the other end of the line, her normally soft, lilting voice far from quiet—or lilting. McKenzie flinched, pulling the phone a little from her ear. Damn, she'd forgotten how loudly her friend could screech. "What am I doing?" She frowned, turning to Aidan. He stood looking at her, all massive broad chest, sculpted six-pack and lean hips. Hell, even the tattoo under his shirt made her sex constrict, its burning form so very much the perfect metaphor for how he made her feel—on fire.

Which is why you were just about to—

"I've just been informed by one of my staff," Kylie went on, assuming a very uptight tone—far more businesslike than any McKenzie had heard her use, "that a reporter from Goss Weekly has been harassing Nick Blackthorne."

McKenzie laughed. "Oh, that."

"Yes, that," Kylie snapped, and McKenzie flinched again. "I invited you here as my friend, Mack, not as a bloody journalist for that shit mag you work for." The words tripped over each other, Kylie's anger turning each one to a sharp report. "Do you have any idea how hard it was even getting to *talk* to Blackthorne's *agent*? And you go and pull this stunt on me?"

"No, it's not like that, Ky," McKenzie said quickly, her friend's rising ire like a blow to the stomach. "I slept with him."

Silence greeted her statement. Not even the sound of Kylie breathing could be heard.

McKenzie licked her lips, her gaze moving to Aidan's, watching him watching her. "I haven't been harassing him," she continued, Kylie's complete lack of response unnerving her. "Well, not since I first approached him, and then Aidan stopped me from—"

"Wait a minute," Kylie cut her off, and McKenzie could almost see her friend on the other end of the line, her eyes narrowing the way they always did when she was processing information she couldn't believe possible, her head tilted to the side just a fraction. "Are you telling me you had sex with Nick Blackthorne?"

McKenzie nodded, a stupid thing to do, given Kylie couldn't see her, but reflex all the same. "Yes."

More silence. Followed by Kylie saying, "You stupid cow."

McKenzie's eyebrows shot up her forehead. "Excuse me?"

"I can't believe you did that." Her voice wasn't just angry this time; it was disappointed. "Why the fuck did you think I specifically told you to bring Aidan to the island? Damn it, Mack. It was because I thought the romance of the island would finally make you see...would finally make you realize how desperately he—"

"Aidan was there."

McKenzie's hurried statement shut Kylie up. Pronto.

"I had my first threesome." McKenzie grinned, holding Aidan's gaze with her own. Her pussy constricted, her belly squirming with a tight sensation she recognized all to well—arousal. Arousal for the man standing watching her. Christ, he made her horny.

"Wait, wait, wait." Kylie's voice was incredulous. "You had sex with Aidan?"

The squirming sensation in McKenzie's stomach grew more insistent, sinking into the warm junction of her thighs. Her nipples pinched tight, the minute reaction drawing Aidan's attention for a split second. His nostrils flared and he returned his stare to her face, hungry desire smoldering in his eyes.

McKenzie nodded again, her pulse beating faster. "Yes."

"Aidan Rogers?" Kylie questioned down the phone line. "New South Wales' firefighter of the year? Eight-foot-five, built-like-a-brick-office-block Aidan Rogers?"

McKenzie's sex contracted, the aroused thrill twisting through her body turning into something else. Something far more wanton. "Yes, Aidan. And Nick Blackthorne."

"Aidan Rogers?" Kylie asked, ignoring the singer's inclusion. "Your best friend? The man you've known for practically ever? The guy who once punched out the school captain for saying you had a fuckable arse? *That* Aidan Rogers?"

McKenzie smiled, her sex fluttering some more. If Kylie was going to tell her she was an idiot for doing such a thing, McKenzie was going to tell her friend to stick it in her ear. "Yes. *That* Aidan Rogers."

Once again, silence filled the connection.

McKenzie's eyebrows pulled into a slight frown. She looked at Aidan, his expression puzzled. And just a little concerned. Any second now he'd come and take the phone from her, she could see it in his eyes and the way his muscles coiled beneath his shirt.

"Are you fucking kidding me?" Kylie suddenly burst out. "Oh, my God!" She laughed, the riotous peals of jubilation forcing McKenzie to jerk the phone away in an effort to preserve her eardrum's delicate integrity. "About freaking time!"

A heavy beat thumped in McKenzie's throat. Damn it, did everyone know how Aidan felt about her, *except* her? Jesus, how ignorant and blind could she be?

She placed the phone back to her ear, her lips curling into a wide grin. "I'm not kidding," she said, watching Aidan walk towards her. She gazed up at him, her lips parting as he stopped directly before her, his thighs brushing hers, his eyes not just smoldering with desire, but positively ablaze. Desire. For her. Powerful, undeniable desire. Bloody hell, how could she have *missed* it?

"Was it good?" Kylie gushed, her excitement thrumming through the connection. "Tell me it was good. Tell me it was amazing. Oh, my God, tell me you're going to do it again. And again. And again."

With a small, lopsided smile, Aidan reached out and took the phone from McKenzie's fingers, raising it to his ear. "And again," he said into the mouthpiece, his voice a deep rumble that sent a shard of wet electricity into McKenzie's core. "Now excuse us, will you Kylie? There's somewhere I have to take Mack. And something I have to do to her. Again."

And as Kylie's squeal of delight exploded through the connection, Aidan threw the phone over his shoulder and lowered his head, his breath mingling with McKenzie's as his lips brushed hers. "Ready?"

She was ready. More than ready. When it came to Aidan, how had she ever not been? So why was her stomach knotting? Why was she feeling...nervous?

Because this isn't just a simple fuck-fest, Mack, and you know it. Which means it's something else. Something more. But with Nick Blackthorne in the equation, with him waiting for you both in his bungalow, with you both heading there now...what does that make that "something else"? What? What?

She didn't know and that not knowing scared her. She *should* know. Hell, Aidan *wasn't* an unknown quantity. He was her best friend. He was her rock, her world, her crutch. He was what put the smile on her face and chased away the tears when life made her sad. But that was the old Aidan, the pre-threesome Aidan. What if that Aidan was gone now? Lost to her because of what they'd shared?

And if *that* was the case, who was the Aidan with her now?

Come to think of it, who was *she* now? Could they ever move on from what had happened in this room? Did Aidan even want to? Did she? Did she even *want* to go to Nick's bungalow? With the irrefutable pleasure waiting for her there, how could she not? But was it pleasure from *two* men worshipping her body, or simply pleasure from Aidan—just Aidan?

Her belly knotted again. Oh God. Too many unanswered questions. She hated unanswered questions. Hated them.

Then find the answers.

Aidan's lips moved over hers, not a kiss but a soft and achingly sweet caress. "Shall we go?"

Tell Aidan you want to stay here. Tell him you want to stay here and make love to him and only him. Tell him you love—

"Nick's probably waiting for us."

A numb calm fell over her body. She'd never felt so confused. When she should be feeling so damn wonderful she'd never felt so bloody confused. She was balancing on the edge of a yawning precipice shrouded in unanswered questions and she had no clue if she was going to fall...

Then step back from the edge for a moment, Mack. Step back.

McKenzie's belly flip-flopped and she pulled in a steady breath, closing her eyes and leaning into Aidan's chest for a heartbeat before pushing herself from his body. She needed space. She needed time. Some way to gain a little perspective, but how could she get that space, time and perspective with Aidan beside her? And with Nick waiting?

"You're right, Aidan." She gave him a slow smile. "He probably is. But I have to go for a walk first."

A flash of worry etched between Aidan's eyebrows, a deep crease she rarely saw on his face but recognized all the same. He wanted to ask her more, she could tell by the way he regarded her. But he didn't. He was still Aidan, after all. She may have discovered he was her very deepest sexual fantasy and even deeper soul fantasy. He may have shared the most amazing sexual experience of her life with her, but he was still Aidan. Even if this new post-threesome Aidan was different, Aidan her best friend knew when to push her and when to let her have some rope, and right now, she needed some rope.

If only enough to walk through the resort's grounds and clear her head.

"Just give me a few minutes, okay?" She rested her hands on his chest. His heart beat under her right palm, a drumming rhythm that vibrated straight into her own body.

He studied her, gaze unwavering, before giving a single nod. "Where shall I meet you?"

Here.

She wanted to say it. She really did. She wanted to say, "Here—just you and me", but she wasn't brave enough. Because what if just "her and him" didn't work anymore? After what they'd shared with Nick, what if what she and Aidan had only just discovered was now...tainted? What did she do then?

And there you have even more bloody questions, Mack. You need to go think about what you'll do if the answers to all these questions aren't the ones you want them to be.

With another smile, this one smaller and much more wry, she slipped from his loose embrace and walked to the door. "I'll meet you at Nick's bungalow."

Aidan's Adam's apple jerked up and down in his throat but he didn't say a word. Not one.

Not even when she turned the doorknob, pulled open the door and left him standing alone.

The early evening air flowed over her body, curled around her bare legs and arms in a warm and humid caress. She drew it into her lungs in a long, slow breath, counting to ten as she did so.

When had she become so gutless? Damn it, she was supposed to be a fearless journalist, for Pete's sake. She'd hounded drug-using actors, wife-cheating politicians and stripper-addicted authors in her time at Goss. Hell, only this morning she'd approached the world's most famous rock star to ask him about his sexuality. Why couldn't she look her best friend in the eye, tell him exactly how she felt about him and ask him how he felt about her? Like, really felt about her? She knew he wanted her sexually, but was that just it? Were they friends with benefits now?

God, Mack, are you serious? Is that what's worrying you? The sex? Just the sex?

No, it wasn't. It was more. It was a life unfolding in front of her with Aidan's place in it unclear. That was a future she'd never, ever glimpsed before and it scared her witless.

She walked away from the suite, heading for the beach. The

sounds of the resort wafted around her, the low murmur of people enjoying the luxury threading through the whisper of the coastal breezes in the lush gardens and the gentle swish of the nearby waves on the sand.

She let out another ragged breath, her bare feet taking her farther away from her suite and the man within it. Kylie had wanted this place to be something magical for her and Aidan, and it had. It truly had. But what happened if that magic didn't follow them back to the mainland? Would it be capable of returning with them to Newcastle and their normal lives when the memory of Nick's part in that magic shadowed them?

Who says it would?

She pulled a face. She did. Every time one of Nick's songs played over the radio she'd be drawn back into the moment both men possessed her body, and she didn't doubt Aidan would be as well. Would they survive that? Or would everything, *everything* just fall apart?

What would she do if that happened? How would she live each day without Aidan in her world, even "just her friend" Aidan? He'd been there for so long, she couldn't imagine a life without him. She knew she wanted more than what they'd had before, her heart knew it, her soul knew it and her body knew it, but what the hell would she do if not even *that* was there for her anymore?

The cool silken kiss of sand through her toes sent a shiver up her spine and she stopped, staring out at the absolute beauty of the Pacific Ocean before her. The water was calm, the setting sun turning the rolling waves a deep indigo-purple, the breaking foam on each a golden pink. Couples strolled along the pristine white sand, hand-in-hand or arms wrapped around waists, hips brushing hips as they made their ambling way to whatever happiness awaited them.

McKenzie closed her eyes on the sight of all that peace and beauty, feeling even more unsettled. What was wrong with her?

"Shall I remind you, you can't surf to save yourself?"

Mason's voice behind her made McKenzie jump and she spun to face her twin, her heart beating far too fast in her throat. "What the hell are you doing here?" she snapped, giving him a narrowed-eyed glare. "Aren't you meant to be out on that bucket of rust you and Trent call a boat?"

Mason's cheeks seemed to fill with a warm pink tinge—or

maybe it was the sinking sun's rays that cast his face in such a blushing light. Either way, he flashed her a somewhat sheepish grin, the action very un-Mason-like. "Yeah, well, with six months of being on *Pleasure* ahead of us, I'm kinda letting my land legs make the most of it while they can."

McKenzie cocked an eyebrow, her brother's passive answer even less Mason-like than his smile. "Why do I feel like you're not telling me something?" She narrowed her eyes on his again. "Are you up to something Mum will have a freak about?"

Mason snorted, his hands finding his hair and scruffing at the thick dark-blond waves. "You could probably say that."

"Oh, goodie." McKenzie wriggled. "Can I tell her?"

For an answer, Mason gave her his own intense stare. "Wanna tell *me* why you're standing here gaping at the surf alone? Where's Rogers?"

At Aidan's name, McKenzie's belly did another little flip-flop. And her pussy gave a tight little flutter. She let out a sigh, turning back to the breathtaking beauty of the beach. Behind her, the resort seemed to settle into the approaching night, the distant sound of someone saying "one-two-one-two" in a microphone peppering the more recognizable sounds of exotic birds calling to their absent partners. "Have you ever done something completely reckless and insane and downright surreal, and then thought, holy shit, what do I do next?"

Her brother snorted again. "Every fucking day of my life of late."

McKenzie shot him a sideward look. His jaw was clenched, his stare fixed on the rolling waves. She suppressed a wry chuckle. Typical. The day she goes and gets herself all fucked-up, Mason decided to as well. No wonder their other brothers always complained about their "scary-shit twin thing".

She gave his shoulder a nudge with hers. "You okay?"

Mason pulled a face. "Nope. You?"

She laughed, shaking her head. "Nope. Wanna tell me about it?"

He laughed in return, shoving her shoulder back with a fraction more force. "Not yet. You?"

"No way. That would be way too weird." She smiled, Mason's presence seeping into the unsettled apprehension gnawing at her bones. If there was one other person on this planet she could rely on apart from Aidan it was Mason. Her twin, however, didn't make her think dirty thoughts. Or warm, fuzzy happily-ever-after thoughts. "Do you think it's possible best friends can share everything, Mase? Like, *everything*?"

"You reading my mind again, girly-girl?" His use of his special childhood nickname for McKenzie made her throat tight. He hadn't called her girly-girl since they were twelve—since she'd nipple-crippled him into stopping. Why had she done that? She couldn't remember now. "I think best friends should know what can be shared and what can't, no matter what the rest of the world thinks."

McKenzie ground her teeth and scrunched up her face. "You're not helping me here, brother."

He cocked her a look. "You and Rogers having problems?"

Mason's question squeezed a ragged sigh from her chest. "Depends on your definition of 'problems'."

"Do you love him?"

Her mouth fell open. "Love?"

Mason rolled his eyes. "Oh, c'mon sis. I've seen the way he looks at you. We all have. He's been in love with you for bloody ever. And honestly, I've seen the way you look at him as well. It wasn't as obvious, but it was there—an affection way beyond that of a mere friend. So I ask you again, do you love him?"

McKenzie swallowed. She hadn't expected that from her brother, but then, she hadn't expected anything that had happened so far since she stepped foot on this island. "I...I..." The rest of her answer caught in her throat, the implications of her answer far too scary to consider.

He gave her a pointed look. "Aidan's your best friend for a reason, sis. Hell, he's the only one I know you let push you around, and to be honest, he's the only one I know who I'd *let* push you around. He's been looking out for your heart since the day he met you, holding it in those massive bloody hands of his and making sure no one hurts it. He would do anything for you, you know that, right?"

"I know. But what if I don't know what that 'anything' is at the moment?"

Mason turned back to the surf, his gaze focused on the gentle waves as if the answer to her question was riding them. "I think, when it all comes down to it, a best friend knows *more* about what's right for you than you do." He turned his attention to her, really looking at her. "That's why they're your best friend, yes?"

McKenzie looked at him back—into his face so like hers and yet so very different. "Yes. That's exactly why."

A heavy beat thumped in her temple. Aidan *was* her best friend, but just as importantly, *she* was his. He may have been holding her heart in his hands, but she'd been bloody well holding his in hers for as long as she could remember, too. And she sure as shit wasn't going to let it go now. Not when she'd finally realized how damn right it felt there. And as for the "anything"? She knew exactly what she wanted that "anything" to be—Aidan in her life. Not just as her friend, but as her lover, and if Nick Blackthorne was the sex toy *du jour* while on the island, she was fine with that. When she and Aidan got back home to Newcastle, they would just go shopping for a different one—maybe some handcuffs? Or a glass dildo? Or one of those funky U-shaped vibrators aimed at couples? Maybe all three? Maybe nothing at all.

It wouldn't matter because they would have each other.

"Your best friend will never ever do anything wrong by you, Mack." Mason nudged her shoulder with his again. "Aidan would die before he did."

With a strangled cry, McKenzie threw herself at him, wrapping her arms around his neck and giving him a tight squeeze. "Thanks, bro," she whispered in his ear, warm pressure holding her chest a fraction of a second before she slapped a noisy kiss on his cheek.

"Eww," he wailed, scrambling for her wrists with his hands. "Girl germs!"

She laughed, skipping backward away from him, the sand like cool satin between her toes. "Freak."

He grinned at her, his teeth flashing white in the mauve dusk light. "Lunatic."

She danced another step backward, her pulse pounding in her neck, her pussy heavy with constricting want. "Gotta go."

Mason's grin stretched wider. "Going to go do something reckless and insane?"

She grinned back. "And totally surreal. You?"

He laughed. "Oh, you better believe it."

Chapter Seven

"*A face of an angel with filth on her mind,*" Nick sang under his breath, studying the smooth amber liquid in the cut crystal glass in his hand. "*I pray to burn in her fire, I pray to die in her arms.*"

The words sent a charge through him, like the electrical energy of a summer storm—crackling through the hazy, eucalyptus-drenched air, making the pulse quicken and the breath turn to shallow pants. It was intoxicating. Potent.

He held his glass closer to his face, watching the rolling waves kiss the white sand beyond his private bungalow's eastern balcony through the still scotch.

"*Yet the arms of her lover reach out for more,*" he continued to sing on a murmur, closing his eyes, his dick—already half erect—twitching in his jeans. "*Like a sinner I will burn in his fire. I will die in his fire as she pleads for—*"

"I don't think she's coming."

Aidan's low voice, spoken from the balcony's doorway, opened Nick's eyes and he lifted his glass to his lips, swallowing the scotch—his first since Germany—in one mouthful. The liquor burned its way down his throat, a river of heat that did nothing to ease the unsettled nerves fluttering in his gut. So much more to his song to be found, to be felt... So much more of it still hidden in the mist.

Letting out a soft breath, he turned to the massive man now standing beside him, casting him a slow smile. "She'll come."

Aidan didn't look convinced. The muscles in his sizable body tensed and he turned to look at the main door.

"She'll be here, Aidan," Nick said, taking in the man's coiled strength and taciturn apprehension.

Troubled green eyes turned back to him. "How do you know?"

"Because she loves you."

At Nick's simple statement, Aidan let out a ragged sigh. "She hasn't told me that."

Nick chuckled, unfurling from his seat and placing his hand on Aidan's broad shoulder. He'd seen the guy buck naked, he'd been witness to his amazing strength and power, but at the feel of Aidan's muscles under his palm—like chiseled marble— another wave of awed appreciation rolled through him. The male form had never turned him on before, but it was impossible *not* to be impressed with Aidan's sheer masculinity. "Her eyes have told you, mate." He fixed Aidan with a steady look. "Trust me, she'll be here. She loves you."

Aidan studied him, doubt etching lines on either side of his eyes. "Damn it, I fucked up." He dragged his hands through his hair as he turned back to the door. "I should have told her—"

A soft knock on the entry door brought him to silence.

Nick's heart leapt into his throat. His pulse rate doubled. He stood and stared at the bungalow's closed door, the knot in his gut twisting tighter. There were two possibilities to what awaited on the other side and as selfish as it was, he longed for only one of them: McKenzie Wood would cross the threshold and he would find the ending to his song. The other was too bleak to consider: she would tell Nick she wanted nothing to do with him again.

The knock came again, softer this time.

He shot Aidan a quick look and found the man standing motionless. "Do you want to get that, or shall I?"

With a start, Aidan moved, his ropey muscles coiling and flexing as he strode to the door. Nick watched him wrap long, callused fingers around the doorknob, watched him twist his wrist, watched his shoulder bunch as he pulled open the door.

A shaky sigh escaped from Nick as McKenzie stepped over the threshold, closed the door behind her with her heel and slipped the soft black shift dress she was wearing from her shoulders.

It fell to an inky puddle of material at her feet, but Nick didn't really notice. Not when she stood before Aidan wearing nothing but a tiny black lace G-string and delicate black patent leather stilettos. Not when her breasts rose and fell with such sublime perfection, their rosy nipples puckered into hard tips, their creamy form swollen with anticipated pleasure.

Not when she looked up at Aidan and said, "And I want to beg but I can't find the words."

The lyrics from Nick's first love song—a song he wrote for the goddess who long ago tore his heart apart—speared into his heart. The song McKenzie had selected when he'd come to them both and asked to be a part of their rapture.

He walked towards the two lovers, scooping the red silk scarf he'd laid out on the bungalow's dining table earlier up as he did so. The cool fabric slid over his fingers in a gentle caress that sent wicked licks of hot desire into his groin. His throat thickened. Oh, what he wanted to do tonight...

He stopped beside Aidan, giving the man—who still gazed down at McKenzie with silent love—a steady look. His heart beat harder. How could they not know how much each loved the other? How could they not *see* it? It was so potent, so undeniable he could barely draw breath. It fueled his arousal like nothing he'd ever experienced before. It moved him, inspired him. Fuck, it rocked him to the very center of his soul.

"Aidan—" he kept his voice steady, "—tie McKenzie's wrists together behind her back."

McKenzie's sudden intake of breath, a hitching gasp, sent another hot surge of hunger into Nick's groin. As did the way Aidan's nostrils flared as the man turned to look at him.

He raised his hand, holding it palm upward, fingers extended. The red silk scarf draped over his palm, vibrant and evocative, as if alive with the future of those in the room.

Aidan studied it for what felt like a lifetime, his jaw clenched, his eyes unblinking. He lifted his stare to McKenzie's face. "Mack?"

The question—just her name but full of unspoken hope— was enough to make Nick's cock flood with hot blood. When McKenzie gave Aidan a single nod, moving her hands to behind her back, her breasts thrusting forward, Nick almost came there and then.

The trust, the faith these two people had for each other... God, it was exquisite.

And so fucking arousing.

Without a word, Aidan removed the scarf from Nick's hand,

stepping behind McKenzie, towering over her.

Nick took his place in front of her, his gaze holding hers as Aidan slid his hands over her shoulders and down her arms, the scarf held loosely between his fingers, caressing her skin as he reached her wrists.

"You trust him, don't you?" Nick's balls rose at the concentrated want in McKenzie's direct blue eyes.

He saw Aidan become still, his head bent, his body pressed close to McKenzie's back, as if he needed to hear an answer he already knew. Perhaps, with Nick there, he did.

A small smile pulled at the corners of McKenzie's mouth. "I trust him."

Nick's balls throbbed and he took a step closer, letting his denim-clad thighs brush her naked ones. "Do you trust me?"

"Yes." She drew in a deep breath, the action causing her nipples to graze the front of his shirt and his balls didn't just throb, they ached. "I do. Besides, I know Aidan will break you in two if you do anything to hurt me."

Nick chuckled. "True."

Aidan's gaze flicked up to his. "True," he said softly just as McKenzie's gasp filled the room and her body stiffened.

Nick's pulse thumped harder in his chest, her reaction telling him exactly what Aidan had done: tied the scarf around her wrists. Bound them together. Rendering her vulnerable.

Fuck, yes.

The urge to kiss her, to capture her lips and plunder her mouth almost overwhelmed him, but he held it in check. Just. Turning on his heel, he crossed the room to the table, retrieving another soft silk scarf waiting there. He heard Aidan's heavy breaths behind him, the sound affirmation the man was as close to breaking point as himself. When he turned back to them both, he found two sets of eyes watching him, both ablaze with a desire so raw his cock jerked in his jeans. Precome leaked from its slit, its warmth slicking his taut flesh.

He walked back, stopping directly before McKenzie, the scarf dangling from his fingertips. *"A face of an angel with filth on her mind."* The lyrics came from him in a low purr. *"I pray to burn in her fire, I pray to die in her arms."*

He reached up and laid the scarf gently on her forehead, holding her stare for a moment.

"Yet the arms of her lover reach out for more.
"Like a sinner I will burn in his fire,
"I will die in his fire as she pleads for..."

McKenzie lifted her chin. "More," she whispered.

Aidan's groan rumbled in his chest, urgent and strained, and it was too much for Nick. Too much.

He pulled the scarf down over McKenzie's eyes, knotted it behind her head and crushed her mouth with his.

The very second Nick's lips found McKenzie's, Aidan's lips found her throat. He tasted her perfume on her skin, he breathed in her clean, delicate scent. From the way McKenzie shifted against him, he knew she was already struggling to control the pleasure in her body. Her hands were balled as fists at the small of her back, her knuckles pressing to the flat plane of his belly, just above his groin. His dick jerked in his trousers, straining instantly and irrefutably for her flesh, her heat.

He smoothed his hands over her body instead, up the curve of her ribcage to the swell of her breasts. His thumbs found her nipples, his pulse quickening at the hitching moan he heard her make through Nick's kiss.

The singer pulled away from her, his mouth journeying down her throat, over her breasts until he captured one of her nipples. Aidan felt Nick's warm lips on his fingers, felt his tongue stroke at McKenzie's flesh. He held her breast for Nick to suckle on it, the soft moans rising in her chest all the evidence he needed to prove she was succumbing to the sensations the man's mouth wrought on her body.

His cock jerked with increasing need. And something else. Something like...

Jealousy?

The thought threw him off kilter. Jealous? Now? Why now? After everything...

Because you love her, Rogers. You love her with every fiber of your being. You always have and you always will.

A low growl rumbled in his chest and he ground his teeth. The idea of Nick making love to McKenzie, of touching her...

Aidan's stomach knotted. Not anymore. Not anymore.

As if sensing Aidan's sudden tension, Nick lifted his head from McKenzie's breasts, sliding his gaze to Aidan's face. They stared at each other for a steady moment, a question in Nick's grey eyes.

Aidan drew in a slow breath, taking McKenzie's scent into his being, feeling her soft body against him. She stood motionless, blindfolded and bound between them, and yet there wasn't an iota of apprehension to her. Her trust in him was implicit. Unquestionable. Oh, Christ, he loved her. So damn much.

He looked at Nick.

Nick looked at him. He didn't say anything, not a word, but Aidan knew what he was going to do. With a smile Aidan could only ever call joyous, the world's most famous, desired rock star lifted his hand to McKenzie's face, cupped her jaw in his palm, and then stepped backward.

Aidan took his place immediately. Silently. He lowered himself to his knees, pressing his lips to McKenzie's flat stomach, exploring her belly button with a series of tiny nips and nibbles.

She hitched in a gasp, and another one when he dragged his lips down farther, his tongue flicking out once to touch her soft, damp folds.

"Oh," she whispered.

Did she know who was touching her now? Aidan didn't care. All he wanted to do at that very moment was fill her with the purest pleasure he could. Give her his heart, his soul, in a simple touch.

He stroked her folds again with his tongue, and again she uttered that whispered word. "Oh."

With gentle hands, he parted her thighs, opening her pussy up to his mouth. He lapped at her cleft, passing his tongue over her clit. Again. Again.

He heard he whimper, a shaky cry that barely left her throat.

He tasted her pussy with his tongue and lips, sucking on her sweetness with gentle pressure before laving her clit once more.

"Oh, yes."

Her moan sent a surge of hot blood to his groin. His balls rose up. He dipped his tongue into her sex again, reveling in the wet heat of her feminine cleft. She tasted... divine.

And he wanted more.

His fingers skimmed over her hips, squeezing her firm arse cheeks for a brief second as he blew a gentle stream of cool air on her flushed, swollen folds.

"Please..." she begged on a trembling breath, rolling her hips forward.

He stroked his tongue over her clit, with a touch more force this time.

A slight shudder rocked through her, vibrating through his hands, down his arms into his chest.

"Please..." she begged again, her voice husky. "Oh, please, please I need to..."

He dipped his tongue deeper into her sex, lapping at her juices.

"I need to..."

The words fell from her in a hitching moan.

He rolled his tongue over her clit, flicked it, sucked on it.

"Oh, oh."

He drew the sensitive nub into his mouth, capturing it with his teeth a split second before suckling on it once more.

"Oh God, please..."

He sucked harder. Flicked his tongue over it. Delved deep into her creamy heat and then sucked on her clit again.

"Oh, please, please."

Her hips bucked forward. Her arse cheeks coiled. He heard her breath turn rapid, shallow pants that turned his balls to excruciating globes of urgent need.

He stroked his fingers over her hips, up her belly, feathered his fingertips over the swell of her breasts, teasing her erect nipples and then returning his hands to her hips. He swiped his tongue over her clit, swirled it around the tip and sucked it past his lips.

"Oh, please." The moaned supplication was barely more than a breath. "Please."

He smoothed his hands back to her thighs, spread her legs wider, granting his fingers, his mouth, greater access to the very center of her heat, and flicked his tongue over and over and over her clit. He slipped his fingers into her drenched channel and stroked the sweetest spot of her walls within.

She came. With a keening cry and a jolting shudder.

Aidan closed his eyes, pressing his face to her center, drinking her release as it wept from her.

He would never tire of this, of giving her this unconditional pleasure. He would never…

"I love you, Aidan."

McKenzie's voice caressed his heart. He opened his eyes, hardly daring to draw breath.

She bent her face toward him, the scarf hiding her beautiful, cheeky, expressive eyes from him.

He didn't move. Did he hear correctly? Did he?

"Did you hear me, Rogers?" she murmured, her lips curling in a slow grin. "I love you. I love you so bloody much I won't thump you for taking so long to tell me you love me back."

Before he could stop himself, Aidan leapt to his feet, a whoop of delight—or some such sound—bursting from him as he swept McKenzie up into his arms and claimed her lips with his.

She kissed him back, her tongue mating with his, fierce and demanding and ferocious. Everything McKenzie-ish. And everything McKenzie-ish was everything he loved.

He kissed her until his head spun and his groin throbbed, and when he feared he would drop her, he lowered her feet to the floor and slipped the scarf from her face. "I love you too, Mack, just in case you haven't picked up on that yet."

She rolled her eyes. "A girl would have to be pretty bloody dense not to."

He laughed, pulling her closer. "Yeah, dense is a good word."

She gave him a mock glare. "Hey!"

"How did you know it was me?" he asked, gazing into her eyes.

She grinned. "Who else would make me feel like that?"

He cocked an eyebrow. "Like what?"

Her grin stretched wider. "Like nothing else mattered in the world but me?"

A soft cough to Aidan's left made him start and he swung around, more than a little embarrassed to discover he'd completely forgotten Nick's presence in the room.

The rock star sat in one of the bungalow's low, leather chairs, ankle resting on bent knee, one arm slung casually over the back of the chair. His body was loose and calm, his lips curled in an easy smile. Across his lap lay McKenzie's dress, his fingers dancing over its soft fabric as if it were the strings of a guitar. "Now that was a thing of beauty."

McKenzie laughed, resting her cheek against Aidan's chest. His heart rate kicked up a notched at the simple intimacy and he wondered if he would ever get used to the wonderful sensation of being touched by her. Unlikely. Hell, he didn't *want* to. Not ever.

He bent his head and kissed the top of hers, for no other reason than he could.

His heart rate tripped over itself again. Christ, he felt amazing.

Nick it seemed, recognized his sheer joy. The man's smile twitched, his eyes sparkling bright grey happiness. "I think I'm allowed to say I told you so at this point, Aidan?"

Aidan smoothed his hands down McKenzie's arms and, with a quick fumble of the scarf on her wrists, released her of her silken binds, gazing down into her upturned face. "Yeah, I guess you can."

A second of silence passed before Nick cleared his throat again. "I have to perform at Evoke in a few minutes." He uncrossed his leg and shifting in the chair until he seemed so far removed from leaving Aidan wondered if he'd misheard him. "But before I go, I have McKenzie's exclusive to tell."

McKenzie stiffened against Aidan, her hands coming to rest on his stomach as she gave her head one sharp shake of disagreement. "No, I don't want it. The world doesn't need to know why you were—"

Before Aidan's jaw could drop, Nick interrupted her with a laugh, holding up his palm. "It's okay, Ms. Wood from Goss Weekly. I *want* to tell you."

McKenzie stood very still in Aidan's arms. Her heart thumped against his chest, quick, rapid. She caught her bottom lip with her teeth, gnawing on it as she considered Nick's offer. The sight of such uncertainty sent an irrational surge of pride through Aidan. Here was the woman who less than twelve hours ago wanted to spill the beans on whatever dark secret Nick Blackthorne was harboring. But now...

"Truly, Mack," Nick said from his chair, the use of her nickname sending an inexplicable ribbon of happiness through

Aidan.

McKenzie turned her gaze to Aidan for a moment, long enough for him to see her waiting for his reaction. A slight frown pulled at her eyebrows.

He shrugged. "You're a journalist, Mack." He gave her a nudge and slight push away, letting her know exactly what he thought of the situation. "Could I stand back and watch a house burn down?"

With a nod, she crossed to Nick, retrieving her dress from his fingers as he offered it to her. She shimmied into it, the fabric falling over her slim body like black liquid. Aidan pulled in a slow breath. Yep, there wasn't a hope in hell he was ever getting used to being in love with her. Not a hope in hell.

"Okay," she said, and he had to chuckle at the sudden brusque tone of her voice—all business and no-nonsense and serious. "Give me my exclusive."

Chapter Eight

"Two years ago I learned I was adopted."

Nick's calm statement made McKenzie blink. That wasn't what she'd been expecting at all. She'd expected...what? Actually, she didn't have a clue. After the last day, nothing about Nick Blackthorne was what she'd thought it was.

"Two years?" Aidan said behind her, and she glanced over her shoulder, noting he'd propped himself against the edge of the table with his ankles crossed. The pit of her belly tightened and she fought the urge to smile. Damn, he looked hot. Hot and fuckable. "Around the time your parents were killed in that car accident?"

The time frame made McKenzie blink again. Her journalist's mind scrambled to connect the dots.

"Yeah," Nick answered, his voice uncharacteristically emotionless. "My adopted status was revealed to me during the reading of their will. Along with the fact I had a brother three years younger than me."

McKenzie's breath caught in her throat. Thirty-five years of not knowing. Thirty-five years of thinking you were one person only to discover you weren't? And then discovering you had a brother you knew nothing of? The tightening in her belly turned to a churning lurch. She thought of her brothers—all six of them. Sure, she'd wanted to kill more than one of them growing up, Mason the most, but not having them in her life? Not knowing about them...? No. She couldn't even begin to comprehend it.

"Jesus."

Aidan's barely audible murmur whispered behind her, but she couldn't take her stare from Nick.

He gave her a wry grin. "To say it was a shock is a bit of an understatement."

Aidan snorted.

"Apparently my parents—" Nick paused, a frustrated frown pulling at his eyebrows, "—my *non-biological* parents tried to adopt him too but the application was denied. I don't know why. It wasn't mentioned in the will and I could never find out."

McKenzie crossed to the seat next to Nick's and lowered herself onto it, perching on its cushioned edge. "But you found out everything else?"

He let out a sigh. "It took me eighteen months of battling red tape but I did. My birth name is Nicolas Schulze, my birth mother was a young German illegally living in Australia and my brother's name is—" he let out another sigh, the breath a harrowing gush of air, "—*was*, Derek."

"Was?"

The one-word question felt like dust on McKenzie's tongue. This was not the exclusive she imagined. That Nick was sharing it with her, on the record, made her throat thick. God, how had the world not known this?

"Eighteen months to find him?" Aidan asked softly. "So, six months ago from today? That was the time you cancelled your world tour."

Nick nodded, giving Aidan a wry grin. "You got a Nick Blackthorne timeline in your head, mate?"

Aidan chuckled. "I bought tickets. Was going to surprise Mack with them."

Nick pulled a face. "Well fuck, 'ey. I hope you got your money back?"

Aidan gave him a grin. "Yeah. Bought tickets to U2 with it."

Nick's laughter bubbled up his chest. "Good, Bono could do with the extra cash." He laughed again, and yet McKenzie couldn't help but notice the mirth didn't quite reach his eyes. They were still...haunted.

"What happened to Derek, Nick?"

Nick's chest heaved with a silent breath. He looked away, his attention seemingly focused on the sweeping views outside his bungalow's open deck doors. McKenzie doubted he saw the Pacific Ocean. "I finally did find Derek in Germany. It took many weeks to establish any kind of relationship with him at all. It would seem our mother—long dead of a drug overdose by this time—hadn't been the most loving of parents. Nor the best role model. Derek grew up being dragged from one commune to another. By the time he was sixteen, he'd been sexually assaulted by more than one of our mother's partners."

The air left McKenzie's lungs in a sharp gasp. She didn't know what to say. Neither, it seemed, did Aidan, who studied the singer with a clenched jaw and flaring nostrils, his arms crossed over his broad chest, coiled and hard.

Nick moved his gaze from the open doorway and the calm, dusk-painted ocean beyond. "He was working the streets in Berlin. He was addicted to just about every fucked-up drug a pusher can sell and fucking anything that offered him a hit."

His voice was flat. He stopped. Swallowed.

"I'm sorry, Nick." McKenzie caught her bottom lip with her teeth. "You don't have to tell me anymore. I'm not—"

He shook his head. "Shush, Mack. There is a happy ending to this tale, I promise."

McKenzie found it hard to believe him. Happy? No wonder the last two years had been filled with reports of Nick Blackthorne acting surly and aggressive. No wonder he'd cancelled all live performances. Shit, with this to deal with?

She frowned at him.

"I did everything I could to help him," Nick went on, holding her gaze. His strength staggered her. "He got cleaned up as much as he could, kicked as many addictions as he could, except..." He wiped at his mouth with his hand. "Derek was bisexual, but one of his so-called 'fathers' tried to beat it out of him at the age of eighteen. A month after finding Derek I had to return to the U.S.—contractual obligations with my record label. By the time I returned to Germany, Derek had admitted himself into the *Vergnügen* sex clinic. He was convinced he was a sick, perverted sex-addict who needed to be cured. Nothing I or the doctors said would change his mind. I spent my days and nights with him in the clinic, doing everything to help the brother I'd never known I had see there was nothing wrong with his sexual choices."

He stopped and looked out the window again. "He committed suicide two weeks ago. I found him in a pool of his own blood on the floor of his room after returning from a meeting with his doctors."

"Jesus," Aidan muttered, making McKenzie jump. She blinked, her eyes prickling, her mouth dry. "There's a happy ending to this?"

"There is." Nick turned away from the window. "You two."

"Excuse me?"

She'd asked the question before she realized it. She and Aidan? How could she and Aidan be the happy ever after to this tale?

Nick smiled, the first truly relaxed action she'd seen from him since he started her "exclusive".

"You two. I'd lost any sense of life, of happiness, you see. Fuck, I couldn't see any color in the world, I couldn't hear any music in the days until I saw you together this morning. I was broken. I doubted real love, real joy existed." He let out a sigh and a soft chuckle. "Your obvious love for each other has mended me and for that, I will never be able to thank you enough."

"Wow." McKenzie couldn't think of anything else to say. Not a thing. Luckily, Aidan could.

"No worries, mate. Remind me to send you the bill later."

The unexpected quip made Nick laugh. Really laugh. He shook his head, grinning at Aidan. "Deal, although I'm pretty certain I can think of something better." He turned back to McKenzie, unfurling from his seat with loose-limbed ease to stride over to her. "And there you have your exclusive, Ms. Wood. All on the record. Just do me a favor?"

She nodded, still unable to find her voice. That Nick had shared that with her and Aidan. That she and Aidan could have affected him so much. That their love for each other...

"Don't write it for Goss." He gave her a look she could only describe as knowing. "I did a quick Google search of your stuff before coming to your suite this morning. Write it for Time Magazine or Rolling Stone. It's where you deserve to be."

McKenzie's mouth fell open. She stared at him, for the third time in twenty-four hours lost for words.

Beside her, Aidan chuckled, the sound a low, easy rumble of content. "She will. Trust—"

The phone rang.

"Shit." Nick shot the watch on his wrist a quick look. "I'm meant to be at Bar Evoke." He looked back at Aidan, giving him a wide grin. "I know the urge to stay here and make long, mad passionate love to the woman is probably fucking overpowering, but promise me you'll control yourself for just another hour or more? You both need to be at this soft-opening party, okay?"

Ignoring the still-ringing phone, he held out his hand to Aidan, who took the long slender fingers with his own strong, callused ones in a firm shake.

"Deal." Aidan nodded, and those green eyes of his slid to McKenzie, his gaze so hot her pussy constricted with an eager throb. "But only for an hour. After that, I'm taking her back to our suite and making love to her until the sun comes up."

Nick laughed, and with a soft kiss on McKenzie's lips, he turned and strolled from the room, scooping up a battered guitar case from the bungalow's plush leather sofa as he made his way to the door.

McKenzie watched him swing the door shut behind him, the faint sound of his humming tickling her ears before the room was silent once again.

"Well." Aidan's hands smoothed around her waist, his arms tugging her slightly backward until she nestled against his large, hard frame. "You promised me the trip of a lifetime, McKenzie Wood," he murmured in her ear, his lips grazing her skin, "and you sure as hell delivered. Remind me never to doubt you again."

Closing her eyes, she leaned into his firm embrace. "Can I have that in writing?"

He laughed, a healthy, contented snort. "Not on your bloody life."

She twisted in his arms, regarding him with a cocked eyebrow. "Excuse me?"

For an answer, his lips brushed hers, his hands finding their way to her backside to cup it in a not-so-gentle caress. "C'mon," he growled, raising his head enough to stare down into her face, "I promised the world's most famous rock star I wouldn't make love to you for an hour and if we don't leave this very room now I'll be forced to break that promise."

And—as McKenzie's pussy began to throb anew with hungry want at his statement—he spun her on her heel and pushed her away from him.

Nick Blackthorne walked up onto the small raised level

Kylie Sullivan had provided to act as a stage, his fingers curling loosely around the handle of his guitar case. Around him, the nightclub thrummed with the sounds of people enjoying the soft opening's offerings—fine food, fine wine and the most stunning vista on the island.

Bar Evoke was, if nothing else, evocative. The resort's main nightclub was lit with warm, muted lights that made the steel and polished wooden surfaces look like liquid gold. One entire wall was made of glass, providing the crowd already gathered in the club an uninterrupted view of the calm Pacific and the deep, purple sky beyond.

Nick wasn't remotely interested in any of it.

He crossed to the lone stool waiting for him in the center of the small stage, placing his guitar case on the floor beside it. It had been almost two years since he'd held any kind of musical instrument, let alone the old acoustic twelve-string guitar resting within the case's battered walls. Two long years. He placed his hands on the closed lid, the darkness of the as-yet unlit stage providing him the concealment to study the guests spread out around him, currently unaware of his presence.

He wasn't interested in them either. Well, not all of them.

A loud cheer broke out to his right, followed by a loud "'Bout bloody time, Rogers," and an equally loud "Good on ya, mate". Nick smiled, watching as two men—one who surreally looked a lot like a male version of McKenzie—slapped Aidan Rogers on the back, the McKenzie carbon-copy reaching up to scruff up Aidan's hair.

Nick let out a soft laugh. "My sentiments, exactly," he murmured, his heart growing heavy when Aidan's lips stretched into a wide grin. The large firefighter ducked his head, and Nick couldn't help but notice Aidan never tore his gaze from McKenzie.

He chuckled, flipping open the latches of his guitar case. Love. Such a raw, inescapable, ungovernable emotion. Complicated and fraught with great moments of absolute terror, love was the single most wonderful gift a person could experience. And for someone like him—the most elemental muse. Who would have thought his muse would take the form of two soul mates born to be so much more? Friends to lovers. A song waiting to be sung.

He watched as McKenzie lifted her face to Aidan's. Watched

as the journalist with his life in her talented hands reached up and tugged Aidan down into a kiss that was both cheeky and full of promise.

"*A face of an angel with filth on her mind,*" he whispered, the words sliding over a rhythm found deep within his soul.

Lifting the lid of his case, he touched his fingertips to the steel strings of his old guitar—tracing the line of one down the neck until he reached the sound hole. The almost imperceptible friction of skin on stretched steel filled him with a deep warmth, his balls rising up, his heart rate quickening before, with a steady confidence, he closed his fingers around the guitar's neck and withdrew it from its worn velvet bed.

A low thrill rippled through him.

He stood and perched himself on the edge of the stool, enjoying the anonymity the dark shadows afforded him. Cradling his guitar on his lap, he sat motionless, watching the guests move around the club, listening to the sounds of them enjoying their meals as they relaxed into one another's company. Time and again, his attention returned to Aidan and McKenzie where they sat with a small group of people, drawing something akin to comfort from their distant presence. His time with them was over, but he would never, ever forget them. They had given him music again.

Given him hope after he thought hope no longer knew his name.

He closed his eyes and let the ambience of the night roll over him, hearing the songs in the guests' conversations, hearing the rhythm in their laughter and the music in their movements.

Ten, fifteen minutes later—he wasn't really sure—he opened his eyes and nodded to a silent man waiting to the left of the stage. With hurried grace, the man stepped up onto the stage, positioned a microphone a few feet away from Nick and then scurried off the stage.

Nick's heart thumped once. Hard into his throat.

He touched his fingertips to the strings of his guitar once more, stroked them and then, with a low clearing of his still-thick throat, tucked the musical instrument's familiar wooden body under his right arm.

A single beam of light revealed his presence on the stage, a hush falling over those selected by Kylie Sullivan to experience the resort's soft opening as they realized he was sitting on the stage.

He heard his name whispered by a dozen voices or more.

He heard his blood roar in his ears.

He heard his heart pound in his chest.

He heard the voice of a ghost from a lifetime ago murmur his name in pleasure, heard the goddess ask him to *sing, sing for me, lover.*

He caressed the strings one more time before lifting his head and gazing out at the quiet crowd. "For McKenzie and Aidan." He smiled at the two people who had changed him forever. "Who showed me love and gave me life. This, ladies and gentlemen, is 'Tropical Sin'."

His fingers found the notes on his guitar, a simple and yet intricate melody, and then the words found his tongue.

A face of an angel with filth on her mind,
I pray to burn in her fire, I pray to die in her arms.
Yet the arms of her lover reach out for more.
Like a sinner I will burn in his fire.
I will die in his fire as she pleads for more.

Like a sinner I will burn in his fire,
I will die in his fire and beg her for life.
Beg her for soul, beg her for heat.
I will die in his fire and beg her for life.
Beg her for soul, beg her for heat.

And the waves sing their song as endless as time,
And the ache in my heart is so sweet.
Like a sinner I will burn in her fire,
I will die in her fire and live in their love.
Live in their love

Until I find you. Again.

About the Author

Lexxie's not a deviant. She just has a deviant's imagination and a desire to entertain readers with her words. Add the two together and you get darkly erotic romances with a twist of horror, sci-fi and the paranormal.

When she's not submerged in the worlds she creates, Lexxie's life revolves around her family, a husband who thinks she's insane, a cat determined to rule the house, two yabbies hell-bent on destroying their tank and her daughters, who both utterly captured her heart and changed her life forever.

Contact Lexxie at lexxie@lexxiecouper.com, follow her on Twitter http://twitter.com/lexxie_couper or visit her at www.lexxiecouper.com where she occasionally makes a fool of herself on her blog.

Look for these titles by
Lexxie Couper

Now Available:

Death, The Vamp and His Brother
The Sun Sword
Triple Dare
Dare Me

Savage Australia
Savage Retribution
Savage Transformation

Bandicoot Cove
Exotic Indulgence
Tropical Sin
Love's Rhythm

Party Games
Suck and Blow

Print Anthologies
Red-Hot Winter

Island Idyll

Jess Dee

Dedication

Viv, it's taken a while, but we finally did it! Woot. (Bet you'd almost given up on me.)

Lex, here's to writing many more books together in the middle of the night. *Yawn*

Ladies—I've had a brilliant time writing the anthology. Looking forward to round two.

Fedora—Thank you. For your sharp eyes, good advice, wise comments and honesty. You realize you've become an essential part of my book writing process?

Jennifer (Editor Extraordinaire)—I'm not sure whether you're crazy or just plain wonderful to have taken on the Bandicoot project, but damn, I'm glad you did!

Chapter One

You Are Personally and Cordially Invited to Attend The Soft Opening of Australia's Newest FIVE-STAR Luxury Resort BANDICOOT COVE on Bilby Island. Bring a plus one if you desire.

All expenses and needs will be catered for as we test our customer services in preparation for the Grand Opening.

(P.S. Can you believe I got this job, guys? Wow!!
See you soon,
Love, Kylie
XXXX)

(P.P.S.—Si! Wait 'til you see who installed our computer network. Your eyes are gonna pop.)

Sienna James drew her arm back, took aim and flung a flattish oyster-colored shell forward with as much gusto as she could manage. It sailed a good five meters in the air, landed with a muffled plop and sank beneath the pristine water surrounding the tropical and oh-so-beautiful Bilby Island.

With a satisfied grin, Sienna buried her feet in the wet sand, the sludgy grains squishing between her toes and leaned down to get another shell. Taking careful aim, she tossed it just as far as before. This time however, as she released the shell, she let out a mighty *whoop.*

Why the hell had she never considered tossing out her troubles before? So far, it was working a treat. With every shell that landed in the ocean, the shackles of her grief loosened, and throw-by-throw, step-by-step, she walked free of them.

Before lobbing the next shell as far as it could go, she brought it up to face level, glared at it with one eye and named it.

"Ben Cowley," she said and let it fly.

Ben sank gratifyingly fast.

"Dead-end engagement," she said to another shell and watched it disappear beneath the surface—just the way her ex-upcoming wedding had. Without even a splutter of breath. Both the shell and the wedding were gone. Never to resurface.

She held up a multi-hued shell, complete with intricate twirls and whorls. "Eight freaking years of my life," she yelled at it. "Eight!" This one flew even farther than the rest, and she had to shake the tension from her wrist as it plopped into the sea.

With every shell that vanished from sight, the burden of her break-up with Ben, which had been weighing down on her shoulders like rotting seaweed, seemed to ease. Tossing her woes aside was exactly what Sienna needed. A kind of ceremonial reawakening. Three months of mourning a dying relationship was long enough. It was time to live again.

Hurling her ex-mother-in-law-to-be into the ocean felt surprisingly good. So damn good, she tossed her in again, just for the hell of it.

The freedom of her actions sang to her. God, she hadn't felt this positive, this liberated, in months. If the water could drown her sorrows so effectively, what could it do to her body?

She was about to find out.

Checking up and down the deserted beach for any possible sign of life—and finding none—she stripped down to her underwear. With one more cautionary glance to her left and right, she ditched her bra and panties.

Whooping again, she rushed at the water. The welcoming sapphire sea engulfed her. Warm, briny water closed around her legs, then her waist, drawing her into its crystal-clear depths. With a gulp of air, she ducked beneath the surface, submerging herself completely. Silence swam around her. Salt burned her eyes. Peace descended.

When her lungs groaned, voicing their urgency for oxygen, she kicked off from the sandy bottom and exploded into the air. Water splattered in a million different directions.

Throwing her troubles away had been a fantastic idea.

Washing them away in this glorious island sea, with only brightly colored fish for company, was the single best idea she'd had in years.

Josh Lye stopped to catch his breath before sprinting back to the hotel. The lack of physical distance on the island bothered him not at all. Laps of four-hundred-meter sprints across an island beach under the tropical Queensland sun beat city-bound traffic-laden jogs hands-down, any day.

One minute to get his heart rate back to normal and he'd head back.

He rested his hands on his knees, leaned forward and took mighty mouthfuls of air.

Four, breathe. Three, breathe. Two, breathe. One and...

What the—?

Was that a dolphin?

Uh, not likely, unless the dolphins living in this water were white, and Josh knew for a fact they weren't. He'd swum out to a pod frolicking off the island just yesterday afternoon, and their sleek skins had been obviously grey. Varying shades of grey, yes, but still grey.

He blinked, looked again, and this time focused properly.

Ah, person. Not dolphin.

Woman, to be more specific.

Wha—? Wait. Naked woman!

Naked woman, wading through the water and...whooping?

One-minute time limit forgotten, Josh stood right where he was and stared, entranced.

Of course she was swimming naked. Anyone with a body quite so bountiful and beautiful *should* swim naked. It should be written into Australian federal law. She should have the political right to display that body to every red-blooded male in the country.

Er, hell, no. She shouldn't.

She should only display that body to him. And only ever in private, away from the prying eyes of any other hot-blooded male anywhere on earth.

Okay, so he wasn't so close he could make out details like cup size and freckles, but his view was clear enough that his dick stood up for a look as well.

"Down boy," he growled quietly. "No way I can run with a woody."

The mermaid rose, facing away from him, and threw her hair back so that glorious, silver droplets cascaded in a shower around her. She let out a gleeful laugh.

Guilt filled Josh. What kind of a perv was he, watching her like this, when she had no idea he was there? He guessed if she did know she'd plunge back down beneath the water and not resurface until he left.

Time to go.

Marching himself and his stiff-as-steel dick down the beach, he hesitated only when he saw the pile of clothes strewn on the shore.

A pair of white shorts—short, white shorts—a black, singlet-type top and a thong so tiny he almost missed it. A matching bra—a back lacy number—lay alongside the clothing.

So, 36C.

If she'd been any closer, he'd have called it easily without the help of the bra.

With a broad grin and the details of her clothing tucked away in his mind, he took a deep breath and sprinted back down the beach, safe in the knowledge that his little mermaid remained completely unaware of his presence.

Chapter Two

Sienna drew back her shoulders, straightened her spine and with a determined air, turned to face the world.

Okay, maybe not the world. More like the poolside bar. Still, the swim and the shell-tossing exercise had done her a world of good. She felt like a million bucks.

"A strawberry daiquiri please. Frozen, double hit of rum." She shot the bartender a dazzling smile and was rewarded with a flirty grin.

Oh, yeah. She still had it. The thought was accompanied by a modicum of satisfaction and a whole heap of surprise. After eight years with one man, she hadn't been sure.

"There you are," an excited voice purred in her ear. "I've been searching for you."

Sienna turned to find Kylie Sullivan standing beside her. She threw her arms around the other woman, and the two embraced like school kids, jumping up and down and squealing, just like they had at fifteen.

"Oh, my God. It's gorgeous, Ky. The most exquisite hotel I've ever seen," Sienna enthused.

"I know! Isn't it wonderful?" Kylie's eyes shone.

"Amazing." Ky had landed with her bum in the butter. "A perfect job. A perfect place. Possibly the most romantic hotel on the planet, and you're managing it."

Lucky Kylie.

Lucky Sienna. If not for Kylie, she wouldn't be here right now. Ky had only sent out invitations to her nearest and dearest in anticipation of the grand opening of Bandicoot Cove. This was the practice run. The make-sure-everything-works-smoothly run. Sienna was only too happy to be one of Ky's experimental subjects.

Kylie shot the bartender a smile. "Whatever she's having, I'll have the same, Stan."

Moments later, the two were stretched out on deck chairs, catching up on the last six months. Large mouthfuls of rum already sat like a warm puddle in Sienna's belly. Combined with the high of seeing an old friend and the glorious late-spring sunshine heating her skin, Sienna was grinning like a fool.

"I just bumped into Mason and TS," she told Kylie. Sienna had seen them as she'd walked off the beach. "Your little brother was looking totally stoked over the woman they were with."

Kylie nodded. "Paige. She seems nice. I've met her a couple of times before."

Sienna agreed. "Nice, gorgeous and skinny." She frowned. "I don't like her. I don't like anyone who's skinny."

Kylie laughed out loud. "You're not looking too bad yourself, Ms. James. I don't think I've ever seen you this thin or wearing such revealing clothes, for that matter."

Sienna glanced down at her shorts and the skintight, black halter-neck. The brand-new items she'd bought after dropping five kilos, post Ben. Missing him, missing the good times they'd spent together, missing the loving, caring, wonderful guy he'd been before he'd gotten so involved with work had killed her appetite, utterly and completely.

See? There were some positives to break-ups. It felt good to wear something skimpy for once. Even if her cleavage tended to spill over the top and she still had another good five kilos to lose. She wasn't one hundred percent comfortable with the lack of coverage, but wearing any more clothes in this humidity was inconceivable.

"Mack arrived a little while ago also," Kylie said about the third friend who made up their tight clique, excitement ringing through her voice. "She's busy exploring the island."

"Cool. I'll go find her later. Did she come alone?" Last time Sienna had spoken to her, Mack had been of two minds as to whether to bring her best friend, Aidan, along or travel fancy-free.

"She flew in with Mason." TS's friend and Mack's twin brother. "Aidan's here too. And he's looking mighty fine, I might add."

Sienna shook her head with a grin. "Think Mack will ever notice he's head-over-heels in love with her?"

"Yeah. One day. When Aidan holds up a banner saying: *Open your eyes, McKenzie. I love you!*"

The two women burst into laughter. As if. Aidan hadn't said a word about the subject in all these years. Nothing was ever going to change.

"It's good to hear you laugh again," Kylie said. "For a while there you worried us."

Sienna's smile faltered before returning with force. "For a while there *I* worried me. But you know what? I'm good now. I'm getting over him. I'm getting over us." Getting over him hadn't been easy. If only Ben had been an arsehole and done something to hurt her—like cheated or treated her like dirt—breaking up with him would have been a whole lot easier. But the truth was, Ben was a good guy. A wonderful man who'd married his job instead of his fiancée. Which meant getting over him was harder than she'd anticipated.

The shells and the sea had gone a long way to help her today.

"I am so pumped to be on the island. So ready to move on. I bet there are a hundred great-looking men here I can move on with." One such specimen walked over to the bar as she spoke.

"There are some, for sure." Kylie's eyes twinkled with mischief. "But not hundreds. Remember, the hotel isn't open to the public yet."

"One'll do me just fine." Sienna grinned. "Someone so hot he'll make me forget all about Ben." A holiday fling was exactly what she needed to get past the love she still felt for her ex.

A smile tugged at the corner of Kylie's mouth. "Funny you should mention great-looking men..."

Sienna studied her friend's face with intrigue. "I've seen that look before. You've met someone, haven't you?"

The small smile broke into a massive grin. The kind of grin Kylie only displayed when she was falling in love.

"Spill. Now. What's his name?"

Kylie's face lit up. Then shut down. Then lit up again. "Not his," she confessed in a whisper. "Their."

Sienna blinked. "Uh, pardon?"

Kylie looked around, as if checking for prying ears. There

were none. "I've met three guys, Si. *Three*. And I think I'm in love with all of them."

Sienna's jaw dropped. Kylie had always enjoyed a healthy romantic life, but three men were a lot for anyone to juggle, even Kylie. "Do they know about one another?"

Kylie's grin increased. "I would say so, since I'm sleeping with all three of them...*at the same time*."

Sienna gaped at her friend. "You're what?"

"There's something about the air out here," Kylie said with a carefree chuckle. "The freedom. It's like magic, intoxicatingly so. It makes you do things you'd never do in Newcastle."

"Three of them?" Sienna spluttered.

Kylie nodded, her face aglow. "Three of them."

For the second time in twenty minutes, Sienna squealed. "I want details. Every last, sordid one."

Kylie blushed. "Uh, mind if we skip the deets for now? I'm still kinda getting used to them myself. But...I could introduce you to all three tonight at the soft opening party at Bar Evoke, if you like?"

"If I like? Sheesh, try keep me away." Wow. Kylie and three men. "I don't know if I'm excited for you or just plain shocked out of my skull."

"I'm still kinda shocked about it myself," Kylie confessed. "But do me one favor. Give the island a chance to work its magic on you. Experience the freedom. Let the air intoxicate you too. Then you can decided if you're shocked—" she winked, "—or just plain jealous."

"Deal." Sienna laughed and sipped her drink, surprised to find it almost finished. "So you think I'm gonna be jealous?"

"Hon, for the last eight years, you've had sex with one man. One. No variety, no choice. Just one ol' guy," Kylie teased. "You are gonna be green with envy."

"Well, how can I argue when you put it like that?" Not that she'd ever had need to complain. As lovers went, Ben was a ten out of ten. Twenty out of ten. Loving, attentive, inventive, adventurous and satisfying. Oh, so satisfying. But since he hadn't had time for sex in the months leading up to the break-up, there'd been a distinct lack of satisfaction on Sienna's part.

"Who knows, Si, maybe you'll meet three men this weekend."

Sienna snorted. "I'd be happy with one. Well, one at a time anyway." Any more than that was not a number she'd feel comfortable juggling. Regardless of the magic island air.

Kylie signaled to a waitress and ordered another daiquiri. "It's for you," she told Sienna. "I have to run. Have another drink. Enjoy the sunshine, relax and forget about Ben. 'Kay?"

"No worries," Sienna answered, the combined effects of the rum and the Queensland heat already deliciously numbing her senses. She patted her bag. "I'm good here. Got my book and my sunnies, and I intend to read, drink and ogle hotties until dinner at least."

"Sounds like a plan." Kylie stood and straightened her tight manager's skirt.

Sienna couldn't let her leave without asking the one question that had been playing on her mind since receiving her beautifully printed invitation. "Hey, Ky?"

"Mm hmm?" Her friend's gaze was focused on the bar.

"I'm dying to know. Who installed your computer network?"

Kylie turned to her with a glint in her eyes. "If I told you it was a lie, would you believe me?"

"If you told me what was a lie?"

"A lie of epic proportions, I might add."

Sienna shook her head in confusion. "You lied? There's no one going to make my eyes pop?"

Kylie turned to the bar again, raised her hand and waved. A man waved back. The same hottie Sienna had noticed a few minutes earlier. Tall with enormous shoulders. He headed towards Kylie.

Kylie watched his approach, then flashed Sienna a wicked smile. "Believe me, Si, this is the only lie you've ever wanted." She checked the man's approach, checked her watch and smiled again. "Gotta run. Later, babe."

And she was gone, her heels tap-tapping over the travertine tiles surrounding the pool.

Dazed, Sienna watched her leave. What the...?

"Bloody hell!"

The stunned expletive had Sienna whirling around.

"Sienna James?"

She raised her head to stare up, up, up at the man Kylie had waved to. Hottie for sure. His white T-shirt hugged broad shoulders, and low-slung boardies highlighted trim hips and long muscular legs. Never mind hot. Scorching!

He pulled off a trendy pair of sunnies and stared at her with exquisite green eyes. Familiar eyes. "It really is you. And you still have your freckles."

Yeah, compliments of the sun. She had a ton of them.

The man knew her, of that there was no question. But damned if she could place him. She looked at him questioningly, taking in the silky hair that casually curled around his neck, as though he hadn't had a chance to cut it in months. Once it must have been pure brown, but the island sun had kissed it, leaving blond streaks woven through the russet strands.

His skin was tanned gold, confirming her assessment of the time he'd spent in the sun, and his lips—full, gorgeous and ruby-red—were curved in a bewildered smile. At least a week's worth of stubble shadowed his jaw and upper lip.

"Hell, Si, you look better now than you did twelve years ago. And man, you looked good then."

Recognition hit, the force enough to take her breath away. Suddenly Kylie's words made perfect sense.

It wasn't a lie she'd been referring to. It was a Lye. Or, to be more specific, a Joshua Lye.

A heart-stoppingly gorgeous, all grown-up Joshua Lye.

"Josh?" she asked tentatively.

He nodded. "In the flesh."

And, oh, dear Lord, what flesh it was. If the teenage Josh had made her blush like a fool, the very adult version made every nerve ending stand to attention. At sixteen, he'd been cute. At thirty, he was full-blown sex on a stick.

He sat with a *thunk* on the deck chair Kylie had just vacated and shook his head in wonder. "Christ, if you weren't the star feature in every wet dream I ever had…"

Her eyes popped open. "If I wasn't *what?*"

"My wet dream every night for years," he said, his gaze roaming over her face. "How are you, Si?"

She blinked several times, processing his words, his presence leaving her staggered.

Josh was here. On the island. Josh Lye. Or, as she, Mack and Kylie had called him, Josh *Lie-With-Me*. Hmm, nope, hang on. She was the only one who'd called him that, and only when he wasn't anywhere near. Ky and Mack had called him Josh *Lie-With-Si.*

Sienna had only had a crush on him the entire way through high school. She'd have shed her good-girl image in a second if even once he'd shown her any interest. Hell, she'd have tossed her much-cherished virginity aside in a heartbeat for just five minutes with him.

God, she hadn't seen him in...twelve years.

"I...I'm okay." She finally found the presence of mind to answer his question. "You?"

His gaze dropped to her chest and then slowly made its way down to her thighs. A grin tugged at his lips. "Good. Never better."

Sienna frowned. "You know, you have some kind of cheek, mister."

He cast her a questioning look. "I do?"

"Where do you get off making me the center of your wet dreams, anyway?"

"Where do I get off?" His lips twitched, as though he tried to repress a bark of laughter. "Uh, you really need me to answer?"

Sienna resisted the urge to drop her head in her hands and cover the blush she knew blossomed on her cheeks. Shit, that was so not what she'd meant. "Listen up, mate, I haven't seen you in forever, and you greet me with an explicit insight into your teenage fantasies. Nice. Real nice." Oh, yeah, real nice. It would have been nicer to know when she was a teenager too. When *he'd* been the main feature of every one of *her* adolescent dreams.

Josh's gaze dropped to her chest again, the exact place where her cleavage spilled over the top, and he let out a low wolf whistle. "Not just a teenage fantasy. I strongly suspect you're gonna be the center of a full-blown adult wet dream tonight as well. Mine."

She gaped at him. "You didn't just say that."

His eyes twinkled as he winked. "I always did like the way you blushed in school. How quickly those cheeks filled with color. Seems like nothing's changed."

Apparently nothing had changed. She'd blushed as a teenager every time Josh had walked into a room, and she was blushing again now. It was like her body couldn't deny her attraction to him.

Josh eyed her sexily. "I still like how you look when you blush. Like a mixture of a Penthouse centerfold and an innocent kid."

She snorted. "I'm thirty years old. Hardly an innocent kid."

"Which leaves just the Penthouse centerfold."

She opened her mouth to retort and realized she was struck speechless.

A rumble of laughter filled the air. "There it is again. The trademark Sienna James blush."

"Damn it, you're doing this on purpose. You haven't changed one bit, have you?"

Josh shook his head. "Nope, I was crazy about you in school, and after spending two minutes with you now, I'm crazy about you all over again."

"Pffft." She dismissed his comment with a flick of her wrist, although she couldn't hide her smile. Or deny the tug of awareness that flickered through her belly and lower. It was the first tug she'd felt for anyone other than Ben in a seriously long time. "What are you doing on the island?"

"Time." He grimaced. "Two months hard labor."

"You work here?" Would surprises never cease?

He nodded. "It's been hell, I tell you. Hell. I'm forced to swim every morning, sail a cat at sunset, dive on weekends and run barefoot along the beach every lunch hour. It's killing me."

She gave him a commiserative nod. "I can see the toll it's taken. You look awful." Awful good. He looked downright lickable. Sienna could only thank her lucky stars the waitress arrived with her daiquiri at that moment. Otherwise, she would, without a doubt, have licked him.

Not all over. Just a little sample of his neck. And maybe his lips. And, if she could just get that T-shirt out of the way, then maybe a nipple as well.

Sienna. Concentrate!

She took a very long sip of daiquiri and shoved all thoughts of licks, lips and nipples aside. "So, what hard labor have you been sentenced to?"

"Installing the computer network." He shook his head and scowled. "Wanna know the worst part of all? They may make it a life sentence. The hotel needs a permanent IT person on staff, twenty-four seven."

He grinned then. An outrageously sexy grin. A grin that made her want to lick him all over again. Everywhere.

"What did I do to deserve this kind of punishment?" he asked her. "What?"

"I'm sorry. You must have been a very bad boy." She laid her hand over his in mock comfort and jerked as a jolt of heat shot through her palm.

"I was a very bad boy." His eyes danced. "And I grew into a very bad man. Want to see proof?"

Yes! Every instinct she possessed yelled in her head. She'd wanted proof when she was a teenager, and she wanted proof now. Hell, proof with Josh would be a fantastic way of taking that final step away from Ben.

She suppressed her base needs and clung to her common sense instead, taking another sip of her drink for fortification. "I'd rather see proof of your sailing skills," she told him. "I saw the cats out on the beach earlier. I'd have taken one out on my own, but since I have no idea how to sail and would probably flip the Hobie and drown myself, I figured I'd better not take a chance."

"Fair dinkum? You wanna go sailing with me?" He turned his hand palm up, and Sienna belatedly realized she'd forgotten to move her arm away. Before she could motivate herself to do just that, Josh clasped her hand in his.

She bit her cheek, refusing to focus on the warmth of his skin as it wrapped around her hand. "That depends."

He raised an eyebrow. "On what?"

"You gonna talk any more about those wet dreams you used to have?"

Josh shook his head almost immediately, the epitome of a well-behaved kid—which he'd never been. "Hell, no. I promise."

Ah. Well, darn. "And you don't have to work?"

"I'm done for the week. Unless there's an emergency, this afternoon and the entire weekend are all mine."

She smiled. "Then if you'd be willing to take me, I'd love to go sailing with you."

He stood and was tugging her up along with him before she'd finished talking. "Ace. Let's go."

"Now?" What if she hadn't given him a choice? What if he

didn't really want to go sailing and she'd just forced herself on him?

He nodded. "Right now."

"Wh-what's the rush?"

He met her gaze with his emerald green one. "You know how I promised not to talk about my teenage wet dreams?"

"Uh, yeah." Why, oh why did she feel like she was walking into a well-planned trap?

His face lit up like a damned Christmas tree. "Well, I made no such promises about my adult ones. And believe me, Si, you don't want anyone within ear distance when I tell you about those."

Chapter Three

Sienna gaped at Josh. Again. Hell, she didn't think she'd stopped gaping since he'd surprised her by the pool. But seriously, the words that came out of the man's mouth were enough to make anyone gawk. And blush.

He sat beside her on the Hobie's trampoline, his legs stretched in front of him, one ankle propped over the other and the tiller caught under his arm. Wind whipped hair around his face, making him look wild, untamed and absolutely beautiful. Mirth and merriment glinted in his eyes like the rays of the afternoon sun glinted on the water.

"You're just saying all of that to make me blush again," she told him accusingly.

He shrugged, looking ridiculously adorable. "I'm saying it because it's the truth."

Sienna straightened her shoulders and decided to call his bluff. She was no longer the tongue-tied kid. She was a mature, experienced adult, and she could give as good as she got.

And if she got good, she gave good.

Suppressing a smile, she glanced pointedly at his groin then ran her hand over the boom beneath the sail, trailing her fingers down the smooth metal. "This hard, huh?"

"That hard." He grinned at her. "But thicker."

She wrapped her fingers around the metal and raised a disbelieving eyebrow.

"You're welcome to compare," he offered generously and shifted his leg, inviting her to move her hand from the boom and settle it on his cock.

Sienna's grip on the bar tightened. Her mouth turned dry. Ben was the only man she'd desired in eight years. Eight long years. She still desired him. That was a hard, unrelenting fact she couldn't deny.

Yet sitting this close to Josh, with the salty, ocean air filling her nose and nothing but crystal water stretched out around them, her belly flipped from one side to the other. Hunger and lust coursed through her veins like an incoming tide. She wanted him. Wanted him with a fierceness that shook her.

Not Ben. *Josh.*

When once she'd lusted after him with all the innocence of a teenager, now very womanly needs tugged at her breasts and pulled at her pussy. Josh's talk about the size of his erection was not helping matters at all. She resisted the urge to pump her hand up and down the boom, doing to it exactly what she wished to do to Josh.

That, and so very much more.

She sniffed. "You realize of course that I would have welcomed the chance to compare when we were at school."

His smile softened. "I'm willing to bet you didn't even know what an erection was when we were at school."

Touché. Still, instead of blushing, she met his gaze head-on. No time like right now to do something about all those desires raging through her bloodstream. "I would've been open to your teaching me."

"Ah see, Si. If the teenage Josh had let you anywhere near his erection, it would have been game over before you'd even touched him once." His eyelids drooped sexily. "Before you'd touched *me* once," he corrected, his voice a whole heck of a lot deeper.

Dear God. Was that simply desire in her veins? Felt more like a raging inferno.

She folded her arms across her breasts, staring at him mulishly as her past and present merged in her mind. "Here's what I don't get."

He looked at her expectantly.

"You knew I had the biggest crush on you for like, oh, *five years.* Heck, I even asked you to the Year Twelve Formal. You turned me down flat." *Ouch.* That had hurt. Big-time.

He merely nodded in agreement.

With a huff, she went on. "You never once, in all that time, acknowledged any kind of returned attraction."

Another nod.

Damn it. Did he have to agree so easily? Could he not maybe lie, and say something like he'd just kept his attraction to her under wraps?

She gave him the evil eye. "Yet here you are, telling me I was your wet dream every night of your high school life. Telling me that seeing me now makes you hard all over again. I don't get it. What did I do so wrong back then that you refused to show me any interest?"

For a second, the laughter and happiness leeched from Josh's face. His eyes...died. Emptied of emotion. And his lips thinned, fine lines fanning out from the sides of his mouth. "Si..."

He shook his head, blinked, and a mask dropped over his face, hiding any sign of the misery she'd just seen.

"Si," he said again. "You were everything good and pure in school. Everything each poor male sap in our year dreamed about. You could have clicked your fingers and had anyone you wanted fall at your knees. You were a...princess."

Er, not quite the way she remembered it.

She'd been a little overweight even then. Not a nerd exactly, but strait-laced and studious enough that she'd never been any guy's first choice. Those privileges had always gone to Ky and Mack. She was the plain Jane, happy to hear about her friends' conquests and determined to do her parents proud.

"You were..." He hesitated, as though searching for the right word. "Perfect. Utterly perfect. The last thing you needed was me fouling up your reputation."

Do not gape at him again! "What the...? What reputation? And how on earth could you have fouled it up?"

"It's never good for the class angel to hang out with the class failure."

"Failure? What the hell, Josh? Are you and I talking about the same school?" No, Josh may not have passed with the Dux of Year Twelve Award, but as far as Sienna knew, he'd always gotten along just fine academically. And just fine with the girls too.

Damn it, even now a sliver of jealousy crept under her ribs.

"You were good, Si. I wasn't. I refused to let my...ways blacken yours."

His ways? Blacken hers? "Seriously, Josh, you're talking rubbish." Hurt and anger assailed her. She could see only one reason he'd spout such crap. "If you didn't like me then, that's okay. You don't have to like everyone. I can even appreciate that having a classmate fawning all over you might make you feel awkward. But don't go feeding me some bullshit about you not being good enough, just to make me feel better."

Damn it, she shouldn't have come out here with him. Shouldn't have forced him to take her sailing. She'd been a burden to him back then apparently, and she'd just made herself a burden all over again. Her and her big mouth. Next time she'd just keep it shut. Every single insecurity she'd ever experienced at school came flooding back.

Cold shivers spread up her arms even though the sun beat down on her shoulders. The sail billowed in the wind, making Josh tug a little harder on the tiller.

"Know why I declined your invitation to the formal?" he finally asked.

She refused to answer. She'd already said too much about their high school years and her ridiculous infatuation with him.

"Because I had no way of paying for the tickets. Besides, if I'd missed work, even one night, my arsehole boss would've fired my sorry arse."

She blinked. "You worked in high school?"

He shrugged. "Didn't have a choice."

"When?"

"Every night. Five to ten, at the fish and chips shop down the road."

She stared at him, stunned. How could she not have known?

"And every weekend. Stacking shelves at Coles."

"Two jobs?"

Another shrug. "Family had to eat."

"And you had to pay for the food?"

"Me and Jarrod."

His older brother. "Wh-what about your parents?"

"Ah, yeah. My parents. Let's see. My old man, well, I have no idea why he never gave us money. Probably because he spent seven of the twelve years I was in school in prison."

She knew her mouth hung open, but somehow she couldn't

close it.

"And my mother? Yeah, she was good for work for a while. Until she discovered the attraction of the bottom of a gin bottle."

Her heart constricted. Dear God, what a childhood. How could she have been so blissfully unaware of the hardships in his life?

She ached for the teenage boy he'd once been. Or maybe she ached for the boy he was never allowed to be. "So you and Jarrod were forced to work?"

He angled the cat to the right, a little too far and too fast, and it tilted precariously. Sienna slid a little closer to Josh, so their legs pressed together. The muscles in his thigh were hard as rock and tense as elastic about to snap.

He righted the cat, muttered an apology and turned the Hobie again, catching the wind. The cat sailed through the water, picking up speed.

Sienna did not move her thigh. Not even an inch. She liked the way it felt resting against his. Liked the way the hair on his legs abraded her skin. Liked the way a tic pulsed in his cheek as he looked at her leg, then his, then up at the sail.

"Josh?"

"Yeah?"

"Why was your dad in prison?"

Big sigh. "Fraud."

"Is he out yet?"

"I'd assume so, since he was given a nine-year sentence almost twenty years ago."

"You don't know for sure?"

Josh shook his head. "Never been interested enough to find out."

"But surely he came back to live with you when he got out?"

His face was once again a blank mask. "He might have. We weren't there."

"Where were you?"

"Jarrod and I moved up north. To the Sunshine Coast."

"And your mother?"

"She moved on with her bottle of gin. To this day I have no idea where they went."

"She deserted you?"

"Pretty much."

"How old were you when she left?"

He bit his lip. "Sixteen."

"Sixteen?" That would have made Jarrod seventeen. "You lived without either parent for the last two years of high school?"

His arm tensed around the tiller, his biceps bulging under his skin. "It was easier alone."

"You never said anything," she whispered, dismayed by his revelations.

"We couldn't. Jazz and I knew if we mentioned our situation to anyone, and DOCS got wind of it, they'd step in. We managed just fine with an alcoholic mother. We managed even better without her."

God, he was so removed, so cold. Discussing the Department of Community Services and his past as though he had no connection to it whatsoever. Did he need to distance himself? To help him forget the pain and the hardships?

"I'm sorry," she whispered, knowing the words were completely inadequate, yet helpless to come up with anything better.

"Don't be." Again, his biceps bulged. "It was years ago. A lifetime ago."

"Still, I wish I'd known..."

"Why, so you could step in and cure my ailments? My woes?"

"I..." She let her words die on her lips. That was exactly what she'd have wanted to do. She'd have tried to help improve his circumstances somehow. And in doing so, she'd have inadvertently revealed the Lyes' living conditions, and DOCS would have stepped in. Exactly what Jarrod and Josh hadn't wanted. "It would have helped me understand you a little better."

"Ah, princess, I never wanted your pity."

She began to object then stopped. He was right again. That's what she would have given him. He hadn't wanted it then, and she was pretty darn sure he didn't want it now. "So, let me get this straight. Your dad was in prison, and your mother was an alcoholic."

Josh nodded.

"You and Jarrod worked every single day to put food on your table and...pay your way through school?"

"Someone had to pay."

"And with all of this shit going on in your life you still managed to pass every exam you ever wrote and get through your HSC?"

Determination glinted in his eyes. "A kid is nothing without a school education."

"So you did all of that, all of it, just the two of you?"

"In a nutshell."

She bristled. "Yet you have the audacity to label yourself the class failure?"

"Compared to you, that's exactly what I was."

"Damn it, Josh, you're not a freaking failure." She poked a finger into his arm. "You're a bloody idiot. I was a pampered kid who got whatever I wanted from a family who loved me. I never had to work a day in my life until I finished my uni degree." *Princess* was a pretty apt description, actually. "You had to support yourself and your family, and you still made it through high school. You're not a failure. You're a freaking legend."

"A legend?" He snorted. "Yeah, right."

She sniffed in indignation. "A real-life hero."

"Heroes aren't real," he pointed out. "They're made-up fantasies."

She looked at him sideways. "You were my fantasy for five years."

"That's the problem with fantasies. They're never as good in the flesh."

She gasped. "You're kidding, right?"

"I never kid about fantasies."

"Damn it, Josh. Your flesh looks good enough to lick."

He said nothing, merely raised an eyebrow in her direction.

Don't blush. Do not blush. "Know what I used to call you back in school?"

"Josh?" he hazarded.

"Nice try." She rolled her eyes. "But wrong. I called you Josh Lie-With-Me."

The eyebrow lifted higher.

"Because all I freaking wanted to do was lie with you. Even for just five minutes."

He threw his head back and laughed out loud, the first genuine emotion he'd shown since he'd begun telling her his sorry story. "See, princess. That's why you and I could never have worked. You and your angelic ways. You had a crush on me for five years, and all you wanted to do was lie with me?"

"No, you moronic halfwit. I had a crush on you for five years, and all I wanted to do, even if it only lasted five minutes, was fuck your brains out."

It was Josh's turn to gape at Sienna.

"*Lie* was a euphemism," she finished with a grumpy frown.

Jesus fucking Christ. The girl who'd usurped his childhood dreams had just confessed she'd wanted him as much as he'd wanted her. The angelic princess, who was so far out of his league it was laughable, had been as hot for him as he'd been for her.

Just as well he'd stayed away from her in school. Preserved her pristine purity.

No girl as perfect as Sienna deserved to be tainted by his kind.

"If it makes you feel any better," she said, her lips swollen in a pout, "I still want to fuck your brains out."

For once in his life, Josh was speechless. He had no witty retort, no quick comeback. He was quite simply stunned all the way down to his toes. And his dick, which throbbed beneath his shorts.

Not a day had passed at school when he'd escaped an embarrassing erection, brought upon merely by seeing Sienna.

Over a decade later, and he was still plagued with the same affliction. Only this time, the adult woman beckoned even more wantonly than the child, making his cock stand even straighter than it had back then. And thicker. So much thicker.

His gaze dropped to her chest. Again. Beneath the lifejacket that hung open over her shoulders, was the tiny little black shirt he'd first seen lying in a pile on the beach. His childhood fantasy was also the perfect mermaid who'd frolicked so freely in the waves.

The way her breasts spilled over the top of the shirt had him stiffening even more. And the fact that her nipples were two taut peaks, staring at him, calling to him, only made matters worse.

The kid he'd been would never, ever have thought to take advantage of the kid she'd been. He'd never felt good enough for her.

The adult he'd become felt no such compunction. The kid had been so way beneath Sienna she'd have balked at his living conditions. The adult had a thriving business, a place in the Sunshine Coast society, and enough money saved in the bank that he need never work another day in his life.

The adult had lived with fantasies of the perfect girl for over ten years. Had enough time passed between now and then to finally allow him a taste of what he'd missed out on as a teen? A taste of Sienna.

"Princess," Josh said, his voice carrying an intentional warning, "I'm not that same kid. If you offer yourself to me now, I am not going to refuse."

It was her turn to raise an eyebrow. "Ah, so you think my confessing that I still want you to fuck me six ways to Sunday is an...offer?"

Good God, her eyes were exquisite. Clear as a summer blue sky. "Is it?"

She flicked a silky lock of flaxen hair over her shoulder and sniffed again. Her eyes flashed, darkening even as her face lit up. "Hell, yeah. And mark my words on this one, you turn me down again, and there won't be another offer."

Chapter Four

It was, without a doubt, the longest trip back to shore in the history of sailing. The mere two hundred meters felt more like a hundred miles.

Josh steered the cat into the shallow depths, jumped into the water and dragged the Hobie onto the beach. Sienna jumped too, not giving Josh the chance to lift her off the trampoline himself and carry her back to his room.

He waved over at Luke, the guy in charge of the boats, signaling their return, then grabbed Sienna's hand and hauled her off the sand.

"My room is just down there." She pointed, her voice breathless.

Ah. A beachside bungalow. Figured. Kylie would have saved the best for her best friends. His own suite was situated in the staff quarters. Nothing to sneeze at, but a million miles away from here. "Condoms are in my room," he told her, wondering why the fuck he didn't carry one around in his pocket at all times.

New rule. From this second on always carry a condom. Always. No question.

Her lips curved into a sexy grin. "I have some."

He faltered midstep. "You do?"

"There's a box in the bathroom. Compliments of the hotel."

"So, they're not yours?"

She shook her head.

Unquestionable relief stole through him. They weren't hers. Which meant she hadn't come here with the intention of having sex.

"I didn't think to bring any," she confessed. Her lips twitched as she looked on ahead, steering him towards her bungalow. "I don't usually use condoms with my vibrator."

Josh tripped. Over his own feet. Fuck, she hadn't even blushed when she'd said that.

Sienna turned to steady him. "You okay?"

Christ, the way her eyes danced, mischief painted all over her delectable face, her freckles standing out... "You said that on purpose," he accused. "Just to get a reaction out of me."

Why on earth had he ever thought her eyes were the color of a summer sky? Right now they looked black. Her pupils were enormous, dark spheres rimmed with navy.

"Did I get a reaction?" she asked with the tiniest hint of a smirk.

Jesus, what happened to the naïve kid he'd known in school? "Did you want one?"

She shrugged sweetly. "Only if it promises more satisfaction than my vibrator."

Enough.

He couldn't take another second of her teasing. Of her subtle scent that drifted through his nose with hints of cinnamon. Of her creamy white skin, so silky, just begging to be touched. He couldn't take one more second.

With more speed than he knew he possessed, he backed her up against the trunk of a palm tree, stepped in close—so close she'd have no doubt of the satisfaction his response could provide—and slanted his mouth over hers.

The little minx was ready for him, her lips soft, warm, welcoming and...parted.

Holy fuck! She'd parted her lips for him, inviting his tongue in, leaving the hot, sweet cavern of her mouth open to his exploration.

Her taste hit him with the force of a cannonball, smashing into his chest, winding him. Sweet and tangy, like strawberries and rum. And salty, like the sea air. Innocence, mischief and...sadness, all rolled into one.

He could taste all that on her tongue? Sadness? Why?

Then she whimpered against his lips, and his thoughts scattered. She twined a leg around his, hooking her foot around his ankle, pressing her groin into his and lining her pussy up with his cock.

He hadn't been kidding earlier when he'd said if she'd touched him, even once, when they were younger, it'd have been game over in a second. Suddenly he was that horny kid all over again. The determined teenager, aroused and desperate for a taste of her, a feel of her, knowing he could never have her.

She slid her hand between their bodies, cupping his dick through his boardies, making him groan savagely into her mouth.

The sound must have motivated her. Less than a second later the same hand was dipping beneath the waistband of his shorts and caressing his bare, aching penis. Here, in the open, standing just on the side of a public pathway, where God knew who could walk past. Anyone.

Anyone. And she was holding his dick in her palm, petting it.

Christ. Fuck. Holy shit.

She was in his arms, pressing her body against him, wrapping her hand around his erection, and damned if he wasn't on the verge of ending the game right now.

He wrenched his lips from hers, his eyes scrunched shut, pain shooting through his balls.

Fuck, release. He needed release. Needed to come.

"Let go. Quick," he rasped. *Whoa. Close. Way too close.* "Say something, anything. Get my mind off fucking you, or it's not gonna happen."

Her hand was an instrument of torture, releasing him in tiny, tormenting strokes. Her breath came in shallow gasps, her breasts scraping against his chest with every inhalation.

Not helping. Not one little bit. "Princess, fuck, say something."

With a long, breathy sigh, she released him, extricating her hand from his pants. "I...I'm getting married."

He clenched his teeth, willing his orgasm into retreat mode, mulling over her words, trying to make sense of them.

Married.

Married?

His erection died a sudden, effective death. Her confession slapped him clean across the face.

Josh stumbled back. "Married?"

No way. No fucking way.

What was he then? Some last minute entertainment before the big day? The last hurrah? A quick spin to tie up any childhood loose ends?

Sienna's face creased with sorrow.

"You're getting married, and you're here? Doing this? With me?" Irrational fury surged through him.

Tears pooled in her eyes. She shook her head. "No. I'm not."

Josh glared, his thoughts reeling. "Jesus, Sienna, what the fuck kind of a game are you playing with me?"

"No game. I'm not getting married." Her voice trembled.

"You said—"

"You told me to say something."

He smacked his fist into his forehead. Christ, he had. He'd practically yelled at her. "So...so you're not getting married."

A tear spilled over onto her cheek. "No." She shook her head. "Not anymore."

He stared at her, shocked.

"We broke up."

Ah. Could that account for the sorrow he'd tasted on her tongue? "When?"

"Few months ago."

"Why are you telling me this now?"

"Because I'm about to sleep with you. I thought you had a right to know. I, er, I haven't been with anyone besides Ben for a very long time."

Oh, great. Just fucking great. "So this makes me, what? The rebound guy?"

"Wha—? God, no!" She looked as shocked as he felt.

"Then you have slept with someone since the break-up?"

"No," she practically yelled at him.

"So I am the rebound guy," he confirmed.

She shook her head viciously. "Interesting perspective. I'd been thinking about you as my salvation."

He snorted. "Salvation. A quick fuck to get over your ex. Whatever. Same thing, no?"

She wiped an angry hand over her cheek, brushing away any trace of her tears. "I just told you I spent five years at school wishing you'd fuck me. That I still wish you'd fuck me. And this is your answer? This is your conclusion?" Emotion flashed through her eyes. Fury? Dismay? Confusion?

"Pretty obvious conclusion, don't you think?" Why was he so angry? Did it even matter if he was her rebound guy?

Her face shut down. Her body cooled beside his, noticeably. "You know what, Josh? I've got enough shit to deal with without you getting all pissy on me." She shoved herself away from the tree. "I've fantasized about you for years. But I guess it's true what they say. The reality can never live up to the fantasy." Shouldering him hard in the chest, she stormed past him.

Pain twanged through his sternum, the aching promise of a future bruise.

"Have a nice life," she tossed back at him and marched off.

He watched her go. Watched her round arse swing with every furious stride. Watched her endless, curvy legs eat up the path. Watched as the woman who'd been the center of every childhood dream disappeared from his life once again.

It was better to let her walk away. He didn't need the complication in his life right now. Didn't need a princess.

He never had.

In fact, the whole sorry situation wasn't worth another thought.

Acting purely on instinct, he sprinted after Sienna. One step, two, ten. Twenty. He barreled into her back, knocking her clean off her feet, the impact taking him down with her.

He twisted a microsecond before they landed, shoving them both onto the manicured lawn and landing beneath her, cushioning her fall.

Another bruise, definitely. This one on his butt, but he didn't give a damn. Without waiting for his breath to return, or her shock to dissipate, he cupped the back of her head, hauled her face down to his and kissed her again.

Their mouths met, clashed, fought, then finally submitted. The anger abated, fury turned to passion and her lips parted, once again inviting his tongue to explore.

Arms twined around his neck as she cuddled in closer, and breasts as round and plump as heaven pressed against his chest.

"I'm sorry, princess," he murmured when she pulled away to catch her breath. "My behavior was inexcusable."

She pressed her mouth to his jaw, leaving a soft imprint of

her lips. "You're not a rebound guy," she whispered. A blush crept into her cheeks. "But you are the first man I've been attracted to since Ben."

"Should I take that as a compliment?"

"I don't know. How do you normally take it when a woman confesses she wants you to fuck her senseless?"

He laughed, a gruff, low laugh. "Contrary to popular belief, it's not every day a woman tells me that."

"I find that hard to believe."

"After hearing about my childhood? Poverty and dysfunctional families don't exactly attract women like flies."

"Are you calling me a fly?"

"You're a princess. You always have been."

"Is that a bad thing?" She held her breath.

"Only for failures like me, who have no chance of catching a princess."

"You're not a failure." She tilted her head to look him in the eyes. "You never were."

"I was never a prince."

"I never wanted a prince. I just wanted you to lie with me."

"Do you still?"

Mischief flashed in her eyes. "Well, I have my vibrator..."

Minx. "Show me."

Chapter Five

"But you asked me to show you."

Uh-uh. No way. He wasn't falling for her innocence all over again. Josh tossed the toy over his shoulder. "I had to get you indoors somehow. Otherwise I'd have fucked you on the very public hotel lawn."

Her eyes lit up.

He groaned, the sound a mixture of disbelief and arousal. "You would have liked that?"

She tugged at the little black top, pulling it over her head and tossing it aside. "I may be a princess, but I'm not the good girl you seem to think I am."

Er, no. The strapless bra she wore, although black and lacy, did not scream good. It screamed *rip me off now and ravage the breasts beneath.* "So what, naughty girls like having sex in places they can be seen?"

Her hands disappeared beside her back and seconds later the bra fell to the floor. "I can't speak for all naughty girls, but this one certainly likes the thrill of knowing she could get caught at any time."

He licked his very dry lips, wishing it were her nipples his tongue caressed, not his own, hungry mouth. "You'd have let me fuck you outside?"

"I've waited so long for this moment, I'd let you fuck me anywhere." Her skimpy white shorts disappeared.

Josh forgot to breathe. Dear God, the woman was a picture of perfection. All lush flesh, abundant breasts, glowing skin and legs that wouldn't quit. "Anywhere?" he managed to choke out.

"Anywhere, anytime, any way."

She stepped out of the tiny scrap of material she had the audacity to call a thong, and Josh had to steady himself by grabbing the back of the couch. Holy hell. Never mind a princess, she was a goddess. Mother Earth.

Curvy enough to bring any man to his knees. As for her pussy, the clean-shaven flesh beckoned him closer. Closer still. Until he was in front of her. Touching her. Hauling her naked form into his arms and kissing her with all the pent-up frustration and need of an eighteen-year-old.

An eighteen-year-old who'd lusted after her for five years.

He scooped her up and carried her into the pristine wood and glass bedroom, laying her down on snow-white Egyptian cotton sheets. "The anywhere we'll leave for later." Sex in public? Not something he'd ever done. Not something he'd discount though. Perhaps when it was darker...? "The anytime is right now." Well, to start with. "As for the any way... Princess, there are so many ways I wanna make love to you, you'll be ninety before we've covered half of them."

"You talk the talk, bigshot. But so far I haven't seen any signs of you walking the walk."

He raised an eyebrow. "You want a sign?"

"No, I want you to stop talking and fuck me senseless."

He pulled off his shirt and tossed it aside. As his pants came off, he acknowledged defeat. How could he not? His dick was a solid pole jutting out before him, the head leaking a steady trail of precome. "You know I'm gonna last all of three seconds once I get inside you?"

"Then it'll be two seconds longer than me," she admitted hoarsely, her gaze glued to his erection.

He tore open a condom, eternally grateful to the hotel for having the foresight he so clearly lacked. With his gaze focused on the juncture between her legs, he sheathed himself. "Show me," he urged, watching as goose bumps popped up all over her skin.

Without hesitation, Sienna bent her knees and spread her legs, offering Josh a view he'd waited almost his whole life to see.

God help him, it was worth every minute of the wait.

Her pussy lips glistened between her thighs, a welcome invitation to the shaft he now gripped tight in his palm. He dragged air into his lungs.

"I can't go slow, princess," he warned. "I've waited too long for this moment. Wanted you forever. If I take a step towards the bed, it's not gonna be for gentle kisses and foreplay. I'm gonna bury myself as deep inside you as I can get and not stop moving until you've come screaming and every last drop of semen has drained from my cock."

A trickle of cream oozed from her exposed lips. "Promises, promises."

Josh pounced.

One second he stood in front of the bed, the next he covered her goddess-like body with his own and helped himself to her mouth. The sensations of her bare flesh clasped against his, of her taut nipples poking his chest and her womanly softness pillowing his harder muscles had him ready to blow.

As their lips melded and their tongues tangoed, she wrapped her legs around his waist and tilted her hips.

Her warm pussy caressed his cock, the evidence of her desire moistening his balls and the tiny bit of exposed flesh at the base of his dick. If he'd thought he couldn't get any harder, he'd thought very wrong.

With one thrust, Josh did as he'd longed to do since his first wet dream about her. Full to bursting, he buried himself in his dream girl.

Sienna pulled her mouth from his with a gasp, her entire body tensing.

Josh froze. *Fuck.*

"Princess?" he growled.

Her answer was a low moan.

His heart pounded. "Are you okay?"

Her breath came in fast gulps. "B-better than okay."

Thank fucking God. "I thought I'd hurt you."

She shook her head and squeezed her muscles around his cock, as though testing his girth—and self control. "You're bigger than I'm used to, is all."

Well, hell. His chest puffed up to twice its normal size. "I'll be gentle," he promised.

"Don't you fucking dare," she warned testily, and rolled her hips beneath him.

Ah. Fuck.

She did it again.

Jesus. No fair. She wasn't used to his size. He had to go slow.

Josh placed his hands on either side of her head and lifted his weight off her slightly. Sweat beaded on his spine, the result of his concerted effort to remain still.

"Josh," she growled between clenched teeth. "Move. Please. Move, now!"

Slow. Just go slow.

"Argh!" With a yell, she arched her back, clasped his waist tight between her legs and rode his dick as fast and as fiercely as her position would allow.

Velvet heat surrounded his shaft, sucked him in deep, stunned him all the way down to his toes, then released him. Fast, so fast. Too fast. He couldn't appreciate it.

Then it was back. The velvet heat. Her pussy. Her hot, wet pussy, claiming him, calling him. Fucking him.

With a wild roar, he lost his control.

Josh pistoned into her, over and over, stroking his cock inside her. Deep. So fucking deep he couldn't tell where he finished and she started. So deep he'd have feared losing himself inside her—if that wasn't exactly where he wanted to be. Where he'd always wanted to be.

She was right there with him, all the way. Meeting every feral thrust, clamping her inner walls around his erection, trapping him inside so every tug out was a delicious struggle.

Christ, three seconds had been an exaggeration. One second and he was ready to explode. His balls were tight knots beneath his dick. His shaft an aching rod, stymied with pleasure.

And Sienna. Lord, she was screaming. And gasping and...coming.

Holy fuck. Jesus Christ. She was coming. And coming and coming and coming. All over his cock.

Clenching him tight. So tight, milking him. Pulling his seed from his balls. Oh, Christ. She was shoving her breasts up high, rubbing them against his chest, muttering mindlessly.

God, she was coming. And... so was he!

Can't stop. Can't hold back.

Not one more second.

Silver heat blitzed through his shaft.

Coming. So hard. So fucking hard.

His entire body convulsed, the muscles in his back stretched tight enough to snap.

But, God. The pleasure. The intense, pure, pleasure.

Just perfect.

Pure perfect pleasure.

Josh sat on Sienna's balcony, his feet resting on the cane table, his butt perched on a ridiculously comfortable cushion on a cane couch. Not ten meters from said balcony, beach sand met lush green lawn. The sea was but a hop, skip and a jump from Sienna's room.

Josh tried to appreciate the sun as it dipped over the water. Tried to enjoy the forty different shades of pink and red that painted the twilight sky. He tried furiously to feel some sense of shame or maybe even embarrassment as a couple strolled along the path, hand in hand, and smiled at him from a short distance away.

In truth he felt nothing but the lips around his cock. The warm heat of Sienna's mouth as she sucked him in deeper, caressing him with her tongue. First, she twirled that sinful tongue around the head, and when she'd sufficiently tortured him enough, she twirled it around the length of his shaft.

Sweat beaded on his forehead and upper lip. Barely a half an hour had passed since his first explosive orgasm, and thanks to the ministrations of the woman kneeling between his legs, he was headed for a second one. Fast.

Josh lifted his arm, heavy as lead, and waved at the couple. They waved back, oblivious to the fact that a luscious, naked goddess perched at his feet, treating him to a little slice of heaven.

She drew her lips off of him. "You waving at someone?" Her voice was husky.

Josh had to clear his throat to answer, and even then he spoke no louder than a whisper. "Yeah. A couple walking past."

She gave a lusty groan and licked him from root to tip. "Think they know what you're doing?"

"I'm not doing a damn thing, princess," Josh reminded her. "And neither are you," he pointed out with a disgruntled sigh.

She'd ceased all mouth movement and regarded him with those darkened blue eyes he was beginning to adore. Her lips were swollen and parted, and every syllable she uttered sent warm breath fluttering over his dick.

"How does it feel," she asked, mischief dancing over her face, "knowing they're so close and have no idea what's going on?"

"It feels..." He let his words drift away as she wrapped her lips around his tip and suckled gently. "Ah, Christ, it feels unbelievable."

She kissed his balls. "What if they knew what we were doing? Or worse. Came closer to say hello?"

He didn't have an answer. Dread fluttered in his stomach, right about the same time a fresh wave of blood slammed into his already engorged member. Precome leaked from his shaft.

Sienna moaned softly. "Can you still see them?"

Josh nodded, almost incapable of speech. "They're...close." Although they'd already walked past the balcony. Josh kept his voice low, praying fervently they didn't hear him. What if they turned around?

"Keep your eyes on them," Sienna told him. "Don't look away. Not for one second."

"Princess—"

"Please." Her smile was devilish. "Do it. For me."

How could he refuse? Josh returned his gaze to the couple, although he really wanted to watch as once again Sienna parted those cherry red lips and pulled him seductively into her mouth.

The woman said something to the man who turned to look at the beach. They stopped walking, not twenty steps away from Sienna's room.

Sienna swallowed his cock.

Josh jerked.

The woman pointed. Josh looked in that direction.

Sienna sucked, her mouth a hot, wet, tight cavern with silken walls.

A dark body broke the smooth surface of the water, spinning once in the air and diving back into the sea.

"Dolphins." The voice belonged to the woman. The rest of her sentence was unintelligible.

Sienna released him, just long enough to mutter, "Keep watching them," and then her mouth was back, consuming him, delighting him, tempting and teasing, rousing and inflaming.

He didn't drop his gaze this time. Watched the couple as they watched the dolphins, sat with his arse plastered to the seat, incapable of movement. Christ, her mouth. It wrenched a groan from deep in his gut, a loud, rasping noise he couldn't control.

The man turned to look at him, his face scrunched in silent question.

Ah, fuck! Caught.

A wave of heat hit him in the stomach, sending goose bumps all the way down his spine. Jesus, why did that thought turn him on so damn much?

Again, he raised his arm, now so heavy with desire he could hardly move it, and pointed to the ocean. "Dolphins," he mouthed. Comprehensive speech was simply not possible.

The man smiled and nodded. Josh smiled and nodded. But not in response to the man. In response to the molten mouth that devoured him, delighted him, fucking dazed him. And to the hand that caressed his testicles, held them, molded them slowly to the shape of her palm.

His balls swelled and tautened. The muscles in his thighs turned rigid. Sienna tightened her mouth, suctioning harder on his dick.

The man gave him a funny look.

"Dolphins," Josh mouthed again with a smile, then threw his head back, opened his mouth, closed his eyes and exploded between Sienna's lips.

His orgasm tore through his body, rocking him, shaking him. Wad after wad of come spurted onto her velvety tongue, and not once did she release him. Her muscles worked around his shaft as she swallowed, dragging even more semen from him.

He didn't have any more to give. Couldn't, not after his first orgasm. Yet the convulsions continued, shudders wracking his shoulders.

Holy fuck. He was so sensitive. Too sensitive. Couldn't take any more of her torturous caresses. Her mouth...

As if sensing his predicament, she pulled off him with a

slow, wet slurp, placed a kiss on his thigh and purred softly.

Inch by inch Josh came back to himself. Reality returned. His neck muscles relaxed and he straightened, opened his eyes and stared across the balcony at the open-mouthed expression of the man. The woman stood beside him, oblivious, as she gazed out at the ocean.

"Dolphins," Josh said again. He smiled dazedly and dropped forward to kiss the hidden Sienna full on the mouth.

Just as soon as he'd built up a modicum of energy, they were going to switch places.

Chapter Six

Sienna stood outside the exclusive, trendy Bar Evoke, leaning against the back of a bench in the exquisite gardens. Flowers blossomed everywhere she looked, their sweet, fresh scent tingeing the air.

Josh had gone back to his apartment to clean up and change, but he'd left with specific instructions to meet here, outside, so they could walk in together. He'd wanted to come back to her room to collect her, but Sienna had reckoned that was a seriously bad idea. If he came anywhere near her bed, they would not make the party. She had to make the party. She'd yet to see Mack and Aidan, and she was dead keen to meet Kylie's men.

Sienna breathed deep of the briny, humid air. The moonless night was thick and warm. Her tiny excuse for a cocktail dress already clung to her damp, just-showered flesh.

The bench Josh had chosen was situated away from the lamps that lit the path. It was the perfect place for a not-so-quick hello before heading indoors. Sienna stood behind it, impatiently awaiting his arrival.

Her heart drummed wildly. Ridiculous she should feel like this, especially so soon after her break-up with Ben, but just thinking about Josh took her breath away. They'd connected today. Connected as a man and woman. Connected sexually, yes, but it went deeper than that. Perhaps it was their shared past that made their communicating so easy, so natural. There seemed to be no shortage of things to discuss. And no inhibitions in revealing deep, dark secrets—or physical needs.

He rocked her world every time she looked at him. The sight made her breath catch and goose bumps erupt over her skin. She'd been convinced she'd never feel that intense lust for anyone other than Ben. She'd been very, very wrong.

Desire, hot and wicked, seeped through her veins, spreading into her limbs, her breasts and lower. The memory of his tongue on her pussy, stroking her clit, sent a gush of hot cream pooling between her legs. So aroused was she, all she need do was press her hand against her clit and she'd come.

Maybe Kylie was right. Maybe there was magic in this island air. Because what she and Josh had experienced today had been pure magic.

She clasped the back of the bench and did not let go.

Sienna sensed his presence a couple of seconds before strong arms embraced her from behind, wrapping around her shoulders and pulling her against a muscular chest.

She let him guide her, stepping back gladly, molding herself to him, relishing the feel of him behind her. His scent wafted into her nose, the spicy masculine aftershave as familiar as her own Calvin Klein perfume. She inhaled deeply, allowing the scent to invade her entire being. It stirred the flames that already flared within.

"Sienna," he rasped and clutched her tighter. "God, Si..."

He sounded...different. Was that awe in his voice? Wonder?

She was awed. Blown away by how right she felt in his arms. How her body fit against his as though they'd stood like this a million times before, her curves pressed into his bulk.

She closed her eyes and dropped her head onto his shoulder, relishing the hard sinew around the bone, enjoying the natural ease of their stance, even if the atmosphere around them had suddenly charged with a million amps of electricity. She rubbed suggestively against the growing erection that pressed into her arse.

A low, masculine moan echoed in her ear, and he held her closer, held her as if she was both a treasured gift and a bird he feared would startle and fly away. His hold was gentle yet determined, and oh, so damn arousing.

"Need to—" He paused. "Have to... Ah, Christ." Soft lips touched her exposed neck, followed by the flick of a warm, wet tongue. Just a whisper, and then it was gone. "Baby," he gasped, and his lips closed over the same bit of flesh and sucked gently.

Baby?

Instinctively she stretched her neck, allowing him better access. "Mmmmm."

Against her back his heart beat a rapid flutter in his chest. It matched her own racing pulse. She grasped his arms in her hands, clutching at his wrists, surprised to find them covered in long, buttoned sleeves.

So formal?

He wore long pants too. In this heat? She hadn't expected that. Neither had she expected the pained growl he emitted before his long, slim fingers trailed ever so lightly against the sides of her breasts, making her nipples bead and her knees weaken.

"Have to touch you," he said on another growl. His thumbs stroked her nipples over her dress, once, twice. And then again.

Dear God. It was too much, too exquisite. She groaned in his arms, writhing against him.

Laughter and chatter erupted in bursts mere meters away, and she tensed immediately. "Oh—"

He cut her off with a soothing, "Shhhh."

The relative darkness might cloak them in privacy, but they still stood in the open where anyone could walk past. A thrill shot through her. "Touch me," she whispered. "Please."

Hot breaths of air tickled her neck and he moved his arm down until he found the hemline of her barely-there dress. His fingers slipped beneath it. Silver heat prickled her leg as his hand feathered over her skin.

She held her breath. Couldn't exhale. Forgot how.

He brushed against her thong.

"Ah!" Her exclamation was a breathless gasp. If she'd been aroused before Josh arrived, she was a livewire now. A pulse throbbed in her pussy, so forcefully she was sure he could feel it vibrating through his hand and arm.

"More," she begged shamelessly, and widened her stance to give him easier entry. She needed his touch. Needed it more than she needed her next breath.

"Si," he whispered, his voice rougher than she expected. But then her own voice had come out a good three tones lower than usual, the result of the carnal desire that held her transfixed. He thrust against her arse, pressing his erection into the cleft, her dress and his pants a sensual barrier she'd as soon weren't there. "God, I missed this. Missed you."

Missed her? In the last forty-five minutes? She'd have laughed at his sentimentality—if she wasn't burning for him. "Please," she begged again. "Touch me. I need...need you to."

His groan was guttural and coincided perfectly with the instant his finger slid beneath the crotch of her thong and brushed against her pussy lips.

Her knees buckled at the contact, and he held her tighter, supporting her, keeping her standing.

"I've got you, baby," he reassured as he ran his finger over the seam between her lips, once, twice, driving her crazy, making every nerve ending come to life. When he dipped it inside, gently, slowly, the liquid that had pooled there oozed out, coating his finger, wetting her panties.

Her jaw dropped open, and she emitted a soundless cry.

"Oh yeah. Just like it should be," Josh murmured. Softly, deliciously, he fucked her, as if he'd been doing this all his life, stroking his finger in and out, adding another, brushing his thumb over her clit.

Good. So damn good.

So unbelievably good.

Her brain short-circuited, refusing to work. Every thought she had fled her mind. She was nothing but a ball of pleasure, a leaf floating closer and closer to the pinnacle of ecstasy.

"Oh, yeah," Josh crooned in her ear. "That's it, baby. Ride my fingers." He thrust again against her arse, in time with movement of his fingers. "Ride my cock."

An unsettled flutter of...something shivered through her, and was gone as Josh caressed her clit, exerting a fraction more pressure than before.

The pleasure was almost excruciating. The bubbles of laughter from close by a powerful aphrodisiac. Sienna burned from the inside out, her pussy the apex of her excitement.

"Come for me, baby," he encouraged. "Come on my fingers."

Tiny quivers rocked her inner walls.

Baby?

Another flutter of disquiet worried her and was gone.

"Anyone could catch us," he whispered. "Could catch you, rocking on my hand."

She whimpered, fear mingling with blatant excitement.

"Let go, baby. Before they find us."

Baby. Not right. Something's wrong.

No, nothing was wrong. Everything was right. Wantonly, carnally right.

"Uh-oh." His voice was even lower than before and softer. His fingers continued their tempestuous strokes. "Someone's coming. Walking off the path. Headed...headed towards us."

Her breath vanished. Her heart raced.

"He's close. Quick. Now, baby. Come, now."

Not baby. Princess!

Sensation overwhelmed her. The quivers detonated into full-on convulsions and Sienna climaxed on his hand. Her pussy pulsed, clasping his fingers within, holding them there even as his thumb pressed harder, making the orgasm stretch out. And out. And out.

She held in the scream she wanted to emit, groaned his name instead. *"Josh."*

The hand inside her stilled. The shoulder her head rested on turned rigid.

"Josh?" he rasped. Ice-cold fury radiated from him, freezing the pleasure within. "Who the fuck is Josh?"

"That...would be me," another voice said. A voice just a little to her right, and almost as cold and angry as the voice in her ear.

Dizziness assaulted Sienna. The world went out of focus.

Baby.

He extracted his fingers and stepped back, leaving her shaky and off-balance.

Spicy aftershave.

She grabbed the back of the bench, clutched it tight.

Long shirt, long pants. Deep voice. Deeper than this afternoon, yet so recognizable. So...known.

She prayed futilely for balance.

The familiarity of it all.

The stars above swung around her, and any oxygen that had once fed the island simply dissolved in the humidity. She couldn't breathe. Couldn't think.

Josh was next to her, not behind her.

Baby. Not Princess. Baby!

Oh, dear God.

She turned her head, knowing what she'd see before she met his gaze. Knowing it would not be longish, sun-bleached brown hair or green eyes.

Knowing the cheeks would be smooth-shaven and the hair cropped short and black as night.

"Ben." The name fell from her lips in a breathless whisper.

What was he doing here? When had he arrived? Why was he here? What did he want? And dear God, why now? Why, why, why?

Chapter Seven

Was this what it felt like to have a panic attack, Sienna wondered as she tried desperately to inhale. Her breath came too fast, too shallow to get in any air.

Someone must have helped her to the bench, because without knowing how she got there she was sitting on it with her head between her knees. A gentle hand rubbed her back, and a voice crooned in her ear. Who the hand and voice belonged to Sienna could not determine. Josh? Ben? Both of them?

She hadn't been able to separate them out two minutes ago, why should she be able to now?

But then two minutes ago she hadn't expected the past she'd put firmly behind her to usurp the present she'd become utterly enthralled with.

"B-Ben," she said, but no sound came out.

Slow down. Breathe slower. Deeper.

Easier said than done.

She would have given up trying if not for the hand on her back. It stroked from her neck to waist and up again. Slowly down, slowly up. A soothing pattern. Something she could follow, adjust her panting to.

The voice helped too, encouraging her, insisting she'd be okay. It spoke with such quiet confidence Sienna had no choice but to believe it.

It took a while—and each time she remembered that the fingers that had been inside her were not Josh's, she had to start again—but she finally managed to set her inhalations and exhalations to the rhythm of the hand.

"That's it, Si. Just breathe easy. Slow and steady," the voice said, and because it sounded in front of her and not beside, Sienna finally established that one man stroked while the other spoke.

"Ben," she rasped.

"Right here, baby," he said from next to her, telling her which man was which.

She didn't look up, wasn't ready to raise her head. The world still swam around her. "Wh-what are you doing here?"

"You didn't know he was coming?" This from the man in front of her. His tone lost the soothing lilt and came out sharp and astonished.

"No." *God, no!* How could she have known? She hadn't spoken to Ben in weeks. Had cut off all communication with him after she'd moved the last of her possessions out of the unit they'd shared into her new, smaller one. The move had cost her every last bit of emotional strength. Talking to Ben would have shattered her resolve, sent her running back to him, apologizing for leaving. Begging him to take her back.

She couldn't go back. He'd married his work instead of her. Left her alone for the better part of a year. Neglected her and their relationship. Not because he didn't love her—he did. But because he'd been trying to establish himself in his new job as an investment banker. He'd just invested more of himself into his career than he had into Sienna-and-Ben. Sienna knew that as he made his way up the corporate ladder, his workload and work dedication would only monopolize more of his time.

She loved him, but she could no longer live as second best. She deserved more than that from the man she gave her soul and her future to.

"Then what *are* you doing here?" Josh asked, the question obviously not aimed at her.

The leg beside her stiffened. "That is none of your damn business," Ben snapped.

Silence ensued as once again Sienna struggled to breathe.

It didn't last as long this time, but it still left her light-headed. She raised her face slowly, fuzzily taking in the shorts and short-sleeved, button-up shirt Josh wore. Smarter than the clothes he'd had on earlier, but still casual, like she'd expected.

Josh raised his hands in submission, but when he spoke his voice was tight. "You're right. This is none of my business. I'll leave you two alone."

What? No!

Before he could take a step, Sienna grabbed Josh's arm. She wouldn't have thought it possible, especially considering how shaky she was, but she held tight, refusing to release him. "Don't go."

She'd only just found him again. She couldn't lose him. Not now. Not this quickly. "I...thought Ben was you," she admitted, shocked all the way down to her bones that she could have made that mistake.

But then Ben wasn't supposed to be here. He hadn't arranged to meet her at the bench. She hadn't anticipated a quick tryst with him in the gardens before joining the festivities inside.

Sienna had been primed and ready for Josh. The idea that he might indulge in a little secret play in public had thrilled and excited her. True, it was Ben who'd taught her about the thrill of hiding in plain sight, who'd introduced her to the danger, the risk and the incredible exhilaration. But it was Josh whose touch she'd expected tonight. She'd responded readily, happily when he'd embraced and caressed her. And she'd felt comfortable, right in her response.

But then who wouldn't feel right or comfortable responding to the touch of a man whose bed she'd shared for eight years? Even if that man was meant to be in Newcastle.

"You mistook me for another man?" Ben asked with a strange hollowness to his voice.

Sienna gaped at him. "You're not supposed to be here. You're not supposed to be holding me. Touching me."

"And he is?" Ben asked with a soft snarl.

Yes! The answer was on the tip of her tongue, but she bit it back. Her answer was not his concern. Once it would have been his concern. Now? No.

Didn't mean his presence wasn't making her heart pound a gazillion miles an hour. Didn't mean she wasn't breathing him in greedily, committing his scent to memory once again, shaking violently from his mere presence. His physical proximity had always affected her like this. Always made her want him so badly her muscles weakened.

"Why are you here, Ben?" she asked, suddenly very tired.

"Don't you know?"

It might be too dark to see his eyes, but Sienna could feel

the full force of his gaze on her. It sent tiny shock waves down her spine. "How could I possibly know?"

"I've come for you."

"Me?" Her heart raced even faster.

"I want you back, baby. I *need* you back."

"Oh." Sienna nodded as if his response made perfect sense. In truth, she was incapable of making head or tails of his words. She chewed on her cheek. "Um...what?"

He grabbed her free hand. "I love you, Sienna. I never stopped. You ripped my heart in two when you walked away. Tore my world apart. I hate living this way. Hate being without you. Come home, baby. Come back to me. Please."

"Um... Ah." Sienna resisted the urge to rub her ear, unsure she'd heard him correctly.

"Make me complete again, Si. Come home." Ben's tone rang with sadness and desperation. This was Ben at his most vulnerable, showing her his insecurities, his fears.

He wanted her back? Seriously? Sienna gawked at him, stunned all the way down to her toes.

The arm she held tugged, attempting to free itself.

Josh! Trying to escape her hold. She tightened her grip, refused to release him. She wasn't ready to let him go.

"Sienna?" Josh said quietly.

She turned to look at him.

"Let me go, princess. I don't belong here."

"Princess?" Ben asked.

"Shut it, mate," Josh told him without taking his attention off Sienna.

"You don't belong where?" Sienna asked.

"Here. With you and him."

"Of course you do." He belonged with her. "We arranged to meet here."

"Did you arrange to meet him too?" Josh asked.

"Don't be ridiculous," she gasped. "I didn't know he was here."

"Yet you happily allowed him to bring you to orgasm," Josh pointed out, anger echoing through his words.

Her silence accentuated her guilt, and the tiny quivers still echoing through her pussy only worsened the situation. "Because I thought he was you," she whispered in shame.

"You would have let me do that to you? Out here?"

"I did let you." Heat crept into her cheeks. "It, uh, just wasn't you."

"No, it was your fiancé," Josh said bitterly.

Fiancé? Ben's words reverberated through her mind.

Come home, baby.

Come back to me.

Impossible. He couldn't really have meant that, could he? She shook her head. "He's not my fiancé. We broke up." Hadn't she told Josh that earlier? Hadn't they fought about it?

"I want to be your fiancé again," Ben told her. "I want to marry you."

Good grief, maybe he was serious. "You w-want to marry me?" The idea made her heart stand still. Made it stop beating. Made hope flare in her belly.

This was Ben, the man she'd loved for eight years, telling her he still wanted to marry her. Even though she'd left him.

Ben. Dear, wonderful, sexy, gorgeous Ben.

"With my entire being," Ben said.

Josh tugged again, reminding her he was there. Reminding her how he'd played havoc with her heartbeat earlier. How he'd made her belly flip-flop with desire.

"What about Josh?" she asked Ben.

"What about him?" Ben asked, as though Josh had no importance in her life.

The question made her bristle. She'd lusted after Josh for five years as a kid, and she'd lusted after him again this afternoon. More than that, something had clicked between them today. Fallen into place. Over the few hours they'd spent together, Josh had come to mean something to her. Ben's dismissal of him got her back up.

"He's important to me." She looked up at Josh, knowing with absolute certainty that she spoke the truth.

Josh seemed to relax. He ceased tugging against her hold and took a step closer.

Ben, on the other hand, pursed his lips. She couldn't see the little lines she was sure edged that grimace, but his anger and dissatisfaction were clear. They radiated off him in waves.

"And me?" Ben asked. "Am I no longer important to you?"

God, she wished she could say no, not anymore. But she'd

be lying if she did. "Of course you are." The words were wrenched from her soul. She didn't want to admit them. Didn't want Ben to know he still had this hold over her. But he did, and denying it was impossible.

Then why would she not let go of Josh's arm?

"Marry me, Sienna," Ben said. "Let's put this hell behind us. We can go back to having what we had before."

Sienna's anger billowed out. Shock had held it in check up until now, but suddenly she couldn't avoid it. She'd left Ben. Put him behind her. Made sure she was moving on. And what had he done? Ruined everything she'd strived so hard to accomplish. Ignored the efforts she'd made to change her world. Come stampeding back into her life, begging her to marry him, again!

Not fair. So not fair. His pleas undermined her will, her wishes.

"Before what?" she bit out. "Before you chose to work twelve-hour days, every day? Before your weekends became work days too? Before you cancelled every arrangement I made for us? Before you started skipping dinners and breakfasts, just so you could get to work on time? Before you forgot I was in your life, waiting for you? Day in, day out? Before all that, you mean?"

Josh's response startled her. He took the hand that had been grasping his wrist in a death grip and held it in his own hand. Offering her...comfort?

She accepted it. Happily. Needing something to hold onto, some sense of stability in the madness that Ben was creating.

"You're angry." Ben nodded, accepting her outburst. "You have every right to be. My behavior was unforgivable. My neglect of you...abhorrent. I know that. I understand what I put you through, because these months without you have been intolerable. And lonely. So damn lonely." He choked out the last words.

Did he want her sympathy? Tough! He wasn't about to find it here. "Whose fault is that?" She didn't wait for his reply. "How the hell do you think I felt all those times you had to work? All those times I pleaded with you to spend a little time together, and you said no? You think the loneliness wasn't unbearable? You think it didn't break my heart?" Uh-uh. Too subtle. "You think *you* didn't break my heart?" Her hand shook as she pointed at him, jabbing his chest with her finger. "*You* broke us. *You* broke you and me. If you're feeling a little lonely now, there's only one person to blame."

Ben's groan was guttural. "You're right. About everything. I fucked up. I broke us. And I was too damn blind to understand it at the time." He rapped his chest. "It was my fault."

He fell silent, as if the words he'd spoken had cost him. It took a few seconds before he continued, and when he did his voice was stronger, more determined. More like the Ben she knew, the man she'd fallen in love with. "I made a mistake, now I'm correcting it. Making things right between us."

She almost scoffed out loud. "Sure. And how do you plan to do that?"

"I've cut back my workload," Ben said. "Taken on fewer clients. I've even told John I'll be spending less hours at the office. He approved it all." Ben squared his shoulders. "I'm fixing what I broke. Making things okay for us. We can be okay. Things will be different from now on. I'll be there for you. For us."

Sienna stared at him, stupefied. "Honestly?" Ben had never tried to cut back his load. Ever. Instead he'd pleaded and apologized, promised to make it up to her. He'd never promised to work less. Yet now...

"Honestly, baby. I had a new contract drawn up, specifying the maximum number of hours I'm prepared to spend at the office. I would have come earlier, told you about it in Newie, but the contract took time because of negotiations. I didn't want to see you until I had something solid and real to offer."

Her anger disintegrated as quickly as it had appeared. Tears welled in her eyes. Three months after they'd broken up, Ben had finally come to his senses. He'd finally offered her, on a silver platter, everything she'd dreamed about for the preceding year. Everything she'd wanted.

This was it. Now. In front of her. If she reached out her hand she could take it. They could go back to the life she and Ben had planned to spend together.

God, she wanted that. She'd wanted it for eight years. Wanted it until her heart had broken into a million pieces.

Joy filled her chest.

She reached out to accept it. To say yes. To take back the future she'd thought lost forever—but found her hand trapped.

Josh held it, and he wasn't letting go.

"Josh?" She looked at him questioningly.

Was she asking for her hand...or for his approval? Because if he freed her hand and she gave it to Ben, then whatever she and Josh might have had would be no longer. In a heartbeat she'd lose the chance she'd wanted with him her whole high school career.

The chance she'd grabbed wholeheartedly this afternoon.

"He's feeding you a line," Josh said with cool disapproval. "He wants you back, and he'll do whatever he can to get you." He shrugged. "I don't blame him. I've only had you for a few hours and I'm loath to lose you."

"Feeding me a line?" Ben? Could he be capable of that?

"Damn straight." Josh nodded. "He's telling you what you want to hear, because it's the only way of getting what he wants."

Josh had a point. The only thing that could ever convince Sienna to go back to Ben was the promise of less of his time spent at work. But was it a line, or was it the truth?

"Si," Ben said. "I neglected you this last year. *I* know that, and it kills me every fucking time I think about it. But I never lied to you. I will never lie to you. *You* know that. You know me."

She did know Ben. If he said he had a new contract, he had a new contract. He'd organized it for her. For them.

God, he'd changed his work habits. For her.

Again she reached out to accept his offer, but this time, more than holding her hand in his, Josh tugged on it, hard enough to pull her up off the bench. The second she was upright he caught her in his arms, pulling her flush against his body, his chest pressing against her breasts.

And there went her heart. Racing in five different directions at the same time. At least that was what it felt like. Her breathing became erratic again, and heat flooded her pussy.

Dear God. Her pussy? Aroused at a time like this?

"You want to go back to him? Then go," Josh said. "I won't stop you. I won't get in your way. But you have to take those steps. You have to walk away from me in order to get to him. Can you do that?"

Without waiting for her response, he kissed her. With the

full force of his Josh Lie-With-Me mouth. His lips consumed, his tongue seduced and his body molded to hers, reminding her of every delicious pleasure they'd shared that afternoon. Every mind-blowing orgasm, every titillating tease. Every laugh he'd wrung out of her and every tear she'd held inside upon learning about this childhood.

One afternoon, and they'd made magic together. Shared a wealth of intimacies. A treasure she only wanted to discover more of.

She kissed him right back, explored his mouth as he'd explored hers, pressed her aching pussy against his hardening cock, rubbing, seeking the pleasure, the release she knew he could give.

She'd waited a lifetime for Josh to acknowledge her, to want her, and now that he had, she couldn't let go of him, couldn't walk away. Didn't want to.

When his mouth finally released hers, his breath came in short, sharp puffs. His erection pulsed against her clit, and his chest rose and fell unevenly—just like hers.

"Walk away, princess," he whispered. "If you can."

She shook her head, but before words could form in her mouth, telling him she couldn't and she didn't want to, hands fastened around her shoulders and twirled her around, out of Josh's grasp.

"She doesn't have to walk," Ben snapped at Josh. "I'll take her."

And take her he did, straight into another kiss, just as forceful and just as exquisite as Josh's. Sienna could have objected, could have said no. If she'd wanted to.

She didn't.

She hadn't kissed Ben for months. The sweet, chocolaty taste of him—he'd always tasted like chocolate to her—swept through her, through her senses, taking her back to the time when she'd been happiest. When she and Ben had been perfect together. When they'd finished each other's sentences, laughed at the same silly jokes, watched the same TV programs, fought over politics and torn off each other's clothes with abnormal speed. The weekends spent naked in bed, separating only to sleep, eat or shower. Making love before sunrise—and before sunset.

And the love. The pure, whole untarnished love of two

people. Ben and Sienna. Sienna and Ben.

She tasted it all in Ben's mouth. Longed for it again. Yearned for it. Wanted what they'd lost in the rise of Ben's professional aspirations. She'd loved Ben for a long time. She still did. Heartbreak and heartache had driven them apart, but still she loved him. Probably always would.

Kissing him brought back every cherished memory she had of him, every iota of passion she'd tried so damn hard to repress.

Already primed from Josh's kiss, and still wet from the orgasm Ben had given her when she thought he was Josh, Sienna was as aroused as she'd ever been. More.

Two men wanted her. Two men lusted after her. Two men she wanted and lusted after.

A jerk pulsed through her when a pair of hands settled on her hips. While Ben's mouth devoured hers, the taste of chocolate rich and sweet on her tongue, Josh tugged gently, pulling her arse backwards by mere inches, until it rested against his pelvis, his erection pressing between her butt cheeks.

Just like Ben's had when she thought he was Josh.

She let him mold her to his shape, pressed back against him, wanting him there. Wanting him there as much as she wanted Ben in front of her.

God, she shouldn't. She should choose one. Or the other. Not both. Not nestle into Josh as she kissed Ben. Not draw Ben's tongue into her mouth as she rubbed against Josh's dick.

"Kiss him," Josh said in her ear. "Enjoy his mouth. But when you come, know who gave you this orgasm, because this time it won't be your fiancé."

O-orgasm? This time? What the—?

Before the thought could solidify, Ben tore his mouth from Sienna's. "Touch her—and die!"

Ben's warning held such malice, Sienna stepped back, straight into Josh. He clamped his arms around her waist, steadying her.

"A little late for intimidation, don't you think?" Josh asked, his voice as sharp as Ben's. "About three months too late?"

Ben's hand tightened into a fist that he'd raised before Sienna could blink.

Shit. He was going to throw a punch.

"Ben," she snapped. "Stop it. Now." Her head spun. He was willing to fight Josh for her? The same man who hadn't had time to eat breakfast with her in the mornings was now gearing up for a brawl?

Breathing hard, Ben glared at Josh. "Give me a reason not to hit him, Si. One reason. That's all."

"You'll hurt your hand?" Josh suggested sarcastically.

"Josh," Sienna chastised. She'd never seen Ben quite this agitated. In his current state, he could easily blacken Josh's eye, or break his nose, or worse. The last thing he needed was Josh egging him on. The last thing she needed was the two men coming to blows.

"One reason, Si." Ben shook, and Sienna knew it was from the effort he used to restrain himself.

"Fine. Do it, princess," Josh said, backing down. "Give him the reason—if you can find one."

Sienna didn't need Josh's permission, but it helped knowing she had it. And she did have a reason for Ben not to hit Josh. A good reason. He'd hate himself afterward, he really would. Despite this new, agitated side of him, he was still Ben.

She'd hate him too if he hit Josh, and she didn't want to hate him. She really didn't. When it came to Ben, she just wanted to...kiss him.

God help her, all she wanted right then was to kiss Ben.

Without thinking twice, Sienna stepped forward.

Josh loosened his embrace, letting her go.

"Here's your reason." She pressed her mouth to his, molding her lips against his, dipping her tongue in his mouth to help herself to a serving of chocolate.

Ben kissed her back almost immediately, but he didn't lower his fist. He still held his arm up like a warning to Josh.

And since Josh was at that very moment rubbing his hands suggestively over her hips, Sienna knew she had to act, fast.

Suppressing a sigh, she pulled her mouth away from his. "Ben C," she threatened, "if you stop kissing me, for any reason whatsoever, I swear to God, I will never talk to you again." She looked him dead in the eye. "Got it?"

It took him a long, tense moment to reply. But then he gave a sharp nod. "Got it."

She gave a sharp nod back. "Good." And this time when she pressed her mouth to his, she didn't pull away.

Neither did Ben. The hand that he'd used to threaten Josh now clasped her neck, pulling her closer, holding her face to his, keeping her there as his lips stole her breath and his tongue plundered her mouth.

Ben did not stop kissing her. Not when Josh's hands found her outer thighs, and not when, using deft strokes, Josh caressed her legs, pushing her dress up over her hips as he did so.

Goose bumps covered her entire body. His hands felt so damn incredible.

Then she remembered Josh's promise: *When you come, know who gave you this orgasm.*

Orgasm?

Dear God, he's gonna make me come.

While I kiss Ben.

The thought made her shiver.

The shiver made Ben try to pull away to snarl at Josh.

Damn it, she should have known Ben wouldn't yield to Josh's presence easily.

Too freaking bad. He'd held the strings to their relationship for the last year. Now they sat in her hand. She had control. She tugged his head back down to hers and kissed him.

Josh rolled her thong over her hips and pushed it down her legs.

He didn't.

God, yes, he did!

The warm breeze fluttering over her nude pussy proved it. She kicked off the thong, groaning into Ben's mouth, pressing her breasts into his chest, her nipples tight, aching beads that longed for a man's touch, a man's wet mouth …

Ben kissed her harder, more passionately, and she groaned again as Josh launched his attack. He spread the cheeks of her arse and pressed his dick in close.

Damn his shorts. She didn't want all that material between them. She wanted his bare, pulsing shaft buried in her arse.

"Next time I make love to you," Josh whispered, "I'm taking you right...here." He thrust once, so his erection rubbed very lightly over her hole.

Sienna nearly fainted from lust.

Josh in her arse? Dear God. She wanted that.

Ben growled into her mouth and broke the kiss again.

"No," Sienna objected vehemently. "Kiss me. Don't stop kissing me. Ever."

Blessedly, Ben obliged.

She needed Ben's kisses like she needed air. Didn't he know that? Hadn't he always known that?

Josh drew his fingers over her pussy. Possessively. Knowingly. He ran his fingers from her clit downwards over her pussy lips, pausing only to dip inside for a second.

"I'm taking you here too," Josh promised as he scooped up the cream that spilled from her channel.

Ben swore viciously as Sienna groaned into his mouth.

"Shh," she soothed, kissing him, stroking her tongue over his until once again Ben took control of the kiss. Ah, she loved it when Ben took control.

And a good thing he did, because Josh used her cream to moisten the cleft between her arse cheeks, providing just the slightest lubrication so he could slide his finger against her anus. When he did it once, Sienna forgot she was kissing Ben. When he did it again, she attacked Ben's mouth with frenzied greed.

Holy heck, it felt good. Freakishly good. So good she could come just like this.

It was Ben who eased her into a less desperate kiss, a more arousing one.

Sienna doubted she'd ever been this turned on in her entire life. Even with her mouth plastered to Ben's, she could smell the scent of her own arousal.

She widened her stance, moaned Josh's name in Ben's mouth.

"*Ben*," her ex-fiancé growled. "*My* name, not his." And he kissed her again.

Josh swept his fingers across her pussy again and again as he caressed her arse with his erection.

Dear God, she wanted that cock inside her. Wanted Josh inside her.

And Ben too.

Then she moaned Ben's name as Ben's thumbs brushed

over her nipples. He'd slipped them in under her sleeveless dress, and because she was braless—deliberately braless, as Josh had requested—there was nothing between her flesh and Ben's touch.

Holy fuck.

She was moaning both of their names. Ben's and Josh's. Kissing Ben while Josh fucked her with his fingers.

Okay, not fucked. Caressed. Aroused. Seduced. Delighted.

Just as Ben's thumbs delighted her nipples.

And meters away, in the exclusive Club Evoke, music began to flow, seeping through the walls and doors as a song she'd never heard before played. She knew the voice that sang, though. Recognized the tones instantly, muted though they were. Aussie rock star, Nick Blackthorne.

How was it possible she recognized the voice of a rock star with no problem whatsoever, yet had trouble identifying the voice of the man she'd lived with for eight years?

It didn't make sense.

Nothing made sense to her. Not anymore. How could it, when she stood between two men who fed her desire, her needs, her basic, primal lusts? Kissed and caressed her in public.

Not one man.

Two!

She couldn't think straight. Stopped trying. She simply felt. Josh's hands. Ben's kisses. Josh's erection. Ben's fingers.

"Remember who gave you this orgasm," Josh whispered, so softly it might have been the whistle of the breeze. When he penetrated her with two fingers, time stood still.

One second she was aroused and aware, the next she was nothing more than a euphoric body, swept away on an exquisite tide of rhapsody. A tide that sent wave upon wave of rapture through her. Over her. Consumed her.

And she let it. Let it carry her away. Far, far away from choices she didn't want to make.

If she was just a floating, rapturous being, then she needn't choose. She could have them both.

Ben and Josh.

Josh and Ben.

Couldn't she?

Chapter Eight

Josh adjusted his shorts as subtly as possible, hoping the other man wouldn't notice the dire situation in which he found himself. Horny as fucking hell and no way to get his release.

No such luck. The soft sneer told Josh that Ben knew exactly what he was going through.

Christ, what had he done? Stripped Sienna in public? Finger-fucked her? And all while she kissed her dickhead fiancé?

Josh hated to admit it, but it was the damn kiss that had prompted him to finger Sienna in the first place. The damn kiss she'd shared with her ex that had given him the erection from hell. Watching Sienna kiss Ben had been a huge, freaking turn-on.

It shouldn't have been. It should have made his cock shrivel up and die. It should have made him want her less. It hadn't.

He needed to come, needed relief. Or he needed to pick a fight with the dickhead fiancé so he had something to concentrate other than the frustration.

No, he couldn't do that. Not to Sienna. Sienna had stopped the fight Ben had tried to initiate. Pity. He'd have liked nothing more than to slam his fist into the dickhead's face.

Sienna still shook with the force of her climax. Ben held her in his arms, supporting her, keeping her upright.

Josh stood behind her, uselessly.

Why was he standing there? Why didn't he get the hell away from the couple? Leave them to sort out their differences and get on with their life together, like Ben wanted?

It would be the right thing to do. The gentlemanly thing to

do.

Fuck that. Josh didn't want to be a gentleman. For five years he'd stayed on the sidelines, never feeling worthy of Sienna. Now that he finally did, he couldn't just give her up. He'd fought too hard to become the man he was today. Fighting was in his nature. And damn it, he was going to fight for the woman.

Something incredible had happened between him and Sienna today. Their years of wanting each other as kids had mysteriously translated into a recipe of instant compatibility as adults.

Compatibility? Hell. Never mind big fancy words. Josh was falling for her like a ton of bricks.

Josh couldn't back down. He owed himself this opportunity. And she was worth fighting for.

He just couldn't throw that first punch. He'd have to fight in other ways. More...genteel ways.

He bent down and patted the ground around Sienna's feet, locating her thong. Kneeling behind her, he coaxed first her one ankle up and then the other, helping her to slip her underwear back on. He tugged the panties up the endless length of her legs and over her hips.

He shouldn't do it—he knew he shouldn't—but he couldn't stop himself from swiping a finger over her naked pussy one more time, feeling her swollen, puffy lips.

She convulsed again, a kind of aftershock, and a fresh drop of her juice moistened his finger.

With a groan, Josh put the finger in his mouth and sucked it clean.

Fuck, she tasted incredible. Like blue gum honey and double thick cream.

If Ben hadn't been there, Josh would have placed his mouth on her pussy and eaten her out, right then and there.

But Ben was there, so Josh adjusted the thong until it fit correctly, then pushed the hemline of her dress down until Sienna was once again properly dressed.

He straightened his legs, still standing behind her, but he kept his distance. If he brushed his dick against her arse, even once, he'd lose control and come in his damned pants.

Ben sneered at him again, then spoke to Sienna,

murmuring in her ear in golden tones.

Yeah, he might be whispering, but Josh was close enough to hear every word, and the arsehole had to know it.

"I love you, Si," Ben said and closed his eyes.

Shit. Even Josh could identify the sincerity in his dulcet voice. Could hear the longing and the affection.

"I love you too, Ben C," Sienna told him, her voice hoarse and roughened from her orgasm. Or could it be from her confession? "You know I do."

The words stabbed straight into Josh's heart, blinding him with pain.

"I miss you. So much. Miss talking to you. Holding you when we sleep. Making love to you. *With* you." Ben cleared his throat. "What I wouldn't do to strip you, right now, feel your naked skin against mine, your juices wetting my finger." He groaned, a soft erotic sound that made Sienna shiver. "And my cock. I wanna be inside you, baby. So damn much, it hurts."

Sienna gave a sexy whimper.

Jesus, Josh should not find Ben's words arousing. He should not be imagining Ben inside Sienna. But he was, and the image made his shaft throb even harder.

What the hell? The dickhead had had eight years to put his cock in Sienna. Josh resented every day of every one of those eight years. Resented every time Ben had been inside her.

Resented? Hell, he fucking hated it. And yet here he was getting aroused at the thought. Fuckwit.

"I love watching you come, baby," Ben said. "Love when you get excited like you just did. I wanna make you come again. Wanna spend the rest of your life making you come."

Josh felt an overwhelming need to do exactly the same thing. Keep Sienna in his life always. Keep her happy. Keep her satisfied. Keep her coming, over and over again.

Him, not Ben.

No matter how goddamn much the idea of Ben fucking her turned him on, Josh wanted to be the only man making love to her.

Fuck this. He couldn't let Ben win. Couldn't let Sienna walk away when they'd barely had a chance to be together. He wasn't ready to lose her—they'd only just found each other again.

With no thought of hesitation, he stepped in close, slid his finger beneath Sienna's skirt and slipped it straight into her panties.

Her body welcomed the invasion with a jolt and a shudder. Not for a second did she tense or pull away. If anything, she relaxed almost instantly into his touch, twisting her hips once, enveloping his finger with her pussy.

As Ben continued to seduce her with his husky voice and romantic promises, Josh fingered Sienna until cream soaked her thong and her breath came in short gasps.

He fingered her while Ben urged her to return home. He fingered her while Ben spoke about wedding bells and fucking white picket fences. And he fingered her as Ben told her how much he fucking loved her.

He fingered her until Sienna was convulsing all over, coming on his hand, trapping his finger inside her, holding it there, refusing to surrender it to him. And when her pussy relaxed once again in post-orgasmic lethargy, he fingered her arse, gently. So damn gently, but it was all Sienna needed. Her climax was harder than before, and longer, and Josh wished to God it was his cock and not his finger inside her.

So focused was Josh on her orgasms, he failed to notice that Ben had quit talking. It was only when Sienna finally gasped for him to please stop that the silence permeated his concentration.

Josh glared at Ben. Ben glared at Josh.

Josh leaned forward, his gaze on Ben, his mouth at Sienna's ear. "You ready to walk away from me, princess?"

Her response was instantaneous. "God, no!" And then her knees must have given way because she simply crumpled.

Ben caught her, as he should have since he was holding her, and swung her up so her legs hung over one arm and her shoulders nestled into the other.

She sighed contentedly in his arms, and although jealousy struck deep in his gut, a smug satisfaction washed over Josh. He was the one who'd given her that contentedness.

"It seems we have a problem." Ben sounded...sad? Dismayed? Determined? "A big problem. But," he murmured, as if he didn't want to say what he was about to, "I may just have a solution."

Ben was a strategist at heart. Planning was his forte:

setting goals and exploring different avenues to achieve those goals. Mapping out every possible course of action and every possible repercussion. It was what gave him the edge at work. Made him succeed time and time again.

Over the last three months, he'd had one primary goal: winning Sienna back. He'd done what he did in any complex situation. Examined the situation, assessed the shortcomings, outlined his goals and priorities, and then set his plan in motion.

Which was why after four weeks of heavy negotiation, Ben now stood at Sienna's feet, begging her to come home. But he'd made a fatal error. He'd failed to take all the variables of their break-up into account. Ben hadn't anticipated Sienna would meet another man this quickly.

Now he had no choice. He had to restrategize, and he had to do it on the spot, under pressure. And the worst part of all? Plan B had to include that other man.

Did he want to share Sienna with Josh? *Fuck, no.*

Did he want to lose her to him? *Again, no.*

But Sienna wasn't letting go of Josh anytime soon. She'd made that perfectly clear. The only solution? Compromise. Work with Josh rather than risk losing the woman he loved.

Damn it, he could barely breathe as he looked at her. As he considered sharing her. Love for Sienna welled in his chest, constricting his lungs and his heartbeat.

She'd lost weight, felt different in his arms. But she still smelled like the woman he loved. Like roses in summer. Like a breath of fresh air. With her he felt like a whole man and not the hollow ghost he'd become after she left.

What kind of an idiot had he been letting her get away? How could he have been so involved with work that he'd failed to notice just how discontented Sienna had become?

He'd taken her for granted. Assumed she'd be there through thick and thin. Assumed, that like him, she was in it for life.

He'd failed to see that the life he'd promised her was not the life they were leading. He'd failed to see that while he flourished and grew in his job, she shriveled and faded in their home.

She'd tried to make it work. Begged him to spend time with her. Begged him to reduce his hours. Begged him for a holiday.

A weekend. An evening. An hour.

He hadn't given it to her. Any of it. Selfishly assuming she was as content as he.

Her graphic design business was thriving, therefore she should be thriving. Only she wasn't. She was withering. Dying inside. And so was their relationship.

Coming home to Sienna at the end of every day was coming home to a little piece of heaven. Coming home to an empty flat was a vicious, cold shock that chilled Ben to the bone. Flayed him. Beat him senseless. Or maybe, finally beat some sense into him.

Life without Sienna was not a life worth living. She was his life, his everything. He needed her back. Needed her like he needed air.

The woman he loved had come to life tonight. Electrified the very air he breathed. Only she'd come to life at another man's touch—or imagined touch—and the comprehension nearly brought him to his knees.

Sienna, coming for someone else. Sienna, orgasming with someone else. Sienna, moaning another man's name.

Fuck, it hurt. Burned so bad, Ben knew there'd be scars.

But it didn't change the fact that for the first time in almost a year, Sienna was the same wildfire she'd been before Ben had destroyed her happiness. And if Josh Whatever-his-name-was was responsible, so be it. Ben wasn't above using him to get what he wanted: Sienna.

He'd had to do a quick recon and alteration of his strategy, but so be it.

Quietly and calmly, Ben outlined his plan.

Not so quietly or calmly, Sienna jumped out of his arms. She stood on her own two feet, her jaw hanging open in disbelief. "All three of us?" she squeaked.

Although every muscle in his body yelled at him not to, Ben nodded, answering Sienna's question. "All three of us."

"At the same time?" Another squeak.

"That depends. Are you going to let him—" *use his name, show respect,* "—Josh walk away just because I've come to the island?" Ben fervently prayed the answer would be yes but knew better.

Sienna studied Ben for a long moment before shaking her

head. "No."

"Then, yes," Ben said serenely, although that was about the last thing he felt. Jealous, aroused, angry, frustrated, desperate... "At the same time."

She must have reached out behind her to touch Josh, because the other man, who currently stood leaning against the bench, his butt resting on the side and his arms crossed over his chest, reached one hand out to her. "I'm right behind you, princess."

Sienna's shoulders seemed to lose their tension.

Christ, Josh spoke with such confidence, such composure, if Ben were Sienna he'd also feel reassured.

But he wasn't Sienna. He was Sienna's fiancé—damn it all, *ex*-fiancé—and he was facing her current lover. Ben didn't know Josh, but he hated the guy. Hated him with a fierce repugnance that made bile rise in his throat. If he could hit him, he would. Without a second thought. Pound the crap out of him. But Sienna would despise him for it, and Sienna already despised him enough.

Her relaxation at Josh's reassurance was exactly what Ben had considered when he'd made his absurd suggestion. The obvious attraction and comfort that flared between the woman he loved and a man he despised.

He shouldn't be aroused, but thinking about Sienna between himself and Josh, both of them fucking her, had his skin tingling.

It wasn't just about the threesome. It was about Sienna. About getting inside her again. Becoming a part of her again. Making her a part of him again.

It was about making love to her so he could make her love him again.

Damn it, he needed her love. Depended on it. He wasn't the same without Sienna.

"Y-you'd be willing to share me?" Sienna's voice quavered with emotion.

What was he hearing? Disbelief? Hurt? Shock? Excitement? Yep, that about summed it up.

Ben braced his shoulders. "Forever? No." *No fucking way.* "For a night? Yes." For a night he could deal. He could enjoy— maybe. Most importantly he could convince Sienna Josh wasn't right for her.

Ben was.

"I..." Her voice trailed off. She raised her free hand in the air, dropped it and shrugged helplessly.

"I know this is hard for you, Si," Ben soothed. "I know you didn't expect me to appear on the island." He'd shocked the hell out of her, no doubt about it. "And I know you're—" Shit, he couldn't say it without almost choking. "I know you're trying to move on. But please. Give us a chance. Give me a chance. Don't throw away eight years without at least trying one more time."

She gaped at him. "And my sleeping with you and Josh, at the same time, will be giving us a chance how, exactly?"

Fair enough question. "You like him. I can see that." It made Ben want to kill the other man. Want to wrap his fingers around Josh's neck and squeeze. Hard. "Asking you to give him up would probably make you hate me."

He took a deep breath, tried his damndest to prevent Sienna from seeing how much his suggestion actually worried him. How threatened Josh made him feel. "I won't ask that of you, Si. So this is an alternative. A good one. Take us both. Have us both. At the same time. Compare. See which of us makes you happier. Decide which of us you want more. This way, you hold the power. It'll be in your hands, completely. He...*Josh* and I will be at your mercy. We'll do whatever you want." He lowered his tone, keeping his voice husky, the way he knew always turned Sienna on. "We'll fuck you however you want us to. We'll make you come however many times you need to come." Sienna came a lot. For her, foreplay and sex were never about chasing that one big climax. It was all about a series of small explosions. One quick orgasm followed by another and another and another. "We will cater to your every whim and fantasy, be whatever you want us to be, so you can make a decision."

"That's quite an offer you're making on my behalf," Josh said softly, dangerously.

Ben shifted his gaze from Sienna to Josh. The man looked...lethal.

Ben raised a brow. Legally, he couldn't strangle the guy, but he could fight him on a different level. "You don't want to cater to her every whim and fantasy?" he asked pleasantly.

"Are those Sienna's whims and fantasies you're talking

about, or your own?" Josh asked, just as suavely.

"My fantasies of Sienna have never included a third wheel." Ben gave him an agreeable smile. "My feelings for her, however, insist I consider it for the first time."

"Your...feelings?" Josh prompted.

"I love her, she loves me." No denying that. Josh would have heard her say it out loud just moments ago. "I won't leave here without knowing I've done everything in my power to get her back." He twisted his lips in a frown, couldn't help himself. "But you're not backing off either, and Sienna doesn't want you to go anywhere." *Fuck, fuck, fuck.* "Which leaves one, two, three of us," Ben counted off on his fingers. "A threesome."

"That's assuming I want to have a threesome with you," Josh said, just as dangerously as before.

Screw the gentleman act. "Mate, you had your dick buried against my fiancée's naked arse, while she kissed *me*. You and I both know that had Sienna given you the okay, you would have buried it *inside* her arse without a second thought. So don't feed me your crap about me and threesomes."

Sienna moaned softly between them.

Ben diverted his attention back to her, ran his hand over her cheek. Her skin burned, heat seeped into his palm.

Aroused. Sienna was aroused.

"You like that idea, don't you, baby? The thought of Josh buried in your arse?"

She didn't answer, but her breath quickened.

Hell, yeah, she liked the idea. "Now imagine Josh buried in your arse—and me sliding into your pussy."

She whimpered.

Blood flowed straight to his cock, so fast it made him dizzy. If Sienna wasn't the most responsive lover imaginable, the most open-minded... There wasn't a single suggestion he'd made she'd rejected. No, she'd taken every one of them and run with it.

Toys? Hell, yeah.

Blowjobs in change rooms? More than a few times.

A quickie in the garden at a dinner party? Okay, only twice.

Dress-up? Sienna liked the schoolteacher outfit the most.

She'd even been willing to try a little BDSM but had laughed too much for that to be successful. They'd enjoyed the props they'd purchased for the attempt though. The restraints and the whips and the feathers. Enjoyed them thoroughly. And regularly.

The suggestion of a threesome? Not something he'd have ever made to her before. But times had changed. Circumstances were different.

Sienna wasn't. She was willing to run with it, just like she'd been willing to run with the other suggestions. Willing and excited.

"Imagine Josh in your arse while I lick your pussy," he told her softly. "Or me in your arse while he licks your pussy." Jesus, he wanted to be in her arse. And in her pussy. Wanted to lick her clit. Taste her cream. He didn't care who else was there, so long as Sienna was aroused. So long as Sienna wanted him there.

Okay, so he did care who else was there, and under other circumstances he wouldn't allow another man near her. But tonight...just tonight, he'd do whatever it took to get back into bed with Sienna.

"Do you want that, princess?" Josh had stolen closer without Ben realizing it. "You want me to make love to you at the same time as Ben does?"

Sienna began to shake. Full-on tremors racked her body. Sienna only shook like this when she was fully turned on and trying to repress it.

"D-do you?" she asked Josh, her voice a breathless rasp.

"I want *you*, princess. You know that. So if this is what you want, then..." He hesitated, squared his shoulders. "Then I'm willing to try it." He stepped even closer. "But it has to be your call."

Sienna didn't answer, but she shuddered violently beneath Ben's hand.

Seconds ticked past. Sienna shuddered again.

"Is it what you want, baby?" Ben asked.

In answer, she reached for his hand, which still rested on her cheek, and pulled it downward. Without saying a word, she lowered his hand to her thigh, then pushed it up under her skirt.

Ben needed no further urging. He shoved her thong aside and slid his finger over her clit.

Sienna whimpered out loud, her body a quivering mess.

He slid the same digit deep inside her, or tried to anyway. What he didn't expect, was to find another finger already in there.

Josh!

Ben looked at Josh. Josh looked at Ben.

Fuck, he hated the man. *Hated him.*

Josh pulled out of Sienna. So did Ben.

The hatred did not stop the heat that filled Ben's balls. Did not slow the flow of blood to his cock.

Josh pushed back inside. Ben did the same, matching his pace to Josh's. He didn't mean to match his pace, but for Sienna's sake it was a good thing.

Josh must have realized it as well, because before he slid his finger out again, he nodded once at Ben, prompting him.

They moved together.

Sienna yelped, the sound yanking on Ben's dick, making it even harder—if that were possible.

Together, he and Josh dipped back inside Sienna, then withdrew. Once, twice, more.

"You doing okay, baby?" Ben asked.

He needn't have bothered. Sienna's pussy was soaked through. Her skin was covered in goose bumps and her breath was coming a million miles an hour. Just like it always did when she was on the verge of orgasming.

"Is this what you want, princess?"

"Yes. God, yes!" And with that, Sienna came, emitting a soft wail as she convulsed. The walls of her pussy clamped around the two fingers inside her, trapping them there, together.

Chapter Nine

The party would have to wait. Meeting Kylie's lovers would have to take place tomorrow. Mack and Aidan she could see anytime. As the last flutters of pleasure washed through her, Sienna turned around and walked away. Back to her room.

Back to the balcony where she'd sucked Josh until he'd exploded in her mouth. The same balcony where he'd knelt before her and licked her into dizzying ecstasy. Three times over. Back to the sheets that smelled of sex. Back to the room where she had slowly begun to fall for Josh...again.

Only this time she wasn't going back to the room with just Josh. Ben came as well. Did she want that? Did she want Ben back in her life? God, she didn't know.

Her heart raced, her pulse drumming in her ears.

Ben. Ben was here. Wonderful, adoring Ben.

The Ben she'd loved so dearly for so long. Not the aloof businessman she'd lived with for a year. Ben. Her Ben.

She wanted him physically. Wanted him in her pussy and in her arse, right alongside Josh, just as he'd suggested. No question about it. There'd never been any question about her desire for Ben. She's always wanted him. But back forever? It was too soon to tell.

If only his presence didn't suffuse her like an aphrodisiac. His scent, his voice, his body, they all combined to reduce her to a quivering mass of need. Of want. Of yearning and lust.

She desired Ben as much as she hungered for Josh. Or maybe she desired Josh as much as she hungered for Ben. More like she wanted them both, equally—and at the same time.

Sienna pushed open the door to her bungalow and tugged

the dress over her head, tossing it to the floor. Her sodden, useless thong followed seconds later.

Both men stood behind her, watching. She could feel the heat of their gazes on her back, making her spine tingle. They'd followed her wordlessly across the resort, their footsteps a soft whisper on the lush island grass.

Naked and aroused she headed straight for the bed. She would have drawn back the covers and thrown them aside if strong arms hadn't grabbed her from behind and hauled her around, straight into a bone-melting kiss. Magic sparked through the room.

Josh. Definitely.

How she'd been unable to tell the difference earlier defied her. His scent was so different from Ben's. Ben smelled of expensive, spicy cologne. Josh carried the scent of the island—eucalyptus and fresh air.

She buried her fingers in his silken locks—his long, silken locks, so unlike Ben's short-cropped hair—and tugged him closer. He clasped her butt cheeks and pulled her flush against him so her clit rubbed against the front of his pants, right over his rock-hard erection, making her giddy with need.

The light growth of his beard tickled her lips. So different from the eternally clean-shaven Ben in every way. Yet both men made her burn. Made her pulse race and her flesh hum. Both had the power to take her breath away and make her heart sing.

Or weep.

Josh kneaded her flesh, rolling his fingers over her buttocks, massaging, caressing, pushing her clit harder against his dick. She let him, moved willingly with him, lifted one leg so she could change the angle, get his erection to rub just so.

Josh. Childhood crush, adult fantasy. A real-life hero. Her savior. She couldn't get enough of him.

Seconds before an orgasm overwhelmed her, Ben plucked her from his arms and pulled her into his own, kissing her as feverishly as Josh had.

His shirt was gone, the formal button-up lying in a heap somewhere on the floor. His bare chest rubbed against her breasts, the dark mat of hair there scraping against the tender flesh of her nipples, driving her insane.

God, Ben. He felt so damn good. So damn real. He was

there. With her. The man she'd loved her entire adult life. Her best friend. Her lover. Her fiancé.

Her throat clogged with emotion. She'd missed him. Every minute of every day. His absence had left a gaping hole in her life. A bottomless pit of loneliness, and now he was there. With her. Again.

She ran her hands over the thick muscles in his arms, up over his shoulders. So broad. So secure. She'd always felt safe, protected when leaning against those massive shoulders.

She still did, although not quite so safe as she once had. The trust and the security had been ripped away. Finding it again, in its wholeness, would take a while.

What wouldn't take a while was her utter sexual surrender to him. She could never refuse Ben. Never wanted to. Physically, she couldn't wait to give herself to him. Emotionally...they'd have to see.

He'd undone his belt and pants so they gaped open. The thickened ridge of his penis rode against her pussy, just like Josh's had. Only the soft cotton of his boxers was more giving then Josh's shorts. More flexible, and within seconds the climax that had begun in Josh's arms peaked in Ben's.

Quick and breathtaking, it flew through her, leaving her panting and boneless.

Ben carried her to the bed, laid her down on her back and lay beside her. Not once did he release her mouth. He kissed her as though he never wanted to let her go. Kissed with a soul-searing intensity. A chocolate-flavored delight that would have usurped her entire heart, her entire being, if Josh hadn't chosen that moment to remind her of what they'd shared just hours before.

"Enjoy his kiss, princess." Josh knelt between her legs. He was naked. Beautifully naked. He must have stripped when Ben had her full attention. "But don't mistake his mouth for the one that's about to show you fireworks." And with nothing more than that warning, he hooked the backs of her knees over his shoulders, leaned forward and buried his nose between her thighs.

A sigh of untold pleasure burst from her lips.

As Ben kissed her, Josh made love to her pussy, licking, nibbling, adoring—just like Ben did with her mouth.

Bliss, sweet and hot, spread like fire through her cells. The nerves in her pussy danced, delighting in Josh's attention to detail. They spun in dizzying circles, reaching higher, harder, faster for that pinnacle of ecstasy.

When Josh flattened his tongue against her clit and laved her, firmly, seductively, those nerves found their target, triggering an exquisite orgasm.

She groaned into Ben's mouth as waves of rapture undulated through her. He kissed her through each delicious convulsion, and she kissed him back, his chocolaty flavor the perfect accompaniment to the sin of Josh's mouth.

"My turn to taste you, baby," Ben whispered when he finally pulled away, and Josh reluctantly ceded to him.

Ben buried his head between her legs and welcomed her home. Whether it was Josh's incredible foreplay, the heat of Ben's attack, the expertise of both men's tongues, or the sheer familiarity of Ben's kiss, Sienna could not be sure. But the second his mouth touched her pussy, she came.

Screaming.

Josh captured her lips with his, inhaling her screams. As his mouth caught hers, the magic sparked between them. He kissed her and kissed her and kissed her, and he would have carried on kissing her had Ben not finally lifted his head and spoken.

"Si," Ben said, and Sienna broke the kiss to look at him. His lips were wet—from her juices—and his eyes dark as night, desire turning them almost black. "Tell us what you want. You're in control, baby. Lead us."

Josh nodded, murmuring in her ear. "I'll follow wherever you take us."

The only trouble with their request was that it meant Sienna had to talk, and since she was a raging mass of hormones, a multi-pleasured sack of bones, speech was not all that easy.

"F-first, kiss me," she told Ben. Knowing she'd need to say only the bare minimum to tell him her needs, she added, "Then flip me over."

Ben was all over her, his lips on hers, his tongue in her mouth. He tasted different now, less like chocolate, more like her. More like Josh had tasted. He tasted sinful. Made her heart fill and her pussy throb.

"J-Josh too…" she pleaded.

Ben nodded once and let Josh take her mouth.

"Generous," Josh murmured with an appreciative nod, before consuming her thoughts with his kiss.

And when Sienna was once again a quivering, mindless mass, Ben took control. "Roll over, baby."

He placed his hands on her hips, helping her flip over. Sienna moved willingly, quickly. Well, as quickly as she could in her mindless state. Josh still lay on the bed, and she knelt on all fours between his legs, crouching down low with her arse in the air and her elbows on either side of Josh's hips.

Her head was centimeters from Josh's erection, and she couldn't help but notice the way he fisted his hands in the doona, his knuckles whitening every time she exhaled.

She'd opened herself up completely for Ben, just the way he liked. Just the way she liked.

Ben skirted around the bed. At some point he'd lost the rest of his clothes, and Sienna's breath caught as she saw him in all his naked glory. Saw every line of his ripped body, every inch of flesh she'd loved so thoroughly.

And then he was out of sight, standing behind her. He swallowed, audibly. "Ah, fuck, Si!" He sounded mindless. "I missed this. Missed you. So goddamned much." He fell silent as once again he buried his face between her legs, this time licking her pussy from behind.

God help her, Sienna loved it when Ben went down on her this way. Loved what he did with his tongue. And his lips. And his fingers.

Oh, God. Those fingers!

When her mind cleared from yet another bone-melting orgasm, and her vision returned to normal, the sight she beheld made her mouth water. The tip of Josh's dick had beaded with precome and the vein on his shaft pulsed wildly. She really didn't have a choice in the matter. She was going to have to lick him.

He tasted good. Bitter and salty and so damn sexy. An addictive taste. Nothing like the chocolaty sweetness of Ben. This was far more elemental, far more dangerous.

She tasted some more. And then a little more. Only it wasn't just the tip of his cock she tasted now, it was the shaft too. The long, hard shaft. As much of the long hard shaft as she could get into her mouth.

Josh groaned. A low, animalistic sound.

And Ben licked her arse.

Holy fuck. He licked her arse.

Swept his tongue right over her anus. He did it again, clasping her butt cheeks and pulling them apart so he could get better access. Then he licked her pussy, but he didn't stop there. He continued up, licking his way back to her arse, where he paused to ream her hole, tickle it, delight it, before heading back to her clit.

Torture, sweet, torture.

Everyone should know such torture. She swirled her own tongue around Josh's shaft, licked him from root to tip and swallowed him whole. With his cock as deep in her mouth as she could take him, and Ben's tongue in her arse, no, her pussy, no...her arse, Sienna came again.

She rode Ben's tongue, thrusting her hips against his head as waves of sheer bliss ebbed through her. Seconds passed, maybe even minutes, before the orgasm floated away, before Ben pulled away, and Sienna returned her attention to Josh. She pushed her hair out of her face and looked up at him as she sucked his scrumptious cock.

He looked back at her, his emerald green gaze glazed. Desire seeped from his eyes. As did something else. Something...sad. Something that grabbed her heart and squeezed tight, leaving behind an answering melancholy.

Even as her body reverberated with the surplus pleasure of Ben's expertise, her heart shuddered, telling her something wasn't one hundred percent right. Josh, as aroused as he might be, was not altogether okay with what the three of them did.

It was up to her to make it okay, to make it as good for him as it was for her. Up to her to remind Josh that the island air had cast its spell around them. That the magic hadn't dimmed one iota since Ben had joined them. She sucked a little harder, swirled her tongue around and around.

"Damn, princess, your lips..." His words were lost as he threw his head back and surged into her mouth.

She relaxed her suction, let Josh take control. He thrust gently. So gently, but she had no doubt he was setting the pace. And she freaking loved it. She'd spend the whole night with her lips wrapped around his cock if she didn't know there were better things waiting for her. For them.

She was on her knees. Ben was in the room with them. There were definitely better things on the horizon.

As the thought crossed her mind, the bed dipped behind her.

Ben was back. He settled between her thighs like he had a million times before this. Only Josh had never been in her mouth any of those million times. His presence intensified her arousal exponentially. No matter how many times she and Ben had made love, she'd never, ever felt this alive. This sexy. This...adored.

The decadence of it, the illicitness, combined to send a thrill careening through Sienna's belly.

Something brushed against her pussy.

Not just something. Ben's cock.

Lord, it felt familiar, pressing against her lips, prodding her entrance.

He felt familiar, perched between her legs, his hands holding her hips.

Josh didn't. Not yet. But who needed familiar when the man's very touch kindled desires Sienna never knew she had?

Again she glanced up at Josh. Caught the look in his eyes at the exact moment Ben entered her. Saw the pain and the anger flash across his face. Saw the lusty gaze turn even hazier.

Josh's cock grew in her mouth. Miniscule, but enough for her to confirm that was desire she'd seen flare in his eyes. Desire and...jealousy?

Shit, she didn't want him to be jealous. He didn't need to be. She'd fallen for Josh all over again. Hard and fast. She should tell him that, should let him know. But...she couldn't concentrate. Not when Ben slid inside her, seating himself to the hilt in her pussy. Moaning her name.

Ben.

Ben was back. Where he was supposed to be. Where he should always have been. Where he belonged.

Inside her.

The sense of familiarity was so overwhelming, tears filled her eyes, and one slipped out before she could stop it. She tightened her mouth around Josh, tried to give to him as much intense pleasure as Ben gave her, but she knew it was a losing battle when the walls of her pussy began to convulse and bliss blinded her momentarily.

How many times had she come already? How could she possibly come again? Her body should be worn out. Overwhelmed. Pleasured beyond human capacity.

Apparently it wasn't, as Sienna witnessed not half a minute later.

Something cold, wet and slippery touched her bottom, and with Josh still in her mouth and Ben still in her pussy, a finger slipped past the tight muscles of her anus and into her arse.

She shuddered in ecstasy.

"Jesus, Si, I have to have you here. Have to take you." Ben pulled his finger from her arse and his dick from her pussy. When he pressed back close, it was his cock at her arse.

Had she not been near mindless and muscle-less from the seven thousand preceding orgasms, Ben's thrust might have hurt. It didn't. Mild discomfort was all she felt before he seated himself fully inside her arse. They'd made love like this too many times before for his actions to be painful.

This time however, Sienna knew it would not have been half as good if Josh's cock were not in her mouth. If he wasn't leaking copious amounts of delicious precome. She would not have been aroused even a quarter as much.

The taste of him, the feel of him, the knowledge that he hadn't walked away when Ben popped up so unexpectedly, warmed her heart. Filled her belly with a gazillion butterflies. And suddenly she didn't want just Ben inside her. She wanted Josh there too. Needed him there.

Kissing his shaft ever so wickedly, she looked up at him again. "Josh," she rasped, her throat almost incapable of forming the words.

"Princess," he rasped right back.

"Make love to me. Please." She'd meant to tease him with her words, tempt him, but the longing in her voice echoed through her ears.

He bit his lip. "You sure you want this? You want us both?"

"One hundred percent sure." She might well die if he didn't make love to her right now.

Josh nodded. Slowly. Like Ben thrust. Slowly.

"Condoms are next to the bed," Ben said.

Josh nodded again. He knew. He'd left them there earlier.

Sienna watched him reach over for a packet, tear it open and roll the condom over his shaft. She had a bird's-eye view. Josh pumped his hand up and down said shaft in time to Ben's thrusts inside her.

The sight was so incredibly arousing, a gush of cream pooled in her pussy.

Dear God, how could she be more aroused than she already was? How could she want more than Ben was giving her?

How could she want them both?

She didn't have any answers. She just knew she did.

"Fuck me, Josh," she pleaded, not wanting to wait one more second to get his cock inside her.

She should be nervous. Should be worried. He was bigger than Ben. Significantly bigger. And Ben was already inside her. Filling her arse. How could she take Josh in as well?

The question was, how could she not? Her pussy felt empty. Achy. Hollow. Something was missing.

Josh was missing. She pulled at his legs, insisting he shuffle down the bed, inserting himself beneath her. It took a couple seconds of awkward maneuvering, all three of them seeking a more comfortable position, but finally he was there. Under her. His mouth level with hers, his dick below her pussy. And Ben was behind her, inside her.

Josh hadn't let go of his shaft, she realized. His hand was still wrapped around it, and he used that hand to tap the tip of his cock on her clit.

Holy fuck. That felt unbelievable.

"Kiss me," she demanded, and dropped her mouth to his before he could object.

He didn't try. He simply met her mouth with his, let his tongue seek entry between her lips, and kissed her so sweetly, another tear slipped from her eye.

The island air spun its magic web around them.

Ben ran his hand over her back, a feathery tingle down her spine. He thrust into her, over and over, his balls bouncing against her pussy. God, her entire pussy pulsed. Her arse too. A million nerve endings had awoken from deep slumber, just for this moment.

Josh used his hand to glide his cock over her clit, stroking it over and over. It swelled beneath his touch, beneath his cock.

Tingled. Shuddered. Exploded.

The cream in her pussy gushed out, soaking Josh's shaft. Her ass clamped around Ben's dick, and Ben swore loudly as he groaned in pleasure.

While her pussy still pulsed, Josh guided himself to her entrance and pushed inside. He stopped halfway in, panting. His eyes were closed, his mouth clenched in concentration.

"Oh, God. Oh, God," Sienna mumbled, mindless. So much pleasure. So much bliss. It was like a frenzy of orgasms for her.

Full. So full.

Josh thrust into her, his hips coming off the bed.

Ben gasped.

Full, so very, very full. She couldn't move. Didn't try.

"Holy fuck! Josh. Do that again." It wasn't Sienna who moaned the plea. It was Ben.

"Anything for her," Josh groaned. "Anything." He drove into her, seating himself fully inside her.

"Fuck, yeah," Ben rasped hoarsely. He leaned over and kissed her neck.

Sienna felt his action deep, deep, deep inside. So did Josh. He moaned the second Ben moved.

Both of them were seated fully inside her.

Full, so full. So good. Oh, God, so good!

"Your go," Josh told Ben, just a second before he took Sienna's mouth, jut a second before Ben withdrew from her arse. As he began to pump back inside her, Josh withdrew, filling her again only when Ben pulled out.

God, they were fucking her in rhythm, filling her one at a time. In her entire life, Sienna had never been more aroused, more alive. She had never experienced such bone-deep pleasure. Had the world ended right then, Sienna would die a contented, happy woman.

But the world didn't end. It continued to electrify and stimulate, continued to provide rapture beyond her wildest dreams.

Josh's lips on hers, his tongue in her mouth. Ben's hands on her hips, his lips leaving soft kisses down her spine.

Whether they made love to her for a minute or an hour Sienna couldn't tell. Time lost meaning. Her world became a multihued mass of color, reds and greens, violets and pinks, purples and blues, all exploding behind her eyelids.

It was Ben's shout of surrender that made her eyes open.

"Coming," he yelled. "God, help me, I'm coming." He jerked behind her, buried himself in her arse and stilled for a second before his dick began to pump inside her. Over and over, emptying itself. "Hard. Coming so fucking hard," Ben gasped.

Josh continued to fuck her, his thrusts faster than before, deeper.

"Josh, fu-u-uck—" Ben groaned, digging his fingers into her sides. "Si! Feels...so...good." He put his mouth to her throat and sucked intently.

Blood roared in her ears. Josh's movements inside her felt as good to Ben as they did to Sienna? Lord, the knowledge melted her insides, made her go all gooey.

"Princess," Josh moaned, pounding into her. He'd stopped kissing her, lost his coordination the second Ben started to come. "Princess," he moaned again, and then he too was coming, his back arching up off the bed, his cock thrust deep inside her pussy, his hips jerking against hers.

She felt the vibrations of Josh's orgasm ricochet through her inner walls. Felt the last jolts of Ben's release echo in her arse.

Felt her own climax begin, like a million bubbles bursting inside before the explosion. Before a wave of blinding pleasure broke over her, consuming her, pulsing from her pussy outward, enveloping her entire body.

She'd come before, countless times. This was an orgasm like no other, an orgasm strong enough to wipe her out completely. This was the ultimate bliss.

Chapter Ten

Josh stepped out of the shower and wrapped a towel around his waist. His head spun.

What the fuck had just gone down? What had he done?

A sense of self-loathing whirled through his stomach, gaining momentum.

He'd fucked Sienna. While another man did too. It hadn't been about making love. It had been about showing his dominance. About proving he wouldn't walk away, wouldn't give her up. And it left him feeling like a piece of shit.

Yeah, the sex had been unbelievable. Orgasmic-type unbelievable. He doubted he'd ever come harder in his life. And yes, knowing another man was inside Sienna at the same time was a turn-on unlike anything he'd ever imagined before. Her pussy had squeezed him like a velvet glove. Squeezed more come out of his balls then he'd ever have believed possible.

Could he have stopped what he'd been doing and walked away? Hell, no.

Did he enjoy what they'd done? Hell, yeah. Physically anyway.

Psychologically? Not so much. Every shred of common sense had told him not to walk this route. Not to compete for Sienna's attentions. But the boy he'd been, the parentless boy who'd desperately craved love and attention, had refused to listen.

His mother had walked away. He couldn't let Sienna do the same. Not when he'd just found her again. He'd stayed, believing he was fighting for her. But fucking a woman at the same time as she fucked her fiancé was not a fight. It was a debauched, twisted sense of logic. A fucked-up kind of a way of proving he was better than Ben.

He wasn't. A better man would have left. A better man would have let Sienna get back to the life she was born to lead. Not stayed on in case her fiancé proved Josh was the one she wanted.

The self-loathing intensified, made him sick to his stomach.

Yes, he'd fallen hard for Sienna. But he'd called it from the first. He was the rebound guy. Sienna wasn't over Ben. She wasn't ready to move on, and her willingness to jump straight back into bed with her ex proved that.

He should have listened to his gut instinct and left her this afternoon after they'd gone sailing. He shouldn't have gone back to her room, and he shouldn't have made love to her. Not then, and not now.

Sienna was too good for him. She'd always been too good for him, and his willingness to share her just proved that.

He slipped silently out of the bathroom, assuming Sienna and Ben had fallen asleep.

He'd assumed wrong.

Sienna lay in Ben's arms, blissfully unaware of Josh's presence, laughing softly at something Ben had said. Ben smiled at her, a smile that lit up the fucking room.

It killed Josh to admit it, but they looked good. They looked...happy. They fit together, like a couple should. Comfortable in each other's arms. Familiar with each other. In love.

They looked so fucking in love, it tore through Josh's chest, ripping at his heart, slamming it against his ribs, bruising it— forever. The pain hit hard, and the air whooshed from his lungs.

Ben looked up. "You're out of the shower?" he asked, oblivious to Josh's torment. "Cool. I'll use the bathroom." He gave Sienna a long, hot kiss before shifting out of bed and strolling across the room naked.

The second the bathroom door closed, Josh striped off the towel and pulled on his undies and shorts.

Sienna sat up, the sheet covering her from her waist down. Her luscious breasts bounced as she made herself comfortable, and it was all Josh could do to stop himself from jumping right back into bed with her.

He raised his gaze higher, noticing a dark splotch on the

side of Sienna's neck.

Ben had left his mark.

It made Josh want to hit him again, but he stayed his impulses, pulling his shirt on instead.

"You're getting dressed?" Sienna asked, confused.

Josh nodded.

"But...why?"

Christ, her lips were all pouty, begging for a kiss. "I'm going back to my room."

She narrowed her eyes, as if she couldn't understand him. "Why?"

Josh slipped on his Havaianas and sat beside her on the edge of the bed with a heavy sigh. He took her hand, brought it to his mouth and kissed it. "When I was a kid, I had a ridiculous crush on you. You weren't just my nightly wet dream, princess. I loved you my entire way through high school." He breathed, an ache in his chest making the very action almost impossible. "Seeing you again today was a fantasy come to life. A chance to realize every childhood dream I ever had."

"It was my fantasy come true as well," Sienna whispered.

"Thing is..." Josh hesitated, unsure how to verbalize his thoughts. "In all my fantasies, I never once imagined being with you *and* another guy. In my dreams, it was only you and me."

"I know." Sienna blushed, the crimson in her cheeks only making her look lovelier than ever. "I never imagined myself with two men either."

Josh took a deep breath. "I fell in love with you all over again this afternoon."

Her mouth dropped open, forming an O. The rounded lips begged him to seal his confession with a kiss.

Instead he continued speaking. "Fell in love the way a man loves a woman, not the way a kid lusts after a girl."

"Josh," she breathed, but he cut her off.

"I can't do this, Si. I can't share you. I can't pretend I'm okay making love to you while you make love to your fiancé." Razor blades seemed to tear at his throat. "I'm not, and I never will be."

Again Sienna tried to speak, but he placed a finger over her mouth, shushing her. "He loves you, princess. I can see that.

You can see that. He wants you back. And the thing is..." *Deep breath. You can do this.* "The thing is, I think you should go back to him." There he'd said it. And he was still alive. His heart may be shredded, but he'd survived. "You love him too. You have for eight years. He's your fiancé. Your future. Go back to him. Go back to your life."

Sienna stared at him with enormous eyes. Disbelieving eyes. Eyes that filled with tears as he watched.

Okay, yes, he was alive. But maybe that wasn't a good thing. Searing heat filled his lungs. Shooting pains blinded him, and every muscle cried out in defiance as he held himself rigid, refusing himself the pleasure of touching her.

"Y-you're walking away?" she asked, her voice nothing but a peep.

Josh shrugged, and considering the way his muscles fought every move he made, that wasn't easy. "You and Ben belong together."

"Do we?" Sienna asked.

Josh nodded. "You know you do. Ben knows it too."

Fuck, he didn't want to believe that. Didn't want to lose her now. But Sienna had spent her adult life loving Ben. She wasn't going to throw that all away, especially not now, when Ben had come to his senses.

Unlike Josh's mother, when Sienna made a commitment, she stuck to it. Or half killed herself trying to stick to it, anyway. She'd been with Ben for eight years. Spent one of those years desperately trying to save a relationship in crisis.

Besides, Ben was a decent guy. Josh could see that. Knew it instinctively. He may hate him, but that was merely a guy thing. No way could Josh ever like a man Sienna loved. It just wasn't possible. His competitive nature made sure of it.

But like him or not, Ben would make Sienna happy. And Sienna deserved to be happy.

Tears spilled over her cheeks. "If you love me, you wouldn't leave."

He shook his head. "I'm leaving because I love you. You've had a few hours to get to know me, princess. You've had a lifetime with Ben. He's the right man for you."

And then, because he couldn't help it, he leaned in and pressed one last kiss to her lips. One last, bittersweet kiss. And this time, the saltiness he tasted on her mouth was not sadness about another man. This time, her tears were for him.

"Be happy," he whispered. "Both of you." Then he walked out of her room, out of her bungalow and out of her life.

Josh had not cried since he was sixteen. Not since the day he'd realized his mother had left and wasn't coming back. That day he'd locked himself in his room, thrown himself across his bed and wept himself to sleep. The next morning he'd vowed never to allow a woman to cause him such deep, unrelenting pain again. He'd vowed never to cry again.

For the first time in fourteen years, Josh broke those vows.

"Where's Josh?" Ben asked as he slipped back into bed beside Sienna.

Josh had only just shut the door behind him.

"He's...gone," she whispered. Her words seemed to echo in her ears, reverberating through the emptiness his departure had left.

"Gone?" Ben looked stunned.

Sienna nodded. "He wishes us happiness. Both of us."

"He walked away." Ben wiped a hand over his face. "Christ, I didn't expect that."

"Me neither," Sienna confessed, and a wave of sorrow hit her. Josh had left. Told her he loved her, then left. Her mind reeled. It had happened too fast. Too suddenly. She hadn't had time to prepare. She'd still been savoring the afterglow of their threesome, and he'd walked away.

Was she ready to let him go? Did she want him to go?

Did she have a say in the matter?

Apparently not.

Her sorrow turned to grief. Josh was gone. She'd only just met him again, and now he was gone. Whatever might have happened between them was no longer a possibility. He'd removed himself from the equation.

Which meant she no longer had to decide who she wanted more, him or Ben. With Josh out of the picture, there was no longer a choice.

There was only Ben.

She turned to stare at him. He stared back at her, awe in his eyes. "You don't have to choose between us," he said, having obviously come to the same conclusion. "You can come home now, Si. There's nothing standing between us anymore."

Sienna blinked. There were no more obstacles. Ben's work was no longer an issue, and Josh no longer stood between them. She and Ben could rebuild their lives. Start again. Or pick up at the point where things had begun to crumble around them. Only this time they could do it right. This time they could live the life they'd planned. Together.

Was that what she wanted? She'd spent three months forcing herself to live a life without him, and now he was here, taking her right back to the very place she'd fought so hard to move away from.

Sienna's heart raced. Her knees grew weak and her skin prickled with emotion.

Did she want to be with Ben? She'd been so overwhelmed to have him back, she hadn't stopped to ask herself the question.

More than that, was she content not to have Josh? Her gut yelled no, but he'd left so fast she hadn't had time to think about it.

And she didn't have time now. Not with Ben grinning triumphantly at her. "We can be together again, baby." The joy and relief were audible in his laugh. "We can be Sienna and Ben."

Sienna and Ben. Ben and Sienna. Together again.

His mouth consumed hers in a feverish kiss.

As his tongue swept past her lips with assertive familiarity, Sienna automatically gave herself over to the demands of his passion—just like she had every other time Ben had kissed her over the last eight years.

He moaned carnally, his arousal evident in every shallow breath, every soft caress.

Sienna opened herself up to his touch and his kisses, and waited for the magic of the island to descend over them, just like it had descended over her and Josh.

Hours later, she snuck out from beneath Ben's arm, slipping away from the heat of his body. Careful not to wake him, she tiptoed across the carpeted floor and closed herself in the bathroom.

For the first time since she'd left her bungalow earlier that evening, Sienna had a minute to herself.

She rested her head against the door, closed her eyes and let out a very long breath, relishing the solitude.

It took a couple of minutes to fill the bath, but submerging herself in the hot water was exactly what Sienna needed. Her body had adjusted to life without sex, which meant that the day of loving had made her muscles ache pleasantly, and her pussy and arse tingle.

The water soothed away her discomfort, lapping over her breasts and soaking up any residual stiffness. It eased the exquisite tenderness that remained from Josh's and Ben's wild and wicked thrusting, and brought an overall sense of calm to her physically.

What it could not soothe was Sienna's underlying sense of sadness.

Sienna should be on top of the world. She should be the happiest woman in the world. She had her fiancé back. She had her life back.

So why did the knowledge that her future was once again melded to Ben's make her want to drop her head in her hands and sob?

Chapter Eleven

Josh's feet pounded across the sand, the tiny grains blisteringly hot from the afternoon sun. His lungs burned from lack of oxygen and his muscles screamed from the torment he put them through. He didn't care. He pushed harder, faster, needing to run through his pain.

He'd tried swimming out to the dolphins earlier, thought playing with them might take his mind off Sienna. But his punishing strokes through the water must have scared them off. When he'd arrived at the spot where he'd seen them frolicking just moments before, they'd scattered.

He'd tried sailing, hoping the wind through his hair would blow the cobwebs from his mind, help him see he'd made the right choice in letting Sienna go. Sitting on the cat had done nothing but remind him of the day before, when Sienna had sat beside him and confessed she'd had a crush on him for five years. Confessed that all she'd wanted to do, even if it only lasted five minutes, was fuck his brains out.

The memory had him bent over in agony. He'd let the anguish wash through him, eat him alive, and then he'd turned the Hobie around and sailed back to shore. He couldn't be there. Couldn't sit in the same spot where he'd sat yesterday without Sienna by his side.

So he ran instead. Just like he ran every day. Four-hundred-meter laps up and down the beach. He ditched his shirt and shoes on one of the deck chairs and sprinted along the shoreline, away from the hotel, away from prying eyes. Away from the bungalow Sienna now shared with Ben—if they hadn't already headed back to Newcastle.

Sienna had gotten her five minutes with Josh, and then

some. He'd have preferred longer, like maybe a lifetime of longer, but things hadn't worked out that way. She was with Ben. Like she should have been all along. Josh had just been a temporary blip in her radar.

Fuck, Lye. Have a pity party, why don't you?

Christ, he was pathetic. A fucking baby, crying over spilled milk. Nah, too clichéd. He was his mother, crying over spilled gin. Or his father, crying over a nine-year prison sentence. Maybe he was both of them, crying over the life he wanted but could never have.

Not the life. The woman. And the girl. Sienna, the princess, so far out of his reach he'd been crazy to dream, even for those five minutes, that he might have her.

Girls like Sienna didn't choose boys like Josh. They didn't choose losers. They chose the Ben Cowleys of the world. And they lived happily ever after.

The figure on the sand ahead of him brought Josh to a careening halt.

She stood alone, at the end of the beach, hurling something flat and white into the sea.

What was it?

She leaned over, picked up something else, aimed and threw it too.

A shell.

Josh edged closer, his heart pounding in his ears. Not from the sprint, although that left him gasping for breath, but from the shock. She shouldn't be here. She shouldn't be alone. She should be in her bungalow, or back in Newcastle, with Ben.

Sienna hurled another shell into the sea, yelling something as she did so. Josh wasn't sure what she yelled—her voice vanished in the wind.

He inched closer still, moving silently, determined not to interrupt her. He listened more intently.

Christ, she was gorgeous. Not that he could see her face, but her blonde curls whipped behind her in the breeze. She'd crammed that luscious flesh into a tight singlet, and again wore shorts that showed off an endless length of leg. Her butt, full and round, was pushed out towards him every time she flung her shells, reminding him he'd never gotten a chance to take her there. Never had the pleasure of burying himself in her arse—even though he'd promised her he would.

There were a lot of things he'd wanted to do with Sienna he'd never have the chance to now.

It was just a sad, sucky fact of life.

Josh heard what she said as she flung the shell this time. Heard the word "Engagement" dancing in the air before it plopped in the sea, just like the shell. The next throw was accompanied by a name. Ben's. And on the third throw he heard his own name.

He waited for the splash, but it never came. Sienna hadn't flung the shell. She held it in her hand now, staring at it. "Josh," she said again, and then there was silence. A long length of silence.

Josh didn't dare breathe or move. He simply stood where he was, waiting. Filling his eyes with the sight of her. Wondering what the hell to do next.

He knew he should turn around and walk away, just liked he'd done last night. But this time something stopped him.

Sienna raised her hand to fling the shell, yelling out Josh's name again. She had to let him go, had to throw the shell in the water. Had to drown her sorrows.

So why couldn't she pry open her fingers? Why were they clasping the shell so tight they'd started to cramp? Why were tears running down her cheeks and her heart beating so hard she thought it might smash straight out of her chest?

She stared at her hand, knowing the answer. She'd known the answer all along. Since the minute she'd recognized the man standing beside her chair at the pool as Josh Lye, she'd known.

"Josh," she said again, wiping her other hand across her eyes. She yelled his name. Loud.

She had to find him, had to speak to him. Now.

"Josh," she screamed, knowing he couldn't hear her, knowing she'd have to look for him, search the whole resort if necessary. She'd do it too, just so long as she got to talk to him again.

"Josh," she called as she took off, racing toward the hotel as fast as her legs would carry her. Tears fell from her eyes, blinding her.

She almost didn't see him, almost ran headfirst into the

man standing mere meters away from her. She managed to stop seconds before crashing into him.

Sienna blinked once, then again, barely believing her eyes.

"Josh?" This time his name was a murmur. It was all she could manage.

"Right here, princess."

She swiped at her cheeks, brushing away the tears.

Josh.

It really was him, standing before her, looking utterly gorgeous. Hot, sweaty, half-naked and utterly gorgeous. "Wh-what are you doing here?"

"Watching you." His answer was immediate, as if he hadn't thought about it.

"Why?"

He ran his gaze over the length of her, the action scorching her from head to toe. "I went for a run along the beach, the same as I do every day. I didn't expect you to be here." Josh looked into her eyes, making her breath catch. "When I saw you, I couldn't walk away."

"Uh... Oh." She'd been about to search every nook and cranny in the resort to find him. Tripping over him one or two steps into her hunt had thrown her for a loop. "You startled me."

"I'm sorry."

"That's okay." It was okay. Very okay.

They stared at each other. Sienna couldn't stop staring, couldn't get enough of him. Josh, the boy of her dreams. The man of her dreams.

"You called my name," Josh said.

She nodded. "I was looking for you."

He narrowed his eyes. "Why?"

Why, indeed? She'd been so desperate to find him, to tell him why, yet now that he stood in front of her, she wasn't at all sure what to say. "There's something I need to say to you. I would have said it last night, but you left too quickly." Lordy, her heart raced so fast she could hardly talk.

He looked at her with an unfathomable expression. "I'm here now. You can tell me if you still want to."

"I do." She nodded, affirming her words.

Josh waited.

She couldn't speak. Couldn't find the strength and the honesty to express what was in her heart.

He let out a long sigh. "It's okay, princess. You don't need to say it. You don't need to say anything." He reached out and stroked her cheek, sending hot thrills through her skin. "Just know that if you should wake up in the middle of the night and not be able to get back to sleep, somewhere out here, there's a man dreaming very adult dreams about you." He ran his thumb over her bottom lip, just once, and then he turned around and walked away.

Oh, dear God. He was leaving her—again. No, no, no! He couldn't. She couldn't let him. Had to stop him.

"I love you too," she yelled after his retreating back.

Josh froze midstep, his foot still in the air. He turned around slowly. "What did you say?"

"I said I love you too." Shit, the tears were back, clouding her vision. She couldn't see his face, had no way of knowing what he was thinking.

Sienna began to shake.

"What about Ben?" Josh asked coolly.

"He's...gone." Sienna wrapped her arms around herself to stop the shivers. It didn't help.

"Gone where?"

"Back to Newcastle." Her skin was covered in goose bumps.

He shook his head, looking confused. "Why?"

She swallowed. "I asked him to leave." It had almost killed her, almost broken her heart all over again, but it had been the right decision for both Sienna and Ben. Hopefully, one day soon, Ben would be able to see that too.

"You did?" Josh took a step towards her.

"Yes."

"Why?"

She chewed on her lower lip. "Because our relationship is over."

Another step. "He came back for you."

"I know." She nodded. "And in doing so, he confused the heck out of me. Made me think I still loved him. Made me think I still wanted a future with him."

"You don't?" His question was a hoarse whisper.

"A part of me will always love him, will always love my

memories of him. But our engagement is over. It has been for a long time." Their relationship had died months before she'd officially ended it. "Seeing him again was a shock. Hearing him say all those things about wanting me back, well, it made me nostalgic, made me long for what we'd once had." Because what they'd once had had been good. "But then you left, and I was alone with him. And I realized the magic wasn't there anymore. Whatever Ben and I once shared has died." While the knowledge was liberating, it still made Sienna terribly, terribly sad. She'd lost Ben all over again. But... "The magic in the room last night was there because of you. Not him."

"Si..." He stepped closer.

"You created the magic, Josh. Not him. It sparked the second I saw you by the pool and exploded into something undeniable when we made love yesterday afternoon. Ben got caught up in our magic. Yours and mine. That's why the sex was so good. It wasn't about him, it was about us."

Josh took one final step, and he stood in front of her, close enough to raise his hand to her cheek and wipe away her tears.

She took a shaky breath, luxuriating in his touch, in the tingles that flowed through her as a result. "I was crazy about you as a school kid, Josh Lie-With-Me. But yesterday I fell in love with the man you've become."

"You did?"

"I did."

He closed his eyes, almost as if in prayer. "And you'd still want that?" he asked, his voice sounding as shaky as she felt. "You'd still want five minutes to lie with me?" He opened his eyes, watched her intently. Waited for her answer

She shook her head vehemently. "No!"

Josh dropped his hand so fast she never saw it move.

She grabbed it, brought it back to her face, held it there. "Five minutes would never be enough for everything I want with you." She smiled, then grinned through her tears and quoted him, word for word. "There are so many ways I wanna make love to you, you'll be ninety before we've covered half of them."

Josh groaned, the sound emanating from somewhere deep inside him. "I wanna make love to you too, princess. But I'm a selfish man. I won't share you. Not ever again. I can't tolerate the thought of anyone else touching you. Can you live with that?"

"If you love me, I can live with anything."

"I do love you." He pulled her into his arms, crushed her against him. "Christ, I've loved you since forever, don't you know that by now?"

Sienna held him just as tight, wouldn't let go. "I'm a slow learner, apparently. But if you could give me a gentle reminder every now and again—"

His mouth cut off the rest of her words. His lips met hers in a kiss so heated, every chill that had wrapped around her skin melted in his embrace.

The kisses they'd shared before faded to insignificance. As his tongue swept into her mouth, claiming her, making her his, Sienna knew this was the kiss to end all kisses. This was the real deal. The kiss that sealed her fate.

She was Josh's. Without a shadow of a doubt.

Her heart belonged to him completely. Him, and no one else. And his mouth told her his heart belonged to her—and no one else. Which was a damn good thing, because Sienna was just as selfish as Josh. She too refused to share.

She smiled as she kissed him, couldn't hold back her joy. She didn't try. Ben was gone, officially a sad memory from her past. Josh was here, with her. He loved her, like she loved him. Happiness exploded inside her, like the sun coming up.

"Josh?"

"Yeah?"

"Will you do me a favor?"

"Anything, princess."

"Lie with me?"

"For the next ninety years at least," he promised as he took her hand, and together they sprinted across the beach, back to her hotel room.

About the Author

To learn more about Jess Dee please visit her website at www.jessdee.com. Or you can drop by her blog: http://jessdee.wordpress.com.

Jess loves to hear from her readers. You can contact her any time at jess@jessdee.com.

Look for these titles by
Jess Dee

Now Available:

Office Affair

Tanner Siblings
Ask Adam
Photo Opportunity

Fire
Winter Fire
Hidden Fire

A Question of...
A Question of Trust
A Question of Love

Circle of Friends
Only Tyler
Steve's Story

Three Of A Kind
Going All In
Raising the Stakes
Full House

Bandicoot Cove
Exotic Indulgence
Island Idyll

Speed
See You in My Dreams
Color of Love

Print Anthologies
Risking It All
Three's Company
Red-Hot Winter
Three of a Kind

Their wolves are howling at the moon.
Their human halves are on different planets.

Black Gold
Copyright © 2011 Vivian Arend
Takhini Wolves, Book 1

Lone wolf Shaun Stevens's automatic response to the words "happily ever after"? Kill me now. Yet with all his friends settling down he's begun to think there may actually be something to this love-and-roses crap.

One thing's for sure: his dream mate will have to out-cuss, out-spit and out-hike him. So he never expected the one to push his forever button would be a blue-blooded Southern debutante with a voice as dark and velvety as her skin.

When Gemmita Jacobs steps off the plane in Whitehorse, Yukon, it's about more than her caribou research project. It's her declaration of independence from an overprotected upbringing. Except there's something in the air she can't quite define—something that unexpectedly rouses her mating instincts.

Moments after their eyes lock, the deed is done—and done thoroughly. When the pheromone dust settles, though, all the reasons they don't belong together become painfully clear.

It's enough to make a wolf learn a whole new set of cuss words…

Warnings: Two strong wolves getting exactly what they deserve. Includes wilderness nookie, shifters being naughty in public places, the Midnight Sun as a canopy for seduction and grizzly shifters on the loose. Oh, and don't forget the sarcasm.

Available now in ebook and print from Samhain Publishing.

PUBLISHING

www.samhainpublishing.com

Green for the planet.
Great for your wallet.

It's all about the story...

Romance

HORROR

www.samhainpublishing.com

CPSIA information can be obtained at www.ICGtesting.com
Printed in the USA
BVOW040957210213

313871BV00001B/18/P